Swan Song

www.**books**at**transworld**.co.uk

Swan Song

ROBERT EDRIC

Doubleday

LONDON · TORONTO · SYDNEY · AUCKLAND · JOHANNESBURG

TRANSWORLD PUBLISHERS
61–63 Uxbridge Road, London W5 5SA
a division of The Random House Group Ltd

RANDOM HOUSE AUSTRALIA (PTY) LTD
20 Alfred Street, Milsons Point, Sydney,
New South Wales 2061, Australia

RANDOM HOUSE NEW ZEALAND LTD
18 Poland Road, Glenfield, Auckland 10, New Zealand

RANDOM HOUSE SOUTH AFRICA (PTY) LTD
Endulini, 5a Jubilee Road, Parktown 2193, South Africa

Published 2005 by Doubleday
a division of Transworld Publishers

A catalogue record for this book is available from the British Library.
ISBN 0385 605781

Typeset in 11/14pt Caslon by
Falcon Oast Graphic Art Ltd.

Printed in Great Britain by
Clays Ltd, St Ives plc

1 3 5 7 9 10 8 6 4 2

Papers used by Transworld Publishers are natural, recyclable products made from wood grown in
sustainable forests. The manufacturing processes conform to the environmental regulations
of the country of origin.

i.m.

Mandy Armitage

1962–2004

requiescat

The last week of summer had turned overnight into the first week of autumn. Yesterday, the men in the warehouse beneath me had been loading and unloading their lorries stripped to the waist. Today they'd built a fire of broken crates in a makeshift brazier, and the pale smoke from this drifted the full length of Humber Street and out over the water. They stood round the blaze in the cool sunlight, holding their hands to it and stoking it while they awaited the arrival of their late deliveries.

I closed both my high windows, wiping away six months of accumulated dust, cobwebs and desiccated insects.

That first cool morning was always memorable, and though the mild days would return through what little remained of September and then October, it was always a sign of the coming winter; just as the first returning days of gentle heat and longer light next February or March would be a promise of the coming summer.

Late the previous afternoon, a wasps' nest had been discovered in a neighbouring warehouse, and hundreds of the creatures, gorged on fruit and sluggish, were swatted and killed. The nest had been burned, along with its slower inhabitants, in the brazier. Some of the insects had come up through the gaps in my floorboards and had flown clumsily against my closed windows. The owner of the warehouse had come to see me, relieved that so few of the wasps had appeared. He said pointedly that it wasn't worth informing the 'environmental people' and I agreed with him. He offered me a drink from his hip flask and I accepted it to seal our collusion.

Six months earlier, a visiting restaurant owner had reported seeing a rat in the same warehouse and a week's work had been interrupted by the arrival of the council exterminators. Only four young rats had been found and killed; dozens more had moved elsewhere along the street until the traps and poison had all been removed.

Handing the flask back to the man, I wasn't certain what it had contained. He took a second drink, looked quickly around my four empty walls, shook his head at some unspoken understanding, and then left me, pleased that my silence had been so cheaply bought.

I was due to meet Sunny at Neptune Street in an hour to take another look at the cellar – 'tomb' the *Hull Mail* called it – in which a dozen hitherto forgotten wartime corpses had recently been discovered.

New foundations were being laid between English Street and the Albert Dock, and during these excavations an underground room had been uncovered with its brick ceiling intact. The workmen had stopped work and lowered a ladder into the space to investigate. And having descended into the darkness, they had found there, covered by tarpaulins and the plaster that had collapsed a long time ago, twelve well-preserved corpses. Seven adults and five children.

One of the workmen had called Sunny at the news agency and he had been there within minutes to take pictures.

Soon afterwards, the official machinery had started to move and the site had been emptied and sealed off. Sunny's pictures, along with Yvonne's short account of the discovery, had appeared in one form or other in most of the next day's nationals.

The most popular photograph showed the corpses laid in a row, all fully clothed and darkened by time, and with the children, two of whom were clearly still babies, settled between the adults. Despite the proximity of the river, the underground room was dry and cold, and the faces of all twelve bodies were clearly discernible. The skulls of the babies looked like dirty tennis balls, and the smallest of these still wore a woollen cap.

Sunny took over a hundred pictures, aware that each would command the price of an 'exclusive' tag from the editors who bought them.

Two days after the discovery, a man came forward who had served as an Air Raid Warden during the war and who, having been taken to the cellar by the police, showed them on a map where a cold store had been requisitioned as a temporary morgue following one of the heaviest of Hull's bombing raids in September 1941. There had been insufficient room at Spring Street, and the smaller hospital mortuaries had been quickly filled, so this cold and cavernous space had been cleared out and used.

The man expressed surprise that the room was still intact. He'd assumed it had been filled with the rubble of the bombed build-ings above. He insisted that all the bodies had afterwards been removed, but could not recall when. No reliable record had been found of the people who had been killed and taken there. The remnants of card tags had been found tied to the ankles of the corpses, but these had long since lost their details. The photos Sunny had taken of the labels attached to the babies made them look like small, unwanted presents.

Soon afterwards, the descendants of people who had died in the bombing started coming forward in an effort to identify and reclaim the corpses. A hundred and forty people had applied to see the twelve bodies.

Hull had had a hard war and there was still some resentment at the anonymous manner – the newspaper and radio reports referred to it only as a 'northern town' – in which this destruction and suffering had been reported. But, overall, its inhabitants looked back fondly now, and the discovery of the corpses was a major event.

Sunny knew that the nationals would soon lose interest, but that there would be sufficient local and regional add-ons and spin-offs to keep the story intermittently profitable for several months to come.

It was time to meet him, and I left Humber Street and crossed the marina towards the Albert Dock. The whole area was now in a constant state of demolition and renewal. Cavernous retail stores filled the razed and levelled spaces; access roads grew roundabouts, from which slip roads radiated towards other, mini-roundabouts. Work was under way on the redevelopment of Island Quay, where the foundations of hundreds of new homes were already laid out in a giant maze of concrete lines and blue and yellow piping.

I walked past Ropery Street to Neptune Street and the cordoned-off hole in the ground.

Sunny was already there, pacing back and forth at the edge of the rubble, smoke from his cigar forming small clouds in the still air.

Following his original good fortune in having been contacted by one of the labourers, he had then been kept away from the exposed cellar by the developers. Hoardings had been erected, and the corpses quickly removed.

'They're talking about DNA testing,' he said as I approached him.

'It makes sense.'

'I'd be happier with a birthmark, a photograph in a wallet or a tattoo saying "I Love Mam".'

'You old romantic. Why are we here?'

'Because the people of Hull – my mandate, so to speak – want to know what's happening. And, better still, they want to *pay* to know what's happening. There's already some anger that everything's being kept out of sight and just that little bit too hush-hush.'

'And you're here why? To capture and articulate that anger?'

'Which could very easily and very quickly turn into, oh, outrage.' Everything he said avoided my question.

I looked around us. Other than the men on the building site, there was no one else there. Few doubted that the corpses would eventually be identified and reclaimed, and that an event would then be made of their burial.

'It's because there are kids involved,' he said. He looked tired. I knew from Yvonne that he'd spent the last two nights at the agency, sleeping at his desk. He took the last inch of cigar from his mouth and flicked it to the ground. 'Outrage, resentment, public demands. The need for explanation. I've already heard people talking about fucking "closure". It all works better where there are kids involved. I can already sense that building wave of recreational grief sweeping towards us.' He continued to stare at the distant hole as he spoke.

'You were almost in tears when you saw the pictures of the baby in the bonnet,' I said.

'Tears of joy at what they would be worth,' he said.

I'd been with him and Yvonne at Spring Bank when he'd transferred the pictures from his camera to a screen. Yvonne, too, had been unable to speak upon seeing them for the first time. The corpses' clothing might have hidden injuries, but there was nothing on any of the dozen faces to suggest how they might have been killed. Their eyes had been closed, and on several of the adults, the coins which had been used to hold them shut were still in place after sixty years.

Standing beside Sunny now, I could sense his disappointment that the story had already lost its impact, and that it was being further obscured by its endless retelling as the few facts and details of the discovery were speculated upon, and then as they multiplied and changed.

I wondered why he'd come back, and why he'd wanted me to meet him there.

He took several pictures of the distant men. Smoke rose from the rubble fires on Island Quay. A succession of dumper lorries poured new foundations into pools of shallow water.

'They're turning it into fucking Slough,' he said.

He had been born less than a five-minute walk away, in a small terraced house in Barnabus Court, off The Boulevard. He hadn't lived that close to the river for the past thirty years, but as with everyone else whose family livelihood had once depended on the Humber and the fishing in Arctic seas a thousand miles beyond it, the river was always a part of him. He had started collecting old photos of the industries and yards there before it was all finally lost to the stores and roundabouts and slip roads.

'Yvonne wants to see you,' he said unexpectedly, making no attempt now to sound casual.

'And she sent you to see me first?'

He turned away from me.

'Does she know I'm here now?'

'Probably.'

'What's it about?'

'Paul Hendry,' he said.

The name meant nothing to me and I shook my head.

'Would "Suspected Serial Killer Fights For Life In Coma" help?' He turned back to face me.

'Are you serious?'

He pulled the cellophane from another cigar. 'What do you think?' he said, and without watching what he was doing, he raised his small camera and clicked the shutter a foot from my face. 'Say "cheese",' he said.

2

We made our way under the dual carriageway to Linnaeus Street.

A black and orange poster outside the Kingfisher announced that it was now open all day with Live Entertainment each night.

'You'd want a definition of "Live" before you started spending,' Sunny said as we went in.

On our short journey neither of us had mentioned his reasons for meeting me.

Two days ago, the body of a nineteen-year-old woman called Lucy Collins had been found in the flat she shared with her boyfriend, Paul Hendry. Shortly before this, the 22-year-old Hendry had been discovered comatose in the closed and ransacked surgery of a local doctor. Hendry, a known drug user, was found slumped in a corner of the room with a half-emptied syringe still hanging from his arm. Early reports suggested that, having killed his girlfriend, Hendry had then broken into the surgery intending to steal whatever drugs he found there, and that he had then succumbed to the irresistible opportunity of injecting himself while there. The predictable speculation was that the drugs he had found had been considerably more potent than what he was accustomed to, and that this had caused him to overdose.

He had been taken to the Intensive Care Unit at Hull Royal Infirmary. Police visiting the address found in his wallet had discovered the body of Lucy Collins. She, too, was a known drug user, and while no autopsy had yet been performed, it was already known that she had been savagely attacked and killed by being stabbed through the heart and lungs.

The comatose Hendry became an immediate suspect.

A second theory was that he had deliberately attempted to kill himself with the overdose after killing his girlfriend. There were few firm details other than these, and the police investigation into the killing and subsequent events had as yet drawn no real conclusions.

This was the third violent killing of a young woman in the city in the past four months. The first had taken place at the end of May behind a store in the city centre; and the second, two months later, on a piece of derelict land on the south side of Garrison Road. Like the long-forgotten air-raid victims, that woman had also been discovered by builders clearing away rubble prior to construction work. And like both the city-centre killing and Lucy Collins two days earlier, this second victim had also been violently assaulted.

At first, the police had been reluctant to link the two previous crimes, but with the death of Lucy Collins there was now a rising public demand for a connection to at least be considered.

I knew little more, except that the summer in the city had been an uneasy one, and that frequent warnings had been given for women to take additional precautions if they were alone at night.

The first victim – a girl called Kelly Smith – was also a known prostitute, and while there was no indication that the woman found off Garrison Road had ever worked as one, there were already rumours that Lucy Collins had been seen soliciting on Anlaby Road and Great Thornton Street shortly before her death. Again, the police were refusing to insist on this as something which connected the murders.

Whatever Yvonne wanted from me, it was unlikely that I would be allowed anywhere near the burgeoning investigation, especially while the police themselves seemed so uncertain of the direction it might now be about to take.

'You'd better tell me,' I said to Sunny when he returned with our drinks.

We were the only people in the bar. The landlord stood with his back to us and watched a quiz show on a television mounted high on the wall.

'She and the boy's mother are friends,' he said. 'Her name's Susan Hendry.'

'Close friends?'

'I think so. The boy hasn't lived at home for three or four years. He's an only child. According to Yvonne, the mother has no illusions about him.'

'Which is unlikely. And, presumably, she's adamant he didn't kill his girlfriend?'

'She knows what he was – what they both were.'

'Including the soliciting bit?'

He clicked his tongue. 'She said they lived for each other.'

'And he supported his habit how?'

'She didn't know. The most she would admit to was that she thought he might buy and sell whatever it was.'

'But not that he'd break into a surgery to steal it, or that he'd let his girlfriend prostitute herself to buy it?'

The landlord turned and looked at us upon hearing the word.

'Yvonne just wants you to talk to her,' Sunny said, lowering his voice. 'I'm not arguing the woman's case.'

'Are the police serious about tying him in to the other two killings?'

'I think that's what scares her the most.'

'It's not very likely,' I said uncertainly.

He shrugged. 'I don't know. Sooner or later somebody some-where is going to make a connection, and when that happens whoever's fixed firmly to one killing might find himself nailed even harder to all three.'

'What are the police saying at their press conferences?'

'What do they always say? The whole thing's further complicated by the arrival of a new chief at Queen's Gardens. He arrived five weeks after Kelly Smith and immediately insisted on being considerably more hands-on than his predecessor.'

'Was it just bad timing?'

'Him coming between the first and second killing? It looks like it.'

'But?'

'But I wouldn't say that he himself sees his arrival amid the rising flames quite so pessimistically.'

'Meaning what?'

'Let's just say that at the last press conference he held, he spoke a bit too enthusiastically for my liking about "seizing the challenge" being offered to him. Something about focusing his attention on all those tens of thousands of hardworking, clean-living, law-abiding citizens out there and doing something for them for a change, and something which would make Hull a better place to live in. His name's Alexander Lister.'

'Another crusade against prostitution?'

'Along with all the bad people who sell them drugs and then murder them, presumably. It's a wide remit. What better way to make a name for himself? Let's face it, things being what they are, I doubt there'll be too many trying to stop him.'

Neither of us spoke for a minute. On the television quiz show a woman won a skiing holiday and jumped up and down at the prospect. She was overweight and a lot of her body went on moving after she'd stopped jumping. She'd never been skiing before and couldn't wait to try it. The quiz-show host told her she was a worthy winner. She'd won the prize by knowing that the Pacific Ocean stretched between Asia and America. She'd had three oceans to choose from.

Sunny took a piece of folded paper from his pocket and opened it on the table. It contained the name of the boy's mother, her address and two phone numbers.

'I'll disappoint both of them,' I said, meaning Yvonne and Susan Hendry.

'I think Yvonne already knows that.'

'You'll be telling me next that the least I can do is agree to talk to the woman and try to make her see things a little more realistically.'

He drained his glass. 'I was going to say that you owed Yvonne at least a thousand favours and that this could repay just one of them.'

'A thousand?' I said.

'Minimum. I told her that you'd probably get in touch tonight.'

'All I'd be doing was holding the mother's hand while the police pushed us both away.'

'It might be enough,' he said.

'And the prospect of her wasting her money?'

'It's hers to waste. Neither she nor Yvonne want any favours from you.'

'What have the doctors said?'

'About the boy? Just that they'll have to wait and see, and that the next few days are crucial. You know the routine.'

'And unofficially?'

He shrugged. 'A lot of headshaking and pursed lips, I should imagine.'

'To say nothing of what might await him if he does make a recovery. He probably won't even remember killing the girl.'

'If it's what he did,' he said.

'Do you have files on the other two killings?' I asked him.

'All the news that's fit to print.'

'What do *you* think?'

'I think it's drugs, and I think that makes anything possible, all bets off. I think that, in all probability, he's an evil little fucker who would let his girlfriend sell three-quid blowjobs in a bus shelter if it got him what he wanted. I think he's capable of everything they're saying he's done. The mother might have got her rose-tinted glasses on – whatever she says – but she's probably the only one.'

'In which case, my involvement might only make things worse for her,' I said.

'So what?' He tapped the piece of paper he'd given me. 'She's been at the hospital ever since he was found in the surgery and taken in,' he said. 'Just her and a couple of uniforms.'

'How much real evidence is there against him?'

'Ask her. All I know is what I write in the papers.'

3

I met Susan Hendry the following day. She and Yvonne came from the hospital to Humber Street at noon. Yvonne had called me earlier to say she'd be coming with the woman.

Susan Hendry was in her early forties, well and simply dressed and wearing little make-up. Dark rings of sleeplessness masked her eyes.

I offered her a seat by the window, but she indicated for Yvonne to sit first and then drew her chair closer to my desk.

'Three chairs,' Yvonne said. 'Going up in the world.' It was a remark intended to put Susan Hendry at her ease, and though she appreciated the gesture, the words failed.

'We've come straight from the hospital,' Susan Hendry said to me. She balanced the small bag she carried in her lap.

'How's your son?' I asked her.

'Exactly as he arrived there. Thank you for asking. The hospital staff and the police are keeping a twenty-four-hour watch over him.'

'He's stable,' Yvonne said, trying to make the remark sound considerably more hopeful than it was.

'Is there any indication whatsoever of when he might regain consciousness?' I asked Susan Hendry.

She shook her head. 'Just a few guesses, that's all. Everyone's doing their best to appear optimistic or non-committal.' She opened her bag and took out a pack of cigarettes.

'I'm sure they're doing whatever they need to do for him,' I said, catching Yvonne's glance and immediately regretting the glib remark.

Susan Hendry saw this and touched Yvonne's arm. 'It's all right,' she said. Turning back to me, she said, 'You can get to the point, Mr Rivers. You're not going to ask me anything I haven't already considered a thousand times over since Paul was found.' She took a cigarette from the pack and then offered them to Yvonne, who threw them to me.

'The official police line is that they're waiting to interview your son in connection with the death of Lucy Collins,' I said.

'I know. They tell me twenty times a day. And, unofficially, they think he killed her.'

'He may know or have seen something connected with her death,' I said.

'They have *spokespeople* who sound just like you,' she said. 'Their only real problem at present is that they can't charge him with Lucy's murder until he regains consciousness. And they're as desperate as I am for that to happen.' She tipped her head back and blew a plume of smoke at the high ceiling. 'Tell me, Mr Rivers, am I what you expected?'

I knew exactly what she was asking me.

'All I know of you is what Yvonne told Sunny to tell me. The two of you are friends. She and I are friends, and I trust her and her judgement.'

'But you still possibly regret the fact that I've come to you *via* her?'

With her, I almost said. 'I won't let it get in the way of any enquiries I make on your behalf,' I said, wondering which of the three of us believed that the least.

'And my first question?'

'I didn't know what to expect,' I said. 'Your son's a convicted criminal and a known drug user. He's lying in a coma in a hospital bed having been found unconscious in a surgery he'd broken into with a needle full of something hanging out of his arm and with his face, chest, legs, arms and hands splattered with the blood of his viciously murdered girlfriend. So, no – while I might already have made a few guesses about your son and his chances, I had no real idea of what *you* might be like.' I held her gaze as I spoke.

'Except that I was a friend of Yvonne's,' she said.

'Except that.'

'And Lucy?'

'I expected you to tell me that she and your son were devoted to each other, or that at least he was devoted to her, and that he could never harm her, let alone kill her. *Was* she working as a prostitute when all this happened?'

She hesitated before shaking her head, and then raised a hand to her mouth.

'But you believe it was possible?' I said.

She nodded once and then composed herself. 'Whether you believe it or not, they *were* devoted to each other,' she said. 'It might not have been devotion as you or I might want to understand it, or have experienced it, but that's what it was. They live in a different world from us, Mr Rivers, that's all. Barely a quarter of a mile from here, and yet a different world entirely.'

'Their lives revolved around drugs and around getting enough money to pay for those drugs,' I said. 'The police and one or two other agencies are convinced that Lucy Collins was working as a prostitute in the months before she died. There may even have been a longer history than that.'

'You seem very certain of yourself,' she said.

'I am.'

The previous evening I'd gone back to the agency with Sunny and he'd shown me all he had on the death of Lucy Collins and the discovery of Paul Hendry, along with reports on the previous two murders.

'What other agencies?' Susan Hendry said.

I gave her their names. 'Both Lucy and your son were in irregular contact with their outreach workers.'

She laughed at the title. 'Who did *what* for them, exactly?'

'Your son started rehabilitation treatment three times in the past two years. A year ago, he went for almost four months using nothing.'

She hadn't known this, and for the first time since entering my office she looked at me with something other than despair or resignation in her eyes.

'Four months?' she said.

'According to one report, both he and Lucy were as careful as they could afford to be when using needles.'

'Shouldn't all that be confidential information?' she said.

'It is. You were either lying to me about not knowing Lucy was working as a prostitute, or you were deceiving yourself. If I'm going to look into what happened, then we at least need to start from the same place. If you keep anything from me now, it might later jeopardize everything I'm doing. The police are already three days ahead of us, and they'll have known all this from the start.'

Yvonne rose from her seat and crossed the room to stand at the window. Susan Hendry watched her.

'Like they've *known* from the start that Paul killed Lucy and then broke into James Weaver's surgery to steal drugs?' she said.

'You know James Weaver?' I said.

The question surprised her. 'Of course I know him. He's my doctor.'

'And Paul's?'

'He was once. Presumably he still is. It's why the police think Paul went there – because he knew how to break in, because he knew where to look for what he wanted.'

Yvonne went from the window to the giant mirror, pocked and blemished over its entire surface, which filled my rear wall, installed when the room had been used as a merchant seamen's outfitters. She looked back at my reflection.

'Do *you* think the fact that Lucy was working as a prostitute might be connected to the other killings?' Susan Hendry asked me.

'I don't know. But if the police are going to find something to connect her death with the previous murders, then they won't be able to ignore it.'

'Even though the girl found off Garrison Road wasn't known to be a prostitute?'

'She was a woman walking alone on wasteland,' I said. 'It might have been enough for the killer.'

'How do the police think they're going to make that same connection between Lucy's death and the other two?' Yvonne said.

I held up my palms to her. 'I don't know.'

'They still found Lucy's blood all over Paul,' Susan Hendry said absently.

'Which doesn't prove he killed her,' I said. 'Just, perhaps, that he was with her when she was bleeding.' I regretted the speed with which we had come from the few and straightforward facts of the case into these more hopeful, and so far unconvincing, outer reaches.

Yvonne returned to sit beside Susan Hendry.

'Why haven't the police said any of this to me – about the prostitutes, I mean?'

'Perhaps because they need to keep their options open,' I said. 'I doubt if anyone's seeing anything straight this close to the killing.'

'Including me?' she said.

I acknowledged this. 'He's your son; he may yet lose his life; he may even have done what they're already suggesting he's done: you're bound to have a different perspective on all this.'

'I told you he had a way with words,' Yvonne said, and Susan Hendry laughed.

After that, she sat with her eyes closed for a moment. Both Yvonne and I waited for her to open them.

'I've never been here before,' she said eventually. 'I've had some bad and hard times in the past, but I've never been pushed this hard against anything before. I don't even know how to begin this thing or what I expect to happen once it's started. What if everything you discover only points even more conclusively to my son's guilt?'

'If he did kill Lucy Collins, then nothing I uncover will alter that.'

'And if he dies without regaining consciousness?'

'The police won't let their investigation die with him. They won't be allowed to. Your son may be as much a victim in all of this as Lucy was, or as those others were.'

'I've been telling myself that ever since they started making their own unofficial suspicions public,' she said.

I knew from my time with Sunny the previous evening that there was a growing concern for the police to work harder at solving the two earlier murders. Whatever happened in the case of Lucy Collins, and regardless of whether Paul Hendry lived or died, they would not be allowed to focus on the apparent evidence of his involvement in her murder to the exclusion of all else. According to Sunny, a squad of detectives was about to be set up under the direct control of the new chief. The original, smaller squads were to be regrouped, ensuring that nothing of any significance from any of the three killings would now be overlooked or dismissed.

'When did your son leave home?' I asked Susan Hendry.

'When did he leave me, you mean? Three years ago. His father walked out on us when Paul was four. He was a good kid, we looked out for each other. I won't tell you he was led astray by others, or that he got into things over his head—'

'But it's what happened?'

She nodded. 'I found all sorts of stuff in his room – stuff I didn't have the faintest idea about. We stopped talking to each other, and before I even knew where we were, we'd passed the point of no return. It really was that simple. It was all so – so unstoppable and irreversible. It wasn't a good time for me. I was struggling to keep my own head above water. The usual things – money, work, mortgage, bills, trying to do the right thing by everybody else. When I was finally able to stand upright and look around me, Paul was gone, walking away from me and not even looking back.'

'You knew about his drug use a long time ago?'

She nodded.

'Did you confront him with it?'

'Did we argue and fight and did he disappear for days on end to his new friends, do you mean? And did he come back after four or five nights looking as though he'd been gone for months? Of course I confronted him. Not that it did either of us much good. They recommend it, don't they – confrontation, clearing the air, keeping things out in the open. Well, I wish they'd given me one or two alternatives to try.'

'What happened?'

'He became more and more detached from me. He'd practically already left home by the time he was sixteen. He drifted. His schoolwork suffered even more, and in the end he seemed to just drift away from that, too. He was an intelligent boy. I always assumed he'd go to university. He could play the piano, the guitar and the violin. He could paint and draw. He abandoned everything. And everything I tried to do for him, he saw as interference.' She paused. 'To be perfectly honest with you, I was actually quite pleased when he met Lucy. She seemed to stabilize him somehow. He brought her home to meet me. He was proud of her. He actually *wanted* me to meet her, and her me. They started coming home regularly – once a week or so – and then they started living together – their own small flats and rooms. They moved into Nelson Court fifteen months ago. It was the first place he'd invited me to visit. I knew, of course, that drugs were still a part of it all, but he seemed to be so much more settled there, with Lucy. I was probably deluding myself, but I honestly believed things were getting better.' She smiled. 'He'd started playing the guitar again, and painting. Lucy told me once that she was proud of him. Listening to her, seeing the two of them together, she helped it make a kind of *sense* to me. And I suppose if I'm being entirely honest, it also allowed me to feel a bit better about myself.'

In the street below, a lorry reversed into one of the loading bays, its alarm breaking the silence.

'What did you know of Lucy's background?' I asked her.

'Not a great deal. I know she had no family to speak of. She wasn't from Hull – somewhere on the south coast, I think. I never really asked. I was so relieved that everything had calmed down for Paul, that he might be getting himself straight at last, that he still might want to pick up where he'd left off. I know now, of course, that that was probably just another of my delusions.'

'It must have come as a shock to discover that Lucy had been prepared to work as a prostitute to support herself and your son.' I meant to support their drug habits, and she understood this. I needed to discover her true feelings on this, knowing what emphasis the police now placed on the fact.

'It did. But you know what, I got over it. Like I say, I'd lived through some desperate times myself.'

'And because she was doing it as much for your son as for herself?'

'I hear what you're saying to me,' she said sharply. 'And you're right – she probably was doing it more for Paul than for herself. His was always the bigger problem, and of the two of them, he was always the one least capable of helping himself.'

'And if the police—'

'The police want everything in black and white,' she said. 'They pretend otherwise, but they've already made their minds up about what happened. Lucy and my son were together for over two years. He wouldn't have survived half that time without her. Whatever happened, I owe her a great deal. I told you before, and I'll tell you again because it's so vital in even beginning to understand what's happening now – they were devoted to each other. *Devoted*. There's no other word. I was never devoted to anyone; no one was ever devoted to me; but they were devoted to each other. Perhaps it's why knowing what she was doing didn't come as such a great shock to me. Perhaps I saw it all as a necessary part of the process which kept him moving until he was through to the other side of whatever it was he was going through. It might sound like just another of my excuses, but until all this, it seemed to be working for them.'

I understood most of what she was telling me. And I had a clearer picture of the pieces I didn't yet fully understand. I knew, at the very least, that what she was doing now was done as much for Lucy

Collins's sake as for her son's. I knew, too, that if I pushed her on the matter, she would admit to wanting to redeem her own sense of failure where her son was concerned. In her eyes, there was a direct line between that failure, Lucy Collins's death, and the condition her son was in now.

I knew from Sunny that the doctors at the hospital gave Paul Hendry no more than a fifty-fifty chance of recovering consciousness. And even were he to come round, then the chances of him suffering some degree of brain damage were higher than that.

Susan Hendry understood this better than anyone, and it motivated and informed everything she was now about to undertake. There was little more I needed from her.

'What happens now?' she asked me.

'I'll start making enquiries, the police will somehow get wind of the fact – supposing they didn't follow you here from the hospital and know already – and—'

'Are you serious?' she said.

'You're the mother of suspect number one. This is your first outing after sitting by his bed for three days.'

She looked at the window, and at Yvonne, who rose and again studied the street below.

'If there's a car, then it probably shouldn't be there. They keep the road and kerbs clear for the vans and lorries,' I said.

'There's nothing,' Yvonne said.

There would be a line of cars parked along Dock Street overlooking the marina. Anyone waiting there would be able to pick up the two women as they left my office.

'Will they be able to stop you from doing your job?' Susan Hendry asked me.

'They might try,' I said. There were a dozen legitimate ways they might stop me, and the same number of unofficial ones which would be just as effective. 'A lot will depend on something turning up in the near future which leads them to start looking elsewhere,' I said. 'I have a few friendly contacts on the force. I'll find out what they really believe.' It was a lie, and I avoided Yvonne's eyes as I said it. 'I can at least keep you up to date with everything they believe is happening.'

'And if you come to the same conclusion they appear already to have come to?'

'Then it might make it easier for you to accept that conclusion.'

'It doesn't sound like a particularly clever thing to do – spend money to confirm my own son's guilt.'

I said nothing in reply.

She looked at her watch. She was surprised by how long she and Yvonne had been there. Then she checked her phone for missed messages. There were none. Yvonne did the same.

'Do I need to sign anything?' Susan Hendry asked me.

I told her she didn't, unless it would make her feel better.

'I only meant to make this official,' she said. 'To prove to the police that you were working for me.'

'They'll know that soon enough,' I said.

'Yvonne told me you were sometimes too smart for your own good,' she said.

'By "smart" I meant, well, not "smart" exactly,' Yvonne said.

'I know what she meant,' Susan Hendry said to me. 'And I want to thank you for the consideration you've shown me, Mr Rivers.'

'It'll be on his bill,' Yvonne said.

Susan Hendry ignored this. 'You said that Lucy was *capable* of doing what she did, and not *willing*, and you knew as well as I did that she did it more for Paul than for herself.'

'I don't really know either of those things for certain,' I told her.

'Yes you do,' she said. She held out her hand to me and I took it. 'Don't worry,' she said, 'I'm not going to get a firm grip on you, look hard into your eyes and insist on your belief in my son's innocence.'

'I couldn't give it to you,' I said.

I walked down to the street with them and watched them go, waiting in my doorway until they'd turned towards Castle Street before following them. I searched the cars parked along the water's edge. Several came and went as the two women moved further away from me, but none followed them or slowed beside them.

4

The next morning I went to Nelson Court. It was a recent development of two dozen small apartments, built by a housing association to provide short-term lets. Only five years old, the yellow brick building already looked run-down. The black and gold paint had long since flaked from its railings, and nothing had survived of the planting in the narrow strip of land between the building and the street. Graffiti covered the lower half of the blank front wall, and several of the ground-floor windows were boarded up.

Crime-scene tape had been fastened across the main entrance, and two constables stood at the outer doorway.

I would achieve nothing by approaching them, and so I waited at the corner of Marvel Street, hoping that someone who lived there might emerge, and who could answer my questions.

Paul Hendry and Lucy Collins had lived there for fifteen months, and Susan Hendry had visited them three times in the past six months.

Occasionally, one or other of the constables left the doorway and walked into the centre of the short street. They would already have made a list of all the parked cars, and perhaps even be noting the registrations of the few passing vehicles now. It was a narrow street, and two cars passing would necessitate one of them mounting the pavement.

I was careful not to be seen by either of the men.

Four days had passed since Lucy Collins's body had been found, and everyone living in the building would already have been questioned. If anything significant had resulted from these interviews, then Sunny wasn't aware of it.

I waited half an hour before one of the constables responded to a rap on the inner doorway, unlocked the door and held it open.

A girl came out. She stood with the two young men for a moment and then crossed the street and came in my direction. She wore a coat with a fur-lined hood pulled over her head, her face deep in its shade. One of the constables called after her, and she turned and waved to him.

I drew back from the corner and waited until she came into Marvel Street before approaching her.

I told her who I was and that I was working for Paul Hendry's mother, and she told me immediately that she had known both Paul and Lucy.

I saw only then that she was pregnant, and just as the hood of her coat had hidden her face, so the padded bulk of it concealed her stomach. An inch of pale flesh showed between her jeans and the T-shirt she wore.

'We were friends,' she said. She drew back her hood and watched me closely. She was eighteen or nineteen, slight, with pale blue eyes and a thin mouth.

'I'd appreciate being able to talk to you about them,' I said. 'Mrs Hendry wasn't as close to her son – to either of them – as she'd like to have been.'

'You reckon?' she said knowingly. 'Besides – more her problem than theirs.'

The remark reassured me. I gave her my card and repeated my name.

'Emily Carr,' she said.

I thought for a moment she was going to hold out her hand to me, but instead she stroked it over the gentle curve of her stomach.

'How far?' I said.

'Four months. I've only just started to show.' She looked down at her hand as she spoke. 'Every time I come out, one of them on the door tells me he bets I can do without all this on top of everything else. Wankers.'

'Have they already interviewed you?'

'All of us. Nobody saw or heard anything, not really. You'd think we'd know everything living in those shoe boxes, but people keep mostly to themselves.' She looked over my shoulder and seemed eager to continue walking.

'Are you going somewhere?' I asked her.

She shrugged.

I suggested a coffee in one of the cafés on Whitefriargate. She considered this, and accepted.

'I was just walking,' she said. 'Does your head in, stuck in there all day, especially with them two on the door.'

'I can imagine,' I said.

'They don't let anybody in or out without some stupid fucking remark or other.'

'It won't last. Do you work?'

The question surprised her, and she considered it, as though she had a choice of answers. 'Used to,' she said. 'Nothing special. Shops. Only casual. I haven't done anything for the past month or two, and I daresay it'll be few years now before I get back to it.'

I wondered what this salvo of vague answers and evasions was intended to hide.

'I'm not necessarily interested in the same things as the police,' I told her, hoping the remark might encourage her to say more.

'And what's that, then?' she said. She looked puzzled for a moment, and then laughed.

We arrived at a café and she went to a table while I went to the counter.

When I took our coffees to her, she was passing an unlit cigarette from her fingers to her lips and back again.

'I've given up,' she said. She pulled up her sleeve to reveal two nicotine patches, one discoloured, one new. 'You know, for the kid. Cigarettes, drink, everything.'

'Everything?'

She sipped at the hot coffee, coating her upper lip in foam. 'Especially "everything".' She looked around us at the few other people in the room. 'You want me to spell it out? I've been clean since I first found out.'

'It can't be easy.'

'The patronizing remarks are the hardest thing to bear.'

'Remarks like "It can't be easy"?'

'I get worse. Actually, it has its ups and downs, and it isn't all that difficult. The first couple of weeks are pretty shit, but after that . . . It makes a difference – you know, having a good reason for doing it. It was something me and Lucy used to talk about. We'd seen each other in passing for a few months, but her finding out I was pregnant was what really got us talking.'

'Was she thinking of it?'

'She said she was. I'm not sure. When you're pregnant, that's all some people ever talk about with you. I doubt she'd fancy it just because *I* got caught out.'

'Is it your first?'

She nodded. 'And before you ask – no, I'm not entirely certain who the father is; but, yes, he could have been one of several dead-beats; and, yes, we'll definitely be better off without him.'

'Whoever he is?'

'Whoever he is.' She drank more of her coffee, finally breaking the cigarette into an ashtray.

'Did Lucy say anything specific?'

'About wanting a kid? Not really. Though I think she might have fallen pregnant already and had a termination.'

'She told you that?'

'But not much more. When I asked her why, she just said that she'd been too fucked-up to deal with a kid. She asked me not to say anything about it in front of Paul. And besides, she said, she wouldn't give much for its chances, not the way things were then.'

'Did she mean things between her and Paul?'

'I suppose so. It was always more him than her, if you know what I mean.'

'I think so. His mother said much the same. She thought they were good for each other.'

She considered this. 'They probably were. Most couples like that are. It doesn't mean they actually *are* good for each other, just that they've each got a reassuring little mirror to look into, somebody to make everything seem normal, to make everything better when things go wrong. I've been there myself more than once.'

'Is that why you don't want anything to do with your baby's father?'

'At least I'll only be looking after the two of us.'

'Is that what Lucy did – look after Paul?'

'It always seemed that way to me. He was just proving a point to his mother, whereas she was living like that because she had no real choice. Hand-to-mouth, that's all it ever was, ever *is*.'

'Not when you take the cost of their habits into account,' I said.

'Fair enough. But it's always a struggle.'

'So would you say you were closer to Lucy than to Paul?'

'Probably, but I knew him from a long way back. We went to the same school for a time. I think my father even knew his father when they were growing up. Hessle Road. They worked on the boats; everybody knew everybody back then. They probably worked in the same places at some point. Whatever, it wasn't until Lucy and Paul moved in downstairs and I met her that I realized who he was. He didn't remember me. Hardly surprising. It had been at least ten years. His dad went off when he was a kid. He won't talk about him. I don't think there was any love lost between his mother and father when it happened. Lucy told me he still got touchy about it.'

'And your parents?'

'What about them? Are they looking forward to the big day, do you mean? Are they going to turn into doting grandparents? Forget it. My father died and my mother went to live in Spain. Three years ago. I was sixteen. She left me with my older sister, and I lived there until last year, when I moved into Nelson Court.'

'Were there problems?'

'Just my sister's supposedly perfect husband who couldn't keep his hands to himself. And before you ask – no, he never did, and it isn't him.'

'Does your mother—'

'Does she know I'm pregnant? Probably. And she'll probably want a few photos to show round to all her orange friends when the big day finally arrives.'

'I was going to ask you if she ever comes home.'

'Not once. Nothing left for her here.' She was distracted by a group of girls passing the café window, and she turned to watch them.

I'd wanted to ask her more directly about what had happened at Nelson Court, but it seemed more important now simply to let her talk and to gain her confidence.

When the girls had gone, she turned back to me. 'They're saying that he'll probably die, too,' she said.

'Paul Hendry?'

'That he overdosed. *Did* he kill her?'

'It's a theory.'

She shook her head. 'Not in a million years. About as likely as him actually breaking into that doctors' surgery in the first place.'

I asked her what she meant.

'I mean it just wasn't him. I know twenty others who'd do it without thinking twice about it, but he never had it in him.'

I asked her if she'd seen or heard anything on the day Lucy had been killed.

'Nothing. Like I said, we might have been living on top of each other, but people kept themselves to themselves. One of the coppers told me that we were the likeliest suspects. They're talking crap. The first I knew was when the police cars pulled up outside – three of them – and they started ringing all the bells. Someone told me that a body had been found, a young woman, but even then I never put two and two together. I couldn't believe it when it was Lucy's flat they forced their way into and then when they kept the rest of us away from it. Anything else I heard was just what the others living there had seen or overheard or been told.'

'*Did* you see anything?'

'No. It was all just Chinese whispers for a few days, that's all.' She looked back to the window as she spoke, and I knew then that she was keeping something from me.

'They believe it might be connected to two earlier murders,' I said.

'Those other women? I don't see how. And not if they *do* think Paul did it. I told you – he'd rather kill himself than do anything to Lucy.'

'That's another of their theories,' I said.

'What, that he killed her and then tried to top himself?' she said disbelievingly. 'I knew him; they didn't.'

'How easy would it have been for someone who didn't live in Nelson Court to get into the building?'

'Easy enough. A key each for the outer and inner doors, and then individual keys for the flats. Plus an intercom for buzzing people in. People were forever pressing all the buttons to get in. Most of us did it without thinking.'

'Did non-residents have keys to the entrance doors?'

'I suppose some must have.'

'And there was nothing whatsoever out of the ordinary on the day Lucy Collins was killed?'

'How many times are you going to ask me? Go and read my police statement, if you like. They told us all to take extra precautions. They're a joke.' She drained the last of the coffee from her cup. 'I've not been much use to you, have I?'

'I don't know,' I told her. 'I've got to start somewhere.'

'What, and you decided to start with me?'

'With whoever was the first out of the door,' I admitted.

She laughed at this.

'I'd appreciate being able to talk to you again if I turn anything up,' I said.

'You'd "appreciate" it?'

'It's the way I was brought up,' I said, and she laughed again.

Then I told her that my own father had worked on the trawlers and afterwards in the refitting docks after an injury kept him off the boats. I told her I probably had more in common with Paul Hendry than I liked to admit, having been raised by my mother, an only child, following my father's premature death.

'Where do you live now?' she asked me.

I told her.

'And your office is on Humber Street? I know it. Is it a first-floor dump smelling of cabbages, or an attic dump smelling only slightly less of cabbages?'

'The first, except some days it's oranges or bananas.'

'My father smelled of fishmeal,' she said absently, the memory having unexpectedly returned to her. 'Meal. Or oil. Something fishy, but stronger.'

I told her I remembered the days when the fishmeal factories were processing and when my mother would insist on securing every window and door in her home in a hopeless attempt to keep out the smell, which soaked into all the furnishings and lingered for days. The same days my father would take me outside and insist on us both turning into the wind and breathing deeply, as though the stink were an elixir and would make us immune to everything. On several occasions, the smell had made me retch, and even as I was being sick, a small boy of six or seven, I knew that I had failed or disappointed him in some way.

In the summer, he had taken off his jacket and shirt and had stood facing into that same stinking wind with his arms raised and muscles flexed. He had seemed almost noble to me then, a man undefeated and to be admired, and I could easily imagine him at the wheel of a trawler rising high and falling hard into a sea the colour of marble.

I was distracted by Emily Carr rising beside me. She zipped up her coat and pulled the hood back over her head. Even close to her, it would be difficult to say for certain whether she was a boy or a girl, or if she was pregnant.

'I'm authorized to pay for information,' I said.

The remark caught her unawares. 'I'm not asking for anything,' she said.

'I know.' I took forty pounds from my wallet. 'Take it.'

She took the notes and immediately put them into her pocket. I thought she was about to leave, but she hesitated.

'You never asked me about what Lucy was up to,' she said.

'About her working as a prostitute? It's why the police think there might be some connection to at least one of the other murders.'

'I know,' she said. 'They asked me if either of the other women had ever been to Nelson Court, and then if I thought Paul was capable of doing it. I told them I'd never seen either of them before and that they should be looking for somebody else.' She pulled her zip to its full extent, leaving her face at the back of a short tube.

And then she left me, pausing outside briefly to look back in to where I sat.

5 _____

I went from Whitefriargate to Walker Street in the hope that I
might be able to talk to James Weaver, the doctor in whose surgery
Paul Hendry had been found.

I knew from my time working with John Maxwell, my retired
partner, that it was important to identify the 'cores' of an investigation, to use these as starting points, and then to work outwards
from them – either from the places at which something had
happened, or from the people involved. Some investigations had
only a single 'core'; some had many. I'd also learned the hard way
that poor investigators either buried themselves in paper too
quickly or ended up doing little more than shadowing the police.
And the police only ever told anyone else what it suited them to
say. We were not on the same side, John Maxwell said, and he told
me to silently repeat this mantra each time our paths crossed. He
also told me that Justice was something for the courts, and that if I
did have anything in common with the way the police operated,
then it was that we were all men running around the streets, mostly
in the cold, and usually in the dark.

The Walker Street surgery consisted of three terraced houses, now standing alone, with an annexe that looked as though it had been dropped into place twenty years ago with the intention of being there for a year. A small and crowded car park stood beyond this, with another at the far side of the houses.

A number of plaques were fixed beside the entrance listing the doctors and agencies working from the surgery. I made a note of these. Some of the plaques were simply pieces of coloured plastic. James Weaver's appeared to be the oldest there, and his name was engraved in polished brass, worn smooth and pale with polishing. A tail of letters followed his name, running to two rows. 'Senior Partner' was inscribed along the bottom of the plaque, and this looked like a more recent addition, the lettering sharp and square.

As at Nelson Court, short pieces of police tape remained tied to the doorway and to the side entrances. A fire escape rose from each of the car parks to doors high on the side walls. A silver birch had been planted in one of the car parks, held securely in place by a support considerably thicker than its spindly white trunk.

I'd timed the walk from Nelson Court to Walker Street. It had taken me twelve minutes. Because of the intervening dual carriageway it would probably have taken me just as long to drive the same distance.

I was still as uncertain and as unconvinced as the police must have been about what, if anything – other than Paul Hendry and Lucy Collins's body – connected the two places. Teams of constables had closed the lesser roads and searched the side streets and pieces of open land between the two locations over the previous three days, but nothing had been found.

There was already speculation that the dual carriageway itself, running within a few hundred yards of the sites of all three murders, and with side-road access leading even closer, might be a further connection. It seemed a simple one to make, and in some respects a pointless one, considering that the road was the major route from one side of the city to the other.

I entered the surgery to find a large waiting room full of people. Young children played on the floor at the centre of the space. Posters filled the walls. I stepped over plastic toys and went to the reception desk, at which sat two young women and a much older one. All three wore the same outfits, each with a lapel badge telling me her name. All three were busy, and I waited where I stood, knowing even before I asked that I was unlikely to be allowed to see either Dr Weaver or the room in which Paul Hendry had been found. I also knew that this was not my true reason for being there.

One of the younger women finally put down her phone and turned to me.

'I was wondering if I could see Dr Weaver,' I said.

Upon hearing me, the older woman turned to look at me, tipping her head to study me over her glasses.

'Are you a patient of Dr Weaver's?' the young woman said.

'I'm here in connection with Paul Hendry,' I told her.

She looked suddenly alarmed, and then uncertain.

I was about to apologize when the older woman – Jean, according to her badge – said, 'It's all right, I'll deal with Mr—'

'Rivers,' I said.

'Well, Mr Rivers, I'm afraid I'm going to have to ask you to leave. I take it you're not with the police, otherwise you'd have come in here behaving as though you owned the place, and as though there wasn't a job of work still to be done here. So I'll assume you're from some newspaper or other and I'll tell you what I've told all the others who've come—'

'I'm neither,' I said, causing her to stop speaking and look at me even more suspiciously. She was not a woman accustomed to being interrupted.

She turned to the two younger women, causing them to return to their work.

Then she took off the headset she wore and came to stand directly in front of me at the counter.

I was aware by then that I was being watched by everyone else in the room. No one there could have been completely unaware of what had recently happened at the surgery.

'I'm here on behalf of Susan Hendry,' I said. 'Paul Hendry's mother.'

She looked over my shoulder at the watching patients. 'So? I'm afraid that makes no difference whatsoever. Whatever your purpose here, you must surely be aware that Dr Weaver is in no position to talk to you. Even if he were free and willing to do so.'

'I'm not doing anything underhand or illegal,' I said, but already feeling as though I were doing both.

'I think others must be the judge of that,' she said.

I wondered if this clumsy formality was her natural manner, or if it was simply in response to the way in which I had chosen to confront her.

'Paul Hendry is in a coma,' I said. 'Whatever intrusions or indignities Dr Weaver might have suffered, or imagines he's suffered, they are nothing compared to what is now happening to that boy,' I said, playing more to our silent audience than to her, and hoping I sounded as pompous and as officious as I felt.

'And *I* can only reiterate what I have already told you, Mr Rivers – which is that we have lost three full days already because of this unfortunate incident, and that Dr Weaver – Dr Weaver personally – has been greatly disturbed and discomfited by these events. Yes, personally, and yet throughout everything, throughout all the upheaval, he has both attempted to continue with his work here and has at the same time placed himself at the disposal of the police, whose own demands upon him have seemed at times both excessive and insensitive.' She paused for breath. There was something approaching reverence in her voice as she spoke of the man.

The two younger women exchanged glances behind her back.

'It is my responsibility and my duty,' she went on, 'to ensure that everything here gets back to normality as quickly as possible, and that the members of the practice are able to carry out their work unhindered by all these unwarranted intrusions. And if you do not believe that that is what is desired by all concerned, then I suggest you ask any of the people sitting in this room.'

I expected to hear a ripple of applause for her, and wondered again at the true nature of this aggressive defence of her employer.

My card lay on the counter between us, and I slid it towards her.

'I'd appreciate it if you told Dr Weaver I called, and if you'd give him this. Tell him I was here on behalf of Susan Hendry, and tell him that I assumed both he and I were as concerned for the well-being of her son as she is.' I'd intended this last remark to sting her, but she was as impervious to it as to everything else I'd said.

She picked up the card. 'I shall, of course, ensure that Doctor Weaver receives it.'

'If necessary, I'll come back,' I told her. 'Because, whether you like it or not, Dr Weaver and your precious little domain here are involved in all of this, and it's my intention to find out as much as I can about what actually happened here. You can obstruct me as much as you like – you strike me as a woman accustomed to bullying others and getting her own way because she thinks either age or time-serving is something to be respected or that it confers a superior wisdom – but, one way or another, and with or without your compliance, I will return and I will get to speak to Dr Weaver. Carry on obstructing me and I'll push even harder.'

She continued to look at me in justified and unfaltering disbelief.

'Well,' she said eventually, 'you must be very proud of yourself.'

'No,' I said. 'But it's a long time since *I* obstructed someone just for the perverse and spiteful pleasure of doing it.'

Behind me, people began to murmur about what I'd just said. Public opinion was clearly on her side.

I apologized to the two younger receptionists for having raised my voice, and then, because there was nothing more to be gained by staying, I left.

Outside, I went to the car park in which designated spaces had been marked out and saw the space from which James Weaver's car was absent.

Then I went to the second car park and climbed the fire escape to where a blue and white alarm box was fixed to the wall. I noted its details and went back down to the street.

6

Sunny called me as I walked back to Humber Street.

'Lister's called a press conference. Three o'clock.'

'Why such short notice?'

'Because he can do what he likes. Too late for today's locals, and there won't be much national interest. Even the stringers are getting tired of it.'

'More work for you,' I said.

'Depends how quickly the last of them lose interest. I suspect he's just responding to local pressure to step up the investigation. This way he gets to have his say, make his presence felt – his steady hand on the tiller and all that – and nobody in the outside world gets to interfere in any of it.'

'Are you going?'

'Of course I'm going. I think you should be there, too. Get a look at the man.'

'Why? Because he'll already know Susan Hendry's approached me?'

'That. And because he may want to impress one or two things on you personally.'

*

I met him at two fifty close to Queen's Gardens. He gave me a press pass with my photo in it.

'You could at least have brought a pencil,' he said.

We walked to a newsagent's and I bought a pen and a pad.

'It's an open call,' he said. 'They won't be checking names on the door. Besides, despite already knowing who you are, Lister will be pleased to see you there.'

'*Has* anything happened that he might want to announce?' I asked him.

'Not that I'm aware of.'

I told him about my unsuccessful attempt to see James Weaver, omitting that the man had been absent throughout.

'Like you were ever going to get anywhere near *him*. What did you expect, a tour of the crime scene, a chance to dip your fingers in the dark, sticky blood?'

'His version of events to take back to Susan Hendry would have been a start.'

He shook his head. 'Not going to happen. I've met Weaver before. He thinks a lot of himself. He's connected, on every local medical body from arthritis action to Zimmer frame allocation. He's one of those men who's watched the world around him turn to shit and who then can't help trying to turn it back while feeling it's all a little bit unfair – *he's* still playing by the same old rules – and that he's no longer being accorded his due reverence and respect. Forget him. If you go within a hundred yards of him he'll shout harassment. Besides, the police won't want you anywhere near him.'

At three, we climbed the steps from Queen's Gardens into the station. A succession of notices pointed the way into the room in which the press conference was being held.

We were among the last to arrive. A woman constable opened and closed the door for each new arrival.

Forty chairs had been set out, but fewer than a dozen were occupied. Sunny paused at the door, quickly identifying the others present. No one had checked my credentials. Several of the men at the front of the room raised their hands to Sunny and he acknowledged them.

'Regionals. Half of them won't use anything they get. They're here for something new and they're not going to get it.'

A line of tables had been set out at the front of the room, a large photograph of Lucy Collins pinned to the wall behind them. A telephone number was repeated across the top of the wall.

A minute later, the door beside the tables opened and a man I recognized as Detective Sergeant Brownlow entered. We'd crossed paths a year earlier. He'd accused me of obstructing his investigation of a girl who had drowned – whose mother, my client, insisted had been murdered – and only the outcome of the case had prevented him from making his complaints against me official.

Sunny also recognized him and knew our history. 'Interesting,' he said.

Brownlow carried a sheaf of papers and he spread these across the tables before looking more closely at his sparse audience. He saw Sunny and me, and we both raised our hands to him. Our presence there together caught him briefly off guard, but he quickly composed himself and started a short speech, thanking us for coming. When this was done, he indicated the door through which he had entered and said, 'Ladies and gentlemen, Chief Superintendent Lister,' at which the door opened again and Lister entered.

'Excellent,' Sunny said. 'He wants an entrance *and* a round of applause.' He raised his hands as though about to do this, and then lowered them.

Chief Superintendent Lister was a tall man, mid-forties, with what my mother would have called a 'military bearing'. He held his shoulders back and his chest out. He tugged at his cuffs as he walked to his seat at the centre of the tables. He stood and looked round at us all before sitting. He was probably as disappointed as Brownlow had been at the small turn-out, but he was careful not to show it.

He wore a well-cut, pale grey suit, a white shirt which looked as though he had only just put it on, and a black and silver striped tie with its insignia a carefully measured distance below the knot.

His hair was white, and cut close and neat. It darkened at the edges, leaving clean lines around his face. He looked freshly shaved.

'I'm grateful you could all spare the time to come this afternoon,' he said.

'You rarely come to us,' someone on the front row said, which raised some laughter.

Only Brownlow looked uncomfortable at this.

Two more officers joined Lister and Brownlow at the tables.

At the back of the room, the door opened and a late arrival entered and sat immediately behind Sunny and myself.

Sunny glanced at the man and wrote 'LAW' on his pad.

'Pressures of work, I'm afraid,' Lister said as the laughter subsided. 'And I'm sure you'd be the first to complain if I was using my resources unwisely.' He held up his palms, as though the gesture might bring silence to the room. When people continued to whisper among themselves, Brownlow rose from his seat and called for silence.

This annoyed Lister, but again he was careful not to let it show.

'Have there been developments?' Sunny asked. It was a tired and predictable question to ask, but it would at least allow the proceedings to begin.

Taking this opportunity to reassert his authority over the briefing, Alexander Lister said, 'I doubt that is what you expected to hear. Lucy Collins's death is still under investigation and Paul Hendry remains in the Hull Royal Infirmary in a coma. In that respect we know no more or less than we were able to tell you yesterday.'

'Then why all this now?' Sunny said.

Lister leaned towards Brownlow, who whispered to him.

'Ah, yes, Mr Summers,' Lister said. ' "All this now", as you put it, is precisely because this is what you've been calling for. Openness, accountability, clarity. I will insist – occasionally against my better judgement, I might add – on keeping the press, and, via you, the public, informed of everything that comes to light during the course of this investigation. I will not be accused – as my predecessor was accused – and nor will I stand by and listen to my officers being accused – of evasion, unhelpfulness or obfuscation.'

'Even if that's what they're doing?' someone said.

' "Obfuscation"?' Sunny whispered. 'It just gets better and better.'

'No one is doing anything of the kind,' Lister said loudly. 'And regardless of your own individual agendas concerning this case – which, believe me, I do understand and take cognizance of – I will neither jeopardize nor compromise my inquiries to suit what your readers might want to read.'

It surprised me to see how quickly this confrontation had arisen.

'He's setting out the ground rules,' Sunny said. 'He wants us all to know who's in charge. He wouldn't have said half of what he's said if the nationals had turned up. All this is just chest-beating.'

Someone asked Lister if he was still convinced of Paul Hendry's guilt.

'I'm convinced of nothing at this point in time,' Lister said. 'But I imagine from your question that you are referring to the fact that, as yet, we have established no definite connection or specific line of inquiry which links the killing of Lucy Collins to the deaths of either or both Kelly Smith and Alison Wilson.'

'It seems to make sense to everyone else but you,' the man said.

Alison Wilson was the girl whose body had been found on the derelict land off Garrison Road.

Lister said something behind his hand to Brownlow.

Only then did I notice the security camera mounted in the corner of the ceiling behind the line of men. A small light flashed and the lens moved slightly. Others saw this too, and a woman rose to ask if it could be switched off.

'That's right – give him an opportunity to change the subject,' Sunny said to me, exasperated.

'The camera is as much for your benefit as for ours,' Brownlow said to the woman.

Sunny rose to his feet. 'Is that an answer, DS Brownlow?'

Angered by this continued provocation, Lister pointed at Sunny and said, 'Mr Summers, you and your colleagues show little reluctance when it comes to pointing *your* cameras at *us*.'

It struck me as a clumsy and unguarded remark to make.

'It's what you're there for,' Sunny said. 'It's why you call these things. Though I don't really see the point of today's little show.'

'I call "these things" because it's my fervent belief that they are of mutual benefit. I call "these things" because I hope that *you* – you, personally, Mr Summers – want to see Lucy Collins's killer caught and punished as much as I and my officers do. If there's any conflict of interest on that particular point, then say so now, in front of your colleagues.'

Sunny listened to all this without responding.

Sitting beside Lister, Brownlow smiled and raised his eyebrows to Sunny and me.

Lister held up his hands again. 'What I refuse to allow happen – what I *absolutely* refuse to allow happen – is for this inquiry to become sidetracked, overloaded or hijacked by those people with their own axes to grind. I understand, possibly better than anyone else in this room, the strength of local feeling about these three killings, and the need to investigate as thoroughly as possible even the slightest connection between them, but I will not – repeat, I will *not* – allow either myself or my investigating officers to be railroaded by public opinion. My priorities are very simple. If a single person is responsible for these crimes, then I will apprehend him. If three separate individuals are ultimately proved to be responsible, then I will apprehend all three.'

The room was silent now. People wrote in shorthand and recorders hummed faintly.

'Grandstanding bastard,' Sunny whispered.

Lister went on. 'It must surely have occurred to even you, Mr Summers, that to insist on a single perpetrator would serve no one well, except, possibly, the remaining two.'

There was some vague concurrence at this, and several of the men at the front turned to look at Sunny. They understood as well as he did the lines both he and Lister had just crossed and then retreated back over.

Lister waited for silence. He motioned for the man beside Brownlow to distribute the press releases he had brought with him. As this happened, he resumed speaking, his voice lower, conciliatory.

'I apologize for any offence I may have caused, Mr Summers, but I will not be swayed in this – not by you, not by any of you, and certainly not by ill-informed public opinion or by all those conspiracy theorists insisting they know best. Read my release. There are a great many unanswered questions concerning the discovery of both Lucy Collins and Paul Hendry, and far too much evidence connecting the two for me to ignore.'

'Have you established any real motive for why he might have wanted to kill her?' someone asked.

'You are as aware as I am that both Paul Hendry and Lucy Collins were known drug users. I am not suggesting that this in itself is sufficient to explain what happened, but it is something we cannot ignore. Nevertheless, our inquiries are continuing and—'

Several hands were raised, and Lister pointed to a woman sitting at the side of the room.

'We've been getting a lot of complaints from local women's groups, and a spokesperson who contacted us on behalf of local prostitutes who believed—'

'Sorry,' Lister said, stopping the woman. 'If you could be more specific. A spokesperson for local prostitutes?' He looked to Brownlow and the two others, all three of whom shrugged and shook their heads.

'Two of the women were known – known by your officers – to be working – however sporadically – as prostitutes. You can't seriously continue to insist that this isn't one of your "connections",' the woman said.

'I insist on no such thing,' Lister said. 'But what I do insist is that our inquiries would be better served by this "spokesperson" ' – he gave the word a deliberately cold emphasis – 'coming directly to me or one of my investigating officers and voicing her concerns.'

'They don't trust you,' the woman said bluntly.

'Me personally?' Lister said.

'Your officers. The law in general.'

'If they have good reason not to trust us, then let them come directly to me and tell me in confidence what those reasons are,' Lister said.

This encouraged a further flurry of note-taking.

'He's started his "new brush" spiel,' Sunny whispered. ' "It might have happened in the past, but it isn't going to happen under me." '

'Has it happened?' I asked him.

'You mean have prostitutes been badly, unfairly or dismissively treated by the forces of law and order in Hull? Guess.'

'And worse?'

'It's not what all this is supposed to be about. Forget it. If you wanted the prostitute angle for Susan Hendry – something to point the finger away from her precious son – then you'd be deceiving yourself as much as her. Stop worrying about that and start thinking about why *this* particular little charade is taking place.'

'Which is?'

He pursed his lips. 'Well, he certainly didn't gather us all together to tell us to stop complaining at the way he's going about things, that's for sure.'

'You think they've turned something up they're keeping to themselves?'

He shook his head. 'I don't know. But this is just not how press conferences happen, or why. They don't work like this. Usually, they feed us their lines and we swallow them. We make a bit of noise now and then, things get said, batted back and forth, but, essentially, it's all a PR job for the cameras or grieving relatives. Usually, somebody gets to cry to camera and to beg and plead for somebody either to come home or come back to life, and the rest of us get to feel just that little bit smug about it not being us doing the crying, the begging or the pleading. Somebody out there either *is* the killer, or they know them, or they have their suspicions. My guess is that Lister's backed himself into something of a corner and he's looking for a way out.'

'Meaning that soon the killings might be connected in a way

no-one can ignore and then he'll *have* to come round to that way of thinking?'

'And meanwhile it won't hurt him to keep his options open until Paul Hendry recovers and confesses all.'

'Or until he dies?'

'Lister will want to prepare himself for either eventuality. He's new here, he's got a mark to make, and he's got ambition. This is either the last thing he wanted or a godsend. Either way, he's still got to work out how he comes out on top, smelling good and with his hands clean.'

'And you think it's going to get worse before it gets better?'

'It's an alternative *he* certainly can't afford to ignore.' He indicated Lister, who, along with Brownlow, continued to answer questions from the men and women sitting closer to them. High on the wall, the camera blinked and moved again, and both Sunny and I followed it.

'Cultivate your paranoia carefully,' he said. 'Don't just let it spread unchecked. It's what the calendar told me this morning.'

'Rich coming from a man who still sticks hairs across his office door.'

'I still do it and it still works.'

I ran my hand over his head. 'Not for much longer.'

'Besides,' he said. 'A little bird tells me that Lister's got his sights firmly set on becoming the next ACC.'

'Soon?'

'Soon enough. A year at the outside. It's a big stepping stone.'

'And you think it might have some bearing on how he's handling all this now?'

'Grow up,' he said. And then he turned to the man still sitting behind us, who had remained silent throughout the proceedings, and said, 'Is that right, detective? Does Chief Superintendent Lister intend slipping on a pair of white gloves and carrying a shiny black baton with a silver head and bowing and scraping to all the minor royals each time they deign to walk among us?'

The man smiled at the remark. 'And what, you'd know how to prevent that from happening?'

'No,' Sunny said. 'But if he's gone to all this trouble to watch *our* backs, then I can only assume that he's going to even more to watch his own.'

The man continued smiling, unperturbed by the remark. 'Oh, of that I would be in absolutely no doubt whatsoever.' He nodded to me and then rose and left the room.

Both Lister and Brownlow looked up from their questioners to watch him go.

'What do you think all that was about?' I said. 'One of Lister's stooges?'

'I daresay all will be revealed,' Sunny said.

At the front of the room, Brownlow was now bringing the proceedings to a close. People began packing away their equipment. Lister remained seated as all this happened, talking to his other officers.

One of these men then came to where Sunny and I sat and said that Lister would appreciate being able to speak with us.

'With us, to us or at us?' Sunny said.

'Fuck you, Summers,' the man said beneath his breath.

'Tell him we'd be delighted to share our thoughts with him. Oh, and you might, incidentally, regret that little *sotto voce* remark on account of the incredibly sensitive piece of recording equipment in my pocket here.' He tapped his empty breast pocket. 'Perhaps you'd also like to identify yourself for the record.'

The man looked uncertain for a moment, and then grinned to himself and left us, returning to Lister and Brownlow.

'The plot thickens,' Sunny said.

Lister came to us a moment later, calling his farewells to the departing men and women, few of whom answered him after their wasted visit. He told the woman who'd raised the concerns of the local prostitutes to call him the following day. She, at least, seemed gratified by this apparent interest and concern.

'Mr Rivers,' Lister said to me, holding out his hand for a firm handshake. 'My apologies if any of this appeared' – he pretended to consider his choice of words – 'unnecessary to you. Mr Summers, I imagine, is somewhat more accustomed to it all.'

'I'm engaged by Susan Hendry,' I said.

'Please,' he said, finally releasing my hand. 'You don't need to explain yourself to me. You're engaged by the boy's mother to ensure he's treated fairly in all of this. And, presumably, because she has some misplaced or uncertain affection for Lucy Collins. This morning you spoke to Emily Carr and then tried unsuccessfully to see Dr Weaver. Whatever Mr Summers here might want you to believe, I'm not here to warn you off, just to remind you that I won't tolerate any interference in my own inquiries.'

'Sounds like a warning to me,' Sunny said.

'On the contrary,' Lister said. 'I can quite understand how our own inquiries and those undertaken by Mr Rivers might be of some mutual benefit.'

'Meaning people might say things to him they wouldn't tell you in a thousand years?' Sunny said.

'Certain people – or should I say certain types of people – yes.'

He was talking about Emily Carr.

The detective who had sworn at Sunny moved from beside Lister to stand close to me.

'I just wanted to make sure that we each of us fully understood our parts in all of this,' Lister said. Turning back to me, he said, 'Give John Maxwell my regards when you next speak to him. I worked with him a long time ago.'

'I will,' I said, uncertain what else the remark was intended to imply.

'No-one is going to prevent you from going about your lawful business, Mr Rivers,' he said. 'But, like I said, I *will* stop you from interfering where I have good reason to believe you are jeopardizing or compromising this investigation or the officers involved.'

'Even officers like DS Brownlow?' Sunny said.

Lister refused to be drawn. 'I'm sure I have DS Brownlow's confidence,' he said. 'And if you have any complaints to make against him personally, then I trust you will observe the proper channels.'

'We've got history, that's all,' Brownlow said.

'Whatever it is, don't bring it in here,' Lister said sharply.

'Can we go now?' Sunny said.

Hearing this, Lister finally lost patience and turned and left us, followed by the two other men.

'I think you're supposed to follow them,' Sunny said to Brownlow. 'You know – like a little dog.'

Brownlow smiled at the remark and then walked slowly away from us.

7

The following morning I called Susan Hendry and arranged to see her later in the day. She'd spent her first night at home since her son had been taken into hospital. There had been no change in his condition, he was still in Intensive Care, still on a ventilator, and there were still two constables sitting in the corridor outside the room in which he lay.

She asked me if I had anything new to tell her and I told her I didn't. She sounded tired, as though my call had woken her. I could only imagine what every ring of the phone might now mean to her.

Yvonne had driven her home after she'd fallen asleep at her son's bedside, and had then stayed with her until she'd finally gone to bed in the early hours. Yvonne must have left after that, she said, because she hadn't been there when she'd woken. She told me everything twice, and in detail, as though this partial return to normality was still as strange as it was vital to her.

An hour later, I left Humber Street and went to the address I'd noted from the alarm box at Weaver's surgery.

This turned out to be a Portakabin surrounded by a high-fenced yard on a small industrial estate where Lime Street curved alongside the River Hull. I parked in the street and went to the gate. Two Alsatians stood guard there, chained to a post and barking and straining to get at me. Several vans stood parked in front of the Portakabin.

At the noise of the dogs, a man came to the doorway and looked out at me. He came towards me, shouting at the dogs, both of which fell silent. He carried a plastic cup and threw the contents of this to one side as he came.

I told him I'd appreciate being able to talk to someone about the Walker Street alarm.

'This is just the depot,' he said. 'Enquiries are all normally done on the phone.' He indicated the sign above the entrance. 'That's the number.'

I took out the forty pounds I'd already folded into my pocket, knowing immediately by the way he then positioned himself between me and anyone who might have been watching from the Portakabin that he would talk to me. I also knew that he'd probably mistaken the forty for eighty or perhaps a hundred. It was something else I'd learned from John Maxwell. The trick was not to hand the money over until the transaction was completed.

'Wait here,' he said. 'I'm due out on a call.'

He left me and returned to the cabin, emerging a moment later with a clipboard and wearing a hard hat. The two dogs stood and watched me in silence during his short absence.

He climbed into one of the vans and drove to Jenning Street, where he pulled up out of sight of the yard.

I followed him there on foot.

He opened the passenger door for me.

'What do you want to know?' he said. He angled the rear-view mirror to face back to the junction of the two streets. 'I'm sick and fucking tired of hearing about that place.'

'Oh?'

'I'm on a warning. Nothing official. Just a warning.'

'Have there been problems?'

'Complaints. It's a doctors' surgery, right? A surgery with a dispensary? Drugs. We have a special package for places like that. Response times, tie-ups. They pay over the odds and we're supposed to provide something above and beyond what everybody else gets.'

'What's a "tie-up"?' I asked him.

'When we get the call that the alarm's gone off, we're supposed to alert whichever of the emergency services are "deemed appropriate".'

'The police?'

'Usually.'

'And they do what?'

'Log the call and tell us they'll get there as fast as they can.'

'Which is usually what?'

'Depends. If they've got somebody in the neighbourhood, they can be there in no time at all. Sometimes they don't turn up until an hour later. The boss just tells us to make sure we log our call to them to cover our own backs.'

'Aren't the alarms wired directly to the police station?'

He laughed at the suggestion. 'Ten years ago, perhaps. You know how many call-outs we get some nights?'

I told him I didn't.

'Fucking dozens.'

'Mostly false alarms?' I guessed.

'You said it.'

'What happened at Walker Street five nights ago?' The money was still in my hand and he glanced at it every few seconds.

'Three times that fucker's gone off in the past' – he took a battered ledger from the dashboard and opened it – 'in the past fifteen weeks. It might not sound a lot, but that's ten times a year, give or take. I fitted that alarm myself. Fitted it, tested it, serviced it, everything. Perfect. Job well done. Two years ago. One call-out six months later – false alarm – and then nothing until four months ago.'

'What's the arrangement?' I asked him.

'What do you mean?'

I wasn't certain. 'Does your response change if the alarm goes off too frequently?'

'Officially or unofficially?'

I told him I understood.

'Officially, they get the same response even if it goes off every fucking night.'

'And presumably they end up paying a higher premium for that.'

'It's all part of their insurance package.'

'So what happened a week ago?'

'I'm getting to that. But what you've got to remember is that the guy in charge of that place, the head doctor, wasn't too pleased about our response on the previous two false alarms. He got there before we did on the second one, just like last time. The system's wired up to his bleeper. The first time we got there ahead of him, but only just. It was late at night, turned one, and he was probably just pissed off at being dragged out of his bed. It was raining.'

'And the second time?'

'There were complications, see. Extenuating circumstances. He might have been there before us, but we had a good reason for being late.'

'Which was?'

'The police had only fucking closed off the dual carriageway from Mount Pleasant to Brighton Street. That, and the Freetown Way at George Street and Beverley Road. Nothing moving any-where, well hardly.'

'Why had they done that?'

He turned the ledger towards me. 'July twenty-second, wasn't it. That girl's body had just been found off Garrison Road. Knee-jerk reaction if you ask me. But they blocked everything off and started questioning everybody trying to drive in or out. The boss phoned the doctor to explain and he calmed down. By the time I arrived it was clear that the alarm was another false one. I reset it for him, got him to sign my call-out slip and we all went home.'

'And last week?'

'I swear to God, I was only ten minutes getting there. A fraction of what it had taken on the first two occasions.'

'And Weaver was already there?'

'Just arrived. He was standing at the front door, waiting. He was dressed up all smart, dinner jacket, said he was on his way to some function or other.'

'Did he say where?'

'He might have done. I was a bit busy. I don't take kindly to being shouted at and called a moron, not by the likes of him. He told me to get on with what I'd got to do while he called his wife and explained what was happening. They were going out together, or he was meeting her there, or something. You have to remember, the alarm was still going off while all this was happening. He said that when I'd turned it off he was going to seriously consider terminating his contract with us.'

'And did he?'

He shook his head and smiled. 'Easier said than done. Happens all the time. The deal is that we fit, service and respond. After an initial deposit for fixtures and installation, everything gets paid off in monthly instalments, which also covers our servicing and response.'

'So once the equipment's installed . . .'

'Exactly. He could buy out of it, but then he'd have to have the whole lot taken out and a new system installed by another firm. None of this comes cheap.'

'And so once he'd stopped swearing at you, everything stayed the same?'

'I think he just got overtaken by events – you know, finding the druggie who'd broken in and all that.'

'Did Weaver find him?'

He thought about this. 'I went round the back to check all the doors and windows. There was a side door standing open. No sign of a forced entry – or none that I could see – but I knew better than to go into the place before the law arrived. I called my boss. He'd made his first call to the police, but said he'd call again now that I'd found an open door. He called me back a minute later to say they were definitely on their way. They got there five minutes later.'

'And all that time, Weaver waited with you?'

'He wanted us to go in, but I told him it was best to wait. Neither of us thought there was anyone still in there, but I knew the law wouldn't want us touching anything. Weaver just went on trying to get through to his wife. Kept leaving messages, stuff like that, telling her he was going to be late. I tried to calm him down, but he wasn't having any of it. He started talking about the last two call-outs, kept saying this was the last straw. And then the law arrived.'

'And they discovered the boy?'

'They asked us who we were, told me to shut the alarm off, and then told us to wait where we were while they went in to check the place out. It pissed Weaver off to be spoken to like that, for the two of us to be treated the same. He asked them for their names. Even wrote them down, behaving like Mr high-and-mighty, as though he was in a position to do something about it. I told him just to be patient while they did their job and he all but fucking hit me. That was when he called me a moron. I was about to tell him where to get off when one of the coppers came out of the side door and ran to his car. He told Weaver to move his car from the car park on to the street and told me to move the van further away. Weaver asked him what was happening, but the copper was too busy making calls to answer him.'

'Because they'd found the boy in Weaver's surgery.'

'The ambulance was there in another five minutes. You could hear it coming all the way from the hospital. Then Weaver started telling the other copper about the dinner he was due to attend and the guy told him it wasn't very likely that he'd be going anywhere. Weaver went to sit in one of their cars.'

'Had others arrived?'

'Two or three by then. Three. That was how I knew it was something serious. The ambulance men brought the boy out after that. They were in, out and off as quick as they could.' He looked at his watch. We'd been sitting together for twenty minutes. He continued to look into the rear-view mirror.

'*Did* Weaver make a complaint against you?' I asked him.

'Nah. Like I said, everything got a bit out of hand after they found the druggie.' He paused. 'In fact, now that you mention it, he actually apologized to me.'

'Apologized?'

'We were in the station together, making our statements. There was a lot of hanging about. He came and said he was sorry for having overreacted. He said that the police finding that boy in there changed everything, that if he'd known it was anything more than just another false alarm, he wouldn't have said half the things he did.'

'What did you say?'

'What could I say? One more complaint after the last time, and the chances are I'd be looking for another job. It's barely above minimum wage as it is, but it's something. There's not that many decent jobs going, and I've probably not got as many framed certificates hanging on my wall as Weaver has.'

We both laughed at this and I gave him the forty pounds. He tucked it into his shirt pocket without counting it.

'Did Weaver show any sign that he recognized the boy when they brought him out?' I asked him.

'Not that I can remember. He was mostly covered up. They wheeled him straight from the door to the back of the ambulance. As I remember it, Weaver was still sitting in his dinner jacket in one of the police cars. I think he'd finally got through to his wife and he was telling her everything that was happening.'

I thanked him for everything he'd been able to tell me and gave him one of my cards. He wrote his own number on a piece of paper and gave it to me.

I opened the door.

'There was one other thing,' he said. 'The police said the side door had been forced.'

'Which had set the alarm off?'

'The control box confirmed it. I filled out a full report form and the coppers took a copy. The one who'd gone into the surgery first said that even though it was clear that the boy had gone in through that door, it didn't look as though it would take much forcing. He was wrong. I fitted that lock myself. If it hadn't taken much forcing, then it was probably because somebody had forgotten to slide the dead-bolts inside. Nothing to do with the lock or the alarm. I was definitely in the clear on that score.'

I left the van and walked to where my car was parked. He drove out onto Cleveland Street and was lost in the traffic there.

I went to the Scott Street Bridge and looked down at the River Hull. Half a mile downstream the same brown, mud-laden water flowed and settled at the end of Humber Street, sucked into the ebb and flow of the estuary as its failing momentum finally died.

8

Later that afternoon, I went to see Susan Hendry. She lived in a large and imposing Edwardian house on Park Avenue, close to the recently painted ornamental fountain. The Avenues had been built for the city's wealthier merchants and businessmen, away from the river and its crowded housing and smells, and to the west of the city, in the path of its clean, prevailing winds.

She was standing at the window looking out as I arrived. The door and window frame were vividly blue, and a century-old pattern of leaves and flowers in coloured glass was set into the tops of the panes. She watched me approach, and then waited until I pressed the bell before opening the door to me.

She was wearing the same clothes I'd seen her in previously, and she still looked exhausted. A pile of newspapers lay bunched behind the door where they had been pushed unread. A scatter of envelopes lay on the carpet. A pile of these had been gathered up and stacked on the broad stairs that led upwards from the door.

The hallway was warm, and wall lights illuminated the paintings there. A mahogany banister ran up the stairs to a balcony landing.

The hallway led to several doorways and was painted dark red, emphasizing its length.

She led me into the room in which she had been standing. It reminded me of Yvonne's overcrowded home: more paintings, and ornaments, plates, bowls and mementoes everywhere, the polished wooden floor covered in rugs and scattered with books and magazines.

'You just missed Yvonne,' she said. 'Sunny called. I think he's angry that she's been spending so much time away from the agency.' She spoke slowly, and her eyes avoided mine.

'That won't worry her,' I said.

'She shouted at him to show some compassion and then hung up on him. "Him, of all people," she said. I told her not to fall out with him on my account. He lost his wife and daughter in a car crash, didn't he?'

'Sarah and Isobel,' I said. 'He and his wife were separated. Isobel was thirteen. It was in Essex, a few days after Isobel's birthday. It knocked him off the rails for the best part of ten years. It's why he came back here.'

'It will have knocked him off the rails for the rest of his life,' she said. 'Yvonne's been very kind. She's told me a lot about you. She thinks a lot of the pair of you, you and Sunny.'

'We both think a lot of her,' I said.

'I can tell. I don't have too many close friends. No family to speak of. A few scattered aunts, uncles and distant cousins, I suppose – that sort of family.' She was talking simply to defeat the silence of the house and to try and keep her mind from her son. A muted television played in the corner. A small table was covered with photographs of her son, and of her and Paul together.

'Have they told you anything new?' I asked her.

'Who – the hospital or the police? The police still behave as though they don't have to tell me anything at all.'

'There's nothing they can do until he recovers,' I said.

'How inconvenient for them.'

'I know it's little consolation,' I said. 'But I don't believe they're as convinced as they're professing to be about Paul's connection to the other killings.'

'And that's supposed to make me feel better, is it? That's supposed to give me hope? They're still insisting he killed Lucy.'

It would be a painful waste of time for her to continue going round in circles and so I said nothing.

She apologized. 'I just sit here,' she said. 'I try and imagine the best that can happen, and then I imagine the worst. And do you know what – there's not that much to choose between them. Yvonne told me about her two sons. She never says it, but she probably feels as lost and as abandoned as I do.'

Yvonne's younger son was at university in Manchester, reading Politics; and her elder, having graduated a year ago, was living with his father in Leeds. Neither place was more than a two-hour drive away.

'I spoke to Emily Carr,' I said.

She looked puzzled. 'Who's she?'

'She was a friend of Paul's and Lucy's at Nelson Court.'

'Right. I think Paul might have mentioned her. I think I met her.'

'She's pregnant,' I said, watching her.

She shrugged. 'So?'

'She told me she knew your son from when they were both children together, at school.'

'Oh. I didn't know. I think I assumed that she and Lucy were friends.'

'Perhaps they were, this time round. She said she hadn't seen Paul for years before he moved into Nelson Court. She said her father had been friends with your husband.'

'With Tony? What was his name? Carr?' It was the first real attention she'd paid to me since my arrival.

'She seemed to think it was a long time ago, long before Paul was born, and probably before you met your husband.'

She remembered nothing definite. 'Next time you see her, ask her his name.'

'I think it was just one of those things,' I said. 'They were common enough when the trawler fleets were still working.'

'I know,' she said. 'It's what killed our marriage.'

I didn't understand her.

'My husband,' she said. 'His grandfather was a trawlerman, his father was a trawlerman – a skipper, in fact – and all Tony ever wanted to do while he was growing up was to follow in their footsteps. It was all mapped out for him, cradle to grave. They knew which company he'd work for, which boat he'd sail on, what he'd do, what he'd earn, where he'd fish, every single little step of how he'd make his way from the bottom to the top.'

'And it never happened?'

'It never happened. I met him in '74. He was eighteen; I was fifteen. One year the docks were full of boats and the city full of fishermen; two years later, there was hardly anything left. Even his dad was laid off. He left school, worked on one boat for nine months, and then he was laid off himself. Never worked at sea again.'

'This was before you were married?'

'Two years before. But we'd started making arrangements by then, and I suppose everything just happened. It's how things worked in those days. His parents and my parents saw to that. Perhaps they thought that by getting married and starting a family of his own, he'd find some new purpose in life. He was an only child, see. We both were.'

'And it didn't happen?'

'It might have worked like that for a few months, but not much longer. They all used to hang around together, him and all the other laid-off deck hands. Like a kind of crippling inertia. None of them knew what else to do. None of them really ever accepted what was happening to them. It was a man's world. They thought more of each other than they ever did of their wives and children. Always had their own priorities. His mother spoiled him, treated him like a little god. It's what he became. I don't think any of them could believe that the world had changed so quickly and left them behind and standing out in the cold, unwanted. I saw the same thing happen ten years later when they closed all the pits. There was plenty of sympathy for the miners, but where was it for ours when the fishing industry was destroyed? Nowhere. Perhaps that girl's' – she fluttered her hand.

'Emily Carr.'

'Perhaps Emily Carr's father knew Tony from then. Perhaps they worked together, or were laid off together. Who knows? There were thousands of them. Everybody kept telling him he was young enough to make a go of something else. But fishing was in his blood. It was all he ever wanted. He never even bothered to train for anything else. Just took one poorly paid job after another – mostly working on building sites. Then he started labouring abroad – *Auf Wiedersehen, Pet* – all that. And after that, we grew apart. I only used to see him every three months. And even then, he'd only be home for a week or so, and he preferred to spend most of it with all his own mates – "spend" being the operative word.'

'How old was Paul while all this was happening?'

'We'd been married five years before Paul was born. Four years before Tony walked out on us.'

'What happened?'

'What happened was that one day he sailed back to Germany on the ferry, and two days later I got a call from him telling me he wasn't coming back. His blessed mother knew about it before I did. He'd got her wrapped round his little finger. She started trying to convince me that it was all for the best, that her precious son needed to make a fresh start and leave everything behind him.'

'Everything?'

'They were a tight-lipped family. I was never good enough for him. And certainly not in her eyes. They all closed ranks. I was the one who wanted him to do something better with his life. For them, of course, that meant working on the boats. I was the one who'd driven him away. I went to see them, to tell them about his call, and it was the last time I ever went there. He was killed in an accident on a building site four years later. Düsseldorf. We never even got divorced.'

I tried to remember what Emily Carr had told me about her own father's death.

'Are his parents still alive?' I asked her.

She shook her head. 'His father died ten years ago, his mother the year after. Heart attack and cancer. They were both in their late sixties. They spent twenty years hanging on, but that's all it ever was. I didn't want Paul to have anything to do with them. Not that they made much of an effort. He was the one good thing to come out of that marriage. The company my husband was working for sent me a box of his belongings. It was pathetic. There was another woman, of course, a string of other women. I searched that box, but there wasn't a single picture of either Paul or me in there. He had a hundred pounds to his name. The insurance pay-out from the German contractors came to me. You can imagine how well that went down with his doting mother. I took the box of stuff round to her – they lived nearby, on Dairycoates Avenue – and she threw it in my face. It was the last I saw of her. I didn't even know she'd died until a few months after it happened.' She stopped talking and took a deep breath. She seemed surprised and relieved by all she'd just revealed to me. It had little bearing on what was happening to her now, but it helped me to understand her better.

She indicated the array of photographs on the table.

'You probably think I'm just the same as her,' she said. 'Overbearing, possessive, overprotective.'

'I imagine there are times when all mothers need to be all those things, and perhaps this is one of them,' I said.

She smiled at the remark. 'Yvonne said you had a weakness for fridge-magnet philosophizing.'

'It's the best kind,' I said.

'I don't think she was being critical. She also said you had the strongest sense of right and wrong of anybody she'd ever met.'

'She means any *man* she's ever met.'

'I took that as read.' She smiled again.

I followed her into the kitchen at the rear of the house, where she made us both coffee. A dozen empty wine bottles and two half-empty bottles of vodka stood on the draining board.

'It helps me to sleep,' she said. 'Sometimes.'

I looked out at the long, tree-lined garden. Leaves already lay in drifts along its edges.

'Emily Carr thought Lucy might have been pregnant at some point during the time she was living at Nelson Court,' I said.

She stumbled at hearing the words, gripping and holding the sink. I put my palm against her back.

'About a year ago,' she said, straightening and releasing her grip on the sink, 'Paul called me, said he was coming to see me, that he had something important to tell me. It was the first time I'd heard from him in weeks.'

'And?'

'He never came. When I asked him later what it had been about, he said he couldn't remember, that it couldn't have been much. I'd learned by then not to push him for answers.' She looked out at the lights of the houses opposite, at the early darkness all around them. 'Christ,' she said. 'It never ends, does it? It never bloody ends.'

Beside us, the kettle steamed for a few seconds and then clicked itself off.

9

Kelly Smith had been found murdered at three twenty in the morning on the twenty-eighth of May. Her body was discovered by a man walking to the taxi rank in Victoria Square. She had been stabbed in the chest and stomach and face, and then dumped behind a row of commercial bins in the yard at the rear of the shops on Chapel Street.

It had been quickly established that Kelly Smith was a known prostitute, and that she worked on either Anlaby Road, Ferensway close to the station, or, more recently, in the city centre itself. Her record showed that she had been arrested on three occasions for soliciting. She died two days short of her twenty-first birthday.

On the night she was killed, she had been celebrating in several bars and clubs with a group of her friends, some of whom also worked as prostitutes. She was wearing a white halter top and a short denim skirt. Her handbag and purse were found intact close beside her, as was the deflated balloon which had been tied to her bra strap announcing her forthcoming birthday.

The man who found her had gone into the yard to urinate, searching for somewhere beside the bins where he might not be seen from the street. The gates to the delivery area behind the shops were unlocked and open. A security guard from Lloyds bank said that a team of men had been working on installing a new lighting and air-conditioning system in the bank and had been there over the previous four nights, working from late afternoon until six or seven in the morning. Everyone engaged in the work had been traced and questioned. No one had seen or heard anything out of the ordinary.

The security guard assured the police that the gates had been open for no more than an hour, awaiting the arrival of a lorry delivering ducting. This had arrived and been unloaded, and none of the men employed in this had seen Kelly Smith's body.

The gates were left open for forty minutes after the departure of the lorry, during which time the man had entered and found the corpse.

It was suggested at the post-mortem that a long and deep wound to Kelly Smith's stomach and liver had killed her, and that this had been delivered prior to the eighteen other wounds that were found, nine more to her chest and stomach, four to her legs and five to her face and neck. There was nothing on her hands or forearms to suggest that she had attempted to defend herself, and no bruises or abrasions elsewhere to suggest that she had been restrained or assaulted prior to being stabbed. It was this absence of other marking that led the police to their early conclusion that, despite having been celebrating her forthcoming birthday, Kelly Smith had later taken the opportunity to make some money, either by soliciting as she made her way home, or – more likely – upon unexpectedly encountering a known client there.

She and the other girls had parted between two thirty and three, and they all said she had been excessively drunk by that time. The last two to see her alive had left her sitting on the rose beds at the end of the pedestrian way at the station end of Carr Lane. She had been walking towards Anlaby Road and her home on Selby Street. Those last two girls had hailed her a taxi, but the driver had refused to take her because he believed she was about to be sick.

The man was sought and questioned. He told the police that he recognized all three girls, and that he knew what they were. There were traces of vomit in Kelly Smith's mouth. A search was made of the area, and of the nine patches of vomit found, one of these was positively matched to Kelly Smith.

The examination of her stomach and blood revealed an excessively high alcohol content. If she *had* been soliciting for business after leaving the other girls, it was suggested, then she would have had little real idea of what she was doing. Some considered this a good thing in light of what subsequently happened to her; and some said it might have been why her killer had chosen Kelly Smith over any of the other women in the city centre that night.

Two hundred and thirty hours of CCTV footage were examined, but other than a brief shot of Kelly Smith in the company of several of the other girls turning the corner of Jameson Street into South Street, there was nothing more of her drunken wandering through the brightly lit streets. It had been a warm, dry night, and most of the camera system was operational. There were cameras covering the whole of the pedestrian area, but nothing keeping watch over the delivery yard. The camera and integrated alarm lights which normally covered the rear of the bank had been switched off during the work taking place there.

Having supervised the various deliveries, it was part of the security guard's remit to stay close to the rear entrance and to watch the yard. When the man was questioned, however, he admitted that there had been times when he had been absent from the door for ten or fifteen minutes at a time. He knew some of the men who were working there, and had joined them during their frequent tea breaks. He had worked at the bank for two years, and in all that time he had never known of prostitutes using the normally secure and private space to bring their clients. The high gates were usually locked by seven in the evening, and the entrance and all the other doorways were checked hourly. It occurred to the detectives questioning the man that he was more concerned about losing his job than he was about what had happened to Kelly Smith less than thirty seconds' walk from his own small room.

Kelly Smith lost a great deal of blood, much of it from the first and most serious of her wounds. A lot of this had simply drained from her body because the wound had been deep and extensive and a great many blood vessels had been severed. There was little wider splatter, merely a pool which gathered around her corpse and spread slowly outwards over the tarmac. She lay on her side, with her legs together and folded at the knees. One arm lay beneath her head and was covered in the blood which had flowed from her neck and chest, and the other was folded beneath her.

What little clothing she wore had not been interfered with, and certainly not removed. Her bra remained fastened, and the thong she wore beneath her denim skirt remained in place.

Her ears, nose and navel were pierced, and each contained a diamond stud. Her friends explained that she was wearing these because she was celebrating. When asked why she was celebrating two days early, and on a Tuesday night, none of them knew. One of the girls had shown the investigating detectives the gifts she had volunteered to safeguard for Kelly Smith once she became drunk. These gifts included more jewellery, three soft toys and a novelty vibrator upon which a face with protruding tongue had been moulded.

The balloon still attached to Kelly Smith's bra strap had been deflated by a single puncture. In the few CCTV frames of Kelly Smith with the others, it was still floating above her head, springing up and down as she walked. The girls had tried to fasten more to her, but another of these had become detached and had floated off into the night. Having a balloon telling everyone it was your birthday was an easy way of being bought drinks all night, they explained.

Kelly Smith's every move was plotted and traced in detail. Detectives visited each of the bars and clubs she'd visited and talked to everyone who remembered seeing her there. Tracing everyone present had proved an impossible task, but most of the bar staff remembered the girls. None of these reported anything out of the ordinary.

The girls themselves recounted in overlapping detail how the night had progressed, and even though most of them later became as drunk as Kelly Smith had been, they all remembered a great deal. They remembered most of the men they met, and who wanted to dance with them and buy them drinks. Several of these men had been present at more than one of the places the party had visited, but this was not considered unusual by any of them. Most people had a set pattern to their nights. Men and women who met early in the evenings arranged to meet again later in other places, and some of them remained sober enough to remember those rendezvous. No one could remember Kelly Smith making any firm arrangements to meet anyone after leaving the others.

Because her body had been found so soon after she was killed, there were hopes initially that the connection to her killer might become quickly apparent. But this didn't happen. The city centre had been a busy place that night. The CCTV footage revealed thousands of people, hundreds of moving and parked cars, several other incidents worthy of investigation, but nothing relating to what had happened in the yard off Chapel Street at the time of Kelly Smith's murder.

Even a cursory investigation of the yard showed that her killer might easily have avoided the cameras which watched over the streets outside. In addition, there were hundreds of figures moving through the darker of the city-centre streets who would never be identified.

Almost three hundred registration plates had been recorded within a hundred metres of where Kelly Smith had died at the approximate time of her death. Every one of these had been checked, and nothing had come of this.

The delivery yard was sealed, searched and searched again for every faint trace or echo of what had happened there. But after thirty-six hours it was reopened, and whatever it might once have held of Kelly Smith's killing was lost for ever.

I went to Selby Street to see Kelly Smith's mother. Nineteen weeks had passed since her daughter's death.

A girl of nine or ten answered the door and asked me who I was. I told her and asked if I could speak to Karen Smith.

A woman's voice called to ask who was there.

The girl was barefoot and wearing only pyjamas with a pattern of Barbie dolls on them. She opened the door wider and let me into the small room overlooking the street.

Karen Smith sat in a padded dressing-gown close to a gas fire. She held a plate in her lap containing several slices of toast. She had been watching the television. She looked from me to the girl and then back to me.

I introduced myself and told her why I was there. I hoped my connection to Susan Hendry might persuade her to talk to me. Nothing had yet been released to the press concerning the police's so far unfounded belief that Paul Hendry might have been responsible for any of the earlier killings. The mantelpiece and every other surface in the room were still filled with cards of condolence, at least a hundred of them.

She saw me looking at these.

'That's how popular she was,' she said. 'Some of them are from people who never even knew her, but the rest are from people who knew what a good girl she was.'

The remark made me uneasy.

A train moved slowly along the tracks on the far side of the street and she turned away from me to watch it.

The young girl followed me into the room, sat beside her mother and picked up a bowl of cereal from the floor. It was almost two in the afternoon.

'I can't eat this,' Karen Smith said to her daughter, and the girl took the plate from her lap. Karen Smith immediately lit a cigarette, blowing the smoke into the gas fire and watching it curl and rise in the heat there. The small room was already stiflingly warm.

'He might just as well have stuck that knife into me and her as well,' she said. She ran a hand over the girl's head. 'Because that's what he's done. I can count on one hand the number of times I've been out of this house since it happened. And Kayleigh's not been to school since.'

The girl ate her cereal and watched the television.

'Go on, read some of them if you want,' Karen Smith said, indicating the cards. She picked up several of those nearest to her and gave them to me.

I read them and gave them back to her.

'When it happened, they were all over us,' she said. 'We had a policewoman – nice girl – practically living with us for three or four days. Came and went at all hours, couldn't do enough for us. But since then . . .' She watched the television briefly. 'We were on that, in the papers, everything. And each time one or other of the detectives came to the house they were full of how soon they were going to catch him and what they were going to do to him when they did. I was on tablets for my nerves and stuff even before all this. God alone knows what I'm taking these days.'

'Have you seen your doctor?' I asked her.

'She comes every few days. It's not that far – Anlaby Road. I do everything she tells me, but it's not easy. How can I sleep? How am I supposed to shop and eat properly like she tells me to? It was hard enough when the three of us were together, but without Kelly bringing anything in, it's nigh on impossible.' She picked up several more of the cards and read them, smiling at the printed messages.

I knew from the newspaper reports that she was thirty-nine, but she looked ten years older. Even in the padded gown she looked thin. The bones of her fingers and her shins showed clearly against her skin.

'Have *you* come to tell me about her?' she said.

I wondered how much had truly been revealed to her upon her daughter's death. It was difficult to ask her anything directly with the girl sitting beside her, but she made no attempt to get her to leave.

'They treated us as though we had everything in common,' she said, contradicting what she'd just told me about the police. 'Fifteen years ago, that was, when Kelly was only half the age of this one here, and six months after her father had walked out on us. Two offences in the space of three months, that's all it was. They think people never change. They took away a photo of her when she was eighteen. She'd had it done professionally, you know, proper lighting, the lot, making her look like a model.'

I knew exactly what the photo made her look like. The *Mail* had printed it almost every night during the first week of the police investigation.

'She used to try and get me to have one done like it. *Me*.' She looked down at herself, waiting for my complimentary remark.

'Is there any chance that Kelly might have known either Alison Wilson or Lucy Collins, or even Paul Hendry?' I asked her.

'The police came back to ask me the same thing after that last one was killed. I told them I'd never heard of any of them. But Kelly was a popular girl. She had lots of friends I never met. If she did know any of them, then *their* families never sent cards or got in touch – you know, when their daughters . . .'

The girl announced that she'd finished her cereal and that she was going upstairs to get dressed. Before leaving, she took the ashtray from her mother's lap and tipped it into a bin beside the television.

'She's a good girl,' Karen Smith said, watching her go.

Amid the cards there were framed photos of her two daughters, and on the wall above the fire were hung two larger portraits of the girls.

'She was an attractive girl,' I said.

'She was beautiful. Lovely nature, never harmed a fly. Do anything for anybody, that was Kelly. I said the same to all the police who came.'

I could imagine their unspoken thoughts at hearing this.

'So what exactly is it you do?' she asked me.

'I'm just trying to make sure nothing's been missed,' I said evasively.

'So you're definitely not the police?'

'No.'

'And do you think they're not doing their job properly?'

'I'm sure they're doing everything they can,' I said.

'I meant on account of Kelly being what they said she was.'

'They had good reason for believing it,' I said.

'But they still treated her differently because of it. You've only got to look at what's happening now to see that they didn't treat it as serious as they should have done.'

'I think you're wrong,' I said, hoping this rebuttal might reassure her.

She seemed not to have heard me. 'I told them that when they caught him, I wanted to be the first to see him. I told them they owed me that much at least. They wanted me to see a counsellor or somebody. They sent someone round from so-called Victim Support. What do *I* want with any of them? They said that if I needed any help with Kayleigh, then I only had to ask. They make it sound as though they're all doing you a big favour, but I can see straight through them. I know what they're up to.'

'I don't think there would be any suggestion of you being separated from your daughter,' I said.

'Shows how much you know,' she said. 'Not that it would make much difference. It's devastated us, this has, devastated us. I don't know how we're going to get over it, not really, not properly. They won't even release her body so we can have a funeral. That's what everybody keeps telling me – get her properly buried, proper funeral and everything, and then I can start to look forward again. When it was just her who'd been killed, there was talk of me getting her body back soon enough, but now they just keep telling me over and over that they can't make any promises.'

I considered this unlikely, that the police and their support services would have done considerably more for her, but that she had chosen to remain the living victim around whom all this now revolved.

'It's just like that woman I told them about.'

'What woman?' I'd missed what she was saying.

'The day before Kelly was killed? Yeah? She told me she was coming out of the Prospect Centre when a woman came up to her and asked her if she was Kelly Smith. Said she'd known her father, Philip, my ex.'

'Who was she?'

'Never said. It was raining, pouring down. Kelly said the two of them were standing outside in it. She said she thought the woman was on her way back to a car parked across the street. Said there was someone waiting for her.'

'And the woman definitely didn't identify herself?'

'If she did, Kelly never remembered.'

'So she didn't, for instance, tell Kelly to remember her to her father.'

'Like I said – memory like a sieve.'

'And you told this to the police?'

'For what good it did me, yes. They seemed to think it had nothing whatsoever to do with what happened to Kelly. Something like that happens, you start thinking the worst of everybody, don't you?'

The young girl reappeared, dressed in trousers with straps hanging from each leg and a pink T-shirt with the word BITCH in silver across her chest. She wore nothing beneath this and her nipples pressed small points into the material on either side of the word.

'I told her not to wear it,' Karen Smith said, smiling at the girl. 'She's too young to really understand what it means.'

'No, I'm not,' the girl said sullenly. She dropped onto the sofa beside her mother and folded her arms across the word.

'What chance do they get, growing up these days?' Karen Smith said, then, 'Listen to me – I sound like my mother.'

'How's she taking all this?' I asked her.

'She isn't. Dead. They both are. She worked thirty years in a frozen-fish plant and then died four weeks after she retired. My dad worked on the William Wright Docks. Boat fitter, a proper engineer.'

Everywhere you went in the city, especially in this part of it, these same distant echoes sounded. The sea was still there, and the tides of the estuary still came and went, and the ghosts of the men and the boys and the boats came and went with them.

History here wasn't a castle or a carefully preserved mound of earth; it wasn't the contrived ruin of a manor house or a plaque commemorating an otherwise forgotten battle. History here was a grown man named after a drowned uncle; a Polaroid of an eight-year-old boy in wide trousers and a tank top, lost ten years later at sea; a model of a trawler on a mantelpiece where a clock might have stood; a print of a lost boat riding a turbulent sea and elaborately framed in gold.

History here was the names of men who had mattered; it was the names of bars; it was lost but fiercely remembered fathers, and men and women separated from each other for too long and too often.

'What's she like?' Karen Smith said.

'Sorry. Who?'

'The woman you're working for.'

'She's going through what you went through,' I said. I think by then she'd confused Susan Hendry with the mother of Lucy Collins, and her next words confirmed this.

'They said in the papers that her daughter – you know, that she was on the game.'

'She was,' I said, reluctant to explain in any more detail.

'I hated her for hearing that,' she said. 'Her being one just seemed to prove everything they were saying about why Kelly was killed. They even want it to be true of that other girl they found, don't they?'

'Alison Wilson.'

'That's her. And yet there's not a single thing to say she was on the game, is there? Not a single thing.'

'No,' I said.

'Right, well then, they can just start watching what they say about Kelly.' She smiled, as though she had just won an argument. She seemed completely unaware of how far beyond her grasp the inquiry into her daughter's death had now moved, how far behind she had been left, how little notice it now took of her, how *unnecessary* she had become to it.

I'd seen and heard nothing more or less than I'd expected to see or hear. Nothing of any apparent significance had been revealed to me, and I had done little more than confirm what anyone else reading the newspaper accounts might already have guessed about Kelly Smith and her life in the years before she was murdered.

I rose to leave, thanking her for having spoken to me.

'Will you let me know if you find anything out?' she said. 'You know – something that might have anything to do with Kelly.'

I promised her I would, but knew how unlikely this would be.

The next she would hear of anything would be when someone was arrested and charged with the murder of her daughter. And even then she would only see his picture in the paper and on the television news; and by then her disappointment and disillusion would be complete, and the capture and punishment of her daughter's killer would prove to be anything but the act of re-demption she now desperately needed it to be.

The girl came to the door with me, closing it behind me the instant I stepped out into the street.

10

Arriving at Humber Street the next morning, I was approaching my office when a car pulled up at the junction with Queen Street and a man got out. He watched me briefly from a distance and then came towards me as I reached my door. I recognized him as the detective who had sat behind Sunny and myself at Lister's press conference.

He stood watching the warehousemen for a moment before speaking to me.

'I imagine they'll be knocking all this down soon and redeveloping it as part of Hull's maritime heritage,' he said.

'You can't have too many skinny-latte bars or Pacific rim restaurants in a place like Hull,' I said.

It was still early, not yet eight, but the sports club opposite my office was already open and music and the sounds of the young sparring boxers could be heard through the open windows.

'It's a kind of gym,' I said.

'Which is probably a kind of sports club.' He took out his warrant card and gave it to me, making the gesture seem casual, unofficial. 'Read it,' he said.

His name was Andrew Mitchell. He was a Detective Inspector.

'Are you here as Lister's messenger boy?' I said, handing it back to him.

He smiled at this, though whether at the remark itself, or its predictability, I couldn't tell.

'An hour of your time and you'll either know that for certain or you'll change your mind,' he said. He waited for me to unlock the door.

Upstairs, the unheated room was cold. Condensation had formed along the edges of each of the windows.

Newcomers to the place often stood for a moment and looked around the sparse and shabby room and then remarked on this, either disappointed or reassured depending on why they were there and the judgement they needed to make of me.

Andrew Mitchell went immediately to the chair in front of my desk and sat down.

'I don't want to waste your time,' he said. He took out his warrant card again and slid it towards me. 'It doesn't say anything about Hull or Humberside Police,' he said. 'James Finch sends his regards.'

I'd worked with Finch a year earlier on a National Crime and Child Protection Unit investigation into a six-year-old case of police corruption during the uncovering of a paedophile ring. If not friends, we had at least become close during our two months together, and I trusted him.

'You're National Crime?' I said.

'Finch spoke very highly of you. He also warned me about Mr Summers. I think "fat, profiteering arsehole" comes close.'

'And there we were sitting side by side as the ten commandments were handed down to us.'

'It's what Chief Superintendent Lister enjoys doing. Edicts from on high.'

'And you're doing what now – infiltrating the fourth estate? Watching his back? I thought he had disposables like Brownlow for that.'

'I'm doing neither of those things.'

'How is Finch?'

'He's working in Dover. He and his wife separated six months ago. He's in a police flat.'

'He has two young daughters,' I said, remembering.

'Martha and Nathalie,' he said fondly. 'And he probably sees them for two hours every fortnight.'

'If you see him . . .' I said.

'I won't. At least not for the foreseeable.'

'After which everything will have changed?'

'After which he'll have become like any one of a thousand other coppers who never learned where to draw the line and who then discover that other people have drawn it for them while they were looking the other way.'

'You, for instance?'

'Me, for instance.'

'Why are you here?' I asked him.

'*Here* here, or here in Hull?'

'The bigger picture might be a better opener.'

He took back his warrant card and slid it into his pocket. 'As I'm sure both you and Mr Summers are aware, Chief Superintendent Lister has ambitions to become Assistant Chief Constable in the not too distant future. Followed by Chief Constable as soon as decently possible after that.'

'And what – you're here to stop that happening?'

He laughed and shook his head. 'I have no power whatsoever to either prevent or assist in that particular piece of corridor-creeping.'

'But that is essentially why you're here – to keep an eye on Lister.'

'I wish it were that simple. Let's just say that the powers-that-be—'

' "The powers-that-be"?'

'Yes, Mr Rivers, *those* powers. They're always there – always watching, always pushing, always pulling the strings and flicking the players off the board. And Lister knows that better than I do. There's nothing I can do or say while I'm up here that he won't get to know about.'

'This visit for instance?'

'And the one I might later make to Mr Summers's news agency, yes.' He rubbed his face, looking suddenly tired, and I waited for him to go on. 'And something else Lister knows better than anyone else is that, as far as he's concerned, these might be the best of times or the worst of times. He's made it clear to everyone that he intends to stamp his mark on this force.'

'And a serial killer at loose in the city will provide him with the perfect opportunity to do just that?'

'If that's what this is, yes. Whatever you or I or Mr Summers may think of him, he's not a stupid man. If everything goes according to his plan, he'll be one of the youngest ACCs in the country.'

'And the people watching him?'

'They're probably as convinced of his success as he is. It isn't my job to prevent any of this from happening, just to ensure that things are done properly – due process and all that – and that everyone is fully aware of Lister's game plan.'

'Meaning he may not choose to seize the serial killer option?'

'No – I mean that he now has to walk a very fine line between proper and current police work and what others might regard as self-serving; between what everyone on the force knows is the best way to handle the killings and everything the God-fearing and law-abiding public is calling for; and between what keeps everything manageable and what throws all the pieces into the wind and creates a storm that just goes on blowing and blowing until everything gets swamped and broken and lost. You know how these things work. The instant he announces he's looking for a serial killer, he'll be buried with useless information and never-ending demands for action. Paper walls and no windows.'

'And if it *is* one man doing all the killings?'

'Your client's son, for instance?'

'Lister doesn't seriously believe that. He even implied at the press conference that he wasn't as convinced as everybody else appeared to be that the three women were killed because the killer believed them to be prostitutes.'

He shook his head slowly. 'Would this be the same press

conference where everybody shouted at him that he was wrong and that his best option now was to change his mind, that he had better start listening to and responding to public opinion, or else?'

I considered what he was telling me.

'So is that what he's going to do – a Man-Of-The-People act?'

'It's what he wanted from the start.'

'And now he's got some sort of mandate or justification for doing it?'

'Provided, to all intents and purposes, by people like Summers and yourself.'

'It's all a bit transparent,' I said.

'I doubt if that's what Summers or any of the others will print after weeks of clamouring for someone to take the serial-killer option seriously.'

'Leaving Paul Hendry where, exactly?'

'Where he belongs. On a charge of killing Lucy Collins. I imagine Lister's known from the start that he had nothing to do with the other killings.'

'But until they get properly investigated and solved, he's still got someone to hang out to dry for part of it all?'

'Oh, the angry, clamouring public does enjoy seeing someone hung out to dry. What Lister has to consider now is how far he can exploit that outrage and clamouring to his own ends. If he goes public too soon with the serial-prostitute-killer option, then the whole thing might blow up in his face later.'

'How?'

'It's what happens. He pretends to be in absolute charge, to be making headway, and then the killings go on happening and he gets made to look foolish and inept and gets left further and further behind. Imagine what *that* would do to his chances of promotion.'

'Whereas if he makes the same announcement and then *does* manage to catch the killer after a high-profile investigation with himself clearly in charge and as the motivating force behind that investigation . . .'

'Precisely.'

'So which option is currently at the top of his list?'

He clicked his lips. 'A couple more murdered prostitutes would certainly help matters.'

'Does he think that's likely? There's still no proof that Alison Wilson had ever worked as a prostitute. Do *you* think it's likely?'

He shrugged. 'The point is, everybody now is looking at only three killings and trying to find a connection.'

'Are you saying there have been others?'

Every question I asked him and every answer he gave me took me further and further from Susan Hendry standing in her dark kitchen mourning the loss of her son.

'No one's suggesting anything,' he said. 'But like you said, there is a broader picture to be considered.'

'Which is?'

He looked from me to the window, to the roofs and sky and river beyond before turning back to me. 'In the last five years, nine women have been killed in this city.' He held up his hands. 'No-one's suggesting that there's anything to connect these killings. Three men have been tried and convicted – two murders and one pleaded-down manslaughter – and two others are still on remand facing trial. Only two out of those five are local men. It isn't a pattern. What *does* constitute a pattern, however, is that seven of the nine women were known prostitutes. Whatever else they were, and whatever reason they were killed, they were known prostitutes. That one simple fact can't be ignored. All three successful prosecutions, and one of the two awaiting trial, were for the killing of a prostitute. Whatever else you want to stir into the mix, there will always be that one undeniable fact. And however imperfect that understanding or emphasis or focus might remain, it will always be there at the centre of any subsequent investigation. In addition to which, it adds a volatile slew of moral complications and considerations to those investigations. Nothing like a "deserving" victim or someone who believes he has a justifiable cause for killing.' He paused for a moment. 'You asked me why I was here. I'm here because there are specialist teams at National Crime which would always be called in or, at the very least, be asked to keep an eye on investigations of this nature. They're too high-profile. There's too much at stake to allow them to get out of control, which is what all too often happens. And there's certainly too much at stake in this particular instance when Lister's personal ambitions are thrown into the equation. The balance on these things has to be struck early on, at the outset of the investigation. You lose the opportunity to do that once inquiries are under way.'

'And if more women were killed?'

'Perhaps. The problem for Lister now is that this investigation can't be allowed to change direction once he's pointed it in the direction *he* wants it to go.'

'Meaning the course of the inquiry might be determined as much by his own ambition as by what might be uncovered?'

'It'll never be that simple. The ball's already rolling on this one. He's the one keeping alongside it; the rest of us are already running to catch up.'

'Does he keep you informed of everything that's happening?'

'Like I said, he's not a stupid man. It's a big investigation; there won't be many secrets. Plus he'll want to appear as helpful and as accommodating as possible. Remember, we can all come out of this smelling badly.'

'You as much as him?'

'I doubt if anyone will even be watching when *I* fall out of the sky, Mr Rivers.'

'Like no-one was watching Finch?'

'He's coping. He was considered for this job, but apparently there's still an odour from when he was here last.'

'And Lister, presumably, needs you on his side as much as he needs everything else to go in his favour.'

'Something like that.' He leaned back in his chair, stretched his arms and yawned. 'Is that the bigger picture framed and painted in to your satisfaction? If it's any consolation, there's also a line of thought which suggests that once this "Big Inquiry" announcement is made, the killer will reconsider his luck and his chances and call it a day.'

'Like the Yorkshire Ripper did, you mean?'

He smiled. 'I wondered how long it would be before that happened.'

'Is that what Lister wants – the Hull Ripper?'

'It's what some of the newspapers appear to want. Another killing or two, and they'll run it regardless of the problems it causes.'

'Especially if any more of those killings involve prostitutes.'

' "Involve"?' He shook his head. 'Or even if they're just young women whose mothers insist until they're blue in the face that their daughters were never anything of the sort.'

I knew then that he'd seen Karen Smith and Alison Wilson's mother.

'And which the public chooses to either believe or disbelieve depending on a thousand other things,' I said.

'Exactly. At least now you're apprised of Lister's predicament.'

'Even though I'm still uncertain *why* you're telling me all this. And if you pretend to shrug and say "No real reason" I'll disregard everything you've just told me and know that everything you go on to say is probably a lie.'

'I wouldn't insult your intelligence,' he said, smiling. 'Finch told me you got DCI Smart to agree to you and a dead girl's father attending her disinterment.'

I nodded.

'He broke every rule in the book to let that particular little no-no happen.'

'They were his – your – rules,' I said. 'Not mine. Which understanding, incidentally, I imagine has some bearing on you being here – *here* here – now.'

'Ah, the smaller picture,' he said. 'Lister, being at either the start of something very big and important, or at the end of something that might have been considerably bigger and considerably more important in terms of his own progress, has thrown only a little caution to the wind and – perhaps only until those next few prostitutes are killed, thereby justifying him donning his full battle armour and climbing onto his big white horse – has chosen something of a middle option.'

'Which is?'

'A policy of zero-tolerance towards prostitution and all its evil and degrading offshoots in this fair and beautiful city. In his eyes, it satisfies the public clamour for action and it provides him with the perfect basis for continuing and then upgrading his investigation into the killings should the need arise.'

'By turning the victims into criminals?'

'By striking repeatedly at the weakest and most vulnerable link in the chain until it is smashed and severed completely.'

'Have things like this ever succeeded?'

He held up his palms. 'They change the shape of the operation, that's all. There have been similar operations in Sheffield, Leeds and Bradford recently. By all accounts, the public enjoys them. However temporarily, things seem to improve.'

I considered the implications of what he was now telling me. 'And with an alleged prostitute-killer on the loose, what better time to help all those poor, misguided women change their ways?'

'That's the line he'll sell via Mr Summers and his ilk.'

'What will the operation involve?' I asked him.

'Everything Lister wants it to involve. And here, of course, he has seized another great opportunity. Prostitution equals drugs in most people's eyes. It certainly did where Kelly Smith, Lucy Collins and Paul Hendry were concerned.'

'So if he misses one target, there will always be another he can't fail to hit?'

'The biggest target of them all.'

'And one which will get him just as much support from the local citizenry.'

'Who *wouldn't* applaud such noble work? Let's face it, there's been enough happen here in the past ten years to bring discredit to this force.'

'And which Lister is also about to put right?'

'No, but if it all forms part of his plan to make Hull a safer, better place to live in, then he's going to get a lot of important locals on his side without having to try too hard, beginning with his own men.'

'Who do you think brought that "discredit" on the force in the first place?'

'A few misguided officers. None of whom are still working here.'

'The place is stuffed full of pompous little time-servers like Brownlow.'

'Some might say you were allowing your own prejudiced opinion of the man to cloud your judgement,' he said, but in a tone which made it clear to me that he shared this opinion. 'Brownlow does what's asked of him. And whatever you might believe, he's honest. Besides—'

'Don't tell me Lister's going to put him in charge of some of this.'

'He announced it to everyone at yesterday's briefing.'

'I bet Brownlow grew an inch.'

'If not two.'

'So this time round, he'll be the one falling from the sky if it all goes wrong,' I said.

'There has to be someone.'

'Do you think Brownlow knows it, too?'

'I imagine so. Like Lister, he's got a lot to either gain or lose depending on what happens next. What I'm saying to you now is that Lister has already made all the right moves to get all the right people on his side.'

'No – what you're telling me now is that he doesn't really give a toss about Paul Hendry, that he never for one instant believed he was responsible for any of the other murders.'

'I thought it might be something you needed to know,' he said.

'Why? Because you're finally going to tell me why you're telling me all this?'

'You're making too much of it. You're involved, that's all. You're working for the mother of Lister's only suspect. Until something better turns up – and it will – Lister's holding on to Hendry and Collins. You should be grateful, because for as long as that happens, you stay involved. The minute Hendry and Collins drop from that bigger picture, then you disappear with them. How long do you think Lister is going to tolerate your interference then?'

I considered all this and knew that everything he'd predicted was likely to happen. 'Lister will want rid of you if he even suspects you of telling me all this,' I said.

'I doubt it. You'd have worked it all out for yourself, and sooner rather than later. He probably even knows I'm here right now.'

'And Sunny?'

'Summers? What do you mean?'

'I mean it can't have entirely escaped either your or Lister's notice that he's got a big mouth and that he makes a lot of noise as far as all the local press is concerned. We all know how important the right spin is on this kind of thing, especially at the kick-off. "Outsider Police Chief Persecutes Local Prostitutes". "New Cop Cleans Up City And Earns Undying Gratitude".'

'I'm not trying to get to Summers on Lister's behalf through you, if that's what you think,' he said.

'I don't. It would never work. Like you said, Sunny will probably wait to see which way the wind blows and what kind of stink it brings with it before he climbs onto his own white charger.'

'Precisely. Let's just say that I personally will look upon both you and Mr Summers as my markers.'

'Meaning you'll be scratching our backs occasionally in the expectation of getting ten times more in return.'

'Perhaps. And, I'll be happier not having to be told every morning by Lister how well everything's going. He's got some good men on his investigating teams. He's not going to waste them. It's unlikely that you're going to find anything out before they do in any of this.'

'Thanks for that vote of confidence,' I said. 'Plus, of course, me finding something out before they do is a chance you can't afford to take.'

He smiled again. 'Right. You think you're the only person that realizes that a previous call-out to a faulty alarm at the Walker Street surgery took place on the night Alison Wilson was murdered. You're going to have to move faster than that.'

'And what significance does Lister accord that particular coincidence?'

'Whatever it is, it'll be divided by at least thirty to account for all the other false alarms that went off that night. And talking of Weaver . . .'

'Which we weren't.'

'Right. He complained to Lister that you'd been round at his surgery abusing his staff and demanding a guided tour of the crime scene, with refreshments.'

'Directly to Lister?'

'Directly.' He held up his hand and crossed his fore- and index finger.

'What did Lister say?'

'Apparently, he persuaded Weaver not to make the complaint official – complicating the investigation already under way and all that – and promised him he'd deal with it himself.'

'And Weaver was satisfied with that?'

'Looks like it.'

'Susan and Paul Hendry are Weaver's patients,' I said. 'Emily Carr knew Paul Hendry when they were children. Her father knew his father.'

'We know that, too. Everybody in this city knows fifty other people, who know at least another fifty unknown to the first person. Imagine how quickly that kind of thing spreads outwards, and then how quickly it bounces back on itself, filling in all the gaps as it comes. I imagine there are some parts of Hull where, now or once upon a time, everybody knew everybody else, living and dead and as yet unborn.'

'That would be the once-upon-a-time side of things,' I said.

'Look, if Paul Hendry did kill Lucy Collins, it would be a good start to try and understand *why* – even if it *was* only a drug-fuelled fit of rage that got out of hand.'

'Even if it derails Lister's big clean-up before it gets off the ground?'

He looked at his watch. It was almost nine.

He rose from where he sat and went to the window, wiping a ring in the condensation and looking out over the buildings opposite, almost as though he was searching for something there amid the weed-filled gutters and peeling brickwork.

'What?' I said.

'Lister's big clean-up,' he said. 'It started four hours ago.' He turned back to me and wiped the moisture from his fingers on his coat.

11

Waiting until Mitchell had gone, I left the office and walked to Spring Bank.

Sunny was out, but Yvonne had been there since seven. I told her I'd been to see Susan Hendry the previous day, but she knew this already. Then I told her what Mitchell had just told me about Lister's crusade, and she knew about that, too. She'd been with Susan Hendry at six that morning when the police had arrived with a warrant to search her home. Paul hadn't lived there for almost three years, but she still had his boxed possessions stored in his old room, and the police had taken these away.

Yvonne had taken photos of the police as they searched the house and had asked each of the men who'd taken part in this for their name and number.

She'd already heard from Sunny what had happened at the press conference. She asked me what I thought the true reason was behind Mitchell's visit, and I confessed I still didn't know.

She'd driven Susan Hendry back to the hospital and left her there. After seven days, there had still been no improvement in Paul Hendry's condition.

'Where's Sunny while all this is happening?' I asked her.

She looked down over the busy road below. The blinds hung at an angle, forced out of alignment by the mounds of paper and magazines piled on the sill.

'He got a call from someone telling him what was about to happen,' she said. 'He called me from Queen's Gardens just before you arrived. It looks like the police have had a busy night.'

'Is he still there?'

'Probably.' She was anxious about what Susan Hendry was now going through, and I guessed that Sunny's lack of interest in this both saddened and disappointed her.

'It's all just Lister's public declaration of intent,' I said. 'I don't think searching—'

'We all know what it is,' she said angrily. 'And we all know what he hopes to achieve by it. The problem is, no-one knows what will actually *happen*. According to Sunny, they've taken dozens in. They left Susan's home looking like a storm had blown through it.'

'The police know Paul had nothing to do with either of the earlier killings,' I said. It was more than I knew for certain, but it was all I had to offer her.

'Are you sure of that?'

I lied and told her I was and she relaxed a little, leaning back in her chair and pushing herself away from her desk.

'But they still think he killed Lucy Collins,' I said. 'It would look a bit negligent – taking in fifty others and not paying a visit to the family home of their only suspect.'

She acceded to this in silence.

'So all this is just for the sake of appearances?' she said. 'Show-of-strength policing.'

I could think of nothing to say to her that wouldn't expose my lie and disappoint her further.

'Sunny should have stayed here,' she said.

'And not jump just because Lister said "jump"? He'll have had his reasons for going.'

And she understood these far better than I did. If Lister was determined to run this campaign solely to his own agenda, then anything which kept Sunny close to its centre instead of outside and sitting in on carefully polished press conferences was going to be of value to him.

I asked her if she knew who had been taken in.

'About thirty girls. Including Emily Carr.'

'Emily Carr?'

'Don't sound so surprised. Why, what line did she spin you?'

'Do the police think she's still working?'

She closed her eyes at the remark. 'Listen to yourself,' she said. 'You think her being pregnant and starting to show *isn't* going to be a turn-on for some of her customers or clients or whatever they're called these days? The youngest was thirteen, the oldest sixty-two. Yep, you heard. Sixty-two. And she was probably just as thin and as desperate at twenty-two as she is now.'

'Lister won't like it that Sunny's already there,' I said.

'So what? Do you think he'll like it any more or less than the fact that Mitchell's already been to see you?' She put a finger to her forehead and pretended to think. 'Oh, I forgot – that's got nothing to do with Mitchell leaking information to you – to you specifically – or you – again, you specifically – being used by Lister using Mitchell as his go-between.'

'It might be of some use to Susan Hendry,' I said, knowing how feeble and contrived this continued to sound.

'Yeah, right,' she said. 'All of this – you, Sunny, the police, Lister, Mitchell, Emily butter-wouldn't-melt Carr – it's all one big merry-go-round of convenience and compromise and looking the other way. You know it, I know it, Sunny knows it, Mitchell knows it. And Lister certainly knows it. So let's not fool ourselves that any of us is doing anything but following his lead in all of this and looking for a way to make us all feel that little bit better about ourselves.'

She slapped her palms on her desk. A pile of papers and padded envelopes slid smoothly across its surface.

She had switched on the answering machine, and since my arrival half an hour earlier there had been a dozen calls from people wanting to know what was happening and wanting something from Sunny.

As the mound of envelopes settled, a woman rang and said she was calling from *Race Today* magazine and wanted as much background as Sunny could provide on the racial dimension of what was currently taking place in the city.

'See, everybody's got their own agenda,' she said.

Then she rose, came to me and held me close to her. I locked my hands in the small of her back.

'You have to put on your cape and your mask and go out there and clean it all up,' she said, her face pressed into my shoulder.

'I can try,' I said.

She stood away from me, her hands clasping my arms.

'Convince the police that some as-yet-unidentified murderer killed all three of those women, and that Paul Hendry was somehow implicated and driven to what he did because he somehow got in the way,' she said. 'I know – two "somehows".'

'And then what? His mother holds his hand and his eyes flutter and against all the odds he comes round?'

'Hey, you can do all that?' she said.

'I'll dig out that cape and mask.'

She released her hold on me and went back to her chair.

I told her I was going in search of Sunny.

'Tell him to get back here and field these calls,' she said.

I found him at Queen's Gardens, sitting on a bench overlooking the ponds there, a short distance from the police station, watching the giant yellow fish come and go through the cloudy water. Most of the reeds and other plants had died back, and ducks sat in small groups on the grass.

He looked up at my arrival beside him, but showed no real surprise.

'Long morning?' I said.

'Interesting morning.' He flicked the last inch of his cigarette into the water, extinguishing it and causing one of the fish to rise and consider it. The fish's mouth opened and closed, swallowed and then spat out the tab. We both watched it. After the first fish, a second and then a third came to examine the cigarette.

'What's Lister playing at?' I asked him.

'He's not playing at anything. He's making sure we all know where we stand in relation to how *he's* going to work on this one.'

'Was Brownlow there?'

'Riding high on Lister's coat tails and enjoying every predictable fucking minute of it.'

Across the park, a group of women left the police station. They congregated on the steps leading down to the empty flower-beds and talked among themselves. I searched for Emily Carr, but she wasn't among them.

'Do you think he'll hold anyone?' I asked him.

'Most of the girls will be out by lunchtime. They'll have found a bit of stuff here and there and will feel the need to act accordingly.'

'So you think this was just Lister making his presence felt?'

'Clicking his fingers and stoking up the fires,' he said.

We both continued watching the distant women as they dispersed.

Several of them came to where we sat. A couple of them knew Sunny and exchanged greetings with him. None of them seemed particularly concerned by what had just happened to them.

'Lend us a fiver for a cab,' one of them asked Sunny, and he gave her the money. She told him she'd pay it back when she next saw him.

'Lister wants the press on board,' he said as the women left us. 'And the press, naturally enough, want whatever Lister is prepared to give them above and beyond the conference tears and crap. Lister also wants to clean up the streets of Hull, and this gives him every justification he could ever need for stunts like today's. In addition to which, the people of Hull also want the place made safer, even if they don't yet fully understand what that might mean regarding the future. They want rid of the girls, they certainly want rid of the men who control them, and most of all they want rid of the drug dealers who keep them where they are. The way Lister's playing it, everything gets tied up into the one neat, convincing and eagerly anticipated package. You can see how clean and shiny everything is starting to look.'

I told him about my visit from Mitchell.

'He was in there,' he said, indicating the station. 'He told you about it *after* it had started. If he is here to keep an eye on Lister, then the only certain thing in all of this is that Lister will be keeping an even closer eye on him. And if Lister thinks you're involved any closer than you deserve to be, then he'll use the fact that Mitchell came to see you behind his back to shut you out completely. Perhaps that's why he came. Whatever, Mitchell will always be more accountable to his own masters than he is to Lister.'

'Has Lister made any announcements about today?'

'Only his intention of holding a press review – *review* – each day to bring everybody up to speed on what's happening and to collate – *collate* – and assess any feedback we may have for him. Apparently, we're as much a part of this campaign as he and his force are.'

'Does he have a name for it?'

' "Operation Pioneer". "Operation Murdered Prostitutes" just doesn't have that same catchy ring, does it? The *Hull Mail* is already on board and cheering loudly from the sidelines.'

It was a reference to the name with which the city had been branded by its latest council-sponsored image-makers: *Hull – Pioneering City*. Even though no-one was entirely certain who – Wilberforce apart – these 'pioneers' were, exactly. Or where they'd come from to be pioneering in Hull; or where they'd gone to from Hull to be pioneering elsewhere.

A second group of women emerged from the police station and skirted the gardens in the direction of the city centre. Workmen on the nearby building-site scaffolding called down to them. The women made gestures and kept on walking. The voices and laughter of the men were amplified in the enclosed space. Shoppers stood to watch the women as they dispersed. I saw then how easy it might be for Lister to get everyone on his side.

I looked again for Emily Carr, but she wasn't among the women.

When I turned back to Sunny, I saw that he remained focused on the station entrance, and I followed his gaze to where

Brownlow was now descending the steps towards the ponds.

He came to us and sat between us.

'Very cosy,' he said.

'Can I help you, officer?' Sunny said. 'You seem to need a lot of help from a lot of people these days.'

'I doubt we need anything from you. You barely seem capable of helping yourself most days.'

'Ouch,' Sunny said.

'And you,' Brownlow said, turning to me. 'Still trying to pretend that the poor little mummy's boy wasn't covered from head to foot with the blood of the girl he'd just killed?'

'I take it all this is off the record,' I said. 'I'm sure Chief Superintendent Lister wouldn't countenance such offensive remarks from one of his most trusted officers. And especially not now that he's insisting on all this – what's the word? – transparency.'

Brownlow laughed. 'It's just words.'

I wondered if, from somewhere high in the station, Lister himself wasn't now watching us.

Believing the same, Sunny said, 'Should we wave to him, do you think?'

Realizing what we were suggesting, Brownlow said, 'Underestimate him at your peril.'

Both Sunny and I laughed at the melodramatic phrase.

' "Peril",' Sunny said. 'A much underused word.' He took out his notebook and wrote in it. ' "Underestimate him at your peril",' he said slowly.

'And as for you,' Brownlow said, turning back to me. 'If you think Mitchell's any kind of insurance in all of this, then let me disabuse you of that right now.'

'Insurance against what?'

Again, Sunny repeated his words and wrote them down.

'So,' he said as he finished writing. 'What did this morning's little display actually achieve apart from stirring a stick through the swill and raising Lister's profile?'

'Who said it was meant to achieve anything? Good use of manpower and resources. The forces of law and order taking the initiative for a change. A lot of people put on notice and wondering what's going to happen next.'

'And everyone else stood around applauding.'

'It can't hurt.'

'Nor is any of it going to put you one inch closer to the real killer of at least two of the women,' Sunny said.

'Two prostitutes,' Brownlow said.

'Not necessarily. But it's interesting that you remain so insistent on the matter.'

'It's what they were,' Brownlow said. He seemed confident of his assertion.

'What did you mean about Mitchell?' Sunny said to him.

'What I said. Lister knows why he's there. Mitchell's not going to have any real part in this investigation, and when it's all over he's going to disappear back to where he came from with his tail between his legs.'

'He's intended to be an integral part of it all,' I said.

'He's got an NC watching brief, that's all. This is a local investigation and we're the ones best equipped to handle it. Not people like Mitchell.'

Sunny laughed. 'Your past record might suggest otherwise.'

Brownlow turned sharply at the remark. 'You know fuck all about it, except what it's worth to you,' he said. He jabbed at Sunny, his finger stopping an inch short of his chest.

Sunny looked down at this and then pushed Brownlow's arm to one side. 'And you're looking to wipe your own slate clean,' he said, his voice low and even. Then he raised his hand and waved to the distant building, antagonizing Brownlow further, and causing him to rise and leave us as abruptly as he had arrived.

'Don't fall in the water,' Sunny called after him.

Brownlow kept on walking.

I hoped all this goading was intended to serve a purpose, but I remained unconvinced.

'At least now we *all* know where we stand,' Sunny said.

'Even me?' I said.

'Even you.'

12

I went later to see Emily Carr at Nelson Court. I still suspected her of knowing more than she'd told me during our first encounter, and I was hoping that what had happened to her earlier in the day might have made her reconsider whatever it was she was keeping from me.

I rang her intercom and waited. The two constables were no longer at the door. There was no answer for several minutes, and then she asked who was there. I identified myself and told her I knew what had happened. She told me to wait, and instead of unlocking the entrance door from her own flat, she came down to make sure I was alone before letting me in.

As I entered, she searched the narrow street on either side of me. I promised her I was there alone and that no-one knew I had come to see her.

'And until five o'clock this morning I might have believed you,' she said.

She locked the inner door behind me and I followed her up the stairs. She wore a black T-shirt and nothing on her feet. Her hair was pulled tightly back from her face.

'Did you know this was going to happen?' she asked me. She switched off a radio and a television, which had filled the small flat with their competing noises.

'It's a new man,' I said. 'He's going to clean up the city for all the good, law-abiding, church-going, honest, tax-paying citizens who live here. Did they charge you with anything?'

'By which you think they probably had a choice of charges. No. Just a warning that if my name or face was brought back to their attention, then I'd be in serious trouble.' She ran a hand over her stomach. 'They thought this was hilarious. The man who was asking me all the questions kept making remarks about the father, about what kind of mother I'd be, about how the *poor* kid would be brought up.'

I asked her to describe him, and she described Brownlow. I wondered if that, too, had been deliberate. Mitchell knew I'd been to see her, and perhaps he'd told Brownlow.

'Do you know him?' she asked me.

'He's got a big part in all this sweeping clean.'

'He kept telling me that he might have to inform Social Services what I was up to, and that they'd probably decide I was unfit to raise my own child. Can he do that? Can *they* do anything about it?'

There were always a number of threatening, anonymous *they*s and *them*s circling the precarious lives of people like Emily Carr.

'It won't happen,' I said, hoping I sounded more convincing than I felt.

'And you know that for a fact, do you?'

She made us both coffee and we sat together in her small kitchen.

'I think you know more about what happened on the day Lucy Collins was killed than you told me,' I said. 'And I also think she confided more in you about her own brief pregnancy.' I had anticipated she might deny this, but her experience earlier in the day had left her tired, uncertain, and apprehensive of the future. I regretted that I was there to capitalize on what Brownlow had started.

'Are you calling me a liar?' she said, but with no real vehemence.

'I'm just saying you didn't know me well enough last time to trust me with everything you knew.'

'What, and now you're my best friend?'

'No. But what happened to you today might go on happening again and again until the killing of Lucy Collins is explained to everyone's satisfaction.'

'You don't think Paul Hendry did it?'

'I think there's a lot of doubt and half-explained connections that still need to be examined,' I said. Anyone else would have laughed in my face.

'The man asking me all the questions seemed pretty certain it was Paul.'

Which was perhaps the only reason she might be prepared to help me now.

'Only because it would make life a lot easier for him,' I said.

'He put his hand on my stomach,' she said. 'And then he ran it right up until it . . . I heard him with some of the other girls. He talked to them like they were nothing. Some of them knew him.' She held her mug in both hands. Its heat rose into her face and she closed her eyes.

'*Did* you hear or see something?' I prompted her.

'They were rowing,' she said, her eyes still closed.

'Do you know what it was about?'

'I could guess. Lucy told me a few days earlier that she'd felt bad ever since she'd had the termination four months ago. I think she was depressed. She told me that there had been other complications.'

'Medical complications?'

'I assume so. I think she said there had been some kind of infection. She was forever going to see the doctor. Whatever it was, it dragged things out for her.'

'Did she ever say anything about the possibility of it not being Paul Hendry's child?'

She opened her eyes at the question.

'You told me Lucy asked you not to say anything about the termination in front of Paul. And if he didn't know about the termination, then he certainly won't have known about the pregnancy.'

'I assumed at first she'd said it because it was still too upsetting for them both.'

'And afterwards?'

'You think she was back on the game? Is that what you're asking me?' She shook her head. 'You're wrong. Christ knows why, but she was devoted to him.'

It was the same word Susan Hendry had used.

'The police know she was working as a prostitute in the months before her death,' I said.

She was about to deny this again, but stopped herself.

'His mother was under the impression Paul had something important to tell her,' I said. 'Something about him and Lucy, but which he never got round to doing.'

'I don't know about that. Lucy told me that *it* – you know, sex – that it hardly ever happened.'

'You sound as though you didn't have much time for him,' I said.

She shrugged. 'He always thought more about himself than anyone else. He was inconsiderate. Leaving the front door open, leaving lights on, banging doors and playing music loud late at night. It wasn't just me – we all used to complain about it.'

'And he never apologized?'

'Apologize? Him? He used to get Lucy to do his dirty work for him. Either he used to send her, or she got wind of what had happened and came to say sorry without Mr Wonderful ever knowing about it. I used to tell her that she was being pathetic, and that he ought to do his own dirty work. All *she* ever did was make excuses for him.'

It was a different picture of Paul Hendry from that painted by his mother.

'Are you certain it was Paul and Lucy who were arguing?'

She thought about this.

'Her voice carried more than his. You could sometimes hear her through these walls when she was just talking. He tended not to get too excited about anything. Usually because he was out of it. His voice was lower, anyway, quieter.'

'*Could* it have been someone else with her?'

'I honestly don't know. He was the only person I'd ever heard her rowing with. She told me beforehand that she was going to have to say something about the termination and that she didn't know what to expect. I offered to stay with her while she did it, but she said she wanted to do it alone. I didn't see what difference it would make, not after four months.'

'Was it a long argument?'

'Not particularly. Like I said, it was mostly a lot of shouting and name-calling coming from her. Then it went quiet and that was it.'

'No door-slamming, no-one on the stairs, no-one leaving the building immediately afterwards?'

'I didn't hear anything. This flat looks out over the back. I wouldn't have seen him if he had stormed out. I thought she might come up to me. I wondered whether I should go down to see her, make sure she was OK, but she'd been so insistent beforehand that she wanted to sort everything out by herself. Besides, like I said, I hadn't heard any doors or anybody on the stairs; for all I knew, he was still in there with her. Perhaps they were even, you know, making up.'

'Perhaps,' I said, knowing that she was talking of a time when Lucy Collins was already dead.

'There's not much more I can tell you.'

'Why do *you* think Lucy kept it to herself when she discovered she was pregnant?'

She shook her head. 'Perhaps because she didn't know how she felt about it.'

'About whether or not it was what she wanted?'

'Perhaps. Perhaps that, or perhaps the longer she kept it from him, the harder it got to tell him. She never said. I think she was just scared about everything.'

Like *she* was scared of everything. I wondered if her own unborn child was capable of bearing the weight of everything with which it was already being invested.

She drained her cup and made us both a second drink. She lit a cigarette and then stubbed it out after a single draw on it.

'I've still got the patches, gum, everything. It costs a fortune.'

I wondered if the remark was intended to prompt another offer of payment, but then saw by the way that she went on making our drinks that it wasn't.

'There's no milk,' she said. She crouched down at her fridge, and I saw over her shoulder that it contained almost nothing. It was one defeat too many in that long day, and she came back to the table and sat with a hand held over her eyes.

I asked her if she'd told the police what she'd just told me.

'Not really,' she said. 'As far as they were concerned, it was all a lot more straightforward. What's going to happen now?'

'That might depend on what you didn't tell them,' I said, guessing.

She turned away from me briefly. 'I think she might have been seeing someone else,' she said.

'You mean seeing them as a—'

'It was only once a week, but I think it was regular. Always the same time, and always when Paul was out. That's why I said she wasn't back on the game, not really.'

'Do you know who it was? Would you recognize him?'

She considered this and then shook her head. 'I might even be wrong about it,' she said, but without conviction, and unhappy at what she had just revealed about her friend. 'What *is* going to happen now?' she repeated.

'I think the man who questioned you is going to go on stirring things up until everyone feels even more unsettled and un-comfortable, and until something happens to justify all the stirring.'

'And if it doesn't?'

'I don't think that's an option,' I said. I asked her if she wanted me to fetch her some milk.

'No cash,' she said.

I took out my wallet and she tried not to watch me.

'What help have I been?' she said.

I took out a hundred pounds. It was more than I needed to give her and more than she had expected to receive.

'It's too much,' she said. 'And don't patronize me by saying it's for the baby.'

'I still want to give you something,' I said.

'How about . . .' she said, and hesitated.

'How about what?'

'How about we go shopping for stuff together, food, milk?'

'You want me to go with you?'

She nodded. 'I don't really want to go out,' she said. 'Not after this morning. And I just thought, you know, it's, like, something *normal* people would do.'

I understood precisely what she was asking of me.

'I can't think of anything I'd rather do,' I said.

'Yeah, right,' she said. She pulled on her voluminous coat with its fur hood and drew up the zipper until it again covered most of her face.

We left her flat, and then the building, securing each of the doors behind us.

On the street, she put her arm through mine and clasped her hands together. It was a cold day and the wind off the river stung my forehead and cheeks.

13

Mitchell called me at home later that same night. I'd fallen asleep in front of the television watching a film about a young boy who, when confronted by the usual array of childhood problems, resorted to barking like a dog.

I answered the phone only half-awake. The boy was yapping behind me. Mitchell asked me what kind of dog I had.

'A quiet one,' I said, muting the television. I asked him what he wanted.

'To get together again as soon as possible,' he said. 'I've someone I want you to meet. Ruth McKenzie.'

It occurred to me that he'd spoken again to James Finch since our meeting that morning, and I wondered if he'd needed to do that before introducing Ruth McKenzie to me.

'I've just come from a meeting with Lister and his squad leaders,' he said.

'At this time?' It was after eleven.

'There's a lot to do,' he said evasively. 'Breakfast at the Royal?' he said, meaning the Royal Hotel at the station, and agreeing a time. He hung up immediately the arrangement was made.

I went back to watching the small barking boy, whose mother was now seriously ill, and who was yapping louder than ever. I fell back to sleep before the film ended.

The following morning, Mitchell was there before me, smartly dressed, reading a paper, and sitting beside a woman with platinum-blonde hair, severely cut, and wearing a long, cream-coloured coat. She was the first to see me enter the room. She was speaking on her phone and tapped Mitchell on the arm to indicate that I'd arrived. He folded his paper and stood up, beckoning one of the waiters to him.

As I approached the table, the woman finished her conversation and rose to stand beside him.

'Ruth McKenzie,' she said. 'Mr Rivers, I'm pleased to meet you.'

'Ruth's on her way back to Leeds,' Mitchell said. 'She's our profiler.'

' "Our" meaning?'

'Meaning not from here,' Ruth said. 'I was called in to give a talk to Lister and his men about the kind of man I think we're looking for, and to impress upon them all the importance of keeping their options open as the profile builds and as it comes a little more into focus.'

'We spent four hours with them,' Mitchell said. 'Lister got everyone there to agree not to put it down on their overtime claims.'

'How very noble of him, considering his own inflated wage packet is unlikely to be affected one way or another.'

'He at least did me the courtesy of listening to what I had to say,' Ruth said.

'He had no choice,' I told her.

'Perhaps, but at least a few things were made clear to him.'

'Things that might change the course of his investigation and everything else that's getting swept along with it?'

'Perhaps.'

'Ruth spent six years with Smart and Finch,' Mitchell said, knowing that I would consider this a high enough recommendation. 'They trusted her implicitly on everything she did with them; I think we should do likewise.' He looked at his watch to suggest the time left to us.

I signalled my apology to her.

The waiter brought our coffee and Mitchell took the pot from him as he prepared to pour.

'We have to make this brief, Mr Rivers, but my main purpose in coming here was to impress on Lister's detectives that serial-killer investigations can always be relied upon to follow one of very few fixed patterns,' Ruth said.

'And one of those fixed patterns always exists?'

'Of course.'

'Ruth wrote the book,' Mitchell said. 'Literally.'

'Even if it's only the random, illogical and seemingly completely unconnected pattern,' she said.

'And even that will tell you something about the killer and his reasons for killing?'

'Usually.'

'But that isn't the pattern emerging here?'

'No. I'm convinced of that. I haven't got time to go into the detailed breakdown I outlined to Lister last night, but what I wanted to impress upon him even more is that, in my opinion, there is almost definitely something here which connects these killings to a single perpetrator, and to a single reason for him doing what he's doing.'

' "Almost definitely"?' I said. It seemed an obvious and all-inclusive remark to make.

'I know what you're thinking,' she said. 'But the killings all have sufficient in common to connect them, however tenuous or as-yet unknowable that connection might be. Believe me, it's there.'

'Even if it's just a man with a grudge against prostitutes?'

'It's more than that,' Mitchell said. 'That's just what Lister and Brownlow want it to be.'

'They weren't all prostitutes,' Ruth said.

'Two out of three.'

She and Mitchell exchanged a glance.

'What?' I said.

'Over a year ago,' Mitchell said, 'last summer, a long time before Lister arrived, a girl called Rebecca Siddal was found hanging in an empty house on the Orchard Park estate. She went missing from home after completing her A levels and getting an offer from Nottingham University. She was missing for three days before a team of council workmen, there to board up the doors and windows, found her.'

I remembered the death.

'There was a post-mortem and a coroner's inquest, and an open verdict was returned,' Mitchell said. 'As you can imagine, her parents never accepted this. She was hanged with her own tights. Nothing whatsoever to suggest that anyone else was involved. No forensic, no witnesses, no nothing. Nothing on her or in her or near her. Her parents still don't accept the verdict. According to every-one who knew her, Rebecca Siddal was a well-adjusted, happy, intelligent girl. She was about to get everything she ever wanted out of life. She even passed on a gap year to take up her place at Nottingham.'

'And you're suggesting she might have been killed by the same man who's killing now?' It seemed unlikely to me, and I wondered where Rebecca Siddal fitted into the history of killings in the city Mitchell had outlined for me earlier.

'We're saying it shouldn't be ignored,' Ruth said. 'That's all.'

I knew from her tone that she and Mitchell were convinced of the connection.

'There was never any suggestion that she was even involved with a boy,' I said. 'Let alone that—'

'That she was a prostitute?' Mitchell said. 'She wasn't.'

'How convinced was Lister that this earlier death was connected to those now?'

'Guess,' Ruth said. 'He was as sceptical as you are. But that's only because he's chosen to look harder at one particular pattern than any other.'

'The pattern with him wreathed in glory at the top of it?'

'It's something none of us should ignore,' Mitchell said.

'And so what you're also telling me is that because only two of the four murdered girls were prostitutes, that particular angle is suddenly of considerably less significance?'

'We don't think it's necessarily the solid foundation on which to build his investigation Lister currently considers it to be, no,' Ruth said.

'So what alternatives did you present him with?'

'We just asked him to keep an open mind,' Mitchell said. 'And perhaps to start looking at other things the victims might have had in common, however unlikely.'

'Such as?'

'Such as their ages, their places in life, where they were killed, how they died, how their deaths impacted on the people around them.' The more he said, the more like a poor excuse his explanation sounded. I could imagine Brownlow's face as he and Ruth McKenzie had asked them to consider all this.

'But you're not completely disregarding the fact that two of them *were* known prostitutes?' I said.

'Of course not. But what kind of prostitutes were they? How did they operate? How long had they been working? How consistently, and under what circumstances? Who were their clients? What was *different* about them?'

'What made them different from the prostitutes who weren't killed, you mean?'

Ruth smiled. 'Something like that.'

'It's an impossible thing to speculate on,' I said. 'Besides, Lister will already have teams sifting through all those things.'

'He has,' Mitchell said. 'And soon they'll be buried in a hundred thousand useless reports and sightings and witness statements.'

'They'll be buried even deeper if you insist on including Rebecca Siddal in the sequence of events,' I said.

'We threw her at Lister,' Ruth said. 'And he threw Paul Hendry back at us. He wanted to know where we thought *he* fitted into what we were trying to sell him.'

'And?'

'And then they all had a good laugh at our expense.'

'They actually laughed at you?' I said.

'As good as. There were certainly a lot of smiles, smirks and whispers around the room.'

'Perhaps if you'd had something more definite to give to him,' I suggested.

'I know,' she said. 'But it's a hard thing to do. Start getting too specific about things and you're likely to end up just as blinkered, only facing in another direction.' She looked at me. 'I *do* realize how all this sounds.'

'Especially to men like Lister and Brownlow,' Mitchell added.

'One thing which did strike me', I said, 'was the complete absence of any DNA material on any of the victims to use as a match if anyone was arrested and charged.'

'It's what got us interested in Rebecca Siddal in the first place,' Ruth said. 'And which in itself may be significant. What are the chances – four brutal deaths, and the only solid evidence of involvement in any of them is still the blood sprayed all over Lucy Collins's boyfriend? Whatever else we may or may not know about our killer, we know he's a very careful man.'

'Your reasoning being that he's as careful in his choice of victim – that he's working to a plan – as he is about leaving nothing behind?'

The two of them shared another glance, and both of them smiled. Ruth took a pencil from her bag and added lip gloss to her lips.

'There's nothing Lister hasn't made clear to us,' she said.

'How far is he going to be able to play this to his own rules?' I asked Mitchell.

'Until he gets results? On the plus side, there was a lot of criticism at the time about how the death of Rebecca Siddal was handled. It was a factor in Lister's predecessor's early retirement, and Lister knows that.'

The three of us sat in silence for several minutes, finishing our drinks and considering all that had just been said.

Eventually I said, 'Are you telling me all this because I'm the one plugging that inconvenient gap between Paul Hendry, Lucy Collins and everything else that's happening?'

'Are we *using* you, you mean?' Ruth said. 'Of course we are. No-one's convinced that Hendry's responsible for the other killings, but he's still connected to them via Lucy Collins. As far as we can see, you're the only one working towards either severing that connection completely or proving Hendry's guilt. Either way, it shaves away a great deal of unwanted baggage as far as the rest of the investigation's concerned.'

'Meaning it allows Lister to perhaps start seeing things your way.'

'Something like that,' Mitchell said. It was less than half the truth, and we all knew this. But perhaps this imperfect understanding was the one which suited us all best.

'I have to go,' Ruth announced.

'Reporting back to base?' I said.

'Don't worry – I'll be back here to hold your hands when something new turns up. Besides, Mitchell wouldn't last five minutes without me.' She leaned across the table and kissed him on the cheek.

'Who, me?' Mitchell said. 'I'm fearless.'

It was clear to me that there was a great deal of affection between them. They reminded me of Sunny and Yvonne.

Ruth left us and we saw her a moment later crossing the marble concourse towards her waiting train.

'You think there's a reason – a *specific* reason these killings are taking place, and taking place now, don't you?' I said to Mitchell.

'Ruth's convinced that, despite appearances, there's nothing random or unconsidered or opportunistic about any of these killings.'

'Even the murder of Lucy Collins?'

'Even her. It's what makes Hendry's apparent involvement all the more inexplicable.'

'And does she also believe that the victims might have been chosen for a reason – the actual girls, I mean?'

He nodded once. 'Do you want to go to the press with that one, or shall I? Let's just say she's convinced it's a very strong possibility. They *mean* something to the killer, represent something. By killing them he's following some plan or design. Random, unconsidered and opportunistic killers leave a lot behind them. All those murders I was telling you about yesterday – every single conviction was pushed through on DNA evidence. Every single one. This guy's above all that. Whatever else we uncover, we aren't going to find a blood-soaked lock-up somewhere with black and white photos of the dead girls on the wall, if that's what you're asking me.'

'How far do you think Lister will be prepared to go along with what Ruth's telling him?'

'He'll see how it plays out and then jump one way or the other depending on what serves him best.'

I told him I'd been to see Karen Smith two days earlier.

'She's a wreck,' he said. 'She couldn't tell them anything because, despite all her wonderful memories of the wonderful Kelly, there was no love lost between them, and she and her way-ward daughter were never close.'

'Like Lucy Collins and her family,' I said.

'But unlike Rebecca Siddal or Alison Wilson, both of whom were exceptionally close to their parents.'

'And whatever Karen Smith might have had to tell Lister, he would always consider her testimony unreliable because of her own previous form?'

'Like mother, like daughter,' he said. 'Besides, she laps up all the attention.'

'Would I be able to go and see the parents of Rebecca Siddal?'

He shook his head. 'They've lost all faith in the powers of law and order. They want nothing to do with any of this. Can you blame them? They're dignified, private people, and they're angry that only now might someone be about to take their claims about their daughter's death seriously.'

'Whereas Karen Smith—'

'Is just going to go on selling her anguish, pain and grief to the last newspaper to want to go on hearing about it.'

It seemed a harsh judgement to make of the woman, but I understood what he was telling me.

'I imagine you tried to persuade Rebecca Siddal's parents that finding the killer of these other girls – *if* he also killed their daughter – might help them to come to their acceptance of her death a little sooner,' I said.

'I imagine I did,' he said. 'And before you start wondering why we've let you in on our suspicions concerning Rebecca Siddal, Lister will be announcing later today that he's prepared to re-consider her death as part of his current investigation.'

'Because it'll allow an even more forceful comparison to be made between him and his predecessor?'

'Like I said earlier, while still wanting the prostitute-grudge scenario to pan out, Lister is more than happy to keep his options open.'

'Meaning that at present he has nothing to lose by at least *appearing* to be happy to include Rebecca Siddal in his inquiry?'

'You're learning fast,' he said.

'What other connections between the girls have you considered?' I asked him.

'You name it, we've considered it. Schools, boyfriends, jobs, friends, likes, dislikes, e-mails, texts, Web sites visited. We've run from one end of the spectrum to the other. All four of the girls used the same bus routes. Two of them used the same perfume. Three of them regularly frequented the same bars. Two of them even banked at the same city-centre branch of a bank. And, no, it wasn't the one behind which Kelly Smith was found. And no, wherever we look, we find no indication whatsoever that any of the four girls knew each other or even of each other's existence.' He rubbed his face, looking suddenly tired.

'So what next?'

'Investigations continue and Lister continues to push his brush along the dirty, crime-filled streets.'

'And your bosses are happy to let him do that?'

'I imagine it's too late now to do anything to stop him.' He rose from his chair and picked up his paper.

'One more thing,' I said. 'Did we meet here because Ruth had a train to catch, or because you didn't want to be seen coming to Humber Street again?'

'Is that your way of asking me if Lister's having you watched?' He walked away from me. 'Keep in touch,' he said over his shoulder.

'He's certainly watching one of us very closely,' I said to myself when he was a long way beyond hearing me.

14

I called Sunny. Yvonne answered and I asked her if she remembered the case of Rebecca Siddal's apparent suicide and told her I'd like to see anything the agency might still have on file. Then I told her about my meeting with Mitchell and Ruth McKenzie, and all that this might imply with regard to Paul Hendry. She asked me to describe Ruth McKenzie in great detail, and when I did this she said I sounded impressed by what I'd seen.

'I'm not going to respond to that because you're a lonely, unfulfilled woman who's going to spend the day compiling a lonely hearts page for every young, slim and attractive single mother with brown hair and green eyes, a bubbly personality and good sense of humour who is seeking romance or possibly more, and who hasn't been anywhere except the bingo with her equally funny, equally bubbly, and equally desperate mates for the past two years.'

'Hmm,' she said.

The page – sometimes two – had grown from a single column a year earlier and had become a profitable part of the agency's work for all the local papers it supplied. Sunny would have nothing to do with all the abbreviated, coded details that were listed. He'd once asked her what 'bubbly' really meant. 'Fat, loose-mouthed and with a tendency towards alcoholism,' she told him.

I arranged to visit them both later in the day. She said pointedly that she'd give my regards to Susan Hendry when she next saw her.

'I was about to say that,' I said.

'Of course you were,' she said, and hung up.

Alison Wilson's body had been found early in the morning on the twenty-second of July. She was twenty-three years old and worked as a clerk and receptionist at a film-developing company on Dripool Way, a cul-de-sac on a small industrial estate running parallel with Garrison Road as it approached the Mount Pleasant roundabout. It was widely acknowledged that this short stretch of road, so close to both the city centre and the major routes leading both north and east out of it, was one of the busiest stretches of road in Hull. Local radio stations reported on the congestion there every morning and evening.

Alison Wilson had left work at her usual time of six fifteen the previous evening. She lived with her family in Bilton, where the city finally petered out into the expanse of Holderness. It was her usual practice to walk from where she worked along Williams Street, Abbey Street and Brazil Street to Holderness Road, where a number of buses were available to her. She knew the timings of all of these, and where they stopped, and she would frequently walk the short distance along Holderness Road in the direction of Bilton to improve her chances of catching one or other of the buses. She usually arrived at her parents' bungalow between quarter to seven and seven.

Alison Wilson had been engaged to be married the following year, and two or three times a week she and her fiancé met up to work on the house they were buying on Beverley Road at its junction with Sutton Road.

On the evening she was killed, both her parents had been away and had not returned to Bilton until one in the morning. They were ballroom dancers and had been in Blackpool taking part in a competition. It was not until the following morning that they realized their daughter had not returned home the previous evening. And it was not until they called her fiancé, a man called David Foxton, with whom she occasionally spent the night on camp-beds in the house on Beverley Road, that they realized something was wrong. David Foxton told them he had spoken to Alison at six the previous evening, and that she had told him she was tired and intended going straight home instead of meeting him as previously arranged. He had not spoken to her again that evening. There were no further calls from him to her, or from her to him.

Both he and Alison Wilson's father contacted the police at the Tower Grange station at eight the following morning.

In one of the reports I read, there was some confusion over Alison Wilson's surname. When questioning the people who had known her, the police discovered that she was known to some of them as Alison Boylan – Boylan being the name of her actual father, from whom her mother had parted, later marrying a man called Wilson. Most of those who had known Alison from when she was a young girl – the time of her mother's first marriage – called her Boylan. Alison had only started calling herself Wilson a year or so after her mother's remarriage.

Fifteen minutes before David Foxton's call to Tower Grange, a call had been received at the Queen's Gardens station from a man manoeuvring a bulldozer over derelict land adjacent to James Street to say that he could see what appeared to be a woman, either injured or lying down at the junction of James Street and Williamson Street. The police arrived ten minutes later, just as the call was being made from Tower Grange to Queen's Gardens to let them know of the missing girl.

Alison Wilson had been savagely beaten with a piece of timber which still lay nearby, and had been stabbed eleven times in her neck and chest. The wound pattern showed no similarity to that found on Kelly Smith eight weeks earlier; equally dissimilar was the beating she had received before she died.

A search of the surrounding area revealed nothing. A second-hand-car salesman had parked his cars on the open ground only yards from where Alison Wilson lay without seeing her. Some of the nearby businesses employed security guards who visited the properties throughout the night, but none of these had reported seeing anything.

It was known for certain that Alison Wilson had left work at six fifteen as usual – she had spoken to a cleaner just arriving – but it was considered highly unlikely that she could have been killed during the next few minutes as she made her way from Dripool Way to Holderness Road. It was July, and light until almost ten. Traffic had been standing for half a mile along Garrison Road, Mount Pleasant and Holderness Road, and of the hundreds of motorists who responded to the police appeal, none of them had seen anything unusual that evening, although eight interviewees spoke of seeing a woman dressed as Alison Wilson had been dressed walking the route she would have walked along Holderness Road in search of a bus. Three of these also said they had seen her with another, older woman, the pair of them talking as they walked together.

Everyone Alison Wilson might have known locally, and especially everyone she might have followed or passed on her short journey, was sought out and interviewed. It surprised the police to discover that, despite the few sightings by motorists, no-one else had encountered or spoken to her that evening.

David Foxton was interviewed. He and his brother, a plumber, had spent the whole of the previous afternoon and evening until ten thirty fitting a new central heating system to the house he and Alison were buying. At ten thirty the two men had gone to a nearby pub for a drink, after which Foxton had returned to the house he shared with two other men on Endike Lane, a five-minute walk away.

Both Alison Wilson's cheeks had been fractured during her assault. There was a fracture to the base of her skull, and her face, back, chest and upper arms were all severely bruised and cut from the beating she had received. Three of her teeth had been broken, and all the missing pieces were eventually found – two on the ground near her head, and one in her stomach. Having found nothing else in proximity to her body to suggest that she had been assaulted and killed where she lay, finding the pieces of tooth so close to her corpse surprised the police, and remained unexplained as their investigation started.

The area around Williamson Street was not known to be the haunt of prostitutes. There was too much traffic, too many people on their way elsewhere, nowhere for cars to cruise and idle. Too many others on their way to or from the city centre watching everything that happened.

And despite some early suggestions that the killing might be linked to the murder of Kelly Smith on Chapel Street eight weeks earlier, there was never any suggestion whatsoever that Alison Wilson had ever worked as a prostitute.

Her stepfather had appeared at several press conferences to appeal for help. He acknowledged the police suggestion that she might have been mistaken for someone else – they meant a prostitute – but insisted that this was unlikely. At the third of these appearances, alongside his wife and David Foxton, he had stated his intention of taking legal proceedings against anyone who repeated the discredited suggestion that his stepdaughter might have been a prostitute. He was taking this extreme action, he said, to protect her memory and to curtail the salacious speculation already appearing in the local press.

Sunny had been at each of the conferences, and had written about the death on several subsequent occasions.

David Foxton was questioned in great detail, his alibis checked, and he was not considered by the police to have had any part in his fiancée's killing.

It was pointed out to the police that two months had passed since the murder of Kelly Smith and that no-one had yet been arrested, let alone charged, for that crime. Allegations of lack of commitment persisted, and these grew suddenly much louder with the murder of Alison Wilson.

None of Alison Wilson's clothing had been removed and, like Kelly Smith, she had not been sexually assaulted either before or after she had been killed.

It was the opinion of the doctor who performed the post-mortem that the blow to the base of her skull had concussed her, and that she had been unconscious while the attack on her had continued. As with Kelly Smith, there were no indications that Alison Wilson had tried to defend herself against her attacker.

In the days following the killing, over a thousand motorists who regularly used Garrison Road were stopped and questioned about their journeys.

Alison Wilson's parents pleaded for the release of her body for burial, but this was denied them. Eventually, the press conferences ended, and they returned to their bungalow at Bilton and maintained their silence and waited.

15

The following morning, I'd been at Humber Street only a few minutes when someone knocked at my door, and then tried the handle before I could answer.

The man who entered looked more disappointed than embarrassed by his intrusion.

'Mr Rivers?' he said. He carried a large black case, worn at its edges, and with lettering across one side I couldn't read. 'I imagined I might be far too early to catch you.'

Then why come?

He came into the room and put the case on my desk. As intended, I read the gold lettering. Dr James Weaver. And then the initials and their neat punctuation.

'Dr Weaver,' I said. 'I was on my way out.'

He looked from me to the door. 'I won't detain you any longer than is absolutely necessary,' he said. He spoke as though he believed I had lied to him, and as though he had no qualms about letting me know he knew this. He was in his mid-fifties, tall, and with a lower jaw which looked as though he was constantly holding it up and out. 'I believe you are employed by Susan Hendry to enquire into the unfortunate circumstances surrounding her son's alleged illegalities and self-inflicted injuries,' he said.

'I believe I am,' I said, wondering what this discursive formality was intended either to suggest to me or to disguise.

He continued as though I hadn't spoken. 'I also understand that, as part of these enquiries, you consider it right and proper to harass the staff at my surgery.'

'I spoke to your receptionist,' I said. I knew he'd already been to see Lister, so his appearance here intrigued me. He struck me as a man who might prefer to sort out his own problems and grievances rather than leave them to someone else. Perhaps he was here because he had been unable to resist coming.

'No – you shouted at her. You abused her. As I said, you harassed her. I'm not here to argue the point with you, Mr Rivers, merely to convey to you that I have already told the police everything there is to know concerning the circumstances of the discovery of Paul Hendry, and that I am more than willing to go on assisting *them* in any way they might require of me.'

That was clear, then. And still no mention of the fact that he'd already complained about my behaviour to Lister. Perhaps Lister himself was wary of this personal connection, and had warned him against saying anything which might later compromise him.

'I would be failing in my obligations to Susan Hendry if I didn't cover much of the same ground,' I said. 'And it's because she has so little faith in the police that she came to me in the first place.'

'Then I must point out that I believe her lack of faith to be unfounded. Alexander Lister is an excellent policeman.'

'By which I take it that you and he are personally acquainted, and that that's the true purpose of your visit here,' I said, hoping to match his formality with some of my own.

'I'm afraid I don't understand you,' he said. 'Please, allow me to make myself perfectly clear on the matter. I cannot and will not tolerate any more intrusion or disruption of my surgery and the work there than is absolutely necessary. As you can imagine, there has already been a great deal of both.'

'And while you might have no choice but to tolerate this when the *official* forces of law and order are involved, you will not extend the same courtesy to me?'

He smiled at the word. 'I believe we understand each other perfectly, Mr Rivers. However, what *you* appear still not to have fully grasped or appreciated, is that you have no legal right *whatsoever* to pursue your enquiries where you are not welcome and where those enquiries take place at the expense of others.'

'Did Alexander point that out to you?'

He appeared to falter for an instant. 'I make no apology for knowing Alexander Lister.'

'You'll be telling me next the pair of you play golf together,' I said. They did. Sunny had already told me. They had posed together at local charity matches even before Lister's return to the city.

'As a matter of fact, we do,' Weaver said. 'Alexander and I have known each other for a considerable length of time. I do not, however, understand what any of this has to do with Paul Hendry and the circumstances surrounding—'

'Surrounding his blood-soaked near-corpse having been found in your surgery with a needle half-full of your drugs sticking out of his arm?' I was beginning to tire of his arrogance and his veiled threats.

'If you'd allow me to finish speaking,' he said. 'What I was about—'

'I don't care about where or when or how all your back-slapping with Lister started. All I'm interested in is to discover what really happened to Paul Hendry and Lucy Collins that night. What you might like or not like to happen, what you want or don't want, is of no interest to me. The same goes for *Alexander*,' I said, knowing that everything would eventually find its way back to Lister.

'My wife was right,' he said, shaking his head at my outburst.

'What does she have to do with any of this?'

'For your information, she is currently the Chair of the Police Community Liaison Committee. And before you choose to make some further scathing or supposedly witty remark on that particular piece of information, it is a post she has held now for almost four years. And she has served on the committee, and others like it, in various guises, and with varying responsibilities, for the past twenty, if not twenty-five years.'

'How very public-spirited of her,' I said.

'Many believe so, though I can see why a person like you might decry such public-spiritedness.'

'And she told you to stay away from me?'

'Only because she believed my motives might be misunderstood or misinterpreted, and that I might in some way compromise Alexander's investigation or her own position,' he said.

'Whatever she believes, our paths would have crossed eventually,' I said. 'You're Paul Hendry's GP.'

'I'm also treating his mother,' he said. 'Susan Hendry has been a patient at my surgery for almost twenty years.'

'Lucky her.'

'Your facetiousness and flippancy do you no favours, Mr Rivers.'

'You'll get used to it,' I said, trying to make the remark sound as facetious and flippant as I could make it.

'What Pauline said—'

'Pauline?'

'My wife. Pauline Weaver.' He said it and paused, as though I would recognize the name, which I didn't. 'Her maiden name was Dunn. Pauline Dunn.' It still meant nothing to me. 'She's the daughter of Paul Dunn. Dunn's supermarkets?'

I recognized the name, but wondered why he'd laboured over pointing all this out to me. Unless it was just something else that was intended to impress me and help me to see things the way he saw them.

'I never shop there,' I said. 'Please convey my apologies to Mr Dunn.'

'Pauline's father died a long time ago.'

'And you're telling me all this now why? Because it tells me how well-connected you consider yourself to be? Or because you want me to know how far up the pecking order you consider yourself to be in relation to where *I* do my pecking? Because I should listen more closely to you than to either the mother or the sister or the next-door neighbour of an allegedly drug-abusing prostitute?'

'No, that is most certainly not what I intended my remarks to convey to you, or what, indeed, I intended to imply. You deliberately and maliciously misinterpret everything I say to suit your own prejudices and preconceived ideas, Mr Rivers.'

'You still wanted to come here and convey to me that you consider yourself and your wife to be influential people with influential friends, and that you'd prefer it if I went kicking through the weeds and mud somewhere else a long way away from you.'

'Alexander warned me that you had a florid turn of phrase and a tendency towards melodramatic self-justification.'

'I'm surprised he managed to pick all that up from our one brief encounter,' I said. 'He must be very observant. Unless, of course, someone else has been extolling my virtues to you behind my back.'

He slapped a hand against his case. 'I am not a suspect in this or any other inquiry. There are the proper and correct channels, Mr Rivers. Perhaps your time and energy might be better spent – to say nothing of Susan Hendry's money – in discovering what they are and then using them. I am perfectly within my rights to refuse to assist you if I believe you have overstepped the mark. Just as I am within my rights to advise the other members of the surgery, junior partners and staff alike, not to assist you in your work at the expense of their own. As I said, I shall do everything in my power to assist the *official* inquiry into the death of Lucy Collins and whatever Paul Hendry thought he was doing, but I can neither condone nor support your own involvement, which, to my mind at least, may actually act *against* the best interest of that other investigation.' It was what he had come to say, and now he'd said it.

'Is that you talking, or Alexander?' I said.

'Of course Alexander and I have discussed this matter, but only in the proper manner and through the proper channels.'

'Which are what, exactly?'

'He is far too conscientious and good a policeman to allow—'

'You already said that bit. Something about compromising himself. Is that what you think I'm doing?'

'I believe I've made myself perfectly clear on the point.'

He hadn't. He'd made lots of other things perfectly clear to me, but not that.

'It's why you came,' I said. 'And, please, tell your wife – tell Pauline – that I tend to agree with her rather than you where all this "compromising" business is concerned.'

He smiled briefly at the remark. 'For your information, my wife has already offered to resign the Chair of the Liaison Committee for the duration of this investigation and her offer was turned down. Unanimously.'

'Paul and Pauline,' I said. 'Were she and her father close?'

He paused for a moment to control his anger at the remark. 'That is none of your business or concern,' he said.

Too late, I thought. *I saw it.*

'And, presumably, she inherited the supermarket millions,' I said, jabbing him again. But by then he was prepared for my provocation.

'Again, that is no business or concern of yours,' he said.

'You're suddenly very evasive,' I said. It wasn't true; he'd never once raised the veil of his formality.

'You may interpret my remarks here today in any way you choose, Mr Rivers. Neither Pauline nor I nor any of my colleagues or staff have anything to hide. My concern – my concern as a doctor – is for Susan Hendry. Believe me, if I thought for one moment that what you were doing would bring her some benefit or relief, or even some temporary ease, then I would not be here now. What has happened to her son and to her is extremely sad and regrettable. But perhaps – just perhaps – because of the nature of my pro-fession, I have acquired a different perspective on, and understanding of, the nature and variety of human suffering from the one you yourself clearly hold. Who knows – perhaps that will change?'

'I doubt it,' I said.

'Me, too. And, please, also bear in mind that, however I might appear to you – however arrogant or pompous or dismissive of the work in which you are engaged – I make no apology for that either.'

'Ouch,' I said. 'You still came.'

'I came only because I considered it my duty to come. And, no, I don't care to hear how outdated or ridiculous you might find such a notion. I also came in the hope of appealing to your better nature and asking you to consider Susan Hendry in all of this and how *her* needs might now be best served.'

'Save that for Lister,' I said. 'It wasn't me who barged into her home at five in the morning to terrorize her and take away all of her son's belongings.'

'I know,' he said. 'And I believe Alexander regrets the necessity of that as much as you or I do.'

'That's all right, then. Pity he didn't regret it sufficiently not to do it, or to at least do it differently. Pity he didn't for once stop thinking about his own public image and career prospects.'

Weaver, I realized, had said everything he'd come to tell me avoiding all mention of the events of the day Paul Hendry had allegedly broken into his surgery. And despite Lister's warnings, and apparently against the wishes of his wife, he had come to tell me things I either knew already or would shortly discover. He pretended he was warning me, but was fully aware that he was powerless to do any more.

And during the whole of our conversation, he had referred only once, and then only briefly, to the wider investigation. His concern rested with the fact that Paul Hendry had been found in *his* surgery and what he imagined this might now imply regarding *his* reputation and standing in the world in which he lived.

He was accustomed to being listened to, taken seriously, and obeyed. He was the single major partner in the Walker Street surgery, and he had made clear to me the distinction he drew between himself and his junior partners, and between them and the other staff there. He wanted me to know about himself and his wife and the people like them, and the circles in which they moved. And he wanted me to know about the distance that would always exist between those people and people like Lucy Collins, Kelly Smith and Emily Carr.

He picked up his bag.

'Impressive-looking letters,' I said. 'Just like the ones on the nameplate at the surgery.'

'I earned every one of them,' he said. 'The bag was a gift from my wife. I, personally, would never countenance such an ostentatious thing, but she insisted. It was her gift to me and it means a great deal to me. I understand you yourself are not married, Mr Rivers.'

'My facetiousness and flippancy puts them all off,' I said. 'And, as you can imagine, leading the exciting life of a private investigator, meeting all the exciting people I meet, I need to be careful of that compromise thing.'

He smiled to himself again at these remarks. And then he turned and left me.

'See you again,' I called after him.

He paused briefly at the suggestion, but said nothing in reply.

I went to the window and watched him walk to his car. He was partially blocking one of the warehouse entrances. A trader shouted to him, but Weaver ignored the man completely. He opened the passenger door and put his case on the seat. And then he closed and locked the door before letting himself in at the driver's side. He sat for several minutes before driving away, impervious to the trader's continuing insults and complaints.

16

I called my old partner, John Maxwell, and told him what was happening, knowing only that he already knew Lister from their time together at the start of Lister's career, but certain that he would already be fully aware of what Lister was now attempting in Hull. Despite being twelve years retired from the force, and having lived in County Durham for the three years since our own partnership had ended, John Maxwell kept in touch with old friends in the city, some of whom were still serving officers.

Here was where he'd been born and grown up, and where he'd worked. And it was where he'd decided he could no longer go on living following the death of his wife. Neither of us had spoken of it, but it was the loss of his wife after a long, hard illness that had persuaded him to retire.

He guessed immediately why I was calling him and asked me what I wanted to know. He was almost seventy, and in all the time I had known him neither his memory nor his judgement had ever failed him.

'Lister said he was seconded to you when he first came to Hull twenty years ago,' I said.

'He was. I think, to begin with, it was a way of cutting him down to size. He was a graduate, a fast-tracker before they existed, a little too keen for his own good or for the good of the people around him. I had a reputation for being thorough. I did things properly, followed procedure. He used to talk about Hull as though it was the back of beyond, couldn't wait to get to the end of his time there and move on.'

'Did you get on with him?'

'Funnily enough, I did. I saw the need for men like him. There was nothing to be gained by smothering initiative and making everyone come up slowly, and sometimes undeservedly, through the ranks.'

'How did he respond?'

'He did everything I told him to do. I gave him enough leeway to use his own initiative, but he always made a point of giving in where it mattered. He knew what counted. Even then he knew that some people mattered to him a lot more than others.'

'Just as they might matter to him now, you mean?'

'Is that a serious question?' he said.

I told him that Lister had spoken of him with respect, affection almost.

'It was probably how he felt after our year together. Being with me opened a lot of doors for him and earned him a few points he might otherwise not have earned. And before you say it, yes, he knew that that was what he'd have to do right from the start. And, yes, he probably believed he was using me because it suited him to do so. He could always read a situation and know exactly where everybody stood in it. I'd say that if you have a problem with what he's doing now, then it's more your problem than his. He's the one who needs a good result in all of this, and whatever problems you might think he's creating, that's not how he'll see it.' He started to cough, and broke off speaking.

Waiting until he'd regained his breath, I asked him if he was unwell. He told me he'd been feeling 'run-down' for a few months.

Three months ago, he'd fallen and broken his arm, he said. I regretted not having known about this and told him he should have let me know about the injury.

'Why?' he said simply.

'I could have sent you some flowers,' I said.

'Flowers belong—'

'In parks and cemeteries. I know.' I asked him if he'd had any thoughts on the three murders. I kept the number at three because Lister hadn't yet announced the inclusion of Rebecca Siddal in his inquiry.

'None whatsoever,' he said. 'And any I did have would have no bearing now on how Lister chooses to conduct his investigation.'

'Did the pair of you work on anything big together?'

He considered this for a full minute.

'Nothing particularly "big". An eight-year-old boy had been found murdered and dumped in the Holderness Drain. No-one was ever caught for it. It was in the days before we had reliable access to all the files or information we needed. I think the station had just got its first computer, if you could call it that. Bigger than a fridge. Anyone with any sense could see that the world was changing.'

'And men like Lister were better able to cope with those changes?'

'Better than men like me, you mean?'

'Did you feel as though you were being superseded?' I asked him.

'Of course I was being superseded.' There was neither anger nor resentment in his voice. 'Things had to change. There was still a place for people who worked like I did, but we all still had to make ourselves ready for what was coming. The Stone Age didn't end because they ran out of stones.'

'Do *you* think he's right to use the murders to embark on his crusade against prostitution and drug dealing?'

'Interesting word,' he said, and nothing more.

So far, there had been a veiled warning in almost everything he'd said to me.

I asked him how police doctors operated.

'Be more specific,' he said.

'Who's available, and how?'

'It varies. Sometimes they work for short periods on secondment, employed by the force. But mostly they're contacted at local practices as and when the need arises. Each station will have a list. Forensic have always had their own operation, and usually postmortems were carried out by people on their lists. Most of the work with doctors during my time involved finding one to examine someone we were keeping in the station cells overnight. Apart from that, there wasn't much call for them beyond what they could provide at their surgeries or in the hospitals. There was a lot of overlap.'

'Did you ever come across a doctor called Weaver, James Weaver?'

He considered this. 'The name rings a bell, but nothing very recent. I can't say that I ever encountered him in any of my work.'

'He's married to Pauline Dunn, daughter of Paul Dunn,' I said.

'The supermarkets? So?'

'I just wondered if you'd come across either of them.'

'I knew *of* her. Everybody did. Especially after her father died and left her either the business or the money from its sale. Something happened to old man Dunn,' he said, pausing in an effort to remember. 'Some kind of family tragedy. He went off to France or somewhere to live for a few years. There was always pressure on him to sell his stores to one of the national chains. He went away – in fact I think the whole family went – and then he died shortly afterwards and the supermarkets were sold. I suppose Weaver's wife must have come back here after her father died.'

'And as she inherited his millions.'

'I suppose so.' He was still trying to remember something. 'I doubt if I ever knew what shook the old man up so badly, but whatever it was, he lost his grip on things. I'll make a few enquiries. There must be someone somewhere who still remembers it all. I probably don't recall it because it was never a police matter. Or at least not in Hull. They had a big family home in Bishop Burton, if I remember. The boy was found in Weaver's surgery. Is there a connection?'

'I don't know. Weaver and his wife know Lister socially.'

'Lister will know everybody who counts socially. And those he doesn't already know, he soon will. People like Lister and Weaver, they feed off each other.'

'Pauline Weaver's on a few of his public committees,' I said.

'I remember,' he said. 'In my days on the force, she was the kind of woman who got herself involved in things. To be fair to her, she was always a well-liked woman. People trusted her, and Lister will know that.'

'And use it?'

'So what? I thought I'd made it clear to you – whatever Lister wants, then that's what he'll get – with or without the recommendation of Pauline Dunn, I mean Weaver.'

'But life would be a lot easier for him if she was with him?'

'Naturally.'

Then I told him about Mitchell and his watching brief on Lister and his investigation.

'You have too much faith in National Crime,' he said. 'They have their own agenda, and what's good for them might not necessarily be good for anyone else.'

'Including me?'

'Especially you. You don't need me to tell you any of this. And besides . . .'

'Besides what?'

'You know as well as I do that if they really do have a single, serial killer on their hands, then sooner or later they'll catch him.'

'Because the more he murders, the more he reveals of himself, and the more likely he is to either slip up or to leave something behind which will eventually implicate him? It hasn't happened yet.'

'I've never known it work any other way. The last girl aside, Lister's time – and yours – would be best spent now looking more closely at the first two murders. If it's a single killer, then there's a connection, and sooner or later, it's going to become apparent.'

It was what Mitchell and Ruth McKenzie had tried to persuade me of in the Royal.

He seemed suddenly exhausted and his coughing resumed.

We spoke for several minutes about the discovery of the wartime corpses in the cellar on Neptune Street, and he reminisced briefly about his boyhood in Hull. The house in which he had lived as a boy had been destroyed in a raid, and his neighbours on both sides had been killed because they had refused to leave their homes for the shelter. He had been sent to live with an uncle in Snaith, near Goole, for the rest of the war.

His father had been killed in Burma, and his death had greatly affected John Maxwell's mother.

I already knew most of what he was telling me, but this was the first time I'd heard him talk of it like this, and so I listened without interrupting him.

After a while, he simply stopped speaking and said he had to go.

I thanked him and told him I'd keep in touch.

Later that night, after ten, I called the mobile number I still had for James Finch, the man with whose recommendation Mitchell had approached me.

The phone rang and was answered immediately.

'Mr Leo Rivers,' Finch said. I heard the voices of other men close by.

'I'm surprised my number's still in there,' I said.

'You shouldn't be. I'll get back to you in ten minutes.' He hung up.

I waited an hour for his call. Plenty of time for him to find out why I might be calling him after all that time.

'Andrew Mitchell,' I said immediately.

'Whatever else you might need to know about him, what might be worth knowing above all else at this point, is that Lister prob-ably appreciates having him there even less than he appreciates you and Summers stumbling back and forth across his path. I assume the pair of you are still joined at the hip where these things are concerned.'

He and Sunny had never got on, and had antagonized each other at every opportunity.

'The second most important thing for you to know is that, come what may, Lister is going to make ACC within eighteen months. Is this the end of our conversation?'

'Sorry to hear about you and your wife,' I said.

He sighed. 'Yeah, well, what can I tell you?'

'Are you able to see your daughters?'

'Not as often as I'd like. We'll work something out. Did Mitchell tell you he put me up for three months when it first happened?'

He hadn't. 'You sound pretty certain about Lister's chances,' I said.

'Nothing like that gets left to *chance*. That's the whole point.'

'So *is* Mitchell here purely on a watching brief?' I asked him.

'Originally I think that was the intention. Something good happens, everybody wants to bask in the warmth.'

'You said "originally".'

'I think all this zero-tolerance stuff took a few of them by surprise.'

'It's already happening,' I said.

'I know. Just remember – however it turns out, Lister is not going to be allowed to come out of it looking bad. Whatever you might think of him, he's popular. He likes to cultivate this man-of-the-people thing that always plays well with the taxpayers and voters. Nothing you or anyone else does is going to be allowed to tarnish that. Mitchell's there to keep an eye on everything, but he's also one of our murder specialists. He worked on the M25 killings and then at Soham. He knows better than anyone what kind of storms these particular investigations get to live inside.'

'The same storms that eventually blow out of control?'

'And Mitchell knows ten times more about that than you do. Have you met Ruth McKenzie yet?'

'Briefly,' I said.

'Trust her. She was sent to Mitchell once Lister changed course and made his big announcement about turning Hull into Disneyworld on the Humber. I've worked with her for five years on and off. The story we're putting out is that Lister requested her from National Crime to help with his investigation. He plays along with us, we play along with him. Where's the harm?'

'But in reality she was forced on to Lister just like Mitchell was, and Lister had no say in the matter?'

'Whatever. Lister's making the best of it. He knows exactly why they're there.'

I heard the snap of a lighter, the exhalation of smoke. It was a degree above freezing in Hull.

'*Is* it a serial killer?' I said.

'Why is Lister still keeping tabs on the druggie in a coma, you mean?'

'Bird in the hand?'

'Confidential medical opinion doesn't rate his chances of a useful recovery.'

' "Useful"?'

'Useful,' he said.

'So Lister's just waiting for another killing?'

'We on this side of that thin blue line prefer to call them "further developments".'

'And, meanwhile, he pushes ever onwards with his quest.'

'Onwards and upwards.'

'Does Lister get to hear about everything Mitchell might say about him?'

'One way or another, yes.'

'And so he'll definitely know Mitchell's been to see me behind his back?'

He laughed. 'He'll probably have transcripts and a few photos. Any of this backfires, and Lister will accuse Mitchell of working against his own interests – probably of betraying him and his duty to the force – and Mitchell will be pulled. Like I said, Lister's being groomed for a very exclusive club. They tend to look out for each other. Plus, of course, the people doing the grooming want Lister with them as much as he wants to push the door open and walk on in there.'

'Is that why he took a chance and launched this campaign on his own initiative?'

'Could be,' he said. 'You're the private detective.'

'Anyone in the frame yet for the killings?'

He laughed again. 'You'd be the first person we'd all ring. Perhaps if I gave you a name and address you could go and arrest him yourself. Lister has all the manpower he needs. They'll turn something up or get a lucky break before too long. You know how these things work. Talk to Mitchell,' he said. He sucked in his breath.

'Cold?' I asked him.

'Not as cold as you,' he said, and hung up.

17

I told Sunny about my encounter with Weaver. He showed no surprise that the man had approached me, only that he'd taken so long to do it.

'Weaver, of course, chose route B to the top,' he said.

'Which is?'

'Get born poor, study hard, pull yourself up by the bootstraps, work, study some more, work even harder, and *then* marry the multimillionaire boss's daughter.'

'And is he at the top? He's still working.'

'It's the top as far as Hull's concerned.'

'Where are we, then?'

'You're hovering close to the bottom, and I'm about a foot above you. We do all that work and study stuff, but it's never enough.'

'He made a big point of telling me all about his social standing,' I said.

'And probably while denying it was what he was doing. It's the kind of man he is. I've met the pair of them a few times. I'd say his opinion of himself is always going to be higher than the man who's got Weaver's finger stuck in his chest.'

'What's his wife like?'

'Lady Bountiful? I don't know. I've only ever come across her in my capacity as chronicler of the good and selfless works of the worthy and the wealthy.'

'I got the impression from Weaver and John Maxwell that there was a lot of that sort of thing.'

'There is. And if you're about to start prodding in that direction, I'd think again. Pauline Weaver is a woman much admired and respected. You'd also be making a big mistake if you saw her only as an appendage to Weaver. She's got clout. Old clout. And the generous donations to back it up. I imagine, for instance, that she and Lister are far better acquainted than Lister and the good doctor will ever be. Weaver might turn up at all the black-tie benefits for form's sake, but she's the one who's committed to everything. Weaver might play the part, but she writes most of the scripts.'

I remembered what the security guard had told me about the Weavers and their interrupted engagement on the night Paul Hendry was found in the Walker Street surgery.

He went on. 'Apparently, she's given away millions of her father's money to all the right charities and foundations.'

' "Right" being?'

'Sick kids. Seriously sick kids. Seriously sick kids who are going to die.'

'And you know nothing else about her, or about him and her together?'

'Dirt, you mean? Forget it. They've got position, privilege, and a vault full of folding to support both. They live like minor royalty. Big house on the edge of Bishop Burton. Forty or fifty acres. Holiday homes in France and God knows where else. They own property all over the city. I know what you're thinking – *his* alarm, *his* surgery, *his* patient – but if you're about to start throwing any dirt at him – let alone *her* – then you'd better be prepared for the JCBs that are going to come and dump it back on you in return. You're right – he's an opinionated, arrogant fucker, and every time he struts around with his chest out he pisses somebody off. This week it's you. Get over it.'

'So I ignore all the connections and coincidences?'

'Do what you have to do,' he said, exasperated. 'But believe me, you're looking at something that isn't there.'

He continued to attend Lister's press conferences, and Lister continued to make no apologies for what he was doing. Someone had accused him of behaving like the Witchfinder General, and despite his protestations, the remark pleased him and the name had stuck. If that's what it took, he had countered, then that's what he would become. The title had accompanied a new photo in that day's late-edition *Mail*.

He made a speech: these were troubled times in a troubled city, and nothing was ever going to be achieved by being forced to end-lessly react to an agenda of events dictated by the lawbreakers. He was convinced he knew what was needed, and that his current campaign was delivering this. His critics would have to wait, and then judge him later, by results. He was sorry if anyone was offended by his aims or inconvenienced by his methods, but he remained adamant that everything now was being done for the greater good. The *Mail* printed the speech in full, with the title 'The Greater Good'.

I read it sitting at Sunny's desk.

'How long will they go along with everything?' I said.

'Depends what kind of results he gets. Most people just appreciate the fact that something's being done at last. A few of the brighter boys on the nationals are beginning to express one or two doubts. But it's not what matters. *Here* is where it matters, and *here* is where it gets to stay front-page news because everybody's too lazy to do anything other than fill their pages with what Lister's telling them. Campaigns attract other campaigns.'

Shrines of cellophane-wrapped flowers had already appeared at Garrison Road, Chapel Street and outside Nelson Court, and no distinction was made between the women who had convictions for soliciting and those who didn't. And because the shrines appeared, so they grew.

The *Mail* photographed these, too. A city shared its grief and concern. A city mourned its murdered daughters. I read the predictable and repetitive articles and I imagined how Karen Smith might now be responding to this gratifying public redemption of her daughter.

'Did anything come of all the raids?' I asked Sunny.

'Lister's had some of the girls and their "clients" back in for further questioning. They're still taking them in, five at a time, day and night. Next he's going to do something about kerb-crawlers. That should be interesting.'

'And the teams dedicated to the murders?'

' "Our inquiries are continuing". It's not good news. They move an inch at a time. And you'd be the first to complain if they went any faster and missed anything. Don't worry – Brownlow's not as stupid or as incompetent as you'd like him to be. He'll do everything by the book, and if that means being thorough for once in his career, then he'll be thorough.'

'He'll make sure his own back's covered before going out on a limb to prop Lister up, you mean.'

He shook his head, but more at the lazy remark than at what I was suggesting.

I remained unconvinced of what he was telling me, and he knew this.

Yvonne had suggested interviewing some of the women whose livelihoods were being destroyed by all this police activity, but he'd told her to forget it. The last thing any of the local papers were going to want were stories which might appear sympathetic towards the prostitutes. Despite the shrines and headlines, there was still the unspoken belief that these were women who had deliberately made themselves vulnerable to the attention of a killer. The *Mail* had even printed a letter pointing out that if the prostitutes did not exist in the city, then prostitute-killers would not operate there either, and that perhaps then the police could spend their time and energy ridding the place of its burglars, car thieves and drug dealers. There was a stark, indifferent and seemingly perfect logic to the argument, and it was repeated in further letters and in calls to the local radio stations.

Lister asked for tolerance and understanding, and then went on publicly and loudly arresting and releasing the prostitutes and the men who provided them with either their custom or their drugs, or both.

Yvonne arrived. She had with her a slender file and she dropped this into my lap as she took off her coat.

'Rebecca Siddal's parents never for one minute accepted the coroner's verdict,' she said.

'They never do,' Sunny said. 'Accept that, and it means they should start to leave everything behind them.' He took the file from me and scanned the few articles it held. 'They're just outline reports on what happened. Probably no more than a repeat of what the police told the coroner and the coroner told the press. "Tragic Suicide". "Girl-With-Everything-To-Live-For" angle.'

'Just like Alison Wilson,' I said.

'Don't get your hopes up. That's all it is – an angle. Message massaged by the medium and all that. And then a few follow-ups when the coroner finally released his wholly expected verdict. A bit unsatisfactory all round, and for all concerned.' He continued reading the few photocopied sheets and pieces of newsprint the file contained. 'Just two more grieving parents demanding that more be done, followed by . . .' He turned over the final page – there were no more than six in total – '. . . a copy of the memorials placed by her parents, family and friends in the *Mail*. None of this is going to tell you anything new.' He handed the file back to me.

'Is there any reason why it's so thin?' I asked him.

'Teenage girl kills herself. The nationals were never interested. And why come to us when they can get everything from either the police or the coroner for free?'

I read each of the sheets more closely. They told me little I didn't already know.

I read the page of memorials to the dead girl, over thirty in total, from every member of her family and many of her friends. She was popular and loved. The messages were the usual well-worn ones offered by the *Mail*, but even these seemed sincere and poignant where Rebecca Siddal had been concerned.

'She gets practically the whole page to herself,' Yvonne said, looking over my shoulder. 'Whoever else had one printed that day must have felt badly done to.'

There were only three other names on the page, each with a single insertion.

I was about to return the sheets to the file and give it back to her, when the third of these names caught my eye. It was a memorial to a man called John – or 'Jock' – Boylan, who had been dead for four years, but who was still missed and remembered by his brother, Jimmy.

'Boylan,' I said. 'Boylan was the surname of Alison Wilson's real father.'

They both looked up at this. It wasn't a common surname.

Sunny then sat with his eyes closed for a moment. 'But this is about Rebecca Siddal, not Alison Wilson, or Boylan. All those memorials were published a year ago, *well* before Alison Wilson was killed. There can't possibly be any connection.'

'I could call the Wilsons and see if they know anything about it,' Yvonne suggested.

'Let him do it,' Sunny said, meaning me. 'Lister's waiting for an excuse to make life difficult for us. Approaching the Wilsons in the middle of all this is probably all he needs.'

There were numbers written on the file and along the margins of some of the articles. Yvonne pointed out the one for the Wilsons' Bilton home.

I dialled.

A man answered after only a single ring. I could hear a television in the background.

'Mr Boylan?' I said. 'My name is Leo Rivers. I'm calling in connection with the investigation into the death of your daughter.'

He was silent for a moment, and then said, 'Is this a joke?' He told someone to turn the television down.

'I'm sorry?' I said.

'For a start, my name's Wilson, not Boylan. That was my wife's married name. Which you should bloody well know by now. And second, we've heard next to nothing from you people for the best part of two months. What — now that there's another girl been found killed, you're all suddenly interested again?' He was talking about Lucy Collins.

'I'm sorry,' I said. 'I must have been given the wrong information.' I hoped he'd hang up on me, but instead he told me to wait.

Sunny motioned for me to put the phone down, but I ignored him.

A moment later, a woman's voice said, 'Is it about Alison?'

'My apologies,' I said. 'I'm afraid I offended your husband by referring to him as Mr Boylan.'

'They did that in some of the first newspaper articles,' she said. 'Have you found something?'

'I'm sorry. No,' I said, already hoping the man had forgotten my name and that our own painful conversation would be over before she thought to ask me for it. 'I'm only calling because it was pointed out to us that someone called "Jock" Boylan was mentioned in the memorial column of the *Mail* a year ago and—'

' "Jock" was John. My first husband. His brother Jimmy puts the notices in.' Her tone grew suddenly much colder. 'Look harder and you'll probably find another for each year he's been dead. I don't want to talk about him. His brother blamed me for everything that happened. John died of cancer four years ago.'

'My apologies for having brought it all up again,' I said, still desperately trying to understand what, if anything, might connect the single notice with the thirty notices for Rebecca Siddal. 'Can I ask if you ever see your ex-husband's brother?' I said.

'Never,' she said quickly, slamming a door in my face. 'Not since the funeral. And, to be entirely honest with you, I only went to that because Alison wanted to attend. There was no love lost between me and John, not towards the end of our marriage. Twenty-two years, it lasted, and that was probably fifteen years too long. We only stayed together that long because of Alison. And even that looks to have been a pointless exercise now.' Her voice broke and she caught her breath and started to cry.

'I know how distressing all this must be for you,' I said, increasingly conscious of the deception I was continuing to perpetrate. 'But your daughter's murder is still being actively investigated.'

'I know – we saw her picture in the paper last week, alongside those other two.' She said 'other two' in a voice which left me in no doubt what she meant, and how unfair she considered this sandwiching of her daughter to be.

'I have one final question,' I said. 'Do you or Mr Wilson, or did your first husband, ever know anyone called Siddal, who lived in Cottingham?'

She repeated the name to the man still beside her. 'Neither of us do,' she said. 'John might have done. I don't know. I never knew anyone of that name when I was with him. I'm not from Hull. John was born and bred here. "Jock" was just a name he was given when he was a boy because his family were originally from Peterhead. His brother still lives in one of the few houses still standing on Woodcock Street, where the pair of them were brought up. Or at least he did four years ago, when I last saw him.'

I mouthed the name to Sunny, who pointed it out to me on the map taped to the wall beside him.

I thanked the woman for everything she'd told me, and she asked me what the name meant. I told her it was just a detail that needed clearing up.

The man took the phone from her and told me angrily that I needn't call them again until I'd got something positive to tell them. Then he hung up.

'Impersonating a police officer,' Yvonne said. 'To say nothing about whatsitting the course of justice or obstructing the police in the course of their thing-ing.'

'Perverting,' Sunny said. He tapped his finger at the map again, drawing my attention to what he was showing me.

Woodcock Street cut through the warren of streets midway between Anlaby Road and the dual carriageway. Most of the houses there were now empty, derelict and boarded-up, awaiting demolition.

Susan Hendry's husband had once lived only a hundred yards away on Dairycoates Avenue.

And Glasgow Street connected Woodcock Street with the Selby Street home of Kelly Smith's mother and younger sister.

More old history, names and places forming and disappearing

like smoke, and without any real meaning or anything more tangible to connect them.

I pointed all this out to Sunny, who only shrugged when I asked him what this coincidence might mean.

'Thousands of people live and lived there. It's probably the only part of Hull where you can still trace the same families back through the same streets,' he said. 'They were the families of trawlermen; it was where they all lived. What do Alison Wilson or Lucy Collins have to do with any of that? Or Rebecca Siddal?'

The Seventies had seen the destruction of Hull's deep-sea fishing fleet. This was followed by the redevelopment of much of the land bounded by Hessle Road and the Humber, and the dispersal of the families into the new outlying estates, including the Orchard Park estate, where Rebecca Siddal's hanging body had been found. But he was right. Many families had stayed put, and some had even gone back to the overcrowded streets when they tired of the clean, convenient emptiness of the new lives they were being forced to live.

'It's too much of a coincidence to ignore,' I said.

'Why is it a coincidence?' he said. 'A lot of people live there. Not as many as when the fishing fleet was operational, but still a lot. It's only a coincidence if you buy into your friend Ruth McKenzie's theory about the killings having something very specific which connects them, and even then only if that connection has something to do with the proximity of those three addresses. And there's still a lot more that doesn't fit neatly into that little hypothesis than does. Plus, you would also have to accept that Rebecca Siddal's suicide wasn't what it seemed to everyone else, and that, despite all the evidence to the contrary, it somehow has a bearing on everything that's happening now. It's a lot to start pushing and squeezing into shape.' He shook his head. 'Start trying to do that, and you're going to seriously sidetrack yourself.'

'And the two memorials on the same page?' I said, knowing how unconvincing and desperate I sounded.

'I don't know,' he said. 'If you think it matters, go and check it out. Lister's predecessor will probably have been there a year before you. It's a coincidence. They happen. Rebecca Siddal died

on the anniversary of John Boylan's death three years earlier. Are
you suggesting there's something everybody else has so far missed
which connects the death of the father with that of his daughter
four years later? The harder you look at it, the less sense it makes.'

'As far as anyone was concerned fourteen months ago, Rebecca
Siddal's suicide was just that,' I said. 'It wasn't connected to *any* of
this until Mitchell and Ruth McKenzie brought it to my attention
two days ago.'

'Surely, someone will have sat down and gone through all the
memorials and old newspaper reports?' Yvonne said.

And if they hadn't?

Sunny slapped his palm on the desk. 'If Mitchell brought
Rebecca Siddal's death to your attention, then he's either convinced she's another victim of the same killer – that she was
actually killed – or he told you for another reason.'

'You only distrust him because he comes from the same place
Finch came from,' I said, immediately regretting the remark.

'Oh, is that right? Well excuse me for not rolling over with my
tongue hanging out in gratitude. Plus, of course, neither Mitchell nor
McKenzie will be telling *you* anything that they feel able to keep from
Lister. Besides, all those memorials – they were only ever in the *Mail*.
Another three submissions for Rebecca Siddal, and Boylan would
probably have had to wait until the following day to get his placed.
Either that or it might have ended up on another page entirely.'

Yvonne put her arm round my shoulders. 'He's trying to think
faster than he can talk,' she said to Sunny. She felt my brow.

'Always a mistake in his case,' Sunny said.

But I knew by the way they exchanged glances, and by the pro-
tracted silence which followed, that they were both beginning to
consider all we had just uncovered.

'If Rebecca Siddal *was* killed by the same man, then it would
require a radical rethink on the part of Lister,' Sunny said eventually. 'It would mean he'd got the sequence of killings wrong, and
all *that* implied for his investigation.'

'Are you suggesting that the killing of Rebecca Siddal might
have acted as some kind of trigger?' Yvonne said.

'Not necessarily. Just that finding out what might possibly connect the death of Rebecca Siddal with that of, say, Kelly Smith, might be a more profitable line of enquiry now than trying to establish what connects either Kelly Smith or Alison Wilson with Lucy Collins via Paul Hendry. It might also be worth Lister's while to try and understand why Rebecca Siddal's death was made to look like a suicide.'

'That, and why nothing happened for another year?' I said.

'And what then led to killings two, three and four in such rapid succession?'

'And why Lister still can't make Lucy Collins's death – assuming he still believes Paul Hendry to have killed her – fit the pattern?'

'It's a lot of "ifs", "might be's" and "buts" based on nothing very substantial,' Yvonne said, ending this breathless, leapfrogging speculation.

'We know that,' Sunny said. 'But the more all these things drift in and out of focus, the more I'm prepared to accept that Ruth McKenzie might have a point in insisting that there's something very specific tying everything together – something no-one's come even close to finding yet.'

'Meaning the killings are taking place for a reason, and that only the killer knows what that is,' I said.

Yvonne patted me on the head. 'Well done,' she said.

'Perhaps the three of you should sit down together again,' Sunny said. 'Let Lister and his teams get on with the legwork and number-crunching while you, Mitchell and McKenzie come at all these connections and coincidences from another angle. Whoever's doing this has so far remained invisible. He isn't going to show up in any of the doorstepping or the paperwork. And he certainly isn't going to be caught sitting in a car with a faulty brake light on the A63. He's somewhere else. He might be here, in Hull, but not even the tiniest part of him has shown up in any of this yet.'

'Except perhaps here, today?' I said.

'Perhaps.'

Yvonne opened a window briefly and let both the cold air and the noise of the traffic into the room.

'I'm going to see Susan later,' she said to me. 'Remember her?'

'This is as much to do with her and her son as any of the murdered girls,' I said.

'Are you sure it isn't just you getting carried away with everything now that you've got all this other stuff to start piecing together?' She put her coat and gloves back on.

Sunny and I sat and watched her.

'Tell her I was asking,' I said.

'I would have done that anyhow. I take it that you don't want me to mention any of this to her.'

I was about to ask her to ask Susan Hendry if she knew any member of any of the families of the murdered girls, but Sunny, guessing what I was about to say, said, 'No. Let him get a proper grip on it himself. Let's see which strings Lister's pulling, and which ones Mitchell's got his own fingers firmly attached to.'

She left us and let the door slam behind her.

'No-one at the hospital reckons much for Paul Hendry's chances even if he does recover consciousness in the near future,' he said. He nodded to the closed door. 'She's doing half your work for you.'

I think I'd understood this ever since my first meeting with Yvonne and Susan Hendry a week ago.

'So – what next?' he said.

'Find the brother of Alison Wilson's real father? See where that leads?'

'The clever money says you'll be wasting your time. Axes will be ground.'

'He might be another of those invisible men you were talking about,' I said.

'Or he might just be one of those men everybody is happy not to see.'

I left the agency and walked along Spring Bank into the city centre. There had been a shower of hail earlier, and the stones lay unmelted on the pavement, rolling and crunching beneath my feet. Fumes from the traffic formed a cloud in the cold air and I could taste it as I walked.

18

I reached the station and briefly considered turning along Anlaby Road towards the hospital. Yvonne was right – I at least owed Susan Hendry a summing-up of all that had happened in the past few days, little enough though this was. But perhaps the hospital wasn't the best place for this, and now certainly wasn't the time. Too much had come to light in the past seventy-two hours – too many vague and unchecked connections, too many coincidences – and I needed time now to work out what bearing these might have on the case against her son.

I walked to Victoria Square, turned alongside Prince's Quay and crossed the dual carriageway. The police still set up regular traffic checks along the road, but so far to no avail other than to build up a database of the thousands of cars, vans and lorries which used it regularly. Mitchell was right: they were becoming swamped with paper and mired in data, every tiny piece of which still kept its secrets. The checks were merely a kind of useless and sapping momentum, and a way of keeping Lister's campaign in the public eye and the pages of the local press.

I walked along the marina. The wind created waves and the

moored yachts rocked and rattled in the darkness there.

I turned into Humber Street to find it deserted. There were lights on in some of the upper rooms, and the sports-club windows were illuminated, but the warehouses and stores at ground level were all as dark as the water. The few streetlights were old and yellow, and the dull glow from these barely penetrated the surrounding night.

As I approached my door, I caught a movement in the entrance opposite. I gave no indication of having seen whoever was there, and moved further into an unlit part of the street. I stopped, pretending to search for my key, my head down, but with my eyes on the entrance. I saw further movement – someone's foot appeared and then withdrew. I heard a faint stamping sound.

I continued walking, ready to turn and confront whoever might come out to me. My first thought was that it was someone sent by either Lister or Brownlow to keep a watch on me, but despite what Mitchell had suggested, I still doubted that either man would have considered the effort necessary, or likely to repay them.

I reached my door, careful not to turn my back completely on whoever was there.

Someone called my name. A girl's voice. I turned to look, and Emily Carr emerged from the doorway to stand in the light.

She crossed the road to me and waited at the kerb.

'I was just about to give up,' she said. She wore the same hooded coat, with faded jeans and open shoes unsuitable for the cold. She rubbed her arms. 'It's freezing. I thought there might be somewhere, you know, I could wait and keep an eye out for you.'

'Has something happened?' I asked her.

'Happened?'

Following our brief trip to the shops three nights ago, we had shared a microwaved meal and a six-pack of drink. At one point in the short evening, she'd said it was the most relaxed and the safest she'd felt since the discovery of Lucy Collins's body. She'd told me everything I'd asked of her and I'd been unable to refuse her invitation to eat with her.

I unlocked the door and held it open for her. She went inside and I followed her up the narrow stairs.

There was no bulb in the overhead light in my office and I switched on my two desk lamps. The glow from these did nothing to counter the room's cold.

She sat at my desk and looked around her.

'It looks better in the daylight,' I said.

'You sure?' she said.

I offered her a drink from the bottle I kept there, but she declined.

'I can't drink that stuff,' she said. 'I thought we could go somewhere.'

She was lonely and she was lost, and nobody else who had been to see her in the past twelve days had shown her the slightest genuine sympathy or consideration. And whatever security she might have felt upon the arrival of the police to guard the doors at Nelson Court, she had lost completely with their return there to take her in to Queen's Gardens nine days later.

'I went to the hospital earlier,' she said.

'To see Paul Hendry?'

'No – for a check-up. Make sure none of this had had any effect on the baby.'

'Did they say it might do?' I felt suddenly tired, wishing I was alone to gather my thoughts before everything once again raced ahead of me, and then so far into the official investigation of the deaths as to be completely beyond my grasp.

'It's a shock, right? You're not supposed to have things like this happen to you when you're pregnant. The last thing I need now—' She stopped abruptly and looked at me. 'I didn't mean to come here and moan at you.'

'*Has* something happened?' I asked her again.

'I don't know. It might be something or nothing.'

'Tell me.' I suspected that whatever she was about to relate might have been contrived to allow her to see me again, to make her feel as though she were needed, a small and vital part of what-ever was now happening. 'But, listen – you don't need for something to have happened to come and see me. Seriously. You can get in touch any time you like.'

'You mean that?'

I crossed my heart and she laughed at the gesture. 'I mean it. And I'm certain Paul Hendry's mother would appreciate seeing you, too.'

The suggestion disappointed her, and she was unable to hide this. 'What you're really saying,' she said, 'is that if I've not got something important to tell you, then not to bother you.'

'No – what I'm saying is that all of this is probably a lot more complicated than anybody at present fully understands. You – anybody – might already know something that turns out to be vitally important.' I tried not to sound too enthusiastic about this. 'You've done a great deal already, and I'm grateful.'

'You're also still very patronizing,' she said. 'And probably unmindful of other people's feelings.'

'Somebody else just accused me of that,' I said.

'Where did that come from – "unmindful"?' she said. 'I've never used the word in my life. That's my mother talking.'

I could hear my own mother, twenty or thirty years older than her own, using the same word.

I suggested leaving the cold room and going for a drink, and she quickly accepted.

We walked to the Minerva at the old ferry pier and had one of the small enclaves there to ourselves. We sat beside a fruit machine with its silent, flowing lights.

She took down her hood for the first time and I saw that she had again fastened her hair back from her face. She wore make-up on her eyes and lips and I was careful not to comment on this.

She told me what had happened at the hospital, but she remained detached from it all, as though she were recounting a visit with a friend.

It was warm in the bar and she took off her coat. She wore a pale green cardigan buttoned to her neck.

'It's only natural that you might feel unsettled in Nelson Court,' I said to her when our small talk – our meal together, the hospital, her unborn child – faltered, and guessing this was the real reason for her visit.

'Everything about the place has changed,' she said. 'People have started laying flowers at the door. It gives me the creeps.'

'Things will soon get back to normal,' I said.

'No they won't. Everything's wrong. Everything's turned bad, sour. Everything's stopped being what it once was.'

It was how Susan Hendry probably felt; how Karen Smith felt; how Rebecca Siddal's parents felt; how Alison Wilson's parents were starting to feel.

'Whoever killed Lucy – Paul Hendry, whoever – won't be coming back there,' I said. 'And eventually he'll be caught and locked away for ever.' I probably sounded melodramatic and unconvincing in equal measure.

'I know all that,' she said. 'It's just the thought that there's somebody like that out there, and that he came so close to me. I've been having bad dreams about it. What if he'd come up a flight of stairs instead of going into Lucy's? What if I'd been coming in or going out just as he arrived?'

I wanted to be able to tell her that I believed the killer had targeted Lucy Collins specifically, but I knew that this, too, would sound unconvincing to her.

'You can't think like that,' I said.

'Why not? *You* might have a choice; I don't.'

'*Has* something happened?' I asked her again.

'I don't know. Perhaps I'm just getting everything out of proportion. Paranoid. Even more paranoid. Earlier today, there was a man walking up and down outside the entrance on the other side of the road. Then I think the same man drove past in a car, one end of the street to the other, first one way, then the other.'

'Did you see him clearly?'

She shook her head. 'I already told you – I don't look out over the front. I only saw him when he reached that bit of the road I can see over from the side of the building.'

'And you're sure it was the same man in the car?'

'I think so.' She described the car, saying only that it was metallic-silver-coloured. She didn't know about makes and she hadn't seen any of its registration.

'Perhaps it was the police coming back,' I suggested. 'Just because they've gone from the door doesn't mean they won't keep an eye on the place from time to time.'

'Because they think that whoever it was might come back?'

'I've told you – that isn't going to happen. No – because it's what they do. Plus, they're trying to appear particularly busy at the moment.'

'Like I'd know nothing about all that,' she said.

'Call me if the same man returns,' I said. 'You've got my numbers.'

The small room filled up around us. It was the bar where people had once waited for the ferry crossing the Humber, many of the travellers coming deliberately early for a drink while they waited and watched the boats going back and forth in broad curves against the running tides.

I offered her another drink, but she declined.

'It's getting late,' she said, indicating the night and the emptiness of the quay and the river outside. It was almost eight.

Women were now being warned daily to take precautions if they were in the city centre at night. Some complained at the restrictions they believed were being placed on them, at the atmosphere of fear and suspicion Lister's campaign had created.

'You think I'm stupid for coming to see you, don't you?' she said, her head bowed as she spoke.

'No, I don't,' I told her. 'Look at me.' She looked up and I said it again.

'One of the coppers who was on the door said I ought to think about getting myself some better locks. Said they'd send someone round to *advise* me. I asked him who was going to pay for it all, and he asked me how much I thought I was worth. He meant with the kid and everything.'

'I know a locksmith,' I told her. 'Let me call him in the morning and arrange for him to come round.' I didn't 'know' the man any more than I knew the plumber or the electrician I had employed to work in my home, but the word and the offer reassured her.

'What about the cost?' she said.

'He owes me a few favours,' I said.

And whether she believed me or not, she was in no position to refuse my offer.

I told her I'd walk her home.

'There's no need,' she said. 'It's probably all in my head.'

'It probably is,' I said. 'But I'm going that way and I'd like to.'

She acquiesced and we walked together through the city centre to Nelson Court.

At the door, I said, 'Give me a codeword?'

'A what?'

'Something I can give to the locksmith so you'll know who he is and be able to let him in.'

The suggestion appealed to her and she considered it. 'Dolphin,' she said eventually.

'Dolphin?'

'It's the first thing I thought when I saw my scan. It looked like a dolphin, like a fish, you know?'

I told her I did, and stood and watched as she secured the door behind her and then climbed the stairs to let herself into her own flat.

Few lights showed along the front of the building. At the sound of the door, someone came to a window on the first floor and looked down at me. Perhaps they saw what Emily Carr had seen in the passing stranger. It was impossible now not to look at the decrepit block – its graffiti luminescent in the darkness – and not to sense something of what had happened there twelve days ago, not to feel the blight with which Lucy Collins's brutal killing had contaminated the place for ever.

19

The following day was Saturday, and I went to Woodcock Street mid-morning in the hope of finding Jimmy Boylan at home. Even if his solitary memorial to his brother appearing on the page full of notices commemorating the death of Rebecca Siddal truly had been a coincidence, then it was still one I could not afford to ignore.

There came a point in most investigations where a balance was tipped – a balance between getting mired and lost in the endless past, and pushing forward into the unknowable future. One too many echoes, one too many whispers, one too many averted glances, one too many coincidences. I'd felt the sudden point of that balance at the sight of Jimmy Boylan's pathetic-looking reminder amid all those notices and tragic farewells to the girl who, with everything to live for, had apparently chosen to live for none of it.

I knew from the directory at the agency at what number Jimmy Boylan lived, and I searched the house for signs of life as I approached it.

Woodcock Street was lined with terraced houses with front doors opening directly on to the pavement. Boylan's home looked run-down, neglected. The paint was peeling from its single ground-floor window frame, and the plastic of its door had turned grey. The number was crudely painted beside the door.

I crossed the road and passed by the house on the far side. Both sets of curtains were drawn and there were no lights. It was another overcast day, and even at that time lights showed in the downstairs rooms of the few nearby houses still occupied.

I walked for a further twenty yards, noting where a narrow alley led to a rear way to the house. This would emerge from behind the terrace in the opposite direction.

As I recrossed the road, a woman came out of a house several doors away and asked me if I was looking for someone. She carried a bag and carefully fastened a headscarf over her hair as she came.

'James Boylan,' I said.

She pulled the door shut behind her. 'At this time of day?' she said. 'You'll be lucky. Jimmy Boylan?'

'Will he be at work?'

She laughed. 'Oh, no doubt. Hard at work at something or other.' She pointed to the plastic door. 'Next time, you'd be better off getting here before either the bars or the off-licences open.' She made a drinking motion with her free hand.

'I see,' I said.

'I'm sure you do. You a *friend* of his, are you?' She invested the word with a cold emphasis and I understood exactly what she was telling me.

'Not really. I just wanted to ask him a few questions.' It was the one answer I usually avoided, but I sensed it might be a useful one now in light of her own obvious hostility towards the man.

'You police?'

'Does he live alone?'

'Of course he lives alone. He was born in that house, they both were. He's been there by himself now for the best part of five years. He has all his cronies round now and then, and you'd sometimes see a woman letting herself out.' She said 'woman' the same way she'd said 'friend'. 'You don't know much about him, do you?'

'I'm grateful for all you've told me,' I said.

She looked at her watch, told me she had a bus to catch, and left me.

I went to the door and knocked. There was no response. I tried again. This time, I heard a sound inside. It sounded like something falling or being dropped. I opened the letter box and called in.

A man's voice told me to stop fucking shouting.

I waited.

Several minutes passed before the door was finally opened a few inches. An unshaven man shielding his eyes looked out at me. He was in his fifties. His sparse, dishevelled brown and grey hair was long at the sides and back, and the stubble on his cheeks and chin was three or four days old. There were dark rings beneath his eyes, and his skin was pale.

He squinted out at me. 'Who the fuck are you, and what the fuck time is it?' He opened the door wider to look along the street behind me.

'It's just me,' I said.

'And I asked you who the fuck you were, smartarse.'

I told him my name. 'I'm enquiring into the death of Alison Boylan,' I said, deliberately using Alison Wilson's original name. 'Your brother's daughter.'

'Oh, is that who she was?' He laughed and I flinched at the smell of his breath. His teeth were small and stained. 'But you're not the law, I can tell that much. The law would have been here in the middle of the fucking night. They were the ones who were always careful after the first cock-up to call her Wilson. Come to fucking dob me in, have you? He was my brother, she died, and so I killed her, is that it? Well, you're too late. Bigger men than you have already been and tried and gone away empty-handed.'

'Have they been to see you recently?' I said, meaning since the death of Lucy Collins.

'Have they fuck.' He rubbed his bare arms against the cold air.

'No, I'm not the law. But I'd be grateful if you'd talk to me,' I said.

'How grateful?' he said, finally opening the door wide enough for me to see into the dimly lit room behind him.

'Grateful,' I said.

He turned away from me and I followed him inside.

The drawn curtains let little light into the room. A gas fire burned. The furnishings were old and bulky, and the detritus of an uncaring man living alone filled every surface. Empty cans, mostly, and bottles, with newspapers, cups and other crockery. There was a smell of something scorching.

He went to the fire and pushed a chair away from it.

'Sit down,' he said. 'Make yourself comfortable.' He laughed at the suggestion that anyone but himself could ever possibly be comfortable in the room.

He sat in the scorched chair and brushed at its blackened arm. There were marks and stains on every other piece of furniture. It was still the house his parents had furnished.

'I'd put a lamp on, but the bulb went,' he said. 'I had a bit of a night.' He began to cough, and this took a minute to subside. He looked around him as though he was about to spit. When he finally regained his breath, he asked me what I was looking at.

I continued looking more closely at the room around me. 'This,' I said.

'It suits me. Next you'll be telling me that that bitch didn't put you on to me.'

'Alison's mother?'

'Who else?'

'Her daughter was killed. I imagine she—'

'She was my *brother's daughter* as well,' he shouted. 'You think I don't know she was killed, and how? You think I don't know? She was the only one who kept his fucking name until a couple of years ago. Alison was our mother's name. That bitch of a wife of his tried to get the girl to drop Boylan the minute she shacked up with Prince fucking Charming Wilson.'

'Her marriage to your brother was over a long time before she married Wilson,' I said.

'Was it? Was it? How the fuck do you know what it was or wasn't?

In fact, how the fuck do you know anything? You never knew him. Or her. So don't sit there pretending you fucking know better than me.'

'No,' I said. 'I never knew him.'

'If you want to blame anybody for killing anybody, then you can start by pointing your finger at her.'

'At Alison's mother? Why?'

'Because she might just as well have put a gun to Jock's head when she took up with Wilson, that's why. He was a proud man. *Her* telling *him* he was second-best. How was he expected to cope with that?'

'Millions do,' I said.

'Then fuck them millions. More than twenty fucking years they were married.' As though this explained, excused and forgave everything.

'Where did he go when she threw him out?'

'Where do you think?'

'He came back here? To live with you?'

'Where else was he going to go? This was his real home. She told the law he was violent towards her and the kid, got an order out against him. If it had been me, I probably *would* have killed her – not the girl, *her*. Eighteen months later, he was dead. Cancer. He didn't even make the first attempt to fight it. Just let it eat him up because he had nothing left to live for.'

'Something else you blame her for?'

He looked at me. 'Think what you like.' He picked up and shook several of the cans beside his chair.

I pointed out a half-full bottle of whisky standing by the television and he picked this up and drank from it. 'And you can think what you fucking well like about this as well,' he said. 'So, I killed the girl, did I? I killed Alison?'

'No-one's accusing you of anything,' I said. 'You put a memorial in the *Hull Mail* on each anniversary of your brother's death.'

'So? No other fucker gives a toss about him.'

'Is there no other family?'

'Not now. Just me and him. Cousins back up in Peterhead, stuff like that, but nobody in regular contact. We don't see each other and we don't mean anything to each other. A far fucking cry from when we lived here with our parents.'

'What was different then?'

He turned to face me. 'Are you taking the piss? Our dad, Jimmy Boylan? Biggest fucking man on this street. A skipper. It was what me and Jock were all set for.'

It was the same story Susan Hendry had told me of her husband. Another of history's fading echoes in that small place.

'Fishing?' I said.

'Are you fucking stupid, or something? Of course fishing. I'd already started work on the Iceland boats. Jock was four years younger, only just starting his apprenticeship. We were going to work together.'

'Follow in your father's footsteps.'

'Try to. It didn't seem too much to fucking ask for or to expect at the time.'

'Until the industry collapsed.'

'Is that what it did? It was pulled from under us by the fucking government. Collapsed? You want to fucking listen to yourself, mate. And not just the fishing – everything went.'

I asked him what he meant, still struggling to understand what might connect the death of his brother, his earlier acrimonious divorce, and the deaths of both Rebecca Siddal and Alison Wilson. The rest was the same old blocking in of the same old story.

He drank some more from the bottle, and the smell of the whisky was added to the room's other odours.

He rose unsteadily, went to the window and half opened one of the curtains. 'It's why I keep them closed,' he said.

'What happened?' I prompted him.

'Our father was injured at sea. Laid off for six months. He was never properly fit afterwards and the trawler owners started passing him over. But there was still my money, and what bit Jock had started bringing in. My mother said she'd go out to work, but we weren't having any of that. Not at her age. So we did what thousands of others round here did, we survived. And then *I* got laid off. I was twenty-one. Laid-off at twenty-one and told it was all over. I found the odd bit of work here and there, but it never paid all that good.'

Again, it was the same story Susan Hendry had told me.

'Then Jock got into a bit of bother with the police. Nothing much, nothing ever came of it, but—' He stopped abruptly, as though suddenly conscious of telling me too much, of lowering his guard; perhaps he even believed he was in some way betraying the memory of his dead brother by recounting this history of failure and powerless, unresisting resignation. 'It was all a long, long time ago. He was just a kid. It probably hit him harder than it hit the rest of us, being laid off like that.'

'What was the trouble?'

'That? Nothing. Him and some of the other apprentices. A fight at closing time. They were all drunk, that's all. The kind of thing that happened every night of the week when the boats were in and the men were home with money in their pockets.'

'Was your brother ever charged, convicted?'

He laughed at the suggestion. 'Nah, it never came to anything like that. The law round here knew what was what, how best to sort things out. But the point is, he was taken in and then kept on remand for six weeks in a Young Offenders' Institution the other side of the river, near Brigg. Knocked the place down years since.'

'Can you remember who else might have been involved?' I asked him.

'Thirty years ago? Are you joking? Besides, it wasn't what mattered. There was never any case against him – no charges brought, no witnesses, no evidence, just a few daft lads with too much drink inside of them who got a bit out of hand. Our Jock was the only one who even got himself fucking arrested. Too pissed to run, by all accounts. The law came and found him throwing up in the street.'

'Was anyone seriously hurt?'

'You're not listening to what I'm fucking telling you,' he said, his exasperation rising. 'You're not fucking listening. Forget what happened – it's not the point. The point *is* that it was while Jock was locked up – while the police took their own sweet time pursuing their so-called fucking inquiries – that our mother died.' He drank again from the bottle and closed his eyes. 'After everything else that had just happened to us. One day she complained of pains and not being able to breathe properly, and the next she just collapsed and died. Wouldn't even let us send for a doctor. She was younger than I am now. Me and Jock were born in this house, and both him and her died in it. They stuck our father in Hull Royal and he died there three years after her. He never worked once in all that time. Christ, talk about the mighty falling. I feel as though I've been falling ever since.'

'Did your brother miss your mother's funeral?'

He nodded. 'The bastards wouldn't even let him out for that. His own mother's funeral. We practically begged them and they just sat there and laughed at us. They knew even then that they'd got nothing to hold him on. Said it served him right, that it might teach him – teach us *all* – a lesson. They treated us like fucking gyppos. The trawler owners sent a wreath. Fucking hypocrites. A fucking wreath with her initials on it. My father took it out of the hearse and threw it down in the street.'

'Didn't any of the others involved with Jock come forward and try to help him?'

'Did they fuck. We never saw them for fucking dust. I can't imagine a single one of them was working the boats a year later.'

'And Jock?'

'They let him out two weeks after we buried her. There was no job for him, of course. He might not have been charged, but the boat-owners didn't want anything to do with him, with either of us, after that. They were laying men off and decommissioning boats left, right and centre for months. This half of the city looked like one giant fucking scrapyard for years.'

'I know,' I told him.

'No, you don't,' he said.

'What happened after that?'

'We lived here, the three of us, me, Jock and our father, until the old man died. And then Jock met that bitch and everything took a turn for the better as far as he was concerned.'

'But not for you?'

'Do I look like a man who's led a rich and rewarding life?'

'You resented Jock leaving you behind?'

'Is that what I did? What I *resented* was the way *she* made him change. She came here once or twice, but then she stayed well away. It changed him, that time being locked up, changed him in ways none of us ever really understood at the time. He used to be full of himself, ready for anything.'

'And afterwards?'

'He just let people walk all over him.'

'People like his wife?'

'I probably overreacted – being the last one left in the house and all that – but I hated that fucking woman.'

'Did you put the memorial in the paper to get back at her?'

'To remind her, perhaps. She probably never even saw a single one of them. No – I do it for him. I put one in for our mother and father as well. You can check. I do it because we stopped being a proper family with a home and a future after everything that happened back then. I do it because we've just been bits and pieces of people clinging to the past since then.'

I noticed how much more eloquent and articulate he had become when talking of his family, how his profanities had almost ceased.

'Even before you got here, did you honestly think I'd had anything to do with Alison's death?' he said.

'Not really,' I said. If he'd been remotely implicated, Brownlow would have continued investigating him.

'You'd be closer to the mark accusing me of killing them because they'd all got the world at their feet, just as me and Jock once thought we'd got it at ours,' he said. He put the bottle down and sat back in his chair.

I saw for the first time that there were framed photographs of a young Alison Boylan and her parents on a sideboard. I remembered the pictures and cards and anonymous messages of condolence with which Karen Smith had surrounded herself.

The dead were with us everywhere, and whoever it was who said they clung to us, got it right.

I took money from my wallet to give to him.

'Fucking put it away,' he said. The expletive now sounded almost affectionate.

'I can recoup it,' I said.

'I bet you can. Besides, I'd probably only spend it on some air-freshener or pot-fucking-pourri.'

'I appreciate all you've told me,' I said.

'Funnily enough, *I* appreciate having been *able* to tell you. I haven't talked about any of it like this for a long time, at least not sober.'

'The police will probably come to see you again when they find out I've been, or when they learn about the stuff you put in the papers.'

'Let 'em,' he said. I'd been careful not to mention it, and he in turn hadn't made any reference to the single memorial to his brother amid the dozens for Rebecca Siddal.

'Have you ever heard of a girl called Rebecca Siddal?' I said.

He repeated the name. 'Never. Who is she?'

'A friend of Alison's,' I said, unwilling to reveal what had led me to him.

'Right. You asked me why I put the notices in. To be honest with you, I sometimes ask myself the same question. I put Jock's in because there's no-one left from those days who gives a toss about him. All his new friends were her friends, *their* friends before she threw him out. Let's face it, nobody's going to weep and wail at *my* funeral. When that happens, everything really *will* be over. Perhaps you and me should drink a toast to it now.' He retrieved the bottle. 'To the end,' he said.

He gave me the bottle.

'The end,' I said, and gave it back to him. 'My father worked for Marr's,' I told him. 'They laid him off in '76. He was thirty-nine.'

He considered this and nodded once. 'Then fuck the lot of the greedy, uncaring bastards,' he said.

I left him and walked to the West Dock Road, to where John Maxwell and I had started out together. Our building, and those surrounding it, had long since been demolished, razed, and the rubble carted away. Now everything was flat and empty and surrounded by a high wire fence. A giant hoarding announced that a new fitness centre was shortly to be built on the site, and three giant women in sportswear and trainers flexed their muscles above me, the rain-soaked paper already peeling from their grinning faces and their tanned and perfect bodies.

20

I went from West Dock Road back to Humber Street, and from there I drove to Cottingham, hoping I might be able to talk to Rebecca Siddal's parents. I wasn't certain what I expected to learn from them, but it was a visit I could no longer avoid making now that their daughter's death had finally been included in Lister's investigation.

I knew from what Mitchell had told me in the Royal that they had never accepted the coroner's verdict that, in all probability, their daughter had taken her own life, but what I didn't know was how Rebecca Siddal's family or history might be connected to the families and emerging histories of the other victims.

I also knew from Mitchell that her parents had kept their silence and their distance from the events surrounding their daughter's death fourteen months ago, and I considered it unlikely that I would have more than this one opportunity to learn anything from them.

En route to Cottingham I went out of my way to drive through the expanse of the Orchard Park estate, where Rebecca's body had been found. I knew the address of the empty house where she'd been discovered hanging, but I was soon lost amid the maze of curving and encircling roads, and among the new mounds of rubble where the thirty-year-old tower blocks and houses were themselves being demolished to make way for yet another impossible vision of the future.

I left the estate and was soon in Cottingham, sitting opposite the Siddals' home on Knowsley Avenue, close to the open land upon which Baynard Castle had once stood.

I watched the windows for several minutes, seeing both a man and a woman cross them. Two cars stood nose to tail in the driveway.

I left my car and went to the front door. Earlier, I'd expected Jimmy Boylan to slam his door in my face. I expected it again standing at the Siddals'.

I knocked and a tall, bald man in his early fifties wearing blue overalls and wiping his dirty hands on an even dirtier towel answered. He was talking to someone behind him as he turned to me.

He looked down at me from the raised doorway, and within the space of a second his questioning expression turned to one of suspicion.

I introduced myself and told him immediately that I was working for Susan Hendry.

He appeared to recognize the name.

'And you're here why? The same as the police – to make a few more reassuring noises, to tie up a few more uncomfortable loose ends after all those empty, wasted months? I have nothing to say to you.'

'All I need to know', I said quickly, 'is why you are so convinced your daughter didn't take her own life.' I wanted considerably more than that from him, but equally importantly I needed him to keep the door open and to continue talking to me.

'And fourteen months ago, when it mattered, I would have given you chapter and verse, Mr Rivers, chapter and verse.'

'But not now?'

'No, not now. What are any of you going to find now that you wouldn't have found ten times more easily if you'd started looking then? How do you think—' He was interrupted by a woman's voice calling to him from inside and he half closed the door on me to talk to her. I presumed it was his wife. He spoke in a low, reassuring voice. He lied and told her I was a policeman, there in connection with the current inquiry. His tone apart, everything he said to her seemed formal, cold, keeping her at a distance.

Hearing what he had to say, the woman left the hallway behind him and went away into the house. Rebecca had been their only child, and I could imagine the life the two of them had lived there since her death.

He finally turned back to me, opening the door no further than he needed to talk to me.

'My wife,' he said. He continued wiping his hands on the dirty towel. He saw me looking at this. 'Lawnmower,' he said simply. He paused in thought for a moment. 'All I – all *we* – ever wanted was for them to look more closely at what had happened.'

'But however hard they looked, they could find nothing to support any theory other than the one that Rebecca had hanged herself?'

'Which was ridiculous to everyone who ever knew her.'

'But not to the police?'

'All they ever knew about was Rebecca's hanging body. She'd been missing, they'd searched for her, and then . . . My daughter could never have done that to herself in a million years. And before you say it – yes, I daresay there isn't a parent in the country who wouldn't insist on the same. What mystifies me now is why the police appear to have changed their minds about everything. It did occur to me that they might want to charge the killer of these recent girls with Rebecca's murder just to add one more to their tally and make themselves look good.'

'They won't do that if they can't prove he killed her,' I said.

'So you say. But they're still not telling *us* anything new. They even behave as though we ought to be *grateful* to them now that they've deigned to believe what we've been insisting on from the very beginning. I'm sorry for those other families – I doubt anyone knows better than we do what they're going through right now – but I'll tell you what I told the detectives – I can point you to nothing that might indicate who killed my daughter or why she was killed. And just as I refused to express my gratitude to the police when *they* finally came back to us, I am likewise not going to indulge you now.' He thought about something for a moment, looking over his shoulder before going on.

'Hendry was the boy,' he said. 'Not one of the victims.'

'He was Lucy Collins's boyfriend,' I said. 'The police are convinced he killed her, but not the others.'

'I imagine they have good reason,' he said.

Just as they had good reason to ignore your own pleas to consider your daughter's death to have been something other than suicide?

The question hung unspoken between us.

'Did Rebecca ever mention knowing anyone called Paul Hendry?'

'I told you, Mr Rivers – I'm having no part of this. But, no, she never mentioned a Paul Hendry or any of the other victims. She was only just eighteen, still a schoolgirl. She wasn't like any of those others.'

'By which I assume that you also object to the fact that the police are now viewing your daughter's death as part of an investigation in which the murders of two prostitutes are also being examined? Even if that's the least of what they were?'

He looked at me in disbelief.

'Perhaps it *would* make more sense to investigate Rebecca's death separately,' I added quickly. 'But that's not something they're going to consider.'

He seemed to sag where he stood in the doorway and he put his hand against the frame.

'I'm sorry,' I told him. 'I only meant to suggest that I can understand how it might seem to you – having your daughter's death considered alongside the more recent ones – not that she might have been—'

'What?' he said. 'A prostitute herself? I know *exactly* what you intended to suggest, Mr Rivers. I've kept myself up to date on what's been happening recently. Even *I* can see that this inquiry and this campaign against prostitution have both become part of the same thing in the public mind. I'm not stupid, and nor are you – we both see clearly enough how the police are using that particular ambiguity to their own ends. So, to avoid any further ambiguity or uncertainty – uncertainty between you and me – I will tell you two things in which you can have absolute, unshakeable and certain belief – firstly, that my daughter did not take her own life; and, secondly, that she was not a prostitute. Rebecca never even had a proper boyfriend. I know some people might find that difficult to believe in this day and age, but it's true. And that's all I want to say to you.'

He started to close the door. He was firm in his conviction, and I believed him.

'Orchard Park,' I said quickly, only the last few inches of the door open between us.

'What about it?' The door stopped closing and he opened it again.

'Even when everyone else accepted that Rebecca had taken her own life, I never understood why she had chosen a derelict house on the Orchard Park estate to do it.'

'Simple,' he said. 'She didn't. She never went near the place. There was nothing there for her and she never knew anyone who lived there.' He waited to see what else I had to say.

'Which reinforced your conviction that she'd been murdered and taken there,' I said.

'Taken there, lured there, whatever. What does it matter? Twenty years ago they used to talk about expanding the place right up to the outskirts of Cottingham. And then even further, until we were surrounded.'

'Something to which you were opposed?'

'Of course we were opposed to it. You only have to go and look at the place.'

'I did,' I said. 'On my way here. 'I was looking for—'

'I can guess,' he said. 'Gone. Demolished. Three months ago.'

'You've been back there?'

He lowered his voice. 'The two of us used to drive there and sit in the car. We went last on the anniversary of Rebecca's death. Most of the houses around it had already been knocked down. We knew it wouldn't be long before everything was gone. We never did anything as mawkish as leaving flowers or teddy bears, anything like that, but I can't deny that we both gained some small measure of consolation, reassurance, whatever, from just being there.' He hesitated. 'To tell you the truth, it made things for me, at least, just that little bit more bearable – knowing that the place was somewhere that Rebecca had never frequented.'

I told him I thought I understood him.

'I'm sure you do,' he said, meaning the opposite. 'At least *we* were able to bury our daughter with proper ceremony and some dignity. We visit her grave most weekends, and evenings in the summer. We have that, at least.' He nodded slightly towards the end of the street to suggest the location of his daughter's grave. 'My wife and I are regular churchgoers. It helps. Not much, yet, but it's something. Never believe people, Mr Rivers, who tell you that the passage of time blunts the edge of true grief. It doesn't. It might blunt or make more bearable a lot of other things, but that's all. All that happens with time is that other things grow back into the empty spaces, and the grief itself is forced to change shape.'

He wiped the dirty towel across his face, across his eyes, leaving smears on his forehead and cheeks, oblivious to what he'd done.

'I ought to be going,' he said eventually, almost apologetically, and he finally closed the door on me.

21

Later, at home, I was still trying to understand what I had learned from those two men – Jimmy Boylan and Siddal – each abandoned in the squandered promise and sudden emptiness of his life, when Sunny called to tell me there had been another killing. He was breathless and abrupt, and I heard traffic and voices all around him, the noise of sirens and someone speaking through a megaphone.

'It's a circus,' he shouted above the din.

I asked him where he was.

'Queen's Gardens. Twenty yards from the entrance to the biggest police station in Hull, Lister's so-called nerve centre.' I heard the uncontainable excitement in his voice.

'Who else is there?'

Yvonne took the phone from him, told me to stop asking stupid questions, and hung up.

I arrived twenty minutes later. Leaving Freetown Way, George Street was closed, and traffic was being diverted either away from the city centre towards Beverley Road, or into the multistorey car park there. I joined the queue to enter it and found a space on the roof. Other motorists congregated to watch and discuss what was happening below. Constables moved among the cars asking questions.

Most people were dressed for their nights out in the nearby bars and restaurants, and some complained at having been herded into the car park and at now being forced to walk to their destinations through the light rain that had been falling since late afternoon.

Leaving my car, I was stopped by a policewoman and asked for details of my visit. I told her I was meeting friends for a drink and she told me to leave the car park.

I made my way along Wilberforce Drive, where I was stopped again at a police cordon. There was a crowd there, too, and the police were having difficulty controlling and dispersing it. A line of police cars filled the road. Two ambulances were parked on Queen's Dock Avenue overlooking the garden, and ahead of them stood a fire engine, directly outside the police station.

Other cordons had been set up around the open space, and crowds had gathered on all four sides of the garden.

I called Yvonne and asked her where she was.

She and Sunny were on Hanover Street, at the rear of the Guildhall, and she told me to make my way to them.

The garden itself was sealed and kept clear of everyone except the police and other services, but it was easy enough to move along the streets surrounding it.

I saw Sunny first, standing on a low wall and holding his camera over his head, taking pictures of whatever was happening below.

Yvonne saw me and came to me. She called to Sunny, who ignored her.

'What's happened?' I asked her.

'Forty minutes ago, someone found what they thought was a bag of burning rubbish from one of the bins,' she said. 'They tried to stamp out the flames.'

'And discovered it wasn't a bag of rubbish after all?'

'It was the body of a young woman, a girl perhaps. We don't know much more.'

Sunny joined us.

I asked him how he and Yvonne had got there so quickly.

'I got a call,' he said, his voice low. 'Security man on the new BBC building. He was in the doorway having a smoke when he saw the fire and the police activity. He's reliable. He called me, told me what he'd seen and hung up. We were already in town. We were here in five minutes, before the fire engine.'

'Do they know who she is?'

He shook his head. 'Nothing yet. And certainly nothing they're letting on to the great unwashed.'

'Do they think it's a message to Lister?' I said.

'No – they think it's a murdered girl's burning body,' Yvonne said sharply.

'Leave the speculation until the morning,' Sunny said. 'We're here for the facts, that's all. It's too late for the Sundays, but most of the nationals will be interested for their Monday morning wake-up picccs.' He moved away from us, pushing through the crowd until he reached the steps leading down into the garden.

'He's trying to find out who else might already be here,' Yvonne said.

'Do the police think the killer might still be around?'

'I meant other press. The more he gets of the good stuff before they show up, the more valuable it is.' She pointed to the part of the infilled dock where the body had been found, and where a vividly white tent now stood. 'We were here before they put that up.' At least thirty detectives and uniformed constables stood around the structure. Men in white suits and face masks waited at the entrance. 'Sunny thinks he might have got a shot of the burning body,' she said. She closed her eyes as she spoke.

She went to join him and I followed her.

Sunny pointed out Lister to me, standing alone in an empty space at the far side of the garden, in full dress uniform, his hands on his hips.

'He's going to have to start answering questions soon,' Sunny said. 'I need to get to him in case he has a few words of hollow reassurance for the press.'

Fifty yards from Lister, further along the raised road, I saw Mitchell standing with several constables. I raised my hand to him.

He saw me, looked to the men on either side of him, and then shrugged to let me know that he, too, knew little of what was happening.

I made a 'phone' gesture and he tapped his pocket and then his watch to suggest he would call me soon, presumably when he was alone.

I went back to Sunny and Yvonne. Sunny was talking to another journalist, who also held a camera above his head and took a succession of shots in the direction of the tent, now blindingly illuminated by a rack of spotlights.

'They used petrol,' Sunny said. 'The man who found the fire said he could smell it, and he only saw the body after he'd started trying to stamp out the flames. Whoever it was, she'd been stuffed inside a green refuse bag.'

'A garden bag?' Yvonne said.

'The word is, the petrol and fire were just intended to get rid of the bag and anything on the body that might have revealed something. Not enough fuel to burn the body beyond recognition. She was dead before she was bagged and burned. Somebody saw a lot of blood, but only after the bag had been destroyed. The body was small, so it might have been—'

'A child?' Yvonne said.

'Just small, that's all. Completely sealed in the bag. They think it was fastened with tape.'

We watched as another group of white-suited men walked from the station to the tent. Inner cordons were now being erected across the paths and flower-beds. There were already men wading through the muddy ponds under the bright lights.

'If there's anything still to be found, they've got to find it now,' Sunny said. 'This rain isn't good.'

'How could anyone have done something like that so publicly, and so close to the station, without being seen?' I said. 'It's practically impossible.' I was more convinced than ever that the proximity of the station was the whole point of the body having been dumped where it was.

'We don't know that they weren't seen,' Sunny said. 'Not yet.

There are a lot of cameras in the park and surrounding the station and car park. They've already started emptying them to see if they've got anything. They're keeping them all operational in case anything else turns up. They think the fire was burning for less than a minute before the guy tried to stamp it out. That gives whoever put a match to it sixty seconds or thereabouts to be somewhere else. And assuming they didn't attract attention to themselves by running, that sixty seconds narrows down the field of play to a reasonably small search area.'

'Are they hopeful?'

'It's technology. They worship it. Of course they're hopeful.'

We both knew how many completely unidentifiable figures the CCTV footage would reveal, how many false leads needing elimination, all of them taking men away from the solitary profitable course they might otherwise have been following. They would see exactly what they had seen in all the footage of the city centre on the warm summer night Kelly Smith had been killed.

'Look,' Sunny said, pointing to where more lights were being erected around where Lister stood. 'He's going to say a few stirring words.'

Mitchell now stood beside Lister, along with half a dozen other detectives.

Sunny told us to stay where we were and to watch the tent, and then he left us, pushing through the thickening crowd to where Lister stood.

Below us, I heard Brownlow's voice as he directed his team of men to start questioning the onlookers. It seemed a pointless and impossible task. He saw me standing with Yvonne and came up the steps to us.

'Mr Rivers,' he said. 'And Ms—' He had forgotten Yvonne's surname.

' "Ms" will do,' she told him.

'You appear to have arrived very swiftly,' he said.

'Along with, oh, five thousand others,' Yvonne said.

'And if you two are here, I'll assume that the vulture Summers is hovering somewhere over the corpse.'

One of his men called to him.

'I have to go now – some real detective work to do – but I'll be wanting a few questions answered as soon as possible, so don't—'

'Questions like, Why did the killer leave this one right under your noses and get clean away with it?' I said.

'The investigation's only just started,' he said. 'Who says anybody's got away with anything?'

'Just going on your track record,' I said.

'This won't be as clever as whoever did it thought it was.'

'It'll still leave you lot looking hopeless, getting nowhere and floundering around,' Yvonne said.

'When I want your opinion, darling, I'll ask for it, right?' he said, his voice low, his eyes never leaving mine.

But by then, several people around us had turned to listen to the exchange, causing him to feel exposed and uncomfortable. Others started to shout questions at him, and realizing that the situation might become suddenly uncontrollable, he turned and left us.

'Charming man,' Yvonne said.

On the far side of the park a crowd had now assembled in front of Lister, kept at a distance from him by a line of constables. He was talking to them, and though Yvonne and I were too far away to hear what he was saying, it was easy enough to imagine. There were already several television cameras pointed at him; flashlights erupted continuously all around the garden. A group of women started chanting at him as he spoke, the chorus of voices growing louder with each repeated phrase.

'They'll blame him and his campaign for this one,' I said.

'Good,' Yvonne said.

Sunny returned to us a few minutes later.

He held his recorder to his ear and said, 'Everything being done, crowds making things difficult, rest assured, vigilance, anyone who saw anything blah blah blah. It's enough for a few quotes. I saw Mitchell. He looked as though he'd been told to look useful and hopeful and to keep his mouth shut.'

'Lister will want to contain as much of this as possible.'

'What, and friend Mitchell might already have alerted his real bosses at National Crime?'

'I'll try to talk to him,' I said.

'And then to me?'

'He'll assume that's what I'd do before he tells me anything.'

'I overheard one of the plods,' he said. 'It was definitely a girl – late teens, he reckoned. Dressed for a night out. It's not much, but it's an angle. Lister, naturally enough, just wants everybody to go away and to leave him to get on with it. Like that's going to happen.'

'That's exactly why it's happened like this,' I said. 'To rub his nose in it.'

One of the ambulances started to move along the road towards the garden entrance, its siren silent, but its spinning lights flickering along the sides of the nearby buildings.

'They don't think she was too badly burned,' Sunny said. 'The fire only did what it was meant to do. It was never going to disguise the body, not in this rain.'

'Hey, that's great,' Yvonne said. 'Perhaps when they find her parents, you can call them up with that bit of reassuring news.' She walked away from us. Neither of us tried to prevent her from going or called after her, and she was quickly lost in the restless crowd.

'I know, I know,' Sunny said to me. 'But it matters to stay in the middle of things like this for as long as possible. Everything's going to get muddied with second- and third-hand telling soon enough.' He motioned to Brownlow and his men. 'And they know that better than I do. That's why they're here now. And why they're going to sit up for the rest of the night and then tomorrow and tomorrow night watching the miles of CC footage.'

'But you think whoever did it is well clear of it all by now?'

'I think if he was smart enough to do what he did – here, now, this close – then I doubt he's going to overlook a little thing like his way out of it all. There might be a lot of cameras, but there are just as many blind spots. And you know as well as I do that a nondescript man walking away with his head down against the rain is just that. I also overheard that they're setting up their roadblocks again on all major routes. Apparently, Lister had a master plan just waiting to be put into action. Every car leaving the city will have been stopped or identified within fifteen minutes of the body being found.'

'And you think that that, too, might have formed some part of the killer's calculations?'

'Perhaps. He's certainly been five steps ahead of Lister on everything so far.' He stopped talking and nodded over my shoulder.

Brownlow returned to stand beside me.

'Wondered how long it would be before you showed your face,' he said to Sunny.

'I've just been listening to your illustrious leader,' Sunny said, clicking on his recorder for a few seconds. 'He doesn't sound too clever. Not enough time to prepare himself, I suppose. No press officers or speech-writers to hold his hand. In fact, I'd say you've all been caught off-guard with this one.'

'You're beginning to sound as though you *want* us to fail,' Brownlow said. 'Is that it? Is that a bigger story for you – endlessly carping at us instead of finding out what you can do to help us?'

Sunny switched off his recorder, which had still been running. 'Thanks for that. I might bring it along to Lister's next orchestrated display of moral rectitude and resolute conviction and see what he has to say about all this hostility towards the press.'

'Fuck you, Summers,' Brownlow hissed at him.

'Apparently,' Sunny went on, ignoring the remark, 'tonight all our sympathy goes out to the family and friends of the murdered girl. I think that falls just the wrong side of "sincere", don't you? Especially considering that no-one even knows who she is yet, and because smart people will already be making the connection between her murder and the way Lister has – what's the word? – *personalized* this campaign.'

'You print any of this—'

'And what?' Sunny said.

Brownlow smiled and took a step away from us. He pretended to laugh. 'Silly me – there I am, treating you like a bona fide journalist, and not some five-line stringer for giant vegetables and bouncing baby shows. Go away, and let the people who've got some proper interest in this get on with their job.'

'Damn, you're right,' Sunny said. 'I was forgetting. Then again, I did get here before most of your lot, and I was here taking pictures – of the burning body, of the crowd – at least fifteen minutes before *you* deigned to walk the fifty yards or so from your cosy little office with food round your mouth.'

Brownlow began to raise his hand, as though to wipe his lips, but then stopped himself.

'One more thing,' Sunny said. 'Before I get back to the giant vegetables and bouncing babies, how far up your list of suspects is Paul Hendry for this one?'

Brownlow turned and left us without answering.

We walked to Victoria Square, where yet another crowd had gathered. A woman with a megaphone was addressing this from the base of the statue. Several constables stood close by, trying not to look uncomfortable at what she was saying. Groups of youths, mostly men together and women together, crossed back and forth across the square, their own Saturday nights just beginning.

On Paragon Street, Sunny told me he had too much to do for me to return to the agency with him, and so we parted.

I waited for a cab at the station.

After a few minutes, one arrived and pulled up alongside me. The driver switched off his engine and wound down his window. He asked me where I was going and then told me I'd get there quicker by walking. He'd just spent an hour waiting at one of the police checkpoints. The city was filled with lines of traffic going nowhere, he said. He'd spoken to other drivers on his radio, and they'd all said the same. He rested his hands on the dashboard, pushed himself back in his seat and swore.

22

I was woken early the next morning by Mitchell. He told me he was with Ruth McKenzie, who had returned to Hull late the previous night.

'Lister's keeping her at arm's length as far as possible,' he said.

'Because he thinks her arrival makes it look as though he needs even more help?'

'He wasn't a happy man last night, that's for sure.' He was still at Queen's Gardens, about to leave. He didn't want to come to Humber Street, and so I suggested meeting him at the end of Bishop's Lane, overlooking the River Hull.

'Do they know who she was?' I asked him.

'Twenty minutes,' he said, unwilling to continue speaking on the phone.

I drove to Humber Street, parked there and then walked the short distance to Bishop's Lane.

Mitchell and Ruth were already there, sitting in his car where the narrow lane came to a dead end overlooking the river. The tide was out and there was little water, only a sluggish channel surrounded by shining grey mud.

Seeing me arrive, they both left the warmth of their car and came to join me. There had been an overnight frost, and our breath clouded in the cold air.

'I called Ruth the instant the body was spotted,' Mitchell said.

'And Lister thinks you should have cleared it with him first?'

'He told me to stay out of everything until his forensic teams have finished.'

'Which could be days.'

He shrugged.

'And he asked me just as politely to stay away,' Ruth said.

'Have they found anything yet?'

Mitchell shook his head.

'But, presumably, everybody knows by now that everything dumped on Lister's doorstep last night was done solely to point out his failings to him.'

'No-one will even suggest as much, of course, but it's more or less accepted that that's part of it,' Ruth said. She and Mitchell shared a glance, as though debating or confirming what else they might be about to tell me.

'Part of it?'

'If only it were that straightforward,' she said.

'Meaning?'

'Meaning that, all this sending of messages to Lister aside, we now have to go beyond even second-guessing what our killer's up to, and that we have to look a long way beyond the obvious if what happened yesterday is going to point us to him.'

'The girl was dumped there to prove a point,' I insisted, but neither of them responded to this.

'Lister's planning a big conference for tomorrow morning,' Mitchell said. 'He'll have a lot to say.'

'He had his chance to say something worth listening to last night,' I said. 'All he's doing now is taking charge again and pressing reset on the agenda and timetabling of it all. He practically goaded the killer into doing what he did.'

Mitchell again shook his head at the accusation. 'They know

who she was,' he said. 'And that matters more now than all the speculation about Lister's motives or methods.'

'Which is why *we*, at least, need to be aware of all those wider implications,' Ruth said. 'From where I'm standing, and whatever Lister might want it to signify, this changes everything. Of course it personalizes things to an extent, but there's a lot more to consider now than there was this time yesterday.'

We sat together on a baulk of timber bolted to the disused quay, each of us with a clear view of the river and the estuary beyond. Church bells chimed in the distance, several peals at the same time. There was no sun, no clear sky, just browns and greys, dull lights and an indeterminate horizon on both the water and the land.

'All the other killings,' Ruth went on, 'took place before the investigation had gained any kind of proper focus or momentum. Everything was after-the-event, everything done and dusted before Lister and his teams even started to consider where in-dividual details fitted into the bigger picture. It wasn't until the death of Alison Wilson that they were even prepared to consider that there might be a single killer at work.'

'And not until a few days ago that they were prepared to consider Rebecca Siddal's death as a possible part of the sequence,' Mitchell said. 'Even now, they're still not a hundred per cent certain where they stand on Lucy Collins and Paul Hendry. In fact, some of them are starting to think it might be a completely unconnected crime. He killed her, and then tried to kill himself, simple as that.'

'They're wrong,' I said.

'So *you* – and you alone – keep saying. But even you have to agree – it doesn't really fit the pattern to date. For a start, we know everything there is to know about the two of them, both prior to and during events. There's no case whatsoever against Paul Hendry for anything else.'

It was an imperfect explanation, and we all knew this.

'In a sense, it no longer matters to know what "fits" or doesn't "fit", Ruth said. 'What matters now is that Lister and his teams don't once again become obsessed with trying to make everything part of a single hypothesized outline. I'm not saying there isn't a single killer or even a single reason for the killings taking place, but what I *am* saying is that if there is any solid connection between the killings, then so far it's something beyond the reach of all the forensic evidence.' It was more or less what she'd insisted on telling me at our first meeting, and something I'd given a great deal of thought to since encountering Jimmy Boylan.

'You said they know who she is,' I said to Mitchell.

He took out a notebook.

'Her name was Tracey Lucas. She was eighteen years old and she came from Goole.'

'Thirty miles away.'

'She lived with her parents, who last saw her at midday yesterday. She told them she was going to Doncaster with friends.'

'In the opposite direction.'

'I know. An hour after leaving home, in a bar on Boothferry Road, she told a girlfriend that she was undecided, and that she might go to either Doncaster or Hull, where she'd probably spend the afternoon and evening before returning to Goole.'

'How was she getting there and back?'

'The girl she spoke to said she thought some other friends might be going to one of the two places, and that Tracey was hopeful of getting a lift with them. Apparently, she was looking for these others in the town-centre bars. We haven't been able to contact any of them so far. The friend wasn't entirely certain of the people Tracey was looking for. She gave us a list of possibles. Brownlow's working on it now. There's a chance they might not have returned to Goole yet.' He paused. 'There's even a chance Lister knew her name before his impromptu and inadvisable little show last night.'

'How?'

'A credit-card wallet in her back pocket.'

'There's never been any attempt whatsoever on the part of the killer to try and disguise or conceal the identity of his victims,' Ruth said. 'The bag in which Tracey Lucas was dumped might have been set alight, but it wasn't done to try and hide her identity, which is why the vast majority of corpses are burned.'

'If he hadn't set fire to it, the bag might have been there for hours,' I said. 'It was burned because the killer wanted it found *then*, not later. He wanted it found *where* it was found and he wanted it found *when* it was found – i.e. immediately after he'd dumped it. He wanted to get as close to Lister as possible.'

'No-one's denying that,' Mitchell said, but making it clear to me that he – that they both – considered my insistence on the point misguided.

'I went to see a man called Jimmy Boylan,' I said.

Mitchell wrote the name down.

I told them who Boylan was, and about the two names – Wilson and Boylan – and about the two memorials on the same page of the *Mail*.

It was the first Mitchell had heard of him, meaning no-one had gone out of their way to tell him of the visits to Boylan since the killing of Alison Wilson three months earlier.

Ruth considered what I'd said. 'I don't know what – if anything – it might signify,' she said. 'But if Lister gets a break on this one, it'll be where he least expects it. The killer knows him; he knows where he's looking and how he's directing his investigation.'

'And last night was certainly too well orchestrated to have left anything of any real value behind for him,' Mitchell said.

'Do you think the killer might be trying to provoke Lister into doing something even more excessive?' I asked Ruth.

'It's a possibility, but I doubt if Lister would be stupid enough to respond, and especially not now.'

'Why? Because you'd tell him not to?'

'Me, and a few of those others he might have to actually start listening to before this gets any further out of hand.'

'He knows that somewhere between the murder of Lucy Collins and last night, both he and the killer stepped in opposite directions over the same line towards each other,' Mitchell said. 'That's one simple fact no-one – least of all Lister – is going to be able to ignore.'

Ruth shook her head at the remark. 'What lines? Who's drawing them? Where? Start pretending Lister's some kind of gunslinger and you're playing the game he wants you to play. If we accept that the killer did this solely in response to a challenge from Lister, then we might as well just sit back and wait for a body to turn up in his private washroom. I don't think any of us wants it on our conscience that Tracey Lucas was killed merely to prove a point. What point were any of the other killings making? *They* had nothing to do with Lister per se.'

'Her parents are at Queen's Gardens now,' Mitchell said. 'They've agreed to cooperate with Lister. *They* certainly don't believe their daughter was killed just to get one over on him.'

'Only because they *can't* believe it,' Ruth said.

We sat in silence for a minute, and then we rose from the timber, as cold as stone, and walked along the wharf towards where the river emptied into the estuary, where the saturated mud met even more saturated mud, and where a flock of scavenging gulls fought over a wrack of litter abandoned by the falling tide.

'He's got twenty men going through the CCTV footage,' Mitchell said. 'They've emptied every camera in the city. It's going to absorb a lot of their time and generate a lot of footwork.'

'None of that concerns us,' Ruth said. 'Except to know that the killer probably knows the city well enough to avoid being captured on film. And perhaps that he knows enough about what Lister's attempting to do to take advantage of the growing public outcry at his lack of success. Kelly Smith, Alison Wilson and now Tracey Lucas were all dumped in fairly prominent places, even if none of them was killed where they were found. Perhaps somebody should start considering what that might signify. And if he has been questioned or crosschecked already, then we might also start to consider why he's aroused no suspicion, why no-one's questioning any recurrent details or sightings. Hull's a small place. Somebody knows him. It might get said every time, but it's always true. This thing is too big, too complex and involved, and it's been going on for too long now for somebody close to the killer *not* to know him and what he's doing.'

'They've had two hundred calls already,' Mitchell said. 'All the usual stuff, and all of it coming to nothing.'

'We know all that's going to happen,' Ruth said. 'So does Lister.

With an investigation this size, this *public*, it's unavoidable. He's not going to be able to avoid it, not now.'

'What more do they know about Tracey Lucas?' I asked them. 'Does the fact that she came from Goole have any significance?'

'Because all the other victims were from here, you mean?' Ruth said. 'I doubt that's the reason they were killed – because they came from Hull.'

'She had a bit of a reputation,' Mitchell said. 'But there's no possibility of her ever having been a prostitute, if that's what you mean.'

'Is that from the parents?'

'Among others. Apparently, her latest boyfriend was one of several. He said they had a relationship, but that it wasn't serious.'

'Was she promiscuous?'

'It looks like it. She frequently stayed overnight in Hull or Doncaster. She had friends in both places. We're already question-ing the people she knew here. She sometimes stayed over with them. Or if not them, then friends of friends.'

'Are we saying she slept with comparative strangers?' Ruth said.

'A few people thought so. No-one thought it was all that unusual. Some of the other girls suggested it was fairly common practice.'

'But definitely no actual prostitution?'

'Not as far as we can tell.' He walked to where the wharf rose above a derelict barge on the river. The vessel had been there since before my arrival at Humber Street.

'We don't know enough about her yet to speculate on anything but the basics,' Ruth said. 'Where she was, what her intentions might have been, who she might or might not have seen or been with, and how she ended up where she did. And remember, it's not just great minds that think alike – everything we come up with, Lister, Brownlow and twenty others will already have taken their fine-toothed combs to.'

'They've got unburned parts of the plastic sack,' Mitchell said. 'And a sample of the petrol that didn't burn. They think she was killed – thirteen stab wounds, two or three of which were potentially fatal – and that the petrol was splashed into the bag and over it – enough for it to burn hard enough and fast enough to destroy whatever evidence the bag itself might contain.'

'*Have* they found anything?'

'Not so far. They think the petrol must have been poured *in situ* to avoid it being present anywhere else, but there's no sign so far of any canister. They even had dogs on the streets to see if they could pick up a scent using the fuel, but nothing came of it. There were too many people at the site, and too quickly.'

'Which is what the killer probably banked on,' Ruth said. 'Along with the rain, and then, possibly, the frost later.'

'Tracey Lucas's parents are staying in Hull overnight. Lister's assigned a couple of constables to them. They've agreed to appear with him tomorrow morning,' Mitchell said.

'At which time they'll no doubt declare their full confidence in him and his methods.'

'Whatever they say, that's how it'll look. He won't let any of the serious questions get anywhere near them.'

'Is that why he made you keep your mouth shut last night?' I asked him.

'He made a live broadcast last night, while everything was still unfolding,' Ruth said. 'Unbelievable. He broke every rule in the book.'

'But the point', I said, 'is that he *knew* what he was doing. He can't help himself, and the killer knows this, too.'

But again she didn't agree with this, and she shook her head. 'This is a lot more than breast-beating on Lister's part,' she said.

Mitchell asked me again about Jimmy Boylan and his response to my approach. He could not now ignore the fact that the two events – my visit to Boylan and the murder of Tracey Lucas and the dumping of her body – had taken place only six hours apart. Ruth was less convinced of there being any true connection between the two events, and I told Mitchell I agreed with her.

'There might be more than one killer,' he said. 'Or one killer and someone watching his back.'

'And Jimmy Boylan is neither,' I said.

Mitchell reached the end of the wharf and stood there with his arms outstretched, as though he might have been about to dive into the mud below.

'Do it,' Ruth called to him.

Out on the Humber, a passing container vessel broke the surface of the water and sent low and dying waves across the banks of mud.

'Can I tell Sunny any of this?' I asked them.

'He'll learn most of it tomorrow morning,' Mitchell said. 'Perhaps you should tell him to ask Tracey Lucas's parents how well they really knew their daughter. I don't think there was much love lost – and certainly not on her part, according to her friends. She spent a lot of time away from home, going into Hull at every opportunity. She certainly didn't think a great deal of whatever Goole had to offer her.'

'It has its good points,' I said.

On the far bank of the river, someone had lit a fire, and there was the smell of burning rubber in the air. Smoke rose suddenly from behind a mound of pallets.

Mitchell lowered his arms and stepped back from the edge.

'And to an eighteen-year-old, fun-loving girl, they would be what, exactly?' he said.

23

I went later that day to see Susan Hendry again. I called her before-hand and she asked me to visit her at her home rather than at the hospital. She sounded exhausted and confused, as though my call might have woken her.

She was standing at the window to watch my approach. Leaves fell all around me the full length of Park Avenue and lay mounded in drifts against the walls and kerbs.

I waited at the door, expecting her to open it, but she never came. Finally, I rang the bell and saw her through the panels of coloured glass coming towards me down the long hallway.

'I'm sorry,' she said. 'I was miles away. Thanks for coming. I've only been back an hour or so myself.' She spoke quickly, nervously, as though she had grown unused to casual conversation.

A fire had recently been lit in the sitting-room grate and still burned vigorously. She went to this and put on more coal from a scuttle.

'Is it cold?' she said. 'I think it is. I haven't been back here, not really, not for any length of time since you were last here. Sit down. Can I get you anything?' She pointed to a tray of bottles on a low table. 'I'm having one myself. In fact, I've had one already.' She retrieved her glass from the windowsill and poured us both drinks.

'How's Paul?' I said.

She shrugged and briefly closed her eyes. 'Yesterday, they thought he might be able to breathe unaided and so the consultant came and they tried to take him off the ventilator.'

I knew by the way she said it that the attempt and all it signified had been unsuccessful.

'He seemed to struggle along for a few minutes and then he just stopped breathing. All sorts of alarms and flashing lights. But the consultant and two of the nurses stayed with him. They switched off the alarms and lights and let him go on trying for a few minutes more.' She sipped from her glass. 'You always want to believe that your own children have got something in them that no-one else's children have got. It's ridiculous, of course, but you never stop thinking it.'

'What happened?'

'After a few more minutes – who am I fooling? – it was probably only ever seconds – they saw that he wasn't going to manage it, and so they put the pipe back down his throat and reset all the other bits and pieces that did his breathing for him. I almost told—' She stopped abruptly.

'Told them not to do it?' I said.

She nodded and emptied her glass, pulling a face at the taste.

'It might sound strange to you, perverse even, but listening to him struggle, listening to him fighting for breath for even those few moments, it gave me hope. Just hearing him, seeing his chest tremble and his mouth open and close like that after all those days of him just lying there. The consultant told me that it wasn't what was really happening – Paul fighting for himself – just that his lungs were responding to having the ventilator taken away. He was trying to be reassuring, but I wished he hadn't told me. I could tell how disappointed he was that they'd had to wire everything back up. If he'd asked me then what I honestly wanted him to do, I don't think I would have been able to tell him.'

'Do you think he was offering you the choice?'

'That's what it seemed like.'

'Meaning he probably believed that *not* reattaching the ventilator might have been for the best?'

'Who knows? It's obviously not something he could have put into words, or even suggested to me, and it was far beyond me ever to ask him if it was what he meant, let alone tell him to do it. He'd been at the hospital all night, like me; we were both exhausted. Perhaps for those few moments, the machine unplugged and with us all standing around Paul's bed like that, it just seemed like an option none of us could ignore.'

'And once the ventilator was working again?'

'Back to square one and we all stepped back from the edge.'

'Has there been no improvement at all?'

She shook her head. 'I try to think of a figure – a percentage, say, by which his chances of making a proper recovery are reduced day by day. Is it ten per cent, or five, or just one? Does the episode with the ventilator mean his chances just dropped by twenty per cent or ninety per cent? I tried to get the consultant to put a figure on it, but he told me it was pointless. He said what they've all said – that it was a coma, and that comas are unpredictable. He told me people had woken up after twenty years in them. Nineteen years and six months after everyone had given up hope.' She laughed. 'But that was in America. Of course it was. When I asked him how long they went on keeping them alive in Hull he changed the subject. I don't blame him.'

'Perhaps in a few weeks, if Paul hasn't recovered, you'll be asked to make the same decision.'

'It's a big "perhaps",' she said. She reached across and touched my arm to signal her apology, and to let me know that it was something she'd already started thinking about.

A small piece of coal fell from the fire into the hearth and she watched it burn itself out.

'I heard all about last night,' she said. 'Where was she from, here?'

'Goole,' I said, and hearing this seemed to reassure her.

'I suppose they've got a lot more to go on now,' she said.

'They're keeping everything close to themselves for today. Lister's holding a press conference tomorrow morning. The girl's parents have agreed to participate.'

'They never asked me to attend one when Paul was found.' As an afterthought, she said, 'I mean Lucy.'

'They prefer the next of kin to do it, with close family to back them up.'

'Lucy's father got in touch with one of Lister's men. Did you know?'

The news surprised me. Neither Mitchell nor Ruth had mentioned it.

'When?'

'Late yesterday. There was just him left. They traced him to Southampton. It's where Lucy was born. They thought he'd left there years ago, but he was still there.'

'Is he coming to Hull?'

'I'm not sure. There was no love lost between the two of them. He more or less threw her out at sixteen, and she was happy to go. There's been no communication between them for all that time. That's all I know. They sent a policewoman to ask me if I could confirm his identity. I said I wouldn't know him. Is it important?'

'It might be,' I said. 'Everywhere you look in these killings, there's something pointing in another direction, and usually into the past.'

No love lost. The same words Mitchell had used when talking about the relationship between Kelly Smith and her mother. And the words he'd used earlier when discussing Tracey Lucas and her parents.

'Is that why you were asking me about Paul's father's life before I met him?' she said. She refilled both our glasses.

'Like I told you, Emily Carr said she thought her father had known him.'

'What else?'

'I'm not sure. Yesterday morning, six hours before they found the body of the girl from Goole, I went to see a man called Jimmy Boylan.' I paused, waiting to see if the name meant anything to her.

She thought about it and shook her head.

'Jimmy Boylan had a brother, John, who later became the father of Alison Wilson.'

'And you think there's a connection going back all that way? I've never heard of either of them.'

'They lived – Jimmy Boylan still lives there – on Woodcock Street.'

'Which was a stone's throw away from where Tony lived with his parents on Dairycoates Avenue when I met him. Is that what connects them all?'

'It was thirty years ago, longer. Kelly Smith lived with her mother on Selby Street.'

'I know. I never knew either of them. Neither Paul nor Lucy ever mentioned knowing the girl. Besides, it was *Lucy* who was killed, not my son. Surely, any connection should be sought between these others and either Lucy's father or something in *her* past.' She closed her eyes again. 'I think the policewoman mentioned something about Lucy's father not being well. To be honest, I missed most of what they said because I was too concerned about what had just happened to Paul. Apparently, her father will formally identify Lucy and then they'll ask him their questions. Perhaps if you can find out what he tells them, it might help you make better sense of what's happening here.'

'It might,' I said.

She looked around her. 'I inherited this house from my husband's only surviving relative,' she said. 'A maiden aunt. His father's sister. The only one in the family who didn't throw everything away on drink and whatever. She bought this house and seven others like it sixty years ago, just after the war. She had a small shop. She saved, bought one house when prices were low, rented it out and bought another with her profits; then another and another until she had all eight. They all came to me. Tony was her only nephew. Nobody else left.'

'What did you do?'

'I sold my own home on Saint George's Road, three of the ones she left me, moved in here with Paul, and I let the rest out to students. It was five years ago. We'd never had anything whatso-ever, me and Paul – and certainly nothing from Tony or his disapproving parents – and then all this. Pity it didn't all come to us sooner. At least it means I can afford—'

'People like me?'

'I was going to say it means I can afford to look after Paul if and when he needs it. But, yes, it means I can afford to employ people like you while I sit everything out.'

'Yvonne never told me,' I said.

'Why should she? We've been friends for twenty years. None of this makes any difference to that. It might have been a lot of money to someone like me, but it—' She stopped speaking and turned away from me.

She'd been going to tell me that it wouldn't now make any difference to the recovery of her son.

She asked me if I thought Lister was right to pursue his campaign against the prostitutes as part of his investigation into the killings.

'Tracey Lucas wasn't a prostitute,' I said. 'Nor was Alison Wilson. They now also think that a girl who died a year ago might have been a victim of the same killer. She wasn't a prostitute, either.'

'What was her name?'

'Rebecca Siddal.'

Again, she thought about this and shook her head. 'Sorry. It means nothing. I thought for a moment you were going to say that you were convinced that Lucy hadn't been a prostitute, either.'

'It would have been a lie,' I said. 'We both know that.'

'I know.'

I asked her how long she'd known James Weaver.

'He's been my doctor for eighteen, nineteen years, perhaps longer. And Paul's. Lucy's too, probably. That's why it came as such a shock to learn where Paul had been found. You surely don't think—'

'I don't,' I said. 'It's just that there are still so many loose ends, and like Lister I could do with eliminating a few of them.'

'Like Lucy's father?'

'He wasn't even on my list of loose ends until ten minutes ago,' I said, and she smiled.

I asked her then what she wanted me to do in the event of Lucy Collins's death being excluded from the serial-killer investigation.

The suggestion surprised and alarmed her. 'Because they're convinced Paul killed her, and her alone? Is that what's going to happen? Is that the real reason you're here?'

'I don't know. But whatever they believe, they're going to have to make their minds up about it soon.'

'I suppose it would make life simpler for them to believe in Paul's guilt.'

'I suspect it's what they'll do,' I said.

'Even though that will leave them with only *one* murdered prostitute?' she said coldly. 'Where will that leave Lister's campaign?'

I said nothing, waiting for her to compose herself.

'I know what Lucy was to him,' she said eventually. 'And I know what she did for him. Whatever the police want to believe, I only want the truth. My son may die. I have to get *something* out of all this.'

I'd gone to see her with the vague and ill-considered notion of telling her that perhaps her son was as much a victim in all of this as Lucy Collins and the other girls had been. But I knew now, having listened to her tell me about the failed attempt to remove his ventilator, that it was beyond me even to suggest this, that it would only unsettle and confuse her further.

It wasn't even something I could properly explain to myself. It was why I'd asked her about James Weaver. It was why I'd deliberately mentioned all those other names and places to her and watched for her reaction. It was why I'd wanted her to recognize at least one of the names and to point me in a direction no-one else had yet started moving.

It was considering all this now that I realized there was something about Jimmy Boylan and his brother that I'd forgotten to mention to her.

'Jimmy Boylan's brother, John,' I said. 'He was known as "Jock". Does that ring any bells?'

And the instant I said the name she turned sharply to me and repeated it.

'The family came from Scotland,' I said.

She continued looking at me. 'Tony had a friend called "Jock",' she said. 'I remember him talking about him. I never knew him, just his name, "Jock". I never even knew his real name. It was before I met him. I think they worked together. Perhaps it was on the boats. Or perhaps they were apprentices together.'

And perhaps everybody in Hull – in England, in the world – who had any connection whatsoever to Scotland was called 'Jock'.

I was surprised that she remembered this, having recalled so little else of her husband's past, and I asked her how she could be so certain.

'There was a photo,' she said. I've probably still got it. "Tony and Jock." It's written on the back. The two of them. They can't have been much more than boys, late teens, that sort of age. I'll try and find it for you if it would help.'

'If it's the same man, then it would connect your husband to the father of one of the murdered girls, and then connect them both – via Jimmy Boylan's memorial to his dead brother – to the death of Rebecca Siddal,' I said.

'I haven't seen it for years,' she said, possibly wanting to put a brake on my sudden eagerness to see the picture. 'I only ever saved a few bits and pieces where Tony was concerned, for Paul's sake. Something to show him if he ever asked. It had nothing to do with him, his dad going off and leaving us and then dying before Paul had any real idea of what kind of man he'd been. *I* might never have wanted to see Tony again, but I wouldn't have kept Paul from him, if that's what he'd wanted. I threw most of the stuff out either when Tony went back to Germany that last time or when I learned he was dead. But I'm almost certain that I put that particular picture in a box with a few others.'

'Are you sure it said "Jock"? Not "Jack", for instance?'

For a moment she seemed unsure, and then said, 'No, I'm

certain. And the reason I remember it is because the name "Jock" had quotation marks round it. I can see it now.'

'Could you find it for me?' I asked her.

'It isn't here. I put a pile of stuff into storage when we moved here. On Waterloo Street. There's a removals and storage depot there. I did it when I cleared out all the houses ready for either renting or selling. They're closed on Sundays. I can go tomorrow and try to find it. It won't be easy. It's a big container and there's a lot of stuff from a lot of places packed into it. I always meant to sort through it and get rid of most of it, but I never got round to doing it.'

And if Tony Hendry and Jock Boylan *were* somehow connected, then why not the father of Kelly Smith, who, judging by what his wife had told me of him, was a man formed in the same mould?

A lot now depended on the two 'Jocks' being the same man.

On the mantelpiece, a clock struck four and Susan Hendry looked at her watch.

'I said I'd go back to the hospital,' she said. 'I've booked a taxi.'

The room had grown dark around us, illuminated now only by the streetlight outside and by the glow of the fire.

'Christ,' she said. 'Four o'clock on a Sunday afternoon in October.'

I told her what Larkin had said about Sunday afternoons in winter.

'He got that right,' she said.

Outside, her taxi arrived and sounded its horn. We both rose from our seats at the signal.

'I won't tell you I hope there's been some improvement by the time you get back there,' I said.

'I know you won't. But?'

'But I do hope that when you next have a decision to make, you'll be ready to make it and have the strength to do it.'

'I will,' she said, and then she held me and kissed me on the cheek.

24

I went with Sunny to Lister's press conference the following morning. We arrived only minutes before it was due to begin and the room was already full. Extra seating was being set out, but this still left people standing. It was the same room in which Lister held all his press conferences, and it was now too small for the purpose.

A giant photograph of Tracey Lucas had been taped to the screens on either side of the low stage upon which tables and chairs had been set out. Microphones stood waiting, and recorders had been laid across the front of the tables.

The camera high on the rear wall scanned back and forth across the assembling crowd.

'He should have held it somewhere bigger,' Sunny said. 'This'll get out of hand and he'll have the perfect excuse to pull the plug – too many people fighting to ask too many questions and all of them getting in each other's way. He'll pull the plug, and it will all be our fault for not knowing how to behave.'

The conference was scheduled to last for only thirty minutes.

We'd tried to persuade Yvonne to come with us, but she'd insisted she had too much to do at the agency.

Lister came into the room, followed by several of his senior officers, including Brownlow, and followed by the parents of Tracey Lucas.

Her mother was a woman in her late forties, her father perhaps ten years older. The woman wore a cardigan embroidered with flowers and buttoned up to her chin. Her husband wore a jacket, a plain white shirt and plain black tie, and looked uncomfortable with all three.

They had both spent the previous day and two nights being questioned by Brownlow and his team. Another squad had been working in Goole during their absence. The movements and whereabouts of everyone who had either known their daughter or who had encountered her on the day she died were being pieced together.

This kind of saturation policing was always more revealing in the gaps it left than in the times and places – the minutes and seconds, the various locations and their connecting streets and alleyways – it actually plotted.

Tracey Lucas's mother looked as though she had just finished crying. She held a handkerchief which she continually tucked into and then withdrew from her sleeve.

Lister whispered something to the father, his hand over the closest microphone, and the man pulled his seat closer to his wife's and then briefly put his arm around her. Neither of them seemed either comforted or reassured by the gesture. An old and faded tattoo covered the back of the man's hand, and equally in-distinguishable letters crossed the joints of his fingers. I looked at his other hand and saw the same there.

The detectives sat on either side of these three central figures, presences rather than participants.

Having looked slowly around the room, Lister called for silence.

The doors were closed. I stood beside them with Sunny. Around the room, cameras started to click and flash.

Lister rose from his seat. 'I'd ask you to wait until the conference is approaching its conclusion before taking your pictures,' he said. 'This is a sad and distressing occasion for all concerned, and I'm sure you will all join me in not wishing to add to the pain or dis-comfort of Tracey's parents.'

'His shot across our bows,' Sunny said.

Lister held up both his hands. 'I'd like to start, if I may, with a brief résumé of what happened on Saturday night. I'm sure that many of you are already in possession of the basic facts of the matter, but I do not intend to allow this conference to become yet another round of unfounded speculation and accusations.'

'Shot number two,' Sunny said.

Lister then described the discovery of Tracey Lucas's body in Queen's Gardens two night earlier. This took him ten minutes, and he told us nothing we didn't already know. The only thing of any real value that he was able to tell us was the fact that Tracey Lucas had last been seen in Goole, leaving the Mermaid bar on Boothferry Road, at twenty past three on Saturday afternoon, and that this therefore left a gap of three hours during which her presence was not accounted for until the eventual discovery of her body at half past six that evening.

There had been no reported sightings of her after that time – either by anyone in Goole or the surrounding district – especially the roads leading to the motorway – or on the Hull CCTV footage.

It was a long time. The journey from the centre of Goole to Queen's Gardens would have taken no more than an hour, even allowing for the traffic at that time of the day and week.

Several people raised their hands, but Lister told them he would answer questions only after Tracey's parents had made their own appeals.

Her mother was the first to speak. She told everyone what a wonderful daughter Tracey had been, how loving and considerate and caring, how *ordinary*. Just another one of those millions of happy-go-lucky, ordinary girls. A girl with her whole future ahead of her. A girl who loved her family and friends, and whose family and friends loved her, and who thought the world of her. She was a special girl who had never harmed anyone in her entire life, and it was difficult for her mother to believe that anyone who knew her – anyone who knew Tracey like she and her husband knew her – would want to do any harm whatsoever to her.

Little of which tallied with what Mitchell had told me the previous morning.

The woman began to cry, and pulled out the handkerchief again. Lister put his arm to her back, clearly wishing that her husband had done this instead.

'Perhaps you might like to say a few words,' he suggested to Tracey Lucas's father.

The man leaned closer to the microphones. 'I'd just like to repeat what Tracey's mother has already said,' he said. 'And to say that if anybody out there knows anything, anything at all, then will they please contact the police. Tracey was a beautiful and loving daughter, and only somebody who had never known her could possibly do such a thing.'

'Oh, please,' Sunny said beneath his breath.

'Whoever did this to our Tracey is sick,' the man went on. 'He needs help. And we're here today, doing this, because we don't want anyone else, anybody else's mother or father, to have to go through what we've been through these past few days.'

His wife, I saw, was looking at him as though he had just delivered a heartfelt and genuinely moving eulogy for their murdered daughter. Perhaps it was the most he'd ever said about her. Perhaps it was the fondest he'd ever sounded. Or perhaps it was just the sight of him in his jacket, shirt and tie and with the attention of the room focused on him as he spoke, which impressed her so much.

Both of them were clearly anxious for the conference to finish so that they could leave.

Lister sat looking directly ahead as both the woman and then the man spoke. It was obvious to everyone in the room that everything had been carefully rehearsed, but even he must have felt un-comfortable at the couple's behaviour, and at the obvious insincerity with which Tracey Lucas's father's words had been delivered.

When the man had finished, and as he sat back from the micro-phones, Lister immediately rose from his seat.

'I believe it is only fair and proper that your questions be directed at me and my officers,' he said. 'Mr and Mrs Lucas have been through a great deal, and I will not prolong their suffering. I ask you all to bear this in mind when phrasing your questions.' He again looked around the room, pausing briefly when he saw Sunny and me by the door.

' "Phrasing"?' Sunny said to me.

'I imagine there are some of you wanting to ask questions about the broader investigation,' Lister went on. 'In which case, I would ask you to wait and to do this following Mr and Mrs Lucas's departure.'

A succession of hands were raised, and Lister began picking out his questioners.

I asked Sunny who else was present and he looked at the men and women around us.

'Too many nationals,' he said, meaning that they were now gathering the news directly rather than relying on him.

Someone asked Lister how he accounted for the missing hours, especially considering that the hours preceding and following this gap were so thoroughly and minutely documented. Lister said it was something they were still working on.

Did he think the killer had abducted and killed Tracey Lucas towards the beginning or the end of this time? How long had passed between her being murdered and her body being discovered?

These questions were causing distress to Tracey Lucas's parents, and Lister saw this and called for a short break in the proceedings while they left the room. The couple immediately rose to go. If Lister had hoped that this might restore order and silence to the room, then he was disappointed.

Before the couple had gone from the room, someone asked Lister where Tracey Lucas fitted into his earlier, spurious theory about the killer selecting only prostitutes as his victims.

Both the Lucases faltered at hearing this. Tracey Lucas's mother put a hand to her mouth. Her father looked over the crowd to see who had asked the question. He was about to shout something in reply, when Lister signalled to Brownlow to restrain him and help him from the stage. The man looked as though he might have rushed into the crowd and attacked the journalist responsible.

'Question,' Sunny said. 'Did he seem more concerned about the slur on his dead daughter's reputation, or on the good family name of Lucas, ha ha?'

'Judging by what Mitchell told me, I'd say the latter.'

'Lister doesn't know half of what's happening in Goole,' he said. 'Don Lucas has got a reputation as a violent man. I asked around. The family used to live in Hull. Moved to Goole a long time ago when the firm he worked for shut its Hull factory. They offered him a job in Goole, and he went.'

'What kind of work?'

'No idea.'

'Where in Hull did they live?'

'Ditto. And besides, it doesn't matter. *He* didn't kill her. A dozen witnesses have him in the fine and various bars of old Goole town all afternoon and evening. In fact, right up until the time the police here called the number they found in Tracey's purse. The guy spent all Saturday night in the Portland Hotel sobering up. He's already told a couple of the tabloids that he's prepared to hang his daughter's killer himself. I think, along with "rehearsed", "restrained" would be a good word for what we've seen today.'

Lister remained standing until the man and woman had left the room. Only the reporters and photographers closest to them fell silent as they went.

When the door finally closed on them, Lister said loudly, 'I asked for your cooperation here today, ladies and gentlemen, I offered you this opportunity to achieve something, and this is what happens. Be as critical as you like of me and my methods, but, please, try to keep things in perspective.'

It struck me as an uncharacteristically clumsy remark to make, especially considering all the preparation that had already gone into ensuring the conference worked in his favour.

'What perspective?' someone shouted. '*You're* the one using this investigation to his own ends. We're here today looking at victim number—'

'Her name is Tracey Lucas,' Lister said firmly.

'*Was* Tracey Lucas,' the man said.

'Answer the question,' Sunny called to him.

'I have carried out this investigation as I have best seen fit to undertake it.'

'In English,' Sunny shouted, knowing how provocative the remark would sound to Lister, and causing an outburst of laughter around the room.

Lister stopped talking.

Others started to ask him similar questions.

A woman asked him how responsible he felt for the death of Tracey Lucas now that her killer appeared to have turned this into something more personal between Lister and himself.

Lister shouted through the rising clamour that he had never heard anything more ridiculous.

Then Brownlow said something to him behind his hand, and Lister clapped twice and announced that the conference was over.

'What a surprise,' Sunny called to him.

'I think you should all – all of you, every one of you – consider your own motives in all of this,' Lister said.

Sunny smiled at hearing this.

Lister and Brownlow left the stage, and then they and the other detectives left the room, ignoring the questions which continued to be shouted after them.

Few others followed them out. For many, the outcome of the conference was now their main story.

'He's going to regret this particular piece of bollocks for a long time to come,' a man said to Sunny.

'Or until some plod checking parking tickets comes up with a bloodstained car, a pool of petrol, the rest of the roll of plastic bags and a street map of Goole,' Sunny said.

But it still seemed uncharacteristic of Lister to have lost both his temper and control of the situation so quickly, and I began to doubt his motives for having ended the conference so abruptly.

I suggested this to Sunny, but he remained sceptical.

'He just wanted it over and done with,' he said. 'He'd expected something useful from the parents, and they were a waste of time. Just like all the CC footage was a waste of time. They've got a minute by minute account of her life last Saturday, from the minute she woke up to the minute she disappeared, and then a great yawning fucking chasm in which absolutely anything could have happened to her. They wanted tighter timings. They wanted something else in there. They wanted one of all those others who said they knew her or said they'd seen her to point a finger at something, anything. *Two* people pointing in the same direction, and they'd have had somebody downstairs answering their questions right now. They thought they'd got something with this one, that they were at the very centre of it. But the fact is, they were as far away with Tracey bloody Lucas as with any of the others. She could have been dead at three twenty-one for all they know.'

'They must still have arrived only minutes after whoever set light to the petrol did it,' I said.

'And by which time, presumably, everything had gone according to plan. The match was struck only because the killer knew he was in the clear, that no one had seen him dump the body, and because he knew his route away from it all was wide open and unobserved. They've not come up with anything from any of the cameras. Imagine that.'

'Nothing at all?'

'Dozens of shadowy shapes and completely unidentifiable figures and unreadable licence plates, but nothing that's going to point them at anything specific. It's probably why they've decided to be so thorough in Goole – because *that's* where they expect to find what they're looking for. Not here.'

'It's probably why the killer abducted her in one place and dumped her in another,' I said. 'To create all the inconsistencies and uncertainty.' Just like he might have abducted Rebecca Siddal in one place and left her hanging body to be found somewhere completely different.

'Makes sense to me,' he said. 'Send everybody one way, and

then, slowly, silently and unseen, start moving in the opposite direction.'

'Why didn't Lister consider that?'

'He did. But finding someone in Goole who'd seen or heard something was always going to be a better bet as far as he was concerned.'

'And all this, here, today?'

'To parade the grieving parents before the howling, uncaring bastards of the press? We should have listened to Yvonne and stayed at home.'

'If we'd done that, then you wouldn't have had the opportunity to push your face back into his,' I said.

'There is that.'

I was about to ask him why he'd done it, when my phone rang.

It was Ruth McKenzie asking when we could meet. When I told her where I was she said she was in the room above me. She asked me why I'd attended and I told her I was there with Sunny.

She asked me again where we might meet away from the station and I suggested the Dock Basin Bridge leading to the Prince's Quay shopping centre.

'Ten minutes,' she said, and hung up.

25

She was leaning over the railings and looking at the water beneath her when I arrived. She looked up as I approached her from Dock Street, and then searched the full length of the road behind me.

She wore a long black coat and a black fur hat. Shoppers passed behind her on their way into the centre. The smell of fried food and the sweet smell of baking drifted out of the building each time the doors opened. She broke up the remains of a sandwich and dropped the pieces to the gulls on the water below.

She turned her back to the railings and leaned against them as I approached her.

'Lister sent Mitchell to Goole,' she said.

'Because he wants him out of the way?'

'How was the press conference?'

'Same as all the others, only shorter. Lister lost control and it fell apart.'

'Helped by your friend?'

'He's been to hundreds of them. I think even he thought this one might be different.'

'And when it wasn't, he decided to stamp his feet?'

'It wasn't just him.'

We watched a girl of sixteen or seventeen pushing a double pram across the narrow walkway. Both the babies were crying.

'What did you think to ma and pa Lucas?' she said.

'I'd say they were talked into showing by Lister, and then regretted agreeing to do it. They might as well not have spoken.'

'Another crying human face to a tragedy?'

'They were probably embarrassed because of their relationship with their daughter.'

She shook her head at the suggestion. 'Mitchell and I were with them all day yesterday after leaving you. Brownlow was the first to talk to them and got next to nothing – Tracey got up at eleven thirty, got herself dressed and ready and was out of the house an hour later. I don't think either of them even spoke to her, or her to them. Mitchell and I had to wait until they'd been brought here before we got our chance to talk to them. Lister's big concession to those people further up the chain telling him to let us get involved. He probably thought there was nothing more to be gained from them. Letting me and Mitchell loose on them was his way of simultaneously "involving" us and keeping us at arm's length from the investigation proper.'

'And you thought there was something they weren't telling him?' I said, wondering where her remarks were leading. 'Perhaps he just wanted them away from Goole while his men did their work there.'

'We both thought there was a great deal they weren't telling him. The mother just sat and cried – though it seemed more for herself than her daughter. And the father just kept pacing the room and making his presence felt. Mitchell offered to take him down to the bar and the man jumped at the offer.'

'Leaving you alone with his wife, who – let me guess – was reluctant to say much in her husband's presence.'

'That's how it seemed to me. And for "reluctant" read scared.'

'Tracey Lucas might have had a hundred stories to tell against the pair of them. Perhaps they knew that the gloss *they* were putting on everything was going to be scrubbed away down to the dirty undercoat when all the neighbours and friends started being interviewed.'

'That's what Mitchell thought. Apparently, Don Lucas did nothing but complain about his daughter when the two of them were in the bar together. Made out he wasn't going to change how he felt about her just because of what had happened to her.'

'That was big of him. And her mother?'

'I don't know. I tried to ask her things, but every time I sensed she was getting close to telling me something, she either clammed up or started crying again. I think the pair of them thought we were just there to keep them company until this morning.'

'You don't believe either of them had anything to do with the killing?'

She shook her head. 'Nothing whatsoever. It was just as though they had something *else* to hide, and as though this sudden exposure had caught them unawares and left them vulnerable, that's all. We already know from several of Tracey's friends that her father sold cheap tobacco and cigarettes in the pubs he frequented. Goole police confirmed that they knew all about it. Him and a dozen others.'

'But you still think it was something more?' I said.

'There was definitely something. He's not a nice man. When he and Mitchell came back upstairs, he and his wife exchanged a glance in which I'm certain he was asking her something. She shook her head and he lightened up and went to her. Went to her and put his arm round her, and she flinched when he did it. He was drunk. He told her she should have gone to the bar with him and Mitchell, that we should all have gone. She was frozen solid all the time he was holding her. She looked embarrassed by it all. She whispered something and he left her and switched on the television.'

'Couldn't you get the woman alone and try again?'

'I suggested as much to Lister.'

'And?'

'And he said the couple were too important to him for *somebody like me* to upset and alienate them by treating them as suspects. I don't think he was convinced they'd go ahead with today until they were actually sitting beside him and the tears were flowing again. Don Lucas even got a new jacket and shirt out of the deal. Insisted on it. He'd been brought from Goole wearing a cheap tracksuit and an England shirt. You can imagine how that would have played to the cameras. Lister even persuaded him to take out his earring before the conference. At first, Lucas refused, said he'd had it since he was sixteen, but Lister prevailed. What you saw this morning was the scrubbed-up version. When they get back to Goole some time today, Lister wants them left alone, but watched.'

I tried to remember what else I knew about the family, but there was nothing, except that they had once lived in Hull and had moved to Goole because of Lucas's work.

'What's Mitchell doing in Goole?' I asked her.

'Helping the doorsteppers. Lister thinks this duty-free tobacco thing might lead somewhere. I doubt if Mitchell shares that particular belief.'

'It still might account for why the Lucases were anxious about something.'

'And if that turns out to be true, then we'll all have been wasting our time.'

A gust of wind caught us where we stood over the water and broke the surface beneath us into a flurry of scattered waves. She pulled her high collar to her cheeks.

'We just thought it was something you ought to know about, that's all,' she said.

'Because I might still be able to go places Lister is expressly forbidding you and Mitchell from going?'

She considered the remark. 'I suspect your own opinion of your capabilities is considerably higher than Lister's,' she said.

I suggested leaving the bridge and going into the shopping centre. A gallery – a *galleria* – of cafés lined the wall overlooking the dock. She looked at her watch and agreed. I had anticipated that she would be anxious to return to Queen's Gardens and wondered if there was something else she wanted to tell me.

I fetched us coffee and we found a table overlooking the water and the passing shoppers.

I asked her about her profiling work and told her I'd be interested to hear whatever she might have come up with regarding the killer. It was something Sunny had suggested to me now that his own news reports on the killings were less in demand. It was something she'd be happy to do, she said, but only once she'd cleared it with Lister.

We sat without speaking for several minutes. A flashing illuminated sign at the end of the gallery announced that there were only seventy-three days to Christmas. I wondered when they'd stopped calling them 'Shopping Days'.

Ruth suddenly grinned, and I asked her what was funny.

'You'll like this,' she said. 'The road cameras tracked James Weaver's car from the end of the M62 all the way along the A63 into the city centre on Saturday afternoon.'

'Between three twenty and six thirty?'

'Between five and six. His car and approximately three thousand others.'

'Where had he been?'

'Relax. Mitchell told me you and him had already locked horns. Weaver hadn't been anywhere. He'd spent the afternoon – the whole day – at Weaver Mansion, gardening.'

'At Bishop Burton?' I said.

'Seriously impressive. Belonged to his wife's family.'

I remembered what John Maxwell had told me.

'OK, so where had *she* been?'

'You can forget that, too. She'd been to visit their daughter in York. She's severely mentally handicapped, has been since birth. In addition to being both blind and deaf. She's thirty and needs round-the-clock care. It's not a secret. They've tried to bring her closer to them, apparently, but each time it's been too disturbing – mostly for the daughter. Pauline Weaver used a big chunk of her inheritance to set up and endow the home – Oriel House, it's called, near Easingwold – to ensure their daughter gets everything she needs. There are a dozen or so others there, and Pauline Weaver's money takes care of them, too.'

'I never knew any of this,' I said, remembering what Sunny had told me a week ago about Pauline Weaver's charitable work and donations.

'Apparently, they refuse to involve or to use the fact of the girl's disabilities in any of their fund-raising publicity. It's another reason why they're happy for her to go on living so far from Bishop Burton. Besides, it's only an hour's drive, less.'

'Has everything been checked out?'

'Twice over. When the car was spotted, especially when it was tracked coming from beyond Goole and into the city centre here, Brownlow was told, who then told Lister. Lister told him to check everything personally. Apparently, he was with the Weavers at a concert at the City Hall on Saturday night when the call came in about the body. Somebody went to fetch him.'

She took a photo from her bag and gave it to me. In it, Lister stood with Pauline and James Weaver on either side of him, all three of them raising champagne flutes to the camera. A banner strung behind them announced the date, the concert and the charity they were all there to support. A sticker in the top left-hand corner announced that the picture remained the copyright of the *Hull Mail*.

'Lister's press officer let me have it. Taken less than half an hour before everything blew up in his face.'

I studied Pauline Weaver more closely, convinced that I had never met her. She was a striking-looking woman, with long dark hair, dark eyes and a slender face. Her smile, like that of both Lister and her husband, looked practised.

I remembered Lister in his dress uniform on the steps overlooking Queen's Gardens.

'Sounds like a great alibi,' I said.

'That's what Mitchell said you'd say. Forget it. They did this one by the book, and thoroughly. Someone called Weaver at home, who gave them his wife's mobile. He told them where she'd been and that he was meeting her at the City Hall later. After leaving their daughter, Pauline Weaver had been shopping in York, and had then driven back to Hull and the City Hall and had met her husband

and Lister there. Everything checks out. Someone called Oriel House. Pauline Weaver was there between two and three. She goes there, at those times, every other Saturday. From what I understand of it, I don't think their daughter even recognizes her. When she was contacted in the city centre at just after six, she told the police where she was parked. Guess what – the boot of the car was filled with the bags of shops in York. She'd bought some clothes and some shoes, some wine, books and a few early Christmas presents.'

'And she had timed and dated receipts for everything,' I said.

She nodded. 'The concert started at seven. Her tickets, along with Lister's – he was their guest – had been booked for weeks. Everybody who's anybody was there.'

'Complimentary tickets?'

'Listen to what I'm telling you. It was a big affair. The Weavers, along with Lister, had each paid a hundred pounds for the privilege of attending and being fawned upon and photographed.'

'No wonder Lister looked unhappy at being dragged out to look at the burning body of a murdered girl on his doorstep.'

'That remark isn't worthy of you,' she said, and I apologized.

'And James Weaver was supposedly gardening all day?'

'He has no independent witnesses to corroborate this, but why should he? The house is fairly secluded, the garden enclosed. He said people would probably remember the fire he'd kept burning all afternoon. Mostly damp leaves. There are a lot of trees. Plus they'd just had some pruning work done – Brownlow checked with the contractor – and he was burning the wood. His wife called him when she arrived at the outskirts of the city, and he got ready and drove in to meet her. There was a reception at the Guildhall before the concert. Weaver arrived promptly at six thirty to shake hands and offer round the canapés. Lots of very respectable and reliable witnesses now, just in case you were wondering.'

'She wouldn't drive from York to Hull along the motorway or the A63,' I said. 'The quickest way would be via Market Weighton. Coming that way would bring her back through Bishop Burton. Why the detour?'

'They checked that out, too. Market Weighton was the route she normally took, but she had no intention of going home before the concert. She'd wanted to get to the Guildhall in advance of everything to help set things up.'

'What held her up?'

'Did she drive into Goole and then back out again, do you mean? No. The traffic held her up. She drove to just beyond Shiptonthorpe and then came down to the M62. What held her up even further was an overturned tractor and trailer at Cavil.'

'Which is something else everybody checked?'

'The Howden police sent a car out at four fifty. It took them half an hour to get the road cleared. Single-file for an hour afterwards. The police were already there when Pauline Weaver arrived at the scene. She even asked the man directing traffic how long she was likely to be delayed. Both Mitchell and I have looked at the footage. It's just her in the car. You can even see some of the bags on the back seat.'

'Give me the address of the home where her daughter lives,' I said.

She shook her head. 'Any animosity you may still bear towards Weaver because of your own little run-ins with the man have nothing to do with this.'

'Paul Hendry still allegedly ransacked and then overdosed in his surgery,' I said. 'Weaver is still Susan Hendry's doctor, and he was also Lucy Collins's doctor when, in all likelihood, she had a termination. You'd have to be blind or complicit *not* to think there was something there.'

'Ouch,' she said. 'I suppose we should all be grateful that at least somebody's seeing all this clearly and rationally.' But I could see she was at least beginning to consider what I'd said, and a moment later she took a notebook from her bag and wrote down the address for me.

'I could have got this from one of a dozen other people,' I said.

'But you didn't, did you? You got it from me.'

I read the address, memorized it, then tore the paper into tiny pieces. I took these to a swingbin full of discarded food and dropped them in.

Returning to the table, I asked her if any of the forensic teams had come up with anything from Tracey Lucas's body or the molten bag. None of them had.

Petrol, unleaded, available from any of at least sixty garages, all of them local. Still nothing on the bag. Still no signs of assault prior to the fatal stab wounds. Still no indication of Tracey Lucas having struggled with her killer. And still no prints, no DNA, no fibres and nothing in the muddy rainwashed garden. A thousand footprints leading nowhere, and thousands of cigarette filters and spent matches. Discarded cans, wrappers, bottles. Bird crap, duck crap, dog crap. Sodden bread thrown for the ducks.

'It's beginning to sound like the perfect place to dump a body,' I said.

'They've looked at every camera overlooking the whole area, and still nothing. Admittedly, there are one or two blind spots. And it was dark, and it was raining.' She looked at her watch again. 'I have to get back. Lister wants a word with everyone.'

'Face-saving,' I said.

'He wants me to tell everyone what kind of a man we're looking for. I'll mention that you were asking me the same, shall I? You never know, he might want the profile making public if it's black enough.'

'I won't hold my breath,' I said.

26

I met Susan Hendry at the Waterloo Street storage depot an hour later. She was waiting for me in her car at the entrance. I pulled up behind her and went to join her. She showed me the keys she'd brought.

I followed her to an old warehouse, inside which a metal enclosure had been erected. The windows and skylights of the original building had been covered over, and fluorescent lighting now lit the interior.

A man emerged from a partitioned office at our approach.

Susan Hendry showed him her keys and said she needed to collect something.

He told her she should have given him some advance warning of her arrival, and was reluctant to let us go any further.

She told him it was important.

'Rules are rules,' he said.

She finally understood what he was telling her and gave him ten pounds.

He took the money, told her he shouldn't, and then said he'd see what he could do.

'And who are you?' he said sullenly to me.

'That's the kind of question I need advance warning of,' I said.

He said, 'Smartarse,' and went back to where he had been sitting watching a small television upon our arrival.

I followed Susan Hendry along a narrow alleyway stacked high with numbered containers. She counted these and then indicated one against the far wall of the enclosure.

'He needed notice in case we needed one of them lifted down,' she said to me. 'Fork-lift. My stuff's been sitting on the floor ever since I put it there.' She turned her key in the container lock and went to a row of portable lights hanging from the mesh wall. She tested one of these and brought it back to me.

She opened the container door and I followed her inside.

Furniture and plastic crates stood piled from the floor to the ceiling on either side of us.

She told me the size of the box we were looking for. 'It's a smaller box inside one of these crates, and marked "photos",' she said. 'I was very methodical about it all. I was always one for packaging the past away, labelling it, putting it in its place and leaving it there. Especially where Tony was concerned. It'll be down this end.'

Most of the space was taken up with the furniture and larger crates marked 'Soft Furnishings', along with the addresses from which everything had been removed, as though – and despite what she had just said – everything might one day be delivered back to the original houses and the past accurately and minutely recreated there.

She showed me mice droppings on the floor. 'They also want notice so they can come and sweep the things clean,' she said. 'The containers are guaranteed airtight and secure.'

She started to search among the smaller crates where she stood, clearing a space and then moving these from one side of the container to the other. She put several to one side, and went on looking.

I helped her to search, climbing the stacked boxes and passing them down to her.

Having searched to the container wall she said that the box we were looking for was almost certainly among those she had put to one side.

We carried seven crates out of the container and into the glare of the fluorescent lights. There was a space containing a metal table and two metal chairs where we were able to sit and look through what we'd retrieved.

Each of the crates held at least thirty smaller packets and boxes, many of them marked 'photos'.

We started searching.

After twenty minutes, she selected a new packet, opened it, and immediately said, 'This is it. It's in here somewhere.'

I cleared the table around us.

She took out a single photo and looked hard at the face of the man looking back at her from over twenty years ago. Then she pushed the picture back inside, closed the flap and laid the envelope on the table.

I slid it away from her to where I sat.

I hadn't said as much to her, but I was hoping that more than just the picture of her dead husband and Jock Boylan as boys or young men together would be revealed to us.

'Can I look?' I asked her.

'Even touching it,' she said, 'I felt something. You think every-thing eventually goes away, but it never does; it's always there, isn't it? Always there and waiting to come back at you when you least expect it to.'

I opened the envelope and spread the dozen or so photos it held across the table. They were of varying shapes and sizes, evidence of her earlier selection; most in colour, but some in black and white. The majority of the pictures had a thin white border, and some were Instamatics whose colours had long since faded.

They all contained the same man. In some he was a boy, in some a young man, and in some he was changing from one into the other.

I quickly found the picture of Tony Hendry standing with Jock Boylan. The writing on the back confirmed this. There were quotation marks around 'Jock'. The two men, both grinning broadly, were standing together at a boat's rail, their arms across each other's shoulders, their free hands thumbs-up and pointed at the photographer.

I asked her if she knew who had taken the picture.

She didn't, but guessed at another member of the crew with whom her husband had started to serve his apprenticeship.

There was a picture of a trawler, full-length and indistinct. Undecipherable in the shot, the name *Arctic Moon* was written on the back of the photo.

'Someone else must have written it,' she said. 'Tony, perhaps.'

She saw me looking more closely at the other pictures.

'You're looking for something else, aren't you?' she said.

'I was looking for the other men your husband might have known.'

'Most of these pictures were taken years before I ever knew him,' she said.

There were other men – other crew members? – in five more of the photos, but, disappointingly, none of these were captioned. Perhaps whoever had taken the pictures had believed that there was no need, that he would know these others so intimately and for such a long time to come that there was no need for captioning.

I passed the pictures back to her and asked her if any of these other men were familiar to her.

None were.

She looked for longer at the pictures of her husband, alone and among these others, grinning usually, but occasionally caught unawares.

She looked longest of all at the two pictures of the man holding their baby son. One of the shots had been taken close to the boy's birth, the other possibly a year later. It was a fragile, fraying thread, and she turned the photos over and laid her hands on them before that thread broke.

Then she slid them back to me.

'It wasn't too long after the last of these was taken that he started to lose interest in me, in the pair of us,' she said.

'There are none of you and him alone, or of the three of you together,' I said.

'Another crate, another box, another packet. Like I said, I prefer that kind of history to be kept in its proper place. Besides, I have thousands of pictures of me and Paul taken in the twenty years since.' She rubbed a hand over her eyes, as though to wipe away what she had just seen. 'Do *you* recognize any of the others?'

I told her I didn't. It was the disappointing truth.

'They'll have changed beyond all recognition anyway,' she said.

Not necessarily, but I agreed with her. And then I asked her again to think hard about any of the other names her husband might have mentioned to her. But there was nothing. Most of these men had belonged to the world he had known before the two of them had met and married. A world which had disappeared. And even during those few overlapping years of the mid-Seventies when the two worlds had briefly coexisted, they were still two separate worlds – men and women, home and away, the sea and the land, family and work.

I asked her if I could borrow the pictures. I promised her I'd take good care of them.

She gathered them together and slid them back into the envelope for me.

'I know you will,' she said. Then she reopened the envelope and took out the shot of her husband holding his newborn baby son. 'Paul's christening,' she said. 'I might hang on to it.' She put the photo in her bag.

We spent the next few minutes gathering up everything we'd searched through and returning the packets and envelopes to their correct boxes. Unseen, the past became the past again.

When this was done, we sat together at the metal table under the harsh lights without speaking for a few moments.

'You think that what's happening now – to Paul, to Tracey Lucas and all the others – you think it has something to do with something that happened all those years ago, don't you?' she said. 'You think it has something to do with my husband and the men he might once have known.'

'I honestly don't know,' I said. 'But almost everywhere I've looked has thrown up something which has pointed backwards, to the past, to thirty years ago. All I know is that something happened – I don't know what, or where, or when exactly, or even who was involved – but there's something which keeps drawing barely visible lines between the killings now and some of the men concerned – the fathers and stepfathers and brothers – who were somehow connected to each other all that time ago.' I knew how imperfect and insupportable all this must have sounded to her.

'Are you telling me it's someone my husband might have known thirty years ago who's doing all this now? That's ridiculous. Thirty years? Nobody would wait that long. It's ridiculous. I'd have known. Besides, none of the girls who've been killed were even born thirty years ago. The oldest was only, what, in her early twenties. The girl they found at the weekend was only a teenager.'

I admitted that what I'd just suggested to her made no real sense, and that I had nothing concrete to back it up.

She was clearly anxious at what I'd suggested, and I knew that it would continue to worry her long after we'd parted.

We returned the crates and boxes to the container, and when we'd finished, she took the light back to its rack on the mesh wall.

On our way out of the building, the man at the door shouted to remind her to call in advance next time.

'Next time,' she said, the words catching in her throat as the man's voice echoed above us in the cavernous space.

27 _____

Ruth McKenzie called me again as I drove back to Humber Street.

'Surprise, surprise,' she said. 'Lister thinks me telling the press what I've got is a good idea.'

'Only because he knows he has to. And because he doesn't think you've got anything. And, presumably, because by "press" you didn't mean Sunny. Not specifically.'

'Not specifically, no. But even Lister must know that nothing gets past the eagle-eyed Mr Summers.'

'And that everything *he* gets to hear about, *I* get to hear about?'

'He called you "Tweedledum and Tweedledee".'

'It could have been worse.'

'It was,' she said.

We arranged to meet at the agency later. She said she'd bring Mitchell with her.

I called Sunny and told him of the scoop I'd just secured for him.

' "Scoop"?' he said. 'How quaint. You do realize, of course, that this is just Lister beginning to cover his own back now that things aren't exactly turning out as he'd planned. The more people guessing wrong, the less isolated he looks. Alternatively, the blacker she paints the killer, the whiter Lister looks when he's finally caught.'

'And if he isn't caught?'

'Name one serial killer they didn't catch,' he said. 'And don't say "Jack The Ripper" because everybody knows who he was.'

'I don't,' I said.

'Everybody except you,' he said, and hung up.

I went to Spring Bank after the early evening traffic had died down. I took with me enlarged copies of each of the photographs Susan Hendry had given me. In addition to her husband and Jock Boylan, four other men featured, either individually or jointly, in eight out of the remaining thirteen shots. I thought I recognized Jimmy Boylan in one of these, but the scowling man with a cigarette hanging from his lips and a V sign pointed at the camera might just as easily have been someone else.

Arriving at the agency, I saw Yvonne emerging from the nearby off-licence carrying a box. She saw me crossing the road and beckoned me to her.

'Our lord and master sent me out for supplies,' she said, shaking the box and rattling the bottles it held. 'The dynamic duo arrived early. The three of them are up there now, getting cosy.'

'Why the hostility?' I said, taking the box from her.

'Because they're "them" and we're "us". And because, once again, everybody's using everybody else to their own ends in all of this.'

'Including me?'

'Including you.'

I resisted the urge to point out that she had brought Susan Hendry to me in the first place.

And as though reading my thoughts, she said, 'And don't try again to pretend that all this is being done for either Susan or Paul. Sunny thinks he's on the inside track at last. And Mitchell and whatsername think they can waltz around doing whatever they like *and* get a pat on the back from Lister for doing it. You can't seriously believe that this stupid fucking trickle-down policy is either a good idea or one Lister genuinely wants to pursue.'

'Perhaps he's letting it happen because he knows we're just as likely to come up with something by digging around in those dusty corners he chooses to ignore as he and his all-singing, all-dancing detective squads are,' I said.

She looked at me in disbelief and then moved ahead of me.

I told her I'd seen Susan Hendry earlier.

'She said.'

'Is that what all this is about?'

She slowed to let me catch up with her. 'The doctors are starting to sound openly less hopeful about Paul's chances of recovery.'

'She told me about the failed attempt to remove the ventilator.'

'It shook her up more than she'll admit. It was like watching him die.'

We arrived at the passageway leading to the agency.

'Better not keep *Ruth* waiting for her Chardonnay,' she said as Sunny let us in.

I wanted to say something reassuring to her, but I had nothing plausible or reassuring to tell her.

Inside, Sunny, Mitchell and Ruth were laughing at something as we joined them.

'Everyone having fun?' Yvonne said, and the laughter died.

Mitchell took the box of drink from her and opened two of the bottles.

We drank from paper cups. Except for Yvonne, who kept a wine-glass and a china teacup and saucer in her desk. She'd bought the wine from the fridge and it was chilled.

Mitchell came to me. 'Lucy Collins's father is a dead end. I spoke to the man Brownlow sent with him to identify his daughter. He's been confined to a wheelchair for the past year. He hasn't seen his daughter since she left home three years ago. He's never been to Hull before, knows nobody here, and has no intention of ever coming here. Apparently, he didn't even ask about the release of the body. Lucy lived with him after his wife walked out on them. She remarried a year later. He wasn't too happy about that, either, and the story is that he took it out on the girl before starting on himself. Lucy left home at the first opportunity. He didn't even know she'd come to Hull until a year after she'd arrived. Everything checks out.'

'Any particular reason for her coming here?'

'She just drifted. She could have ended up anywhere.'

Which made her different from all the other dead girls, all of whom, and whose families, had a history in the place.

'The father was awarded full invalidity benefit three years ago. MS. Whatever you might want him to be, and wherever you want him to fit into all of this, he isn't and he doesn't. He hadn't heard once from Lucy in all the time she'd lived apart from him.'

Sunny attracted our attention and said he wanted to hear what Ruth had come up with. He switched on his recorder and pointed it towards where she stood.

Yvonne applauded.

Ruth refilled her plastic cup and moved to stand at the window.

'Lister wants a psychopath,' she said. 'He's used the term inadvisably on more than one occasion in his briefings. I doubt if he's doing himself any favours. A true psychopath is devoid of conscience, remorse and self-restraint. Not our man. Having said that, however, he is not *in*capable of self-control, and in fact is often rigidly in command of his emotions.'

'First he's one thing and then he's another,' Yvonne said.

Ruth turned to face her, refusing to be drawn. 'What the true psychopath lacks is empathy, the capacity to genuinely understand or *care* what others feel. If we go out there looking for a textbook example, we're not going to find him. He's not disoriented or out of touch with reality; he doesn't experience delusions, hallucinations, or any of the other forms of intense distress that characterize certain other mental disorders.' She paused. 'What I would say about our man, however, is that – and this he does share with the common-or-garden psychopath – is that he is rational and completely aware of what he's doing, and *why*. It's why Rivers's so-called patterns interest me so much. No-one yet knows *why* any of this is happening. Our man's behaviour is the result of choice, freely exercised.'

'No voices from God, then?' Yvonne said.

'Unlikely. Prove that a pattern – a reason – exists for these killings – these women specifically – and you'll confirm everything I'm telling you now.'

Mitchell refilled all our cups.

'What really separates our man—'

'Can we stop calling him that?' Yvonne said.

'What really separates the killer from, say, the true psychotic is that he understands right from wrong.'

'And it still makes no difference?' Sunny said.

'None whatsoever. Because he's doing what he's doing for a reason that makes perfect sense to *him*. In extreme cases, you might say it was his *raison d'être*, his whole reason for living, not just for killing.'

I saw that Mitchell watched and listened to her intently, that he trusted her judgement implicitly. He must have heard her say all this a hundred times before, and so presumably he knew how accurate the vague-sounding assessment really was.

Ruth went on. 'This man kills not because he doesn't understand the difference between right and wrong, but because he doesn't *care* for the consequences of his actions, and certainly not insofar as others are concerned or affected by those actions.'

The remark made me consider all the people I'd seen or spoken to in the past twelve days – Susan Hendry, Karen Smith, the Wilsons, the Siddals, the Lucases, Jimmy Boylan – and I began to think that, in this assumption at least, she might be mistaken.

'His inability to feel guilt for his actions may in fact be his most distinctive trait.'

'Are you suggesting he may even feel *justified* in doing what he's doing?' Sunny asked her.

'Oh, certainly. And when we finally discover what connects the killings, then that self-justification will be loud and clear. Because, believe me, you won't hear any expressions of remorse.' She drained her cup. 'On the plus side of all this, we have also to remember that, in addition to being deceitful and manipulative, the killer certainly likes to exercise power over others, will undoubtedly possess good social skills, and be highly persuasive.'

'Christ, it could be me,' Sunny said.

'Especially the bit about exercising power over others,' Yvonne said.

'And he won't be concerned when his crimes and deceits are finally exposed,' Ruth said. 'If one lie is uncovered, he'll spin another and be just as convincing. These people always prefer grand, long-term strategies and fantasies to anything short-term or too realistic. They're superior beings, and they've probably known it all their lives.'

'Anything more specifically personal?' Sunny said. He checked his recorder.

'A tendency towards narcissism, usually with an inflated view of their own self-worth and importance.'

'Like Lister?'

'Exactly like Lister, but on the other side of the mirror,' Ruth said, her tone even and serious.

'And the body being dumped on his doorstep was the killer flagging up his superiority?' I said.

'Among other things.'

'So the killer thinks he's the centre of the universe?' Sunny said.

'You're angling for a headline,' Ruth told him. 'But, yes. The centre of his own little universe, egocentric, and with a strong sense of entitlement.'

'What does that mean?' Yvonne said.

'It means he feels he's owed,' Mitchell told her. 'It means he's getting what he believes he richly deserves.'

'By killing the girls?'

'He may lack the range and depth of the feelings other men possess,' Ruth said. 'But he feels more than justified by living according to his own rules. And whatever happens to him – whether he remains uncaught until he dies, or if he's caught tomorrow and is locked away for the next fifty years – he will see no reason to change his behaviour or his belief in himself and what he's doing.'

'You'd think these people would stand out a mile away,' Sunny said.

'Some do,' Ruth said. 'But they possess all these traits and then never break the law. The world's full of little tinpot tyrants taking everything out on their uncomplaining families, wives and kids, and who then present themselves as Mr Wonderful to the world at large.'

'Is that what this one's doing?' Sunny said.

'He's certainly not running round with his knuckles trailing on the ground and slaver pouring from his mouth,' Mitchell said.

I told Ruth that a number of the men I'd come across over the past days fitted at least part of the picture she was drawing.

'But the one trait most of *them* actually have in common is that they're dead,' Yvonne said.

Jimmy Boylan wasn't dead. Don Lucas wasn't dead. Martin Siddal wasn't dead. Lucy Collins's father wasn't dead.

No-one spoke for a moment.

'Do you still think he's being protected by someone?' Yvonne asked Ruth.

'Family, friends. Somebody knows him. They might not know for certain what he's up to, but they know him and they must have their suspicions.'

'Lister's teams still get twenty calls a day telling them who the killer is,' Mitchell said.

'Most of these men go on doing what they do because the people around them make allowances for them, out of loyalty, fear, whatever,' Ruth said. 'And because they're allowed to go on behaving as they do, so they feel justified in continuing. It's another of those vicious circles. As far as they're concerned, if they go unchecked or unpunished, then they *deserve* to go unchecked and unpunished. It makes perfect sense to them.'

Sunny changed the tape in his machine. 'Anything else?'

Ruth shook her head. 'That's it. That's the outline. That's what I told Lister and his men. It would defeat the object trying to fill in any more detail. Lister might hope I'm going to come up with the killer's initials, but it's this broad outline that's going to serve him best, especially where all his public pronouncements are concerned. One more thing to bear in mind, though – and this relates to *all* serial killers, not just the psychopathic ones – is that a serial killer invariably either *knows* his victims or he knows something supremely relevant about them. And he checks their movements beforehand. *Nothing is left to chance.* Factor chance or random opportunity-taking into this particular equation and you start moving in completely the opposite direction to the killer. Everything he does, he does for a reason.' She looked at me. 'And, yes, allowing for that, it's likely that these specific women were chosen by him for a very particular reason.'

Mitchell went to her briefly and put his arm round her. And only then did it occur to me that he and she had sat in front of these men she was talking about. Sat in front of them and spoken to them, listened to them tell their self-justifying lies and breathed the same air these men were breathing.

I glanced at Yvonne, and saw that she, too, had perhaps come to the same realization.

'One last thing,' Ruth said, waiting until she had our attention. 'These people do not recover. It is never an option. It is not what they want. Recover from what? They do not get "better" and change into you or me. And they cannot be "cured". The world and everyone else in it is wrong. The world and everyone else in it is mad or evil. *They* are not.'

Yvonne took a second wineglass from her drawer, wiped it, and then went to Ruth and poured the wine from her cup into it.

'You've got two?' Sunny said. They had worked together in the agency for seven years.

Ruth thanked her with a nod.

'What was Lister's response to all this?' I asked her.

'The impression I got was that he thought everything was a bit too all-inclusive – something he, Brownlow and the others might just as easily have come up with themselves if they'd had the time to put their heads together over a few drinks. When you're obsessed with evidence, evidence is all you look for.'

'And evidence isn't proof?'

'It's the first thing they teach us,' Mitchell said.

'You amass details, facts, figures, statistics, timings, distances, places, who knows who, who did what to whom, and where, when and why,' Ruth said. 'The best I can do is stand back from all that pictures-on-the-board and arrow-drawing stuff and hope that somewhere in there one of my own indeterminate and messy outlines begins to emerge. It might not be any help in actually finding the killer, but it will come into its own once he's caught and all the after-the-arrest stuff starts.'

'Do you think he'll confess to everything if he's caught?' Sunny asked her.

'It's more than likely. Except it won't be a confession as such, more a triumphant justification, an attempt to persuade everyone else to see the light.' She seemed suddenly exhausted by everything she'd just told us and she wiped a hand across her face.

'And Lister would swap all that for a single-witness photofit of a middle-aged man of medium height and medium build, brown eyes, brown hair, wearing brown trousers and a brown top,' Sunny said.

Ruth left the window and went to sit beside Yvonne.

Sunny asked her if he could use her name in the articles he wanted to write.

'Lister said it would be OK.'

'He'll probably pull out all the stops and refer to you as "Top Police Profiler",' Yvonne said to her.

I gave Mitchell copies of the photographs and he studied them as I told him what I thought they contained. He wrote on the backs of them and asked me what I wanted him to do with them. I asked him to show them round and to try and identify the unknown men. I told him how old the pictures were.

Then I gave Sunny copies. He, too, recognized none of the men.

I showed Yvonne Susan Hendry's husband. She had never known the man.

She looked hard at his young and smiling face. 'All I know is what Susan's told me,' she said. 'You wouldn't guess anything from looking at a picture.' She touched her glass to Ruth's. 'To serial-killing men,' she said.

'Women have done the same,' Ruth told her.

'To them too, then,' Yvonne said.

28

I drove to Oriel House the next morning. The building lay a mile from the A19, two miles south of Easingwold. Following Pauline Weaver's route of three days earlier, I timed my journey via Goole, Cavil and Shiptonthorpe from the centre of Hull, and even with the York ring road traffic, it took me less than an hour and a quarter.

The stone-built house stood in its own grounds, and was completely hidden from the road by an enclosing belt of tall, dark pines. It was an impressive-looking building of three floors with a porticoed double doorway, six high windows at ground level, and seven on the floors above. With its meticulously kept lawns and flowerbeds, it continued to look more like the family home it had originally been than the institution it now was.

Car parking was in a hedged compound to the rear of the building.

Mitchell had already spoken to the man on Brownlow's squad who had visited the place two days ago, and he in turn had passed the details of Pauline Weaver's visit on to me.

I didn't know exactly what I was there to confirm or discover, but the whole story of Pauline Weaver's visit and return journey and arrival in Hull city centre on the night Tracey Lucas's body was dumped there continued to ring false to me. Just as the security guard's recollection of being called to the alarm at the Walker Street surgery on the night of Alison Wilson's killing continued to sound its own wrong and echoing note. Even though, as yet, I had no real idea what these distant coincidences might signify.

I parked at the end of a row of cars and walked to a rear entrance. There was an intercom and a combination lock on the door, and I was about to press the buzzer when a man pushing a wheelbarrow emerged from the path running alongside the car park.

'Help you?' he said to me, apparently unconcerned at seeing me there.

'I tried the front,' I lied. 'No answer. Same here.' I touched the doorframe beside the buzzer.

'They'll be busy. You've come at a busy time.' He came closer to me, and then turned on to a path leading beyond the cars.

'Everything looks good,' I said, indicating the garden and stepping away from the door.

'I'm just maintenance, really,' he said. 'They have contract gardeners, but I usually end up going round for an hour after them clearing up their mess. Who are you here to see?'

'Mrs Ellis,' I said. She was the woman in charge of the place. Her name appeared alongside Pauline Weaver's as both manager and a trustee on the letterheads.

'Not one of the patients, sorry, *residents*?'

'I'm here in connection with Mrs Weaver's visit last Saturday.'

He grew considerably more interested.

'I told that other man they sent that they ought to leave that poor woman alone, that what they were implying was ridiculous.'

'It was she who insisted I came,' I said. 'Everybody knows what a waste of time it is, but she insisted she didn't want any special treatment just because of who she was. Me being here is just a technicality, really. You seem better informed than most.'

'Covering her back, so to speak?' he said.

'Something like that.' I left the doorway, anxious now not to be seen by anyone inside. 'You sound as though you think a lot of her,' I said, encouraging him further.

'I do,' he said. 'We all do. I tell you – she's the nearest you're going to come to a saint, that woman.' He, too, looked anxiously at the building, as though someone might be watching him. 'Look,' he said. 'I can't stand here; I'm meant to be working.'

'I'd still appreciate being able to talk to someone who knows the ins and outs of the place,' I said. 'I'd hate to get in the way of any of the nursing staff. In fact, I'd probably get a better feel of everything from you than from Mrs Ellis.'

He smiled at this, and continued walking beyond the car park, pausing slightly to ensure that I was following him. The lines of raked gravel which radiated from the building were as clean and as neatly edged as the lawns and the flower-beds.

We passed a paved area lined with bins and several skips, and beyond that, concealed even from the hidden cars, was a small, square brick building with a green metal door and a solitary mesh-covered window. He unlocked the door and pushed his wheelbarrow inside.

I followed him in.

He closed the door behind me and switched on the light.

He indicated the machinery the building housed.

'Emergency generator. Hardly ever used these days. I'm meant to be testing it.' He hung up the tools from the wheelbarrow and sat on a bench beneath the window.

'So Pauline Weaver was definitely here,' I said.

'Of course she was. Comes every other Saturday. Always looks me out to say hello. Most of the rest of them treat me like I count for nothing.'

Mrs Ellis included, presumably.

'But not Mrs Weaver?' I said.

'Always makes a point of coming for a chat. Usually it's only for a minute or two, but she always comes. Especially recently. I think it's probably on account of how she felt about all that other business.'

I resisted asking him what he meant.

'It was all on file,' I said. 'Came up when her registration was run through the computer.' I feigned a lack of interest.

'Yeah, well, let's all hope we've heard the last of that. For all our sakes.'

'Agreed,' I said. 'Especially hers.'

'Right.'

'The file just repeated mostly what Mrs Ellis had told everyone.'

'I'll bet it did. Yours truly got raked over the coals, of course. They're always prepared to listen to some and not to others.' He did nothing to disguise the sense of grievance he still felt at whatever had happened.

'You could give *me* your side of things,' I suggested.

'It's got nothing to do with what's happening now.'

'I know that. But it might just help Mrs Weaver,' I said, hoping he wouldn't question the logic of this connection.

'She was the only one who stood up for me,' he said angrily. 'Not even her—' He stopped abruptly, suddenly conscious that he might have said too much.

'Not even her husband,' I said. 'I know. It was all there in the file.'

'He said their daughter should never have been allowed to come in here in the first place.'

'In here? This was where it happened?' I looked more closely around his small domain.

'Where they *said* it happened. She used to sit in her chair on the lawn. She needs constant attention, of course, but she's not as *demanding* as most of them. I used to talk to her. No response, naturally, but she knew I was there, and you can easily kid yourself that something of what you say or do is getting through to her. I used to wheel her round here to listen to the generator when I started it up each week. Supposed to be deaf, but she always used to get excited when I started the thing up. Perhaps it was the vibrations. I used to put her hands on it for her. She used to slap her palms on the casing. It's practically the only time I ever saw her respond to anything.' He paused. 'Who knows – I might be imagining it all.'

'And the place was definitely out of bounds to her?' I said.

'Of course it was. Once a week, that's all. And even then she was only here for ten or twenty minutes. I always used to wheel her round and then take her back to wherever she'd been. Have you seen her yet, Angela?'

'No.'

'It'll shock you.'

'Her disabilities?'

'It's more than that. You'll know what I mean when you see her.'

'How did it happen?' I asked him.

'There was a delivery. Kitchen. It came late and there was nobody else to see it in. It was four boxes. It only took five minutes, and most of that was walking there and back.'

'And you left Angela Weaver alone in here while you went?'

'I pushed her to the open door. She can't do anything for herself. She certainly wasn't going anywhere. Five minutes, I was away. Five minutes. Ten at the very outside.' Meaning it was probably closer to twenty.

'It's all in the report,' I said.

'Is it? And is it in the report that that fu— that that man must have been watching and just waiting for me to leave her, that he must have known she was here all along?'

I shook my head.

'Thought not. He'd only been here a month, new arrival. Came from a hospital in Cardiff or somewhere. Rooms in this place are like gold. He could walk. Hated being cooped up inside, apparently, so they let him out into the grounds. Supposed to be someone keeping an eye on him. I don't suppose *that* particular bit of negligence was in the report, either.'

'Not that I remember,' I said.

'Yes, well, it was still me who got it in the neck for wheeling her in here in the first place. And then for leaving her – *abandoning*, they said – for those few minutes.'

'Sadly, it was long enough,' I said.

He looked at me angrily for a moment. 'I know it was long enough. But what do they all think happened in that time? "Sexual

Assault"? Don't make me laugh. She was twisted up in that wheel-chair tight as a fist. There were restraints holding her in. Her clothes were all . . .' He tailed off.

'The report said her clothing may have been disturbed.'

'I bet it did,' he said. 'But it was just her top' – he patted his chest once, dismissively – 'just that. It wasn't anything, you know, more serious.'

'The report said Angela was very distressed.'

'I'm not denying it. But that doesn't mean to say she had the faintest idea of what was happening to her. That bastard had just gone in and surprised her. She didn't know who he was. Everything just got blown up out of proportion after that.'

'And you're convinced no actual serious sexual assault took place?'

'When I tried to tell them that a year ago they just said that *any* assault – sexual or not – was serious under those circumstances.'

'And, presumably, Pauline Weaver's husband endorsed that view.'

'Christ, did he blow a fuse. If it wasn't for his wife telling him to calm down and consider what was best for their daughter, I'd have been out on my arse there and then.'

'What happened to the other patient?'

'Sent back to where he'd come from less than a week later. Good riddance. Old woman Ellis had already involved the police – had to, I suppose – but Mrs Weaver managed to persuade everybody that their priority now ought to be her daughter.'

'And you think things got brushed under the carpet?'

'There's nothing so certain. It's the only reason I got to keep my job.'

'Even though you were still the one everybody held responsible for what had happened?'

'Ellis certainly did. Mrs Weaver came to see her to tell her not to blame me. She stayed on for a week or so, just to make sure that what had happened hadn't, you know, had any effect on her daughter.'

'And did it?'

He shook his head. 'How could it? A day later and she was exactly the same as she'd always been. It was just something that had caught her unawares and scared her because she didn't know what was happening. They all have their routines, see? It's how they get from day to day, what keeps them happy.'

'But you believe Doctor Weaver continued to hold you responsible for what had happened?'

'His wife said not, but that was the impression I got. He came with her the day it happened and was here for a couple of days afterwards. Then he went while she stayed on. They have a room here. Christ, I've never seen anyone so angry. He looked as though he wanted to punch me when he found out how I'd left her like that. When Mrs Weaver tried to make him see sense, he even shouted at her – in front of everybody – and told her not to tell him what to do. To be honest, it was all a bit embarrassing. Ellis was there, the police were there. I felt sorry for his wife. I felt angry for myself and sorry for her. It was why it meant so much to me afterwards when she came to tell me that *she* didn't blame me and that my job was safe. I remember it was the day before my birthday – the fifth of August – and she even said Happy Birthday to me when I told her.'

'What happened after their argument?'

'It wasn't much of an argument, as such. Just him shouting at her.' He thought for a moment. 'He waited until the police were finished and then he just drove off without her. She stayed with their daughter. To be honest, I was just glad to see the back of everyone that day, give things a chance to blow over.'

'There was never any follow-up,' I said.

'I know. Will you tell Mrs Weaver you talked to me?'

'Of course.'

'Give her my regards. Tell her how much I still appreciate everything she did for me.'

'Did you speak to her last Saturday?'

'Briefly. She said she was going out for the evening. Some big do in Hull. She told me how much she was looking forward to it. She said the traffic coming had been heavy and she asked me if I thought going down to the motorway would be a faster journey back into Hull.'

'What did you tell her?'

'I didn't know. I rarely go to Hull.'

We were interrupted by a sudden loud ringing from beside the silent generator. It was a phone I hadn't seen.

'Internal,' he said. He picked it up and listened as someone spoke to him.

Hanging up, he said, 'They want me at the front. They want the leaves clearing off the drive.'

'Where will Angela Weaver be?' I asked him.

He looked at his watch. 'Day room, probably. They won't be outside on a day like this. But I doubt they'll let you see her. At least not without Ellis checking with Doctor Weaver. That's been the arrangement ever since it happened. Besides, what good is seeing her going to do anybody after all this time?'

'It might be preferable to having to sit through Mrs Ellis's word-perfect story all over again.'

He smiled, and then he indicated that it was time for us to leave the small building. I saw again what a refuge it was to him.

'She was never allowed to come back in here after that,' he said sadly. 'Understandable, I suppose, but I bet she misses coming. Ten minutes, once a week, that's all it was.'

We went outside, and he told me that if I still wanted to talk to Mrs Ellis then I ought to return to the front door.

I told him there didn't seem much point after all he'd been able to tell me, and I asked him which of the rooms was the day room.

He indicated three windows at the far side of the building. 'They won't like it if you go sneaking round, trying to look in,' he said.

'At least I could tell Pauline Weaver that I'd seen her daughter,' I said, again exploiting his high regard for the woman.

'Follow me,' he said, and he led me to a laurel hedge which bordered a path close to the building. He pushed his head into the glossy foliage. 'You can see in from here.' He stood to one side, allowing me to look through the gap he'd created.

The day room was large and lined with empty chairs. A television stood at one end. Several of the patients sat around the room, most of them sitting apart and alone.

'Is she in there?' I asked him.

He looked through the gap beside me.

'By the door,' he said. 'Where she always sits.'

I looked at the woman sitting beside the door. She was slumped in a wheelchair, her body twisted to one side, and her head down against her chest. Her hands were bunched into loose fists and folded back on her forearms. I knew she was thirty, but at that distance, and seeing what little I could of her, her age seemed indeterminate. She might have been eighteen or she might have been fifty-eight.

'Wait,' he told me, and I continued watching.

After a few minutes, the woman slowly raised her head, blinking her sightless eyes, and turning from side to side as though she were listening for something. Her mouth was open and her tongue lay on her bottom lip. Her hands began to agitate.

'Get a good look,' he said. 'She won't hold it up for long. Now you know what I meant when I said you'd be shocked if you hadn't seen her before.' He stood back from the hedge.

I knew exactly what he meant.

Despite all her disabilities, and despite the uncontrollable tremors which shook her, the woman I was looking at was the younger image of Pauline Weaver.

'I knew that'd get you,' he said.

I'd only seen Pauline Weaver in the photograph Ruth McKenzie had given me, but there could be no mistaking her in the features of her daughter. As I watched, the woman's hands stopped shaking and she slowly lowered her head until it was again resting on her chest.

'You've only got to look at her mother to see what she might have been,' he said. 'How hard must *that* be for the pair of them to see each time they come, especially Mrs Weaver?'

I stepped back from the hedge.

'If that was my daughter, I wouldn't—' He stopped talking as the door beside Angela Weaver opened and a woman entered the room. 'It's Ellis,' he said.

The woman came directly to the window and looked to the hedge.

'Can she see us?' I said.

'She can see through brick walls, that woman.' He walked quickly away from me to where the hedge abutted the building and then turned the corner. I could hear his rapid footsteps across the gravel.

I walked in the opposite direction, back to my car.

When I reached it, Mrs Ellis was there ahead of me, talking on her phone. As I approached, she moved to stand directly in front of me.

'I don't know who you are,' she said. 'And I'm not interested in hearing your lies.'

'I'm following up Mrs Weaver's account of her movements on Saturday afternoon,' I said.

'And you do that by talking to *him* instead of me, do you?'

'We were chatting, that's all.'

'Of course you were. And now you'll probably tell me the same lie you told him and pretend you're from the police.'

'I'm not,' I said.

'Then I shall ask you to leave and not to return without the proper authorization. I shall, of course, inform Doctor Weaver that you were attempting to see his daughter. What's your name?'

I told her and gave her one of my cards. She was surprised by my compliance and stood to one side as I got into my car. She reminded me of the overprotective receptionist I'd encountered in Weaver's surgery. Perhaps the woman then had been thinking of Weaver's daughter when she'd referred to my 'insensitivity' in questioning Weaver concerning the discovery of Paul Hendry. It was unlikely that she wouldn't have known about Angela Weaver. And perhaps it was why Weaver and his wife employed people like her and Ellis – to safeguard their interests and to patrol that carefully maintained and measured distance between their private lives and the lives they lived in the glare of all that equally carefully cultivated publicity.

I wound the window down. 'I don't want to cause Angela Weaver any more distress,' I told her. 'I hope you're able to reconsider talking to James Weaver on that understanding.'

'I think that's *my* decision, don't you?' she said.

I left Oriel House and drove back to Hull, this time returning via Bishop Burton. The journey to the village took me forty minutes.

29

There was a call from Emily Carr waiting for me on my return. She said she wanted to see me. She sounded scared. I'd completely forgotten about my promise to find her a locksmith after our drink together four days ago.

I called her back and she answered immediately.

'I just called to let you know that I'm going away for a few weeks,' she said. 'Living here is doing my head in.'

'Where are you going?'

'I've got some mates who live out at Withernsea. They rent a holiday chalet there for the off-season. It'll be a squeeze, but they've said I can go. It won't be for long.'

'Has anything happened?' I asked her. I tried to sound concerned, but in truth I still believed she was overreacting to what had happened, and my mind was still full of everything I'd just discovered at Easingwold.

'What do you care?' she said.

I apologized to her. And for not having organized the locksmith. 'Something important may just have turned up,' I told her.

'What do *I* care?' she said, and then she, too, apologized.

I asked her to give me the Withernsea address and her mobile number. She gave me both and I wrote them down. I asked her when she intended leaving and then offered to drive her to her friends. It was a forty-five-minute journey from Nelson Court.

'I can manage,' she said. 'I've got a few things to do before I go.'

'I'll call you if anything turns up – anything to do with Paul or Lucy.'

'I doubt if it'll make any difference,' she said. 'Not now.' She hesitated. 'I think that man came back.'

'What man?'

'The one I told you about. The one trying the door.'

'You have to call the police,' I told her.

She laughed. 'Yeah, right. Why should I? Even you don't believe me. That's one of the reasons I'm getting out for a few days. Perhaps when they catch whoever it is, then I'll come back.'

'It's not that I don't believe you,' I said. 'It's just—'

'It's just that you don't believe me and because you think I'm being ridiculous. Well, I'll tell you something else that sounds ridiculous – remember I told you I thought Lucy had been seeing someone regularly before all this happened?'

'I remember,' I said.

'Well, I can't be a hundred per cent, but I swear that the man I saw this morning is the man she was seeing. I recognized the coat he wore.'

'Are you sure?'

'I just told you – I'm not completely certain; it's just the coat. I was on the stairs and he couldn't see me. He was definitely looking in, though, as though he was hoping for someone to open the door for him.'

'If you tell the police all this, and that you think Lucy was see-ing someone other than Paul Hendry – for whatever reason – then at least they'll have a record of the fact.'

'Very good – "for whatever reason". And then they'll probably think exactly what you're thinking now. Right, like I said, things to do, places to go.'

'I'll call you,' I said.

'You said.' She hung up. She'd expected more of me and I'd let her down. I considered calling her back and insisting on driving her to Withernsea when she was finally ready to go, but I knew she'd check to see who was calling and then deny me both my apology and this pathetic attempt to redeem myself.

My phone rang the instant I put it down. It was Brownlow.

'Congratulations,' he said.

'What for?'

'I take it that was you at Oriel House two hours ago.'

'Who's suggesting that?'

'Oh, please.'

'Did you know – did *anyone* know – that James Weaver's daughter was sexually assaulted there last year?' I said.

'Hey, we all missed it. All ten thousand of us. Thank God for real detectives like you. Of course we knew about it. And "alleged" is the word. What's it got to do with anything now? The man involved has been in a secure unit back in Cardiff ever since it happened. Hey, guess what – we checked.'

'And?'

'And he's still there. I'll ask you again – what do *you* think it's got to do with anything now?'

I admitted that I had no idea.

'*Did* you know?' I asked him.

'York CID dealt with it. They told us everything. It had nothing to do with us. Just like it *still* has nothing to do with us. It had nothing to do with us then, and it has nothing to do with us now. I don't know if I can make this any clearer for you.'

'It happened five days before Rebecca Siddal was found after allegedly hanging herself,' I said. 'Remember her? And remember the coroner saying she'd probably been dead and hanging for at least three days?'

'What the fuck has she got to do with any of this? Is this Mitchell and his big mouth? Jesus Christ, I've seen people grasping at straws before, Rivers, but this is going straight to the top of my list. And not only are you grasping, you're grasping at something you don't even know is there. Christ Almighty.'

'And you're making this courtesy call, why? To tell me to stop upsetting people beyond your jurisdiction? I don't think so. Go on, admit it – you're doing Lister's dirty work for him. Again. Ellis calls Weaver, Weaver calls his good friend Chief Superintendent Lister, and Lister, understanding the protocol of these situations better than any of you, decides to wipe the dirt off on you.'

'York police might still want to talk to you,' he said.

'I doubt it. Not now the funny-handshake route's been taken. Ellis could have called them while I was there. Makes you think, doesn't it?' I hung up before he could say anything in reply.

Sometimes you could move round and round a problem in ever decreasing circles, holding everything at arm's length; and sometimes it was better to get close, poke it hard and then step quickly back out of reach. It seldom mattered to know which approach might produce the best results.

An hour later, following a walk to Victoria Pier and the aquarium to clear my head, I called John Maxwell, hoping he might have found out more about what had happened to Pauline Weaver's father thirty years ago. But there was no answer.

I left him a message saying that I'd been to see Weaver's daughter, uncertain what part her own blighted existence – or whatever might or might not have happened to her fourteen months ago – played in any of this, but convinced now that, along with all those other, lesser echoes of the near and distant past, it meant *something*.

30 _____

Hoping to avoid a visit from Brownlow, I left Humber Street and drove back to Bishop Burton.

I called the Walker Street surgery from the car and asked to speak to Weaver. The young receptionist who answered told me that he had a number of patients waiting to see him, and that talking to him was out of the question. Having confirmed that he was there, I told her it was a private matter and that I'd try again later.

It was a crisp, bright afternoon fading quickly to darkness, and the road through Bishop Burton was bordered with fallen leaves. The yellow streetlights were already on around the green and the pond and amid the naked trees.

I had avoided visiting Pauline Weaver because so far she had seemed to play no part in what was slowly unravelling in front of me; because everyone else involved knew what I thought of her husband and might consider any approach to her in the same light as they were already seeing my 'persecution' of him. And because, despite her own pleas to be treated no differently to anyone else caught up in Lister's rapidly burgeoning and unwieldy investigation, it seemed unlikely to me that she wouldn't still possess a direct line to Lister himself – either through her own friendship with the man, or via any of the members of the various committees on which she served. The photograph of the three of them together holding up their champagne flutes on the night Tracey Lucas's body had been dumped and set alight convinced me of that.

My visit to Oriel House and discovering what had happened to her daughter there meant that leaving her out of my enquiries was no longer an option.

I pulled off the road a few minutes from her home and called her.

She answered immediately, and I knew from her tone of voice – enquiring, anxious – that she had been expecting someone else.

I told her who I was and that I would appreciate being able to see her. From what I already knew of her husband, I imagined neither of them were people who appreciated being confronted un-expectedly or directly.

She told me she was at home. I also knew from her tone that she already knew that I had been to Oriel House, and that she had in all likelihood been forewarned of my probable arrival in Bishop Burton – either by Mrs Ellis or by Lister himself. I wondered if this also meant that her husband knew I was on my way there, too. My hope was that she would want to talk to me alone. Alerted of my likely approach, she could just as easily have left the house and remained out of contact all day.

She gave me directions to her home.

It was a house similar in many ways to Oriel House: imposing, set apart, hidden, perfectly maintained, and possibly saying every-thing anyone looking in from the outside would ever need to know about its owners.

The high, wrought-iron gates were open as I arrived. A camera and sensor registered my arrival, and as I turned into the drive, the gates swung silently shut behind me. I followed the drive around a giant Cedar of Lebanon and a bed of glossy rhododendrons to the house.

A solitary car stood parked at the front. The drive continued for at least two hundred yards beyond the house to a group of distant outbuildings. The smell of burning leaves filled the cold air.

I rang the bell and waited. Another camera mounted beside the door registered my arrival there. The intercom clicked and Pauline Weaver told me to come in and to walk directly ahead. She was in the garden at the rear of the house.

I saw her through the glass of two doors and a conservatory. She stood beside the smouldering mound of leaves.

Entering the conservatory, she came in to me, taking off her gloves and scarf.

I had anticipated some hostility – a degree of reluctance or reserve at the very least – but she smiled at me and offered me a drink. She pressed a button on the conservatory wall and ordered tea for us. Then she indicated where we might sit. It was a warm room. Vines grew over our heads, still dotted with small bunches of unpicked and immature grapes.

She was a tall, elegant woman, with the well-preserved looks common to the wealthy. I guessed her to be in her mid-fifties. She was lightly and evenly tanned, and her dark hair was cut to rest on her shoulders. She wore no jewellery, not even rings on her fingers, and the first thing she did upon removing her gloves was to rub these with cream. Her teeth were even and white, and when she smiled, the small muscles of her cheeks rose in her face.

'Mrs Ellis called me,' she said. 'I imagined you'd come.'

Which meant that either Brownlow or Lister had confirmed who I was.

'She said you had no wish to cause our daughter any more alarm. I'm afraid Angela is more or less delighted and alarmed entirely at random and for no good reason one way or the other these days, but I appreciate your intentions.'

'Are you saying the assault on your daughter was more traumatic for you and your husband than for her?'

' "Assault"?' she said. 'It always sounds considerably more than it probably was.'

'It was enough to have the man concerned taken away.'

'I know. But what alternative was there? *I* might have been prepared to give him a second chance—'

'But your husband wasn't?'

'Neither he nor Mrs Ellis considered it wise to allow him to remain there. There had already been other complaints made against him. They were only doing what they believed was best for Angela. Did you see her – Angela, I mean?'

'Only through the window.'

'It was probably enough. I fool myself into believing she recognizes me – us – but it's a long way from the truth of the matter. It's perhaps just something that I *need* to believe in. Otherwise why bother visiting?' She turned and looked out over the garden. The mound of leaves still smoked vigorously, the column of pale smoke rising thirty feet into the cold air before flattening out and falling again. It already lay in vaporous patches across the grass.

A woman came into the conservatory with a tray. Pauline Weaver thanked her and told her to leave it. She asked the woman about her husband and the woman answered her like an old friend.

'He works for us in the garden,' Pauline Weaver said to me when the woman had gone. 'But he suffers. His back, his legs, his chest, various joints.' She almost laughed as she said it.

It struck me only then that she was little different from Susan Hendry: each of them looking after children already lost to them; each of them shaped and defined by those children and those losses.

'You went alone to see Angela last Saturday,' I said.

'I often do. James is a very busy man. He needs to relax. I'm afraid he's considerably less deluded than I am where Angela is concerned. Perhaps because of his profession. Besides . . .'

'You appreciate the opportunity to be alone with her?'

She nodded, her eyes still on the smouldering leaves. 'I can talk to her and pretend she hears and understands me – even that she's answering me – when it's just the two of us. James spends just as much time questioning Mrs Ellis and the staff as he does with Angela. He assesses and makes changes to her medication, her regime.' She paused and turned to me. 'Tell me, Mr Rivers, did it shock you to see her?'

'I was surprised by the resemblance,' I said.

'Most people are. Not that she has many visitors, of course. Some people, I imagine, still prefer to believe we keep her at arm's length, but since we found and established Oriel House when Angela was only three, we've always believed that her being there was for the best. Both James and I lead very busy lives.' She indicated the wellingtons and scarf. 'This is one of my rare Lady-of-the-Manor days.'

'Tell me about Angela,' I said.

'I thought you were here to lay your suspicions concerning my husband before me,' she said.

'I still can't ignore the fact that Lucy Collins was one of his patients, as Susan Hendry still is, or that her son was discovered in his surgery, apparently having ransacked the place.' It was as much as I was prepared to reveal to her, and she considered this.

'I understand all that, but why do you – and you alone from what I understand of the matter – insist on still seeing that as part of what's happening elsewhere? Susan Hendry had been James's patient for twenty years, and Lucy Collins for several years at least.'

'Because it isn't happening *elsewhere*,' I said. 'It's happening *here*. And I know that what happened to Paul Hendry and Lucy Collins might appear to be a separate and self-contained case, but I still believe it isn't something that should be dismissed entirely from the wider inquiry.' I was conscious now of revealing something that Lister might not already have told her.

'Even if all it does is continue to confuse the issue?' she said.

'A week ago, the police were still releasing statements telling the world that Paul Hendry was their only suspect.'

'Just as Alexander Lister believes now that you are adamant that the boy's overdose following the killing of his girlfriend is part of this because it's the *only thing* which still connects my husband to the overall inquiry.'

'What, and that as personal vendettas go, it has no real foundation?'

'I know my husband,' she said. 'I can imagine his response to your accusations and inferences. It's the way he is. He makes no claim to wanting to be a likeable man. He does what he does, and he does it well, and thousands of people benefit from that. He has always insisted on working, ever since he qualified. It would have been easy for him, having acquired all this, to have chosen a completely different and equally fulfilling path in life.'

'I understand all that,' I said, wondering how much her defence of the man was intended either to suggest or to conceal.

'And I certainly won't apologize to you on his behalf,' she said. 'I'd probably need to set aside a day every week if I was serious about appeasing all the people James upsets or offends. And nor will I deny that I often wish he could see his way clear to doing it on his own behalf every now and then.' She held her saucer almost to her chin and drank her tea. 'I went alone to see Angela on Saturday because I wanted to take the opportunity to go into York and find something to wear that evening. It was why I went earlier than usual – to give myself more time. I returned via the motorway because it was never my intention to come back here. I went directly into Hull and met James at the Guildhall before the concert at the City Hall.' She closed her eyes for a moment. 'Mahler, Mr Rivers?'

I shook my head.

'A pity. He's a favourite of mine. Alexander was there, of course.' She opened her eyes. 'But you know all this already. I must have arrived before the body was found because I had no trouble in making my way through the centre and parking.'

'And your husband met you at the Guildhall?'

'He did. He'd been here all day.'

'According to him.'

'Of course.'

'You were driving his car.'

'My own was being serviced. I believe Detective Sergeant Brownlow has already been in touch with the garage. They sent someone to pick it up on Friday and then they brought it back yesterday. I took James's car because he had no intention of going anywhere. Later, when it was time for him to meet me in Hull, he called a local taxi firm.'

'Which Brownlow will also have checked.'

'James gave him the name and number. I assume someone checked. I can give you the number, if you like.'

I told her it wasn't necessary.

'As you please,' she said.

She'd diverted me from the girl once. I asked her again to tell me about her daughter.

She took a deep breath and brushed her arms, as though she had grown suddenly cold in the overheated room.

'We were informed that Angela would be born with some degree of disability, but we were not aware of the true extent of that disability. And before you ask – no, abortion was never considered because we found all this out far too late in the pregnancy. It might only have been thirty years ago, but it was a different age altogether as far as that kind of diagnostic capability was concerned. We were told there was a strong likelihood of brain damage, but none of us had the faintest idea of what this might amount to until *after* Angela was born. Whereupon, of course, it became immediately and unavoidably evident to us all how she was likely to be affected and what form her own particular combination of sufferings would take.'

The story sounded like one she had told often, but I still heard the distant notes of affection and disbelief in her voice as she told it.

'Angela was born seven weeks prematurely,' she said. 'And that, along with everything else that was clearly wrong with her – I think that was the word: "wrong" – suggested to everyone that she would not survive for very long. Everyone was warned about this, and so everyone made the most of the short time we were likely to have with her. For twenty-four hours she was completely silent. And then she cried. A nurse remarked that she was hungry and that she was letting us all know this.'

Her breathing became deeper, as though this was a small but vital part of the story, and one she had not so often told.

'What did you do?'

'What else *could* I do? I fed her, of course. I fed her and she stopped crying. James was with me all the time. And my father.

James was still a medical student, and my father had been unwell
– his heart – for years. He was sixty-seven when Angela was born;
forty-four when my mother gave birth to me. I told both of them
what I intended to do – to feed a crying child – and they both
concurred with my decision. I think I did it as much for their sakes
as for Angela's.'

'Or your own?'

'Yes, or my own. I fed her and she survived. That was all it took.
After forty-eight hours they told us she'd be lucky to survive for a
week; and after a week they told us a month. Even at her twenty-
first birthday they were telling us that there was still a strong
possibility that she would die prematurely. It was clear to us even
then, during that first precarious month, that she was going to
require round-the-clock attention for the rest of her life. James
finished his studies, qualified, and then he and I moved abroad, to
Belgium, for three years. My father had a house and business
interests there. The birth of Angela shook him up. He wanted to
do whatever was best for her. He knew a doctor, a place in Brussels
that could care for her. James and I were on our knees after everything that had happened, and we agreed to go with him.'

'And three years later, you came back here. Why?'

'Because my father died, Mr Rivers.'

I regretted having asked her. I tried to remember if I'd already
been told the reason for their return.

'And because, after three years of waiting, after living with my
father, James was anxious to start work, to set up his own practice
if possible. He couldn't do that in Belgium. This was still the
family home. I think we both just wanted and needed some
stability, a way of moving forward again, and to be somewhere we
knew we *belonged*. For me, that could only be here. My father's
funeral took place in the church here. There's a family plot.'

'Is that why you relinquished your hold on the supermarkets?'

'That happened when my father died. The big chains were keen
to buy him out. Without him, it more or less just happened.
Shareholders. Neither James nor I were against selling up. They
were worth a considerable amount – more than enough to allow us

to buy Oriel House and set up the foundation there. Certainly enough for all our needs and to ensure the best possible treatment for Angela for the rest of her life – however long, or short, that might prove to be. The truth is, we'd been away too long, and despite having acquiesced to my father's wishes concerning Angela, we'd probably not done the right thing in going away and cutting ourselves off from all this. Angela's disabilities meant that it hardly mattered where she was cared for or treated, but both James and I felt the growing need to come home and to begin to rebuild our lives here. I'd say that, on the whole, we've been successful in all we've set out to achieve. We both love Angela, and we are both aware that she may now outlive us.'

'Did you ever consider having further children?' I asked her.

She put down her cup and saucer before answering me. 'I wasn't able to.'

'Because of Angela's birth?'

She smiled at me. 'I've answered all your questions, Mr Rivers, and I'm quite prepared – despite my husband's antipathy towards you – to accept that you believe in your convictions, but there are some things you have no right to ask of me or to pry into.'

I apologized for the question.

'Do you believe that Angela's birth and the upheaval this caused had some bearing on your father's death?' I said.

'Of course it did. And of course it's entirely unprovable – is that a word? – and something that no-one else could ever possibly understand.'

And again the similarity between herself and Susan Hendry struck me: two women and two children, all four of them the remnants of families sustained by history and tradition, all of which had all suddenly and unexpectedly ended.

'I ought to get back to the leaves,' she said. Outside, it was now more night than day. The remark was her signal that our conversation had ended.

She had told me nothing that a dozen other people wouldn't be able to verify or confirm.

I put down my cup, and was about to stand when the front door opened and then slammed shut, and James Weaver shouted to ask where she was.

Pauline Weaver showed no alarm at this sudden and unexpected appearance, and she called back to him, her composed tone deliberately tempering his own.

I rose to confront him. He appeared at the conservatory door. He was clearly angry, and looked ready to grab me and push me from his home.

He came quickly to me and stopped a pace from me.

'Why didn't you call me?' he said to his wife, his eyes fixed on mine.

'Because I knew this was how you'd react,' she said. She remained seated, further defusing this confrontation.

'And so instead I have to hear from Mrs Ellis via the surgery.' He held his finger to my chest. 'You had no right – no right whatsoever – either to attempt to see my daughter or to come here and make your ridiculous accusations to my wife.'

'He didn't,' Pauline Weaver said. She raised a hand to his arm to calm him. 'He wanted to know about Angela, that's all.'

'And you *told* him?'

'Of course I did. I hope I also made it clear to him that we refuse to treat our daughter as though she were a dirty little secret, something to be hidden away.' She gave a slight but telling emphasis to the word 'our', as though to remind him of his own obligations to the girl.

He lowered his finger and grew calmer.

'You shouldn't have left the surgery,' she said.

I wondered why he hadn't called her and told her to stop talking to me. Perhaps he wanted this confrontation. Or perhaps he wanted to know, in my presence, what I might have already revealed to her.

He took several paces away from me.

'Then I apologize, Mr Rivers,' he said reluctantly. He stood for a moment as though he was going to hold out his hand to me, but the gesture was beyond him, revealing his true feelings.

'See?' Pauline Weaver said to me. 'He can be a perfectly decent, rational human being when he puts his mind to it.' She smiled fondly at her husband, but Weaver made no attempt to return this conciliatory gesture.

'I was just leaving,' I told him. 'I appreciate all you've told me,' I said to Pauline Weaver, and shook her hand.

'Believe me, both James and I want to see an end to these terrible events as much as you do,' she said. She looked to her husband for his agreement, but he was no longer listening to her, and was now standing at the window with his back to us watching the burning leaves.

'James?' she said.

'Of course,' he said, unable even to turn and face me.

31

Despite all that Pauline Weaver had just revealed to me, I was still unwilling to accept that no connection whatsoever remained between the assault on her daughter fourteen months ago and the alleged suicide of Rebecca Siddal only two or three days later. Nor was I ready to accept as coincidence Jimmy Boylan's solitary memorial to his long-dead brother amid the page full of tributes to Rebecca Siddal, and especially not now that Susan Hendry had confirmed her own dead husband's long-lost friendship with Boylan's brother.

I was also convinced that there was a great deal that Jimmy Boylan hadn't told me during my visit to Woodcock Street. In particular, I wanted to know more about his brother's brief period on remand, about the events leading up to that imprisonment, and about the others involved.

I felt as though I had the two halves of a torn picture in my hands – two halves which looked as though they should fit perfectly together, but which didn't, which revealed when they were matched up that a thin missing strip still kept them apart and the whole picture incomplete.

I felt discouraged by the fact that I was even allowing myself to think like this. Yvonne, I knew, preferred the missing-pieces-of-the-jigsaw approach to detective work; or, failing that, the unravelling-of-loose-ends approach. I knew what convenient and misleading metaphors these were, as deceptive as they were supposedly illuminating, and far more readily accepted by others than by any of the people involved. Yvonne had once accused me of taking all the mystery and romance out of what I did. I'd said the same of her own Lonely Hearts compilations.

I drove to Woodcock Street. It was five in the afternoon and the bars would be long open. I wasn't hopeful of finding Jimmy Boylan at home. Here, too, between Hessle Road and the Humber, the narrow streets were lined with leaves, but unlike in Bishop Burton here they were already flattened and dirty and wet, settling in the gutters like old snow.

I knocked on Boylan's door and heard movement inside.

I knocked again, kicking the plastic panel and shouting to be let in.

After a minute, he shouted to ask me if I was alone. His words were mumbled and I hoped he was more sober than he sounded.

I told him that if he didn't open the door I'd go to Brownlow with my suspicions concerning his involvement in the death of his niece, and see where that led us all.

He laughed in relief and disbelief at hearing this, which was no more than the empty threat deserved.

The door opened a minute later, delayed by its two chains – neither of which had been engaged at my last visit – and Jimmy Boylan tilted his head to look out at me through the gap. He told me to stand to one side to allow him to check that I was alone. I continued to feel encouraged by everything he said and did.

It was difficult to see him clearly in the dim light, but it was immediately obvious to me why he was so reluctant to see me. One of his eyes was closed completely and lost beneath a dark bruise the size of an egg. His other was barely open, and there were bruises on both his cheeks and cuts on his forehead and chin.

He slid out the chains and opened the door fully, stepping

behind it as I entered. Once inside, he immediately locked it and replaced the chains.

Around me, the already untidy room was now in complete disarray, its contents overturned and scattered.

And seeing him like that, I knew immediately that another important connection had just been made, that the past and present had yet again moved unexpectedly and violently together and collided in this small, dilapidated house.

He mumbled because his mouth, too, was swollen and cut. Fresh blood still showed on his lips and was smeared on his cheeks. He held his arm awkwardly against his chest, as though it were already in a sling.

I asked him if he wanted me to take him to the hospital.

'What do *you* think?' he said. He kicked aside the clutter between the door and his chair beside the fire.

'Was it Wilson, Alison's stepfather?' I asked him.

'It hurts when I laugh at stupid questions,' he said. 'So stop coming the fucking innocent. You probably even told him where I lived.'

Three days had passed since my previous visit. I'd told no-one except Sunny, Yvonne, Susan Hendry and Mitchell that I'd seen him or how I'd found him.

'I didn't tell anyone,' I said.

'Yeah, right.' He dropped into his chair and picked up the near-empty whisky bottle from beside it. 'You'll be telling me next that you and me are on the same side,' he said. He touched the side of his mouth with his finger and looked at the blood there. There was a cut where his lips joined which refused to stop bleeding.

'When did this happen?' I asked him.

'Earlier. What a surprise, you turning up a few hours afterwards. Come to make sure the job was done properly? Come to make sure you got your money's worth?'

'Whatever you think I did, you're wrong,' I said. 'Tell me who did it.'

He looked at me closely. 'First you tell me why you thought it was that fucker Wilson,' he said.

'I didn't. I just couldn't think of anyone else who might know where you were. Except the police, of course; and I doubt if even Brownlow would be stupid enough to leave you looking like this. And because I knew how you felt about Wilson taking the place of your brother. I thought you might have contacted him. Unless what you told me was just another of your lies.'

'I never lied to you,' he said angrily.

'Perhaps – but you still only told me the smallest part of what happened to your brother. Just enough to satisfy my curiosity and to keep me at arm's length from everything.'

He'd been no different from any of the others in that respect – either telling me what they thought I wanted to hear; or only providing me with information that might have been easily verified by any number of others.

'Everything you told me about Jock, you said it as though you hadn't been with him. "Too pissed to run, *by all accounts*," you said. You were lying. You knew exactly how drunk he was, because you were with him. Besides, you didn't really tell me anything, except in the barest outline. What were you hoping I'd go away believing – that everything had been lost in the "mists of time"? You lied to me, or at the very least you told me only a tiny part of what had happened – which meant you were hiding something.'

'I told you—'

'You told me nothing that led to anything. You also said that there wasn't anyone left from thirty years ago who still *cared* for your brother – not that there wasn't anyone who didn't still *know* him – and you – after all that time. You said you'd never heard of Rebecca Siddal, which was probably true, but I bet the name rang a bell because of her father.'

'And that's why you came back, is it?' he shouted. 'To get the rest of that endless fucking story?'

I indicated his face and arm and the room around us. 'It looks as though somebody else already knows everything there is to know,' I said. 'Who was it? *Was* it Brownlow?' I needed to keep prompting him.

'Him? Ten minutes he spent here, the day after Alison was

found. Ten fucking minutes. Just long enough to confirm that I hadn't seen any of them for the past three years. What the fuck did *he* care about anything except his own fucking part in it all?'

'I know this has nothing to do with him or the Wilsons,' I said. 'But I also know that it has everything to do with *why* your brother's daughter was killed – and probably why the others were killed, too – and one way or another you're going to tell me. And you can either do that now, here, just the two of us, and I can then take what you tell me and add it to everything else I've found out and tried to put together in the past fortnight. Or I can send Brownlow round again and let him see all this – you – and make up his own mind about how involved you are in everything that's happening. Believe me, he'd come. He's a desperate man with a lot to gain and even more to lose.'

I sounded more confident than I felt.

He put down the bottle and sat with his face in his hands for a moment, wincing at the pain this caused him.

'None of it's going to bring either of them back, is it?' He meant his brother and his niece.

'Nothing was ever going to do that.'

'It was Don Lucas who did this,' he said eventually.

'Don Lucas?'

'Told me he'd stayed over after Lister's press conference especially to see me. Said it was all he could do to stop himself from accusing me publicly in front of all the cameras.'

'Accusing you of murdering his daughter?'

'I didn't even know her name. I didn't even know he *had* a daughter.'

'You had nothing to do with her death,' I said.

'Try telling *him* that. Two of his mates drove from Goole to meet him here. Said he'd found me in the phone book. Besides, he remembered where I lived.'

'Remembered?'

'From all those years ago, from when him and Jock worked the boats together.'

'He knew your brother?'

'Long time back. I recognized him from the picture in the papers. I tore it out and put it on the mantel. It was the first thing he saw when him and the two others pushed their way in here. He said it was all the proof he needed. He accused me of having gone to the law. That's when all this happened.'

'But why does he blame you for the death of his daughter?'

'He doesn't, not really. Punch first, work things out later, that was always Don Lucas's way. It's how he operated thirty years ago, and it's how he goes on doing things today.'

'But all this *is* connected to what happened thirty years ago?'

' 'Course it is. It's why he left Hull and went to Goole in the first place. His father had a bit of clout. *He* was the one who applied for the transfer for his son. Everybody pretended the offer had come because all the work here was being run down, but it wasn't. He went because his father thought it best to get him out of the way until everything died down.'

' "Everything" being?'

'That trouble I was telling you about.'

'The trouble connected to your brother's arrest and imprisonment?'

He nodded and retrieved the bottle.

'And Don Lucas escaped while your brother was locked away and missed your mother's funeral.' I tried to remember everything else he'd told me.

'Everybody said afterwards that it was Jock getting into trouble like that which broke her heart and killed her. They never said it to my face, of course, but I could always imagine them whispering it behind my back.'

'Tell me what happened,' I said.

'Why should I?'

'Because sooner or later, Brownlow or Lister is going to hear about this, and then you'll have to tell it all to them – probably in a room at Queen's Gardens while Brownlow tries to make *you* fit into all the empty spaces he's currently looking at.'

'That'll happen anyway,' he said. 'What good will telling you now do me?'

'Because perhaps I already know enough about what happened,' I lied. 'And because I can go from here with whatever you tell me and continue pushing elsewhere, and by the time Brownlow gets to you I might have something or someone more interesting for him to look at.'

'Someone like Don Lucas?' he said dismissively.

'You're not stupid,' I said. 'You know that the minute Brownlow gets wind of what happened here, you'll be his number-one suspect all of a sudden and all anyone will do then is sit and watch your bruises change colour while they wait to charge you with something. Even if it's only perverting the course of justice. And that's still a big charge in an inquiry like this.'

'And he'd get wind of it because you'd tell him?'

'Lick your lips,' I said. 'That's blood you can taste. Who do *you* want to come back to you? At the very least, I can tell Brownlow that you told me Don Lucas did this to you. Not very good PR for Lister to have his public-sympathy figure number two going round doing this behind his back. Plus, of course, whoever *is* responsible for the deaths of Alison and the others moves further and further down Lister's list of suspects. You're in the spotlight, they're back there in the shadows. Men get convicted and imprisoned unjustly; others, the ones with blood on their hands, walk free for the rest of their lives.' Yvonne would have been proud of me.

He considered all this. He passed the bottle from hand to hand and then shook it towards me. I took it from him.

'Wipe the top,' he said.

There was blood on the rim. I wiped it and drank from it. It was a gesture, but an important one, and I knew as the first raw burn of the cheap spirit caught my throat that he would tell me what he knew. The beating had scared him, and Lucas had no doubt threatened to return.

'I was still on the trawlers,' he said, and this opening sounded almost mythical, Hull's Once Upon A Time, a story belonging to everyone. 'Jock was on another boat. He was the youngest of them all. Lucas, Tony Hendry, Philip Smith and Martin Siddal were in the same crew. There were others, but they're the ones I remember. There must be pictures of them all somewhere.'

'There are,' I said. 'And apart from Lucas and Siddal, they're all dead,' I said, already making more guesses and calculations than I could properly grasp or fully understand.

'Give the man a cigar,' he said. 'And don't forget me – I'm still alive. Just.'

'Were you ever in the same crew?'

He shook his head. 'No, I never worked on the same boat as Jock. The owners didn't like it – not two men from the same family on the same boat. It would have come, but later.'

'Except there never was any "later"?'

'I was just his older brother looking out for him.'

'What about Lucy Collins's father?' I said.

'Never heard of him. Nobody called Collins ever had anything to do with any of this. Listen, those six names are seared onto my brain. If there was anyone called Collins involved, then I would have remembered him. Are you listening to me, or what?'

I nodded. I had other questions for him, but first I needed to hear what he had to say.

'They came back from a trip and sailed to Grimsby instead of back here,' he said. 'There was a salvage yard interested in the boat. The *Arctic Moon*. The owners wanted rid of it. They'd been away for nearly three weeks. The first any of them knew about the boat being decommissioned was when they reached the Humber. Most of the crew came off at Grimsby and the owner sent a bus for them. It was before the bridge, and a long way round. Jock and the others were told to stay with the boat until the salvage man had been to see her. She wasn't going to be broken up there and then. They'd unload her and then bring her back to Hull a few days later. They were all just lads, really.'

I passed the bottle back to him.

'I had a car, an old Ford. I drove round to them. I wasn't working. Jock rang me to let me know what was happening and then suggested that I go to meet them. He said they were having a night on the town. It was what we'd planned to do in Hull when he got back.'

'So you went to Grimsby instead?'

Before the Humber Bridge, this involved a round trip of over seventy miles, following the estuary inland and then back seaward to Grimsby. Despite facing each other across the water, Hull and Grimsby were foreign places to each other.

'I met them in a bar close to the docks. It was early, seven-ish, but you could tell they'd already been drinking for a good few hours. I was never really one of them, not properly, on account of not working on the same boat, but they were happy enough to have me there – probably because I'd got the car. They were staying on the boat overnight. I was going to stay with them and then come back to Hull the next day. Jock was going to come with me.'

He paused, composing himself. He seemed surprised by how easily he was able to recount all he was remembering, and I was grateful for this.

'And something happened that night?' I said.

He nodded. 'The pubs shut at eleven. By which time they were all drunk. Drunk? A couple of them could barely stand. Jock had already been sick twice, but he kept on drinking so as not to lose face. They were fishermen on their first night ashore, lads playing at being men. They all thought then – regardless of what they were doing there – that it was what lay ahead of them until they retired or died, that it was all going to last for ever.

'At eleven they were out on the streets. Someone – Tony Hendry, I think – said they should go to a club. Some were for it, some against. Don Lucas said he had a better idea, said they should all go and look for some women. He was a year or two older than the others – my age – and he said he knew Grimsby and where to start looking. They all pretended to be keen on the idea – what else could they do? – and so they followed him towards the town centre.'

'Looking for prostitutes?'

'I suppose that's what they were. I just went along with it all – as much for Jock's sake as my own. It was clear that Lucas didn't particularly want me there, but he wasn't in a position to do anything about it.'

'And did they find any women?'

He laughed. 'They arrived where Lucas said they'd all be queuing up, and there wasn't a single one in sight. He asked a man swilling out a pub doorway where they all were and the man told him they were too late, that there was a navy boat in and the sailors had all arrived hours earlier. When he saw the look on Lucas's face, he laughed at him, and Lucas head-butted him, knocked him to the ground, into all the water and sick, and then started kicking him.

'After that, they all ran back in the direction they'd just come. Jock was still barely able to stand upright and so I helped him and we followed on behind. We could hear them running and shouting and cheering themselves ahead of us. Neither of us knew where we were, but all we had to do was follow their voices to where—' He stopped abruptly.

The room around us was now in almost total darkness. He sought the lamp which had stood by his chair and switched it on. It lay on its side. The shade had become detached from the base and the bare bulb cast long shadows all around us. He turned up the fire and held his hands close to the grille.

'There was a woman,' he said, his voice lower. 'Young. A girl, really. Lucas and a couple of the others started shouting to her. She crossed the street to get away from them. It must have been obvious to them that she wasn't a prostitute. It would certainly have been obvious to Lucas, who was doing most of the shouting. The trouble was he was desperate to save face in front of the others. He crossed the road to her, talking to her, telling her not to be scared. He told her he had money, that they all did. She began to panic. She told him he'd made a mistake. I don't know why, but I got the impression she was lost, that she shouldn't have been where she was, that she didn't belong there. I expected her just to tell Lucas to fuck off, but she didn't. Instead, she started trying to explain herself to him, trying to reason with him. Fat lot of good it did her. Everything she said to try and keep him away from her, he took it personally. She didn't even *sound* as though she belonged there. It was like Lucas thought she was making fun of him in front of the others.'

'Was there no-one else around who could have done anything?'

'It was a street somewhere between the docks and the town centre, not residential. There was a high wall and lots of entrances to yards. Industrial. It's probably why I thought the girl was lost in the first place.'

'Did *you* try and intervene?'

'I tried. It didn't amount to much. I'd had a fair bit to drink myself. I was more concerned with getting Jock back to the boat. I probably made Lucas even madder than he already was. You've seen what he's capable of now. This is nothing to what he was like when he was younger. They were all scared of him. Even then, he had a reputation as a hard man. Anyway, by then Jock was being sick again and I had my hands full looking after him. I suppose I thought Lucas would have his fun and then leave the girl alone.'

'And that didn't happen?'

'He had his hands on her by then. He told her he knew exactly what she was and what she was after. She went on trying to reason with him, trying to convince him that she wasn't what he thought she was. I couldn't really hear much of what she said because her voice was low and she'd started to cry. All I could really hear was Lucas yelling at her. He took his wallet out and pushed it in her face. I think one or two of the others might have been having second thoughts by then, but none of them were either brave enough or sober enough to stand up to Lucas. I don't suppose any of this lasted for more than a few minutes.'

'It probably seemed a lot longer to her,' I said.

'I don't need *you* to tell me that. He hit her. She said something to him that I didn't hear and he just hit her. Punched her hard in the face. And after he'd punched her once, he went on punching her. Face, stomach, everywhere. He pulled her coat open and started groping her. I think that by then we all knew things had gone too far. Tony Hendry tried to pull him off, and so Lucas hit him, too. By then the girl was on the floor. She might even have been unconscious. Lucas went back to her and kicked her. Hard. Like he kicked me this morning. She was trying to push herself upright, off the ground, and he kicked her again before turning back to the rest of us.'

'Did *none* of you try to help her?'

He shook his head once. 'Like I said – I had my hands full with Jock.'

'It's an excuse,' I said.

'I know it's a fucking excuse. I know I should have fucking done something. But I didn't. OK? And I'll tell you something else I fucking know – I've been paying for that one act of cowardice for the rest of my fucking life. Jock paid for it then, and I've been paying for it ever fucking since.' He paused and calmed down. 'And now it looks as though we're *all* being made to pay for it.'

He meant all the dead daughters of all the men involved.

'What happened then?' I said.

'We heard a siren and legged it. I don't know, somebody must have seen or heard something and called the police. Probably thought it was just another fight in the street. Lucas was the first to start running. Everyone else just followed his lead. The car was there seconds later. The girl was still on the road where Lucas had knocked her down, and Jock was still sitting on the kerb being sick. I tried to get him to stand up and start running, but, like I said, he was incapable.'

'And so you left him there?'

'I didn't know what else to do, not then, not with the siren and the lights and everything, and not with the girl lying on the ground twenty feet away. I just told Jock not to say anything, that I'd find him later, and then I ran after the others.'

'And so your brother was the only one the police got their hands on.'

'I thought they'd see how drunk he was – how young – and that it would be obvious to them that *he* couldn't have done anything to the girl. They must have known there were others involved. They must have seen us, or at least have heard us running away. I expected them to come after us in the car, but they never did. I suppose they had to stay with the girl. And with Jock sitting there looking at them from across the street where she lay, I suppose they imagined they'd got all that they needed to leave everything else until the morning.'

'Did the rest of you get back to the trawler?'

'We were up the rest of the night while Lucas told us what to tell the police when they came. He wanted us to tell them it was all Jock's doing.'

'They wouldn't have believed that,' I said.

'They might have done if we'd all said it.'

'And you refused?'

'Of course I fucking refused. What do you think I am?'

I let the question hang between us for a moment, until he lowered his head and rubbed a painful hand over his face.

'How soon afterwards did the police come?' I asked him.

'That's just it – they didn't. We waited, but they never came. Lucas called the boat owner the next afternoon and told him we were all done with the salvage people, and the owner told him to bring the boat home. The original plan was that the skipper would drive round and bring her home, but it was only across the water and Lucas was more than capable. They sailed at six that afternoon and no-one tried to stop them, no police, no harbour master, no nothing. I saw them off and then I drove home.

'When I got back I told our parents what had happened – I lied and just said we'd been involved in a fight, and that Jock, though having nothing to do with it, had been the only one to get caught. My father even laughed when I told him about it. I suppose I didn't really think it mattered *what* I told them, that the Grimsby police would be in touch fast enough when they'd worked out what had happened. I still expected everything to catch up with us on this side of the water.'

'And it never did?'

'That's the next strange thing – no-one ever came looking for the rest of us. Jock went straight from their cells to the magistrates' court to the detention centre at Brigg because the Grimsby police refused to grant him bail.'

'Pending their investigation and the likelihood of him being charged and tried for assault?'

'If there ever was any investigation, then neither he nor I ever heard about it. That's what I'm telling you – *nothing happened*, there was no follow-up. We all just scattered, got our stories straight, kept our heads down, and *nothing happened*.'

'Why do you think that was?'

'Lucas tried to persuade us it was because he hadn't really hurt the girl and that she'd been a prostitute all along, and that the coppers who found her would know that.'

'And because no-one pressed charges on her behalf?'

'Perhaps it's the kind of thing that happened all the time. Perhaps it's just the kind of place Grimsby was.'

There was some truth in what he was suggesting, but he was still making excuses. And looking at his own cut and bruised face now, and having seen Lucas at Lister's press conference, I couldn't believe that his attack on the girl hadn't left her similarly injured, if not worse. Similarly, and regardless of whether or not she had been a prostitute, I couldn't believe that someone wouldn't have wanted her attackers prosecuted.

He saw that I remained unconvinced by these vague explanations.

'I'm only telling you what happened,' he said. 'The next thing, our mother was bad. She'd been suffering for some time, but all this – especially when we heard that Jock was being sent to Brigg – had a serious effect on her.'

'Did you ever tell her what really happened?'

He shook his head. 'Not then. And not afterwards when people started saying that what had happened to Jock was what had killed her. How could I? If anyone knew the truth of it, they'd say we'd *both* had a hand in her death. I never even knew the girl's name. Lucas said she might have been under-age, and that even if an investigation *was* being carried out, they probably wouldn't name her.'

'And none of you were in a position to try and find out what was happening.'

'We were all just relieved to be back on this side of the water and away from it all. We started to believe everything Lucas told us –

that she couldn't have been badly injured. And when Jock was released after six weeks and came home to just me and our father, we were all convinced it was over and done with. A near call, but that we'd scraped through because no-one over there was pressing charges or even looking for us to find out what had really happened.

'It was bad enough then, just after our mother's funeral, but the next few months and then years got a lot worse. All three of us were out of work for years at a time.'

He stopped talking after that, his story over, the past ended, its aftermath endured, and the long and disappointing decline of the present still being lived. He again raised the bottle to his lips, but by then it was empty.

It was hard to accept all he had just told me. It tied all the murdered girls together, and for that I was grateful – it gave me leverage over both Lister and Mitchell – but I still couldn't believe that no-one had insisted on the Grimsby girl's assault being properly investigated and her attackers brought to justice.

Or perhaps he was right – perhaps everything *had* happened like Lucas had persuaded them, and perhaps Grimsby was just that kind of place.

I also understood something of the tangled knot of guilt, remorse, complicity and responsibility he himself now felt – not only for what had happened to his younger brother, but also for what had happened to their mother and the family she had held together; and then for what had happened all these years later to his brother's only child. If he did feel any guilt for what had happened to the girl in Grimsby, then it was nothing compared to the guilt he now felt for all these other deaths.

'There wasn't even anything in the local papers,' he said. 'There or here. One useless detective showed up to ask us a few questions, but that was only to do with Jock being in Brigg, to check on the details he'd given them, and nothing to do with the assault itself. I didn't see Don Lucas again until at least two years later. He'd settled in Goole by then. Most of the others were already out of work. Lucas couldn't help himself: he was still bragging about what they'd gotten away with. He got my back up. I hated him for what he'd been prepared to allow to happen to Jock.'

'Not for what he'd done to the girl?'

'That, too. But if I'm being honest, it was mostly for what might have happened to Jock. I told him then that if the police ever did come sniffing around, I was going to come clean and tell them exactly what had happened. He told me I was bluffing because of what would happen to me and my precious baby brother if I did.'

'And because then your father would have known.'

'I know. And perhaps he, too, would have blamed us for his wife's death. I know.'

I rose from my seat, already starting to calculate the significance of all he'd just revealed, and where it pointed me.

'What will you do now?' he said, as though reading my thoughts.

I told him I didn't know and made no effort to make the remark sound like anything but the lie it was.

'Will you tell all this to Brownlow or one of the others?' I asked him.

He nodded. 'It's hardly going to hurt Jock now, is it?'

'I doubt if it's going to hurt any of them,' I said. 'Lucas included.'

I counted off the names on my fingers: Martin Siddal, Philip Smith, his brother, Tony Hendry and Don Lucas. In that order. Four daughters, one son. Four dead girls and one boy dying slowly in a coma. And all that time and wasted energy directed at Lucy Collins because she was a girl and a known prostitute.

Then I remembered a remark he'd made earlier.

'Who was the sixth man?' I said.

'What?'

'Six names,' you said. 'Six names seared into your brain.'

He thought about this and counted on his own fingers. 'Billy,' he said suddenly. 'Billy Carr.'

And I felt the name like a blow.

'What?' he said.

'I've met his daughter. I spoke to her only a couple of hours ago.'

But he seemed unaware of what I was telling him, or

unconcerned, lost in the confusion of his own thoughts and blighted memories.

I left him, and outside I called Emily Carr's mobile, but it was switched off. I left her a message telling her to get in touch with me as soon as possible. I gave her Sunny's number and told her that if she didn't want to speak to me, then to call the agency and talk to either him or Yvonne. I told her that if she was still in Hull and didn't want to go back to Nelson Court, then to go to the agency on Spring Bank and tell Sunny that I'd sent her.

I had no number for the friends she had said she was going to stay with in Withernsea, only their address. I heard her telling me that her own father and Paul Hendry's had known each other before either of their children was born.

Then I called Mitchell and left him a message telling him I needed to see him urgently.

I called Sunny, told him what I'd just told Emily Carr, and said I'd be there to see him in a couple of hours. I told him I was on my way to Withernsea to try and find her, and that if she turned up at the agency then he was to keep her there and to remain with her, whoever called or arrived. I told him I didn't have time to explain myself and hung up as he started questioning me.

Then I went briefly back into the room where Jimmy Boylan still sat beside the fire, starkly illuminated by the bare bulb of the lamp, and still with the empty bottle wedged between his knees. He was sobbing convulsively, and shaking.

Five months ago, there had been him and his niece, the last two members of that dwindling family. And now there was only him, and he was old beyond his years, and more alone than even he had ever believed possible. The remorse and guilt he had contained for all those years were like savage dogs inside him, and it seemed to me now, watching him there, crying and shaking in the wreckage of the house in which he had been born, that he had finally decided to stop trying to keep those dogs from tearing him apart and destroying him completely.

I told him I was leaving, but I doubt if he heard me, and I pulled the white plastic door shut on him.

32

The drive to Withernsea took me forty minutes. The city traffic was at its worst, but it thinned by Salt End, and beyond Hedon, out in the flatness of Holderness, the roads were empty.

I continued to call Emily Carr as I drove, but there was still no answer. I left the same message each time, knowing how alarming I was beginning to sound with every repetition.

Arriving at Withernsea, I quickly found the holiday camp she had mentioned. Only a small number of the caravans and chalets were currently occupied and I soon found the couple I was looking for.

The man who answered my knock said Emily had never showed up. He was unconcerned, at once dismissive and suspicious of my own concern. A girl Emily's age came to stand beside him. Both of them had long hair fastened in clasps. He had three piercings in his left eyebrow and she had three matching rings in her right. The right-hand side of his nose and upper lip were pierced, and again she mirrored this with left-hand studs. The pair of them stood framed in the warmth, music and aroma of the small room behind them.

'Stop bothering us,' the girl said. If Emily showed up, then that was cool. If she'd decided not to come, then that was cool, too. 'What's your problem?' she said.

'I think Emily may be in danger,' I told her.

'Yeah, right,' she said. 'And you're the only one who can help her out, right? Fuck off.'

'What kind of danger?' the man said, making a joke of the word.

I didn't have time to persuade him. I gave him my card and sixty pounds. 'If she calls or shows up, tell her I was here and tell her to call me.'

'And the cash is ours whatever happens?' the girl said. 'Cool.'

I ignored her. 'Keep the card handy and tell her to call me right away.'

He gave me their number and I left them and ran back to where I'd parked my car at the centre of the site.

It was almost seven when I arrived at the agency. A wind had risen, and this blew the rain hard against one side of the car.

Mitchell and Ruth were already waiting there for me. Mitchell started asking me questions the moment I arrived.

I asked Sunny to check the answering machine.

'She hasn't called,' he said.

Mitchell persisted with his questioning and I told him to wait while I called John Maxwell.

He answered after a dozen rings. To avoid repeating myself, I motioned for Sunny to make a note of what I said.

I asked John Maxwell if he knew anyone on the force who was working in Grimsby in the autumn of seventy-five. There was a long silence while he considered this.

Beside me, both Sunny and Mitchell started making notes.

I told John Maxwell about the assault on the girl and I recited the names of the six men involved. Sunny and Mitchell exchanged glances, both starting to make their own guesses about what I'd uncovered.

John Maxwell told me he'd do what he could for me.

'It needs to be done now,' I told him. 'Tonight, as soon as possible.'

He didn't ask why. I gave him the agency number and told him I'd be there for only a short while before returning to Humber Street.

Hanging up, I gave Yvonne Emily Carr's number and the number at Withernsea, and told her, whatever happened over the next few hours, to ring both continually to see if Emily had arrived there.

She, too, accepted this without question.

Ruth McKenzie took the list of names from Mitchell and studied it.

'You're saying these are revenge killings for something that happened thirty years ago? That all these men are connected through something in which they were all involved, and that the present killer – presumably someone connected to the *victim* then – is getting his own back only now?' She did nothing to hide her incredulity at the suggestion. 'After thirty years? Why? It makes no sense. If the killer knows what he knows, why not do all this thirty years ago or let the police in on what he knows? You haven't thought this through. Whatever you've worked out, you've worked out wrong. This doesn't happen. You're wrong.' She looked to Mitchell for his support, but he said nothing, and I saw by the anxious glances they then shared that she too was not as convinced of this as she tried to sound.

'Tell us,' Mitchell said to me, and I repeated everything Jimmy Boylan had just told me.

Sunny said he had a reliable contact in the Grimsby police force. He found the number, dialled it, asked for the man and then hung up. His contact was off-duty. He dialled again, and this time the man answered. He told him what little I'd just told John Maxwell and then listened closely as the man spoke to him.

Hanging up, he said, 'He isn't hopeful. Everything was fully computerized twelve years ago. Partial reorganization five years before that. The National Police Computer was still in the process of being set up in seventy-five. Even twelve years ago it was still almost a twenty-year-old crime.'

'And then only if it was an ongoing or open investigation,' Mitchell said.

'Which it probably wasn't,' I said.

'Or if they have fingerprint or DNA evidence waiting to be tested and matched.'

'Equally unlikely.'

'Or if there was a coroner's inquest for any reason and an open verdict was returned,' Ruth added.

'Ditto. So far, nobody died.'

'There might still be some paper record of it all,' Yvonne suggested, but without any real conviction.

'We don't have time to waste on that kind of outside chance,' I told them.

Yvonne asked me who Emily Carr was in relation to Billy Carr, and I told her.

'The last child on the killer's list,' she said.

'Her father was definitely involved,' I said.

'Six men,' Mitchell said. 'Including Hendry and Collins, there have already been six killings. Carr would make seven.'

'I don't think Lucy Collins's murder was part of the sequence,' I said. 'I'm not saying the same man didn't kill her, but I think her death was something unplanned, something spontaneous and necessary to the killer because of her connection to Paul Hendry. I don't know how those two deaths are connected, but they are, and through Hendry's attempted murder they're connected to the others. Paul Hendry was the killer's real target, not Lucy – it was *his* father involved in the original assault, not hers. All the other men had daughters somewhere down the line. Tony and Susan Hendry only had one child, a son, Paul.'

Ruth started to make a call and Mitchell stopped her.

'What?' she said.

'Don't let any of this get out yet to where Lister or Brownlow might be listening,' he told her. 'Brownlow had his chance with Boylan, and Boylan didn't tell him a thing, except about how he felt about his brother's death and about his hatred for the man's ex-wife. He could have spilled all this then if he'd wanted to, but he didn't.'

She accepted what he was suggesting to her and put her phone down.

Yvonne called the two numbers I'd given her. There was still nothing.

'Do you seriously think this Carr girl's in danger?' Mitchell asked me.

'Of course she is,' Yvonne said angrily.

'The last outstanding debt,' Sunny said.

'If we could find her . . .' Mitchell said.

'What?' Yvonne said. 'Tie her up in a clearing and wait for the killer to come to her?' She apologized for the remark, and afterwards no-one spoke for several minutes.

I finally broke the silence by suggesting that I needed to return to Humber Street in case Emily Carr called or came back there.

Mitchell said he and Ruth would come with me. He asked me if I was certain that Jimmy Boylan wasn't the killer, seeking some delayed and perverted revenge for how his brother had been treated in the years before his death.

'It would account for the time delay,' Sunny suggested.

'And it would make sense,' Ruth said. 'This way the original crime and its victim become almost academic as one of the perpetrators turns on the rest of them. And Jimmy Boylan was always part of the gang, don't forget. The killer seems particularly well informed of everything that happened that night and who was involved.'

It was something else I'd considered and dismissed as I'd left Woodcock Street and driven to Withernsea. All I could conclude – setting aside the fact that Jimmy Boylan was unmarried and childless, and that he appeared to care more about what had happened to his brother than what was now happening to himself – was that if anyone had tried to find out who the men ashore that night had been from the trawler-crew lists, then Jimmy Boylan's name would not have been among them. And perhaps anyone looking would have known that only a single Boylan was likely to have sailed.

'So now we need to know who the girl was,' Ruth said suddenly. 'And why, as seems likely – and which to me is the bigger question

– no proper investigation was carried out and no charges were ever brought.'

'Jimmy Boylan said none of them ever knew who the girl was,' I said. 'Just that Lucas had mistaken her for a prostitute, and had then gone on insisting that's what she was to save face in front of the others. That's what all this was about for all of them – saving face in front of their mates. It's why they were all drunk, why they all followed Lucas, and why none of them tried to stop him when he went too far. And there was nothing to identify the girl on the TV or in the papers in the days afterwards. Apart from the solitary detective checking the facts on Jock Boylan, there was no follow-up whatsoever. I'm convinced Jimmy was telling me the truth,' I said. 'He expected to learn everything from the Grimsby police when they discovered who else was on the boat and then came to arrest them all the next day. He was as mystified and as relieved as the others when that never happened.'

'The man asking questions might not have been a detective,' Mitchell said. 'If those six names were never officially linked to what happened that night, then whoever wanted to find out who they were would have had to use his own means.'

'Jock Boylan to Jimmy Boylan to the trawler company to the crew list?'

'Or the same route via the salvage merchant. It wouldn't be difficult to trace the boats leaving Grimsby the next day. Perhaps nothing got back to Jimmy Boylan or the others, or even to the press, because whoever went looking for them made sure of it.'

'Perhaps it was the same man who's paying them all return visits now,' Yvonne said, silencing us all.

The phone rang and Sunny answered immediately and listened without speaking. Then he thanked the caller and asked him to go on looking.

'My man,' he said. 'There's nothing on the computer for any kind of assault in October seventy-five. Plus nothing whatsoever on any of the six names for five years after that date. He thinks it's all too long ago. He's going to keep on looking, but he isn't hopeful.'

'They scattered,' Mitchell said. 'First they came back to Hull and then they scattered and kept their heads down. Everything fell apart around them and they never got back together. Perhaps even then Lucas knew there would be weak links in the chain, someone to point a finger at him as the ringleader and main perpetrator.'

'They had bigger things to worry about,' Sunny said. 'The industry was lost and they were thrown to the wind anyway. It was a different country, then, Grimsby, the south bank. No bridge, no motorway, no unitary authority. A different place completely. And the two police forces certainly weren't known for their friendly cooperation. Nineteen seventy-five? I imagine all eyes then were focused westwards, looking for the Yorkshire Ripper.'

'Which must have been another reason for the Grimsby police being happy to keep shtum,' Mitchell said.

I told him it was time for me to return to Humber Street.

Yvonne promised me she'd stay at the agency overnight and continue trying to contact Emily Carr.

'If John Maxwell calls here first, tell him where I am,' I said.

'He wouldn't tell us anything anyway,' Sunny said. There was an old, unbroken antagonism between the two of them, one which had endured since John Maxwell's days on the force.

Mitchell asked Sunny not to do anything now that might bring any of what I'd uncovered to Lister's attention. 'It'll be too much for him to resist,' he said. 'He'll go in heavy-handed, arrest Jimmy Boylan and Don Lucas, kick up a lot of dust, attract a lot of attention, and achieve absolutely nothing. Same for Brownlow.'

'I could probably have worked all that out for myself,' Sunny said. 'What I can't work out is why you suddenly want the Hero-of-the-Hour badge all for yourself.'

'Believe what you like,' Mitchell told him. 'You usually do.'

Yvonne tried the numbers again before our departure. There was still no response from Emily Carr.

I wondered how long I could go on silently repeating the words 'still' and 'not yet' to myself before I accepted them as the forlorn hopes they truly were.

I tried hard to remember everything she'd told me about the man she was convinced had returned to Nelson Court, the man who might or might not have been seeing Lucy Collins when she was working as a prostitute.

My thoughts were interrupted by Ruth, who told me she and Mitchell were ready to leave.

They followed me through the almost deserted city centre back to Humber Street.

Most of the warehouses were closed for the day, and the only sign of activity was a small group of men unloading a van at the far end of the street. Even the boxing club seemed unnaturally silent.

All the way back, I'd hoped that Emily had changed her mind about Withernsea, and that she would once again be waiting for me somewhere in the shadows, out of sight of the warehousemen.

Arriving at my office, I searched around us, but saw nothing.

Ruth saw this and asked me what I was looking for.

'Nothing,' I told her.

'Did you think the girl might have come back here?'

'She came before,' I said.

'What else?'

'She's pregnant,' I said. 'Four months.'

She exchanged a glance with Mitchell.

'It doesn't necessarily mean anything,' he said, but making no attempt to hide his concern at this news.

I said nothing, and the three of us climbed the stairs to my office.

The high room was cold. I switched on my two desk lamps and the small and largely ineffectual fan heater I kept there. We sat close to this in our coats.

I checked the answering machine, but there was nothing yet from either Emily Carr or John Maxwell.

'It's possible that the fact that the girl who was attacked in Grimsby was believed by Lucas to have been a prostitute has some bearing on the killings now,' Ruth said.

'Because two of the dead women now had records for prostitution?' I said, unconvinced. 'It's the least of what they were.

Besides, like I said, Lucas was saving face, not acting on the strength of his conviction.'

'All of which may be worth considering now,' Mitchell said. 'As might Lister's campaign – targeting the city's prostitutes and creating some confusion in the public mind concerning this, and why the current victims are being singled out.'

'Does it matter *what* any of them were if we know *how* they're connected?' I asked him.

'Possibly, possibly not. But it might help us to make some sense of why all this is happening *now* – now as opposed to then or at any time in between – why so much time has passed.'

Ruth agreed with him. 'You've seen or spoken to all the families involved,' she said. 'Tell us what they all had in common.'

'Just people grieving their losses,' I said. 'And trying to come to terms with the unimaginable. To begin with, I thought that the killer might have been waiting until all the attackers were dead before he started taking his revenge, that perhaps that was his way of ensuring that no-one ever made the connection.'

'Apeman Lucas is still alive,' Mitchell said. 'Martin Siddal is still alive. Jimmy Boylan is still alive.'

'So why was the murder made to look like suicide in Rebecca Siddal's case?' Ruth said.

None of us knew.

'Both Rebecca Siddal's parents and Alison Wilson's parents said that their daughters had had everything to live for,' I said. 'I know it's what everyone says, but they said it and meant it. In fact, all the deaths hit the surviving families hard in one way or another.'

'Perhaps it's why the killer waited,' Ruth said. 'He wanted the families to hurt as bad now as he and his family did then when the girl was attacked.'

'Which suggests what?' Mitchell said. 'That he was definitely related to the girl? My guess is that she didn't die, and that she wasn't seriously injured in the attack. If either of those things had happened, then the police would have had no choice but to pursue the thing.'

'Are you suggesting something might have happened to her later, afterwards, as a result of the assault?' Ruth said.

'I don't know. But there are a lot of little things that just don't add up. If no-one died then, why the killings now?'

'Apart from Kelly Smith, they were all only children,' Mitchell said. 'Something over which the killer could have had absolutely no control whatsoever. It's why Paul Hendry was the only male victim – because there was no other choice.'

'And the fact that he isn't actually dead?' I said. But the remark had caught me unawares, and I started to reconsider what we knew about the circumstances of his discovery and the events in which he had allegedly been involved beforehand with all the connections we were now able to make.

'So do you think now that Hendry's overdose was staged by the killer – perhaps knowing that he'd pumped enough into him to ensure he never recovered – and that Collins was killed because she'd witnessed this or found out about it?' Mitchell said. 'That will only work if the entire sequence of events is reversed.' He, too, started to reconsider those events and connections.

'Whatever,' I said, 'Lister only ever wanted Hendry in the frame for the killing of Lucy Collins. *We* now know that *Hendry* and not Lucy Collins was always the intended victim.' And even as I said it, I began thinking how I was going to later say the same to Susan Hendry.

Mitchell said he considered it significant that Rebecca Siddal had just gained her A levels and was preparing to go to university when she was killed. Equally significant was Alison Wilson's impending marriage and the fact that she and her fiancé were preparing for their future together in their own home on Beverley Road.

I wondered aloud if there might be any connection between Emily Carr's pregnancy and the fact that Lucy Collins had had a termination only months before she was killed. It seemed unlikely – again, it was something far beyond the killer's control, and had nothing to do with what otherwise connected Lucy Collins to the other victims.

'It might suggest that the girl who was assaulted was pregnant,' Ruth said.

'Jimmy Boylan never mentioned it.'

'Perhaps it didn't show.'

Mitchell shook his head. 'What, and the killer would wait thirty years to ensure that that particular detail matched up?'

'How old would the girl who was attacked be today?' Ruth said. 'Late forties, early fifties?'

'Suggesting the killer might be the same age?'

'It's a possibility. Alternatively, it might just as easily be her son, and that's why the thirty-year gap exists. Perhaps she died recently, and her son was waiting for that to happen before exacting his revenge for whatever had happened to her and which had blighted her life for ever afterwards.'

'If that's the case, then Rebecca Siddal died fourteen months ago. If, when we find our man, we discover his mother died shortly prior to that, then it might give us an opening.'

I called Sunny and he told me to be patient. I asked him to call his contact in Grimsby again and he said he would.

I knew there was no point in ringing John Maxwell again, that he accepted my urgency without question, and that he knew I was waiting for him.

At ten, Mitchell went out for a Chinese takeaway.

While he was gone, I asked Ruth if she thought he was relaying everything we'd uncovered and discussed to one of their superiors at National Crime.

She considered this likely, but was unconcerned by the fact. And by the fact that she and Mitchell were keeping all this from Lister.

'If you keep any of it from him for much longer,' I said, 'he'll have every right to come down on you when—'

'When Emily Carr's corpse turns up? Like Mitchell said, Brownlow had his chance with Jimmy Boylan. He could have done his job properly and started piecing all this together then. However . . .'

'What?' I said. 'You still think Boylan only told *me* what he did because it was in his own best interest to do it that way?'

'It's still a possibility,' she said. 'Especially seeing as how everything's coming back out into the light now whether he wants it to or not.'

'And because of what Alison Wilson's stepfather might do if he found out why she'd been murdered?'

'Among other things,' she said.

Mitchell returned, and I asked him immediately who he'd called. He promised me he had told no-one who would tell Lister.

'Or at least not until it becomes expedient to do so?' I said.

'It was always going to happen,' he said. 'You need to cover your own back in case any of this blows up in your face.'

'Or Lister's? Or in the faces of the men who want him sitting at the high table with them?'

He refused to be drawn by this and started laying out the food.

'How long did you think you were going to keep all this to yourself?' he said eventually. 'Apart from which, you may possibly have been the last person to speak to Emily Carr before the killer himself whispered in her ear. And knowing what you now know about her place in the overall scheme of things, I reckon that makes you considerably more vulnerable than most to charges of withholding and perverting.'

After that, we ate the food, and none of us spoke for ten minutes.

The room was barely warmed by the heater, and our tired reflections looked back at us each time we went close to the windows, where a thin frost was already forming along the lower panes.

It was one o'clock when John Maxwell finally returned my call.

Ruth had fallen asleep by then, and she woke with a start.

'Whatever you wanted to find in Grimsby's records isn't there,' John Maxwell said immediately. 'If it wasn't active, pending or open it didn't get transferred during local-government re-organization. There are no evidence bags on record and nothing in any file relating to the time you want.'

I told him I was switching him onto public address and he asked me who else was there.

'No-one directly connected to Lister?' he said.

I began to explain to him what we'd come up with.

He interrupted me. 'If you're not letting Lister in on any of this, then don't tell me. A good defence brief will get everything ruled inadmissible. Ask Mitchell. He knows that better than anyone. National Crime are still using you as a buffer between themselves and Lister for if all this – along with Lister's prospects of promotion – goes wrong.' He was talking more to Mitchell than to me.

'It won't,' Mitchell said. 'Not if you tell us what else you found. What you've told us so far wouldn't have taken you ten minutes to dig up.'

I told John Maxwell that we believed another girl's life was in danger.

'If your man's gone fourteen months without being suspected or detected and without leaving a single piece of evidence behind him, then I imagine "danger" is something of a euphemism,' he said. He paused. 'Tell me, why did you ask me about old man Dunn and his son-in-law?'

I felt a sudden jolt at hearing the name.

Ruth and Mitchell both moved closer to the speaker.

Ruth took out her pad and started writing.

'Because I had a run-in with the son-in-law,' I said. 'Added to which, I saw him again, with his wife, earlier today – I mean yesterday.' He knew the rest of the story involving Paul Hendry and Weaver's surgery.

'What else?' he said.

'The Weavers have a daughter,' I said. 'She's severely handi-capped. She's cared for in a home at Easingwold. The place was paid for and is supported now by the money Dunn's daughter inherited from him when the supermarkets were sold.'

There was another silence.

'I know a man called Farrell,' he said eventually. 'Michael Farrell. He was a lifetime sergeant in Grimsby when I started work on the Hull force. I forget how I met him, but I did, and we got on. He's in his seventies now, lives in Spain, near Alicante. I called him earlier. He's been retired over twenty years, but he was in Grimsby all through the seventies. I told him everything you already knew and asked him if he remembered anything at all that might shine some light on what Boylan had told you. He got back to me, and the first thing he asked me was if this was about old man Dunn. I remembered you mentioning the name to me and so I told him it was.

'Apparently, in early October seventy-five, someone called in a fight in Railway Street, close to the docks. A car was sent and a man arrested. Farrell couldn't remember his name. Drunk, barely able to either stand upright or to string two words together. There was a woman lying across the street. The two men they sent reported hearing others running away. They radioed for an ambulance for the woman, and when this arrived they took the man back to the Victoria Street station. He couldn't tell them anything. No-one believed he'd had anything to do with the assault on the woman.' He paused. 'I assume by your collective silence that all this is making some kind of sense to you.'

'I know who the man on the kerb was,' I said.

'Good. Keep that to yourself, too, and let me finish. The station was short-staffed. There was a navy ship in harbour and everyone was being kept busy elsewhere. By the time anyone was sent to the hospital, the girl's father was already there. Her father and her fiancé. Don't ask me how they knew, or how they'd arrived there so quickly, I don't know. Farrell thinks about an hour passed between getting the call and them turning up at the hospital. The father was trying to make arrangements to have the girl taken to a private hospital on the other side of the river, but the doctors in Grimsby weren't having it. They told him his daughter would have to stay with them for at least another forty-eight hours, perhaps longer, depending on what they found. Apparently, she was conscious by then. She was tearful and upset, but either couldn't or wouldn't say anything about what had happened to her. The constable who'd been sent to see her said she was hysterical.'

'The father?' I said. 'Was it Dunn?'

'Paul Dunn,' he said.

'Which means—'

'Don't,' he said loudly. 'Listen to what else I've got to say and then start speculating when I've finished. Dunn went on insisting that his daughter should be treated elsewhere. Farrell can't remember how old she was – somewhere in her late teens, he thought.'

'Jimmy Boylan just said she looked like a girl.'

'Perhaps she did. Anyway, when old man Dunn saw he wasn't going to prevail over the doctors, he insisted that she be taken to a private room at the hospital. She might have been little more than a girl, but she was already engaged to be married, and her fiancé was also there throughout all this, doing everything Dunn told him to do. No-one else had got wind of anything. There was no press, nothing to splash over the papers.'

'Did Farrell tell you what was done about the assault?'

'He said the boy they'd taken into custody was remanded by a local magistrate the following morning. I imagine they held him because everyone assumed an investigation was about to get under way.'

'And that never happened?'

'Not according to Farrell. I know it seems unlikely, but apparently the girl herself, the father and the fiancé all refused to press charges.'

'Meaning the father refused and the others did as they were told?'

'That was the impression Farrell got. Dunn just went on insisting that he wanted what was best for his daughter, and that that didn't include leaving her in Grimsby any longer than was absolutely necessary. Nor did it include putting her through a painful investigation and trial. Farrell says he was sympathetic to what the old man was suggesting and that he didn't press him too hard to reconsider. Two days later, the girl was well enough to travel and her father arranged for a private ambulance to take her home. That's as much as Farrell can remember about any of it. There was no comeback, no repercussions, nothing to suggest to him that the girl hadn't recovered, and that the father hadn't been right all along in doing what he did for her.'

Mitchell put his hand over the phone. 'Ask him if Dunn's daughter was pregnant,' he said.

I shook my head and pulled his hand away. 'What was the extent of the girl's injuries?' I said.

'I don't know. I asked Farrell, but he could only guess. But they can't have been too serious if the hospital let her go after two days.'

'There was no lasting damage,' I said. 'Like I said, I met her, I know her. She married James Weaver.'

And I also knew her near-identical daughter.

And now I might even have known the cause of her daughter's disability.

And if I knew both of those things, then I also knew the killer, and why he was doing what he was now doing.

Mitchell and Ruth were making these same hurried and scarcely credible calculations, and my mind was so full of these half-formed convictions and reckonings, that I almost missed what John Maxwell said next.

'You're wrong,' he said. 'You haven't met her,' he said.

'What?'

'I said you haven't met her. You don't know her.'

'Her name's Pauline Weaver,' I said. 'Pauline Dunn as was. Angela's mother; Weaver's wife.'

'No it isn't,' he said. 'Her name was Anna Dunn, and she died two years after the attack. In the summer of seventy-seven. She was nineteen.'

All three of us looked hard at the receiver.

'Died?' I said. 'How?'

'I don't know. Farrell said he remembered seeing it in the paper. Nothing big, just a notice. Apparently, it had more to say about her father, about the family name and business, than it did about her. And that's it – all there is to know – beginning, middle and end.'

'Weaver's wife is called Pauline,' I said, still unable to accept how suddenly and completely everything had moved beyond my grasp. 'She answered every question I asked her about her father, about the disabled girl and about the family business.'

'The girl who was attacked, and who died two years later, was called Anna,' he repeated.

Ruth waved to attract my attention. She held up two fingers. 'Dunn had two daughters,' she said.

'Listen to her,' John Maxwell said, overhearing the remark.

I switched off the public address and thanked him for all he'd done. He told me he'd send me a bill for the call to Alicante. I knew he would have been forced to reminisce with Michael Farrell, and I knew it was something he disliked doing.

He said it was late and that he was tired, and then he hung up.

Mitchell and Ruth both sat and faced me across the remains of our meal, our warm breath still clouding the cold air.

Before either of them could say anything, I called Sunny. There was still no word from either Emily Carr or the couple at Withernsea.

When I turned back to Mitchell and Ruth, they were both on their phones, speaking in hurried whispers. I could hear those whispers all the way back to Lister.

It was two in the morning, and out on the deepwater channel of the Humber Road a waiting tanker sat directly upon the reflection of the full moon.

I needed time to myself. Time to reconsider, and to stop having to second-guess everything that was happening. I told them I was going for a walk.

'We'll be here,' Mitchell said as I went, his phone cupped and hidden in his hand.

33

Five hours later, at seven thirty that same morning, I stood and looked at Pauline Weaver through the ornate stained-glass door of her Bishop Burton home. She appeared at the far end of the wide hallway, a cup and saucer in her hand, a newspaper beneath her arm, and looked back at me. I'd been about to press the bell when she'd appeared and seen me there.

We stood like that for several minutes, looking at each other, each of us working out what was about to happen next, each of us knowing only one thing – that the past and the present had once again come to this abrupt and unstoppable collision in the short distance between us.

She continued looking at me, the cup and saucer in her hand, the paper tucked beneath her arm, and I looked at her. And those sharp, pressing fingers of the inescapable past drew us together.

I'd returned to Humber Street at three in the morning to find that both Mitchell and Ruth had gone, and I doubt if any of us had slept in the hours since then.

Pauline Weaver came towards me and the newspaper fell from

beneath her arm. She paused briefly to look where its pages lay scattered on the tiles at her feet.

She stopped again as she reached the door and put down the cup and saucer, our faces now only a few feet apart through the patterned glass. Her hand rose mechanically towards the lock.

I'd called Mitchell from my office at six and told him I was going to see her alone.

He told me immediately that neither he nor Ruth had revealed anything of John Maxwell's revelation to Lister. 'But now it's time for him to be told,' he said. 'Think about it. It's the only way forward.'

'You *have* to see it like that,' I told him, knowing he was right, but still determined to see Pauline Weaver alone before everything was taken away from me, and before either Lister or Brownlow took all the responsibility and credit for whatever happened next.

I needed to hear everything Pauline Weaver now had to tell me about her dead sister, not to hear it retold and repackaged at one of Lister's self-serving press conferences. And certainly not at the gathering at which he finally rose above all the criticisms and complaints, smiling and triumphant, and bathed in the warm golden glow of his own beckoning and richly deserved future.

Ruth took the phone from Mitchell. 'I could come with you,' she suggested.

'And anything Pauline Weaver told him in front of you would be ruled inadmissible as evidence,' Mitchell said, taking the phone back.

'However and whenever James Weaver is arrested,' I said, 'the likelihood is he'll confess to nothing, at least not immediately, and certainly not fast enough to do Emily Carr any good.'

'That's if—' Mitchell said and stopped.

'I know,' I said. 'If she's still alive. But either way, Weaver's going to clam up. Anything we're going to get now, we'll get from his wife, not him.'

'All of which might prove just as inadmissible,' he said.

'Perhaps. But by my reckoning, she's in this as deep as he is, and if she's prepared to come clean about her own part in everything, then it's going to shine a dirty light on him when *his* part in it all comes to be investigated.'

Neither of them spoke for a moment.

'And once they're arrested, they'll be kept apart,' Mitchell said eventually. 'And if Pauline Weaver is as forthcoming as you seem to think she will be, then neither of them will stand an earthly of walking on bail.'

'So what makes you think the good wife will be ready to confess all?' Ruth asked me.

'Because we already know too much, and because when she understands and accepts that, her first thought will be for her so-called daughter.'

'And you'll use the girl – the girl who hasn't even recognized her for thirty years – to get her to talk?'

'Tell me your better plan,' I said.

By then it was almost seven.

After returning to my empty office in the night, I'd gone back out and walked for a further hour along the Humber, from the aquarium to the open, empty space of the West Wharf and back. There had been no news of Emily Carr in all that time, and I began to accept that, in all likelihood, she was already dead.

'And Weaver himself?' Mitchell said. 'Lister isn't going to listen to what you or I have to say and then just rush straight in and arrest him.'

'No. But Brownlow might. Think how good that will look for him on his own clumsy little scramble up the greasy pole.'

He considered what I was suggesting. I didn't want anything to alert Weaver to what I was preparing to do at Bishop Burton. At least not until it became impossible for him either to extricate him-self from the events about to be set in motion there, or to contact his wife before his own arrest.

'Lister would give Weaver too much warning,' I said.

'The old pals' act. Whereas Brownlow might prefer his much-loved and tested bull-in-a-china-shop approach?'

'Especially if we convince him beforehand of Weaver's guilt,' Ruth said.

The pair of them had considerably more to lose than I did if any-thing now went wrong with this simple plan. They both knew this, but neither of them used it against what I was proposing.

It had been a cold and cloudless night, and waiting at Humber Street, I'd watched the first of the fruit lorries arrive at four. I'd encountered some of the traders upon my return from the West Wharf and they'd assumed that I'd spent the night drinking, or that I'd stayed somewhere close by, and they shouted to me as I walked the length of Humber Street trying to imagine where Emily Carr's corpse might already lie waiting to be found.

At seven, I left and drove to Bishop Burton.

En route, I called Sunny, who was woken by my call. Yvonne was still asleep beside him, he said. I asked him to wake the couple at Withernsea and check their messages. I told him I'd get to the agency later in the morning when everything was over.

He didn't ask me what I meant by this, saying only, 'Good luck'.

Yvonne woke, took the phone from him and asked me what I was doing.

'Wish me luck,' I told her.

'You don't need it,' she said. 'You lead a charmed existence.' And then she said, 'Good luck,' because not to have said it might have cost us all considerably more than we would ever be prepared to lose.

Arriving in Bishop Burton, I parked where I could see the entrance gates to the Weavers' house. On the higher land, away from the green and the pond, there was a light mist, thickening in the headlights of the few cars that moved through it.

Weaver left the house at twenty past seven. The gates remained open behind him.

I left my car and walked to the churchyard. A short search of the more impressive stones brought me to the grave of Paul Dunn. His wife, parents, two brothers and a sister lay beside him. And along-side these, beside an old and twisted hawthorn tree, lay the grave of his daughter, Anna, born 1958, died 1977.

I crouched down and wiped the dust from her sculpted name. It was a small stone, flecked black marble with simple gold lettering. Something private and unassuming. There were no other details on the stone, only the word 'Beloved'. The weight and sorrow, joy and despair of the world in a single word.

It was all I needed to see.

Pauline Weaver finally opened the door and then shivered involuntarily at the rush of cold air into the house. Her eyes held mine for a moment, and then she looked over my shoulder at the mist and rising light behind me. The gravel drive again lay banked with leaves. There were no fires on that damp morning, but the smell of burning still clung to the place.

'I came from the graveyard,' I told her.

'I see.' She closed her eyes for a moment.

'Where's Emily Carr?' I said. She knew why I was there, and I saw no sense in either of us pretending otherwise.

She opened her eyes. 'The pregnant girl?' she said. She said it dismissively, almost irritated, as though neither the name nor the girl nor her unborn child were of the slightest consequence to her. 'I thought she might have been somewhere safe by now.'

The remark surprised me, and I wondered if she meant because that's what *I* should have ensured by then.

'Like Tracey Lucas was somewhere safe when you drove your husband's car to York and back via Goole to act as a kind of decoy while he abducted and killed her?' I said.

'Is that what I did?' she said absently.

'What did your husband do – go to Goole in another car knowing that the cameras would pick up and identify his car with you and your perfect little alibi driving it?'

'Make up as many stories as you like,' she said.

'They're not just *my* stories,' I said.

She took several steps away from me and told me to come in.

'I know all about your sister,' I told her. 'I know about the baby she had, that she died, and that you pretended afterwards, coming home from Belgium after those three years abroad, that the baby was your own.'

She stumbled at hearing the words and held the post at the bottom of the stairs for support.

'Then you know it all,' she said, her voice again even and calm.

'Not all,' I said. 'But I do know that Angela was your sister's child, not yours, and that your sister was assaulted in Grimsby thirty years ago, and that the men who did that to her are the fathers of the recently murdered girls, and of Paul Hendry, a boy and only child.'

She walked ahead of me into the conservatory. Lights shone on the walls above us, but beyond these the garden stretched into darkness. The buildings at the far end of the lawn were barely visible through the mist.

'If you know all this, why are you here alone?' she said. 'Why hasn't Alexander Lister surrounded the house with cars and flashing lights?'

'Call him,' I said. 'Call him and tell him I'm here. I'm sure he'd send someone to throw me out for harassing you.'

She considered this. 'By which I take it that there *is* someone somewhere waiting to pounce when you click your fingers, and that you're here alone because you believe I'm going to tell you everything you want to know before that happens. What is it – poor deluded wife charmed by Svengali-like killer? Am I just another victim in all of this?'

I guessed at the unspoken calculations and guesses she was already making as she spoke. And I remembered then that a motorist on Holderness Road had said he thought he'd seen Alison Wilson walking with another woman towards her bus stop. And I remembered what Karen Smith had told me about the woman approaching her daughter the day before she was killed and telling her she'd known Kelly's father. The woman in the rain and the man sitting in the car waiting for this one final act of confirmation to be completed.

'No,' I said. 'But you're the "mother" of a daughter who, in all probability, may never see you again. Or you her.'

This suggestion shocked her and I saw her hands tighten on the arms of her chair.

'And you're in a position to give me that?' she said disbelievingly.

'In more of a position than Lister would be if he knew I was here and what was happening.'

She let her hands fall into her lap.

And then she reached beneath a magazine, pulled out a photograph and gave it to me. It showed her and Anna standing together, teenagers, grinning, with their arms around each other's waist. They wore similar dresses, and Pauline Dunn wore a necklace of large beads. She was only an inch or two taller than Anna, and her head was tilted down at her sister. Their smiles were identical, and I saw by the creases in their dresses that they clutched each other rather than merely held each other close for the photograph.

'I dug it out after your last visit,' she said.

I looked at the picture for a moment longer and then handed it back to her. She laid it face-up on the table, a third and whispering presence in all that now happened between us.

'How many months pregnant was your sister when she was attacked?' I asked her.

A minute passed before she was able to answer me. 'Five. Anna herself was only seventeen. She hardly showed. They punched and kicked her. She was engaged to James. He was five years older.'

'And your father made sure—'

'My father knew nothing about it. He only found out later that night, in Grimsby hospital, when he came barging in with James in tow demanding to know how badly injured his daughter was. My father and James had been invited to dinner in the town by one of his biggest suppliers. Anna had insisted on going too. Then she and James had argued – probably over what she regarded as James's willing subservience to my father – and she'd stormed off. It was what she usually did. She stormed off, leaving everybody to worry about where she'd gone, and then she got lost. It was that simple. The police called our housekeeper, and she called the supplier, who told my father his daughter had just been taken to the hospital. *That* was when *he* found out about her being pregnant. No-one could tell him for certain what harm might have been done to the unborn child. It was why the Grimsby doctors wanted to keep Anna for longer than he was prepared to let them. The baby's heart was still beating, it was still there. But beyond that, they couldn't tell him anything. He insisted he wanted Anna treated by specialists, here, this side of the river, privately – doing what he always did and throwing his name and his money at the problem. And when the Grimsby doctors finally agreed to release her – and only then because *she* appeared to have no lasting injuries – he brought her home and then flew her to Brussels and had her cared for there. Angela was born almost two months prematurely seven weeks later.'

'Was the pregnancy accidental?'

'Of course it was. She was seventeen. She was in the middle of exams. After which she'd go wherever she wanted to go, do whatever she wanted to do. He'd see to that. Whatever Anna wanted, Anna got. She was always his favourite, always that little bit more willing than I ever was to bend to his wishes.'

Everything to live for. Like Rebecca Siddal, Alison Wilson and Emily Carr had everything to live for. Everything. Education, marriage, home, children, future. Everybody said so.

'And Weaver?' I said.

'What about him? He went back to Edinburgh and carried on with his studies. He might have been the father of precious Anna's precious child, but my father didn't want him anywhere near her. Especially not knowing what he now knew. I suppose you might say that we both felt excluded, pushed away. James wrote to me, asking me to help him. I'd known about the pregnancy for a month. He and I started seeing each other.'

'And Anna?'

She looked at me. In the glass all around us, her reflection turned in several directions. 'You don't really know very much at all, do you, Mr Rivers? Anna took her own life two years later. When Angela was born, she couldn't cope. The extent of the child's disabilities was too much for her.'

'So everything you told me about "your" daughter was—'

'I never said Angela was mine. I told you how she survived, how I cared for her, how James and I went on caring for her. When Angela was born, my father took charge of everything. Private nursing homes for Anna and Angela, the best medical treatment, constant reassessment, constant changes, always running to keep up with everything new that was discovered, never quite catching up with anything as she grew and as things changed, usually for the worse. While he lived, he made that child his main priority in life.'

'To the detriment of his business interests?'

'What did *they* matter to him then? He sold out to the first of the big chains to approach him. Everyone assumes now that the stores were sold on his death. They weren't. *He* sold them. All that mattered to him were his daughter and granddaughter. You'd think they were the only family he had.'

'And you believed your inheritance had been lost?'

'Hardly. The stores were still worth millions. What did *I* care? He died of a heart attack when Angela was two.'

'And Anna took her own life a few months later?'

'She couldn't cope without him. She became a neurotic recluse. Pampered, indulged, hidden away. Without him to do everything for her, to tell her every day that everything was all right, and that everything would go on being all right in the years to come, she couldn't cope. She hanged herself. It wasn't the first attempt. She'd tried to kill herself a year earlier with an overdose.

'Hanged like Rebecca Siddal "hanged" herself,' I said. 'And overdosed like Paul Hendry was "overdosed"?' With everything she said, another stark and awful piece of the slowly emerging pattern fell into place. Just as thirty years ago Don Lucas had convinced himself that Anna Dunn was a prostitute. And just as anyone who read the papers or watched the television news reports now saw only two prostitutes when they looked at Kelly Smith and Lucy Collins.

'And in the meantime?' I said, prompting her to continue.

'In the meantime, James and I had grown together. He'd lost a fiancée and a wealthy prospective father-in-law, and I'd lost a sister, my father, and a family firm I'd hoped one day to take over. What were *any* of us in those years but survivors clinging to the rapidly disintegrating wreckage?'

'And Weaver planned to do all this all that time ago?'

The question surprised her.

'All I know is that he went looking for the men involved. My father told him not to, to leave everything alone, and certainly not to get the police involved again.'

'Why?'

She shrugged. 'His shame – him being who he was, at having a seventeen-year-old pregnant daughter? He was an old man, even then.'

'But why *didn't* the police do something?'

'Because we all refused to press charges at his say-so? Because no-one could actually prove who was responsible? Because they knew that even the one boy they did manage to catch had been incapable of doing what had been done to Anna? Because my father was a powerful and influential man? Because the police were going to look incompetent or inefficient for not having immediately gone after the others? Because everything seemed cut and dried, and because Anna seemed unhurt by the attack? I just don't know. How many reasons do you want? They certainly weren't as keen then as Alexander Lister is today to attract every kind of publicity imaginable to what's happening. Anna was never named; her attackers – with that one brief exception – were never sought and punished; James went back to Edinburgh to continue his studies; and me, my father and Anna went abroad, where Angela was born. Three years. My father would have kept us in Brussels longer if he'd lived.'

'And after Anna's death, you decided to bring Angela back here and pretend she was your own child – yours and James Weaver's,' I said.

'James came often to Brussels. I sent him the money. We were married at a civil ceremony three months before we returned. The same month he qualified as a doctor. As for pretending Angela was our own child, you'd be surprised how easy that was. We had the money. We'd bought Oriel House and set up the foundation by then. Who in their right mind was ever going to question what we were doing? Who was even going to suspect the slightest thing?

One look at Angela, and all James and I received was help and sympathy.

'He wanted us to go and live somewhere else, but I insisted on coming back here. We'd been back a year earlier to bury my father. No-one here ever even knew that Anna was pregnant when we went away. We buried her here two years later and then came back to the house a few months after that.'

'When did your husband finally decide to start taking his revenge?'

'We talked about it all the time we were in Brussels together. He'd been surprised at how easily he'd found out the names of the men involved. They'd only cost him ten pounds from a secretary in the trawler-owner's office. After that, he just checked that the men concerned were the men whose names he'd bought. He was as angry and as frustrated as I was at my father's refusal to let the law run its course. I suppose you could say that James threatening to go back to the police with the names gave him some sort of power over my father, made him some kind of threat.'

'And afterwards?'

'Afterwards things just got blunted. We got sick and tired of lurching from one painful crisis to another. You think money keeps you away from all that? Well, it doesn't.'

'Did you ever try to persuade your husband *not* to take some kind of revenge?'

'If you want me to say "yes" and start pleading or bargaining with you, to start putting some distance between the two of us, then you're going to be disappointed. Everything just sat there and festered. Like *we* just sat there and festered. And as all those years passed we knew that we'd come together – been forced together, you might say – for all the wrong reasons. This hasn't been a real marriage for the past ten years now. It just stayed alive through inertia. And because of all those other things that just pile up on the outside and hold everything upright and in place. Even at the very beginning, when we thought we were both mourning Anna, we were each mourning the loss of something completely different – him the death of his fiancée and the mother of his child; me, the loss of my sister and a niece – the only member of the new generation – who would never see me or hear me, or even, literally, know that I existed. James saw even then how much my own love and concern and feelings for Angela outweighed her true mother's.' She paused. 'Imagine that – brought together and clinging to each other with all those corpses between us. What chance did we really have, what chance at all?'

Which was why she hadn't stopped her husband? Why she'd acted as his accomplice or protector? Because what he'd done, then and now, had seemed like some vital and justifiable act of redemption for all that had so randomly and inexplicably and unfairly happened to them? Because it had somehow atoned for everything as they'd struggled to rebuild their lives together? And perhaps because if she hadn't been so insistent on returning to the family home and they'd gone to live elsewhere, then none of this would have happened now?

'Did you ever believe that if you'd left James after Angela was born, he might have done something then?' I asked her.

'You sound as though you're offering me excuses,' she said. 'I'm making none for myself.'

'Then I'll ask you again – where's Emily Carr?'

'I don't know.'

'You're lying,' I said, but the words were little more than a reflex.

'In which case, you could insist that unless I tell you where she is, I have no prospect of ever seeing my daughter again. Yes, "my" daughter, because her real mother never once so much as held her or nursed her or sat by her bedside all night when the real crises came. All I know is that James went back to Nelson Court a few days after the Collins girl had been found there to make sure Carr was still there.'

I looked beyond her to the flock of starlings scavenging across the wet lawn.

'*Has* James already been arrested?' she asked me.

'They'd have come for you at the same time.'

'I suppose so.'

I remembered the way she'd spoken to Weaver when he'd

barged in during my last visit. I remembered how she'd emphasized the word 'our' when talking of Angela as their daughter. It was her signal to him that she'd revealed nothing to me. It was what had caused him to calm down, to lower his hand and turn away from me without giving anything away.

She pointed across the lawn towards the distant buildings, visible now through the growing light. 'The gardener's car. It's in there. We let him keep it there in the winter. He's been in hospital for the past fortnight. It might be on the CCTV footage somewhere between Goole and Hull.'

It had never been my intention in seeing her to hear details of the killings. Partly because there wasn't time, but mostly because I wanted either her or her husband to reveal these directly to Lister.

'*Do* you have someone waiting to arrest James depending on what happens here?' she said.

I nodded. Her mention of the gardener's car reminded me of the handyman I'd spoken to at Oriel House.

'Was it the assault on Angela that convinced your husband that the time had finally come to do something?'

'You can't imagine how we felt. First Anna, and now, all these years later, Angela. It made us both physically sick even to think about it. You've seen her. How would you have felt if she was *your* daughter?'

Rebecca Siddal had been killed and hanged only three days after the assault on the girl, while Pauline Weaver was still with her daughter in Easingwold, and while Weaver was alone at home in Bishop Burton.

'You sent the man who assaulted Angela back to Cardiff,' I said.

'Yes – once again we threw our name and money at the problem and made it go away. We just wanted to make sure Angela was safe.'

'Something your father never managed to achieve for Anna.'

And only then did I fully understand what a convoluted knot of obligation, responsibility, impotent regret and remorse had been pulled tight by those four people, each with their own flawed understanding and needs, and with the unknowing and uncaring child at their centre all those years ago and still at their centre now.

She looked at her watch. 'If I'm going to be able to go and see Angela, I need to give Mrs Ellis an hour's notice.'

'Call her,' I said, and she made the call, pretending to Ellis that she was in York unexpectedly and was taking the opportunity to visit Oriel House and see her daughter. She was a practised liar. 'Thank you,' she said to me when she'd finished.

'The court or your lawyers might soon want to insist on some distinction, but you're as guilty and as culpable as your husband in all of this,' I said. 'And whatever the judge or the press might want to insist on, you'll spend just as long as he does behind bars.'

'I know all that,' she said. 'It doesn't matter. All that matters to me now is that I can see Angela. None of this was ever fair to her. James wanted to pretend that he was doing it all for her, but he was lying – to himself, to me – and I knew that all along. And if I'm being entirely honest with myself, I doubt I was ever anything more than a substitute for my sister, a surrogate mother for James's child.'

I checked the time and promised her I'd wait until eleven before letting Mitchell tell Brownlow what we knew, and letting Brownlow get to her husband at the Walker Street surgery.

'What about me?' she said. 'Aren't you afraid I'll just run away from everything?'

'It can't happen,' I said. 'Not these days.'

'Not like it could happen thirty years ago, you mean?'

'I'll get Brownlow or Mitchell to call the York police, tell them where you are and that you'll be waiting for them.'

'Thank you,' she said again.

She went upstairs and returned a few minutes later wearing a coat, scarf and gloves and carrying a handbag, in which she searched for her car keys as she came back down.

I walked with her to her car.

'Will you be there?' she asked me as she waited to leave. She meant at the Queen's Gardens station, where she would be taken upon being brought back to Hull.

'I doubt it,' I said.

'I see.'

I told her that her husband was being watched, and that I'd know if she tried to warn him about what was happening.

'I won't,' she said. She took her mobile from the bag and gave it to me.

'There are lots of public phones,' I said.

'You have my word. You could call the York police at any time and have me picked up before I even got to Angela.'

I stood back from the kerb and she swung the door shut.

She sat looking out at me for a moment before finally moving away.

I watched her as she followed the rising road out of the village, and then as she disappeared into the mist which still lay draped over the low surrounding hills.

34

I drove back to Hull, to Spring Bank, where I told Sunny and Yvonne everything that had happened in the last twelve hours.

There was still no word from Emily Carr.

Whatever now happened in Easingwold and at Queen's Gardens, the police would not release the news of Weaver's arrest until later that afternoon. This gave Sunny a six-hour start on all the other journalists.

'Another fabulous coup for the North's premier news agency,' Yvonne said. 'And another thirty or forty empty, shitty years for that girl in Easingwold.'

I asked her what she meant.

'She means that if the victims' families sue Weaver through the Civil Courts,' Sunny said, 'then the foundation that keeps Oriel House open may be stripped.'

It was something I hadn't considered.

'Pauline Weaver will have made provision,' I said. 'She must have known all this would happen one day.'

'Must she?' Yvonne said. 'It's good that you can convince yourself so quickly.'

'You do realize that you're going to have to persuade Brownlow to arrest Weaver *before* the time you promised his wife,' Sunny said.

'I know,' I told him. I'd worked everything out on my slow drive back from Bishop Burton.

I called Mitchell and told him where I was.

He told me immediately that Brownlow and his squad were at their daily briefing. He spoke in a whisper, suggesting he was in the company of some of the men. 'Plus, we have the unexpected bonus of Lister being away for the day. Conference. London. Apparently, a fair number of his peers and soon-to-be equals like the way he's going about things up here. They're going to listen to what he has to tell them and then sit around a table and see if they can't come up with a more consumer-friendly name for "zero-tolerance".'

In Lister's absence, Brownlow was even less likely to resist the opportunity he was about to be given.

'Make sure someone lets slip to Weaver that I'm with his wife,' I told him. 'Me, personally. Now.'

'Because she'd be the first person he'd call? They must have a contingency plan for something like this.'

'They probably did. And I probably just tore it to pieces.'

'He'll start screaming about his civil liberties, about due procedure, about using his wife and daughter to get to him.'

'Let him,' I said. 'It'll keep him on the back foot. Take him in without any leverage whatsoever, and he'll claim his right to remain silent and then sit back and wait for his very expensive lawyers to build a wall around him.'

He knew this already. 'Plus, of course, it gives you a chance of keeping your own foot in the door when Lister and Brownlow try to slam it shut on you.'

I pretended this had only just occurred to me. 'Why, so it does.'

'You should leave him to them,' he said. 'I'm serious. They have more than enough. Anything you try and cook up with him now might only make things easier for Weaver later.'

'Without Pauline Weaver's promise to turn herself in and tell them everything she knows, they've got nothing,' I said.

'Oh, right,' he said. 'You still think Weaver's going to tell you where the Carr girl might be. You still think you're going to fly through the sky with that clock ticking down to zero.'

'No – but *he* might feel it's something worth bargaining with,' I said.

He was silent for a moment. Both he and Ruth McKenzie were convinced that Emily Carr was already dead.

'He had no compunction whatsoever about killing the others and putting them on public display within minutes,' I said. 'Emily Carr has already been missing at least twenty-four hours.' I knew how desperate this reasoning sounded.

'Or perhaps it's just that no-one's found her yet,' he said.

'Perhaps.'

And perhaps her being pregnant had made Weaver reconsider killing her. Perhaps Lucy Collins died *instead* of Emily Carr; perhaps *she* made up the numbers.

'The fact that she hasn't turned up yet must mean *something*,' I said.

'OK,' he said. 'Ruth just arrived. She agrees with you. I'll go to Brownlow now.'

'Tell him that if he doesn't act immediately, then Sunny will start sending stories down the line.'

'Great. Threats. Lister won't like it.'

'Lister won't know. At least not in time to do anything about it.'

' "Down the line"?' Sunny said. All the time I'd been talking, he'd been making notes.

'Right,' Mitchell said, and hung up.

'Is this you making amends for not listening to the Carr girl?' Sunny asked me.

I didn't answer him.

'Do you really believe this has got something to do with them both – Anna Dunn and Emily Carr – being pregnant?' Yvonne said. 'Because if you do, then I hope for your sake as much as hers that you're looking at every side of this.'

'She's right,' Sunny said, after which none of us pursued the subject.

Mitchell called back thirty minutes later from the Walker Street surgery. 'Brownlow has his hand round Weaver's upper arm as we speak,' he said.

'And Weaver?'

'Calmly feigning that trusted blend of shocked surprise and oh so slightly arrogant indignation. Telling his receptionist to inform his patients of his absence. And telling Brownlow that his career just ended.'

'But?'

'But it's him. He's sending all the right signals in the wrong direction, and all the wrong ones where they shouldn't be going. He's smiling, still a thousand miles above it all. Brownlow's got ten men around him. They're holding onto every part of Weaver they can get their hands on. Time to go. See you later.'

I relayed the news to Sunny.

Yvonne came to sit beside me.

'I hadn't thought about what might happen to Angela Weaver,' I admitted to her.

'Weaver didn't give a toss about what happened to Susan Hendry,' she said.

'Pauline Weaver will be with her now,' I said. I took out the phone she'd given me and laid it beside my own on Yvonne's desk. It rang almost as soon as I'd put it down.

Yvonne picked it up and identified the caller as James Weaver. She held it for a moment, letting it ring. 'Whatever else you do, get this bit right,' she told me.

I took the phone from her. 'Doctor Weaver,' I said. 'How may I help you?'

'Put my wife on. I know you're with her.'

'I can't do that,' I told him.

'I said *put her on*.'

I waited a moment before answering him. 'I think your days of having people jump just because you tell them to jump are over,' I said.

'Where is she?' he said. 'Where? Tell me.'

'Where's Emily Carr?' I said.

He was silent for a few seconds, and then he laughed.

'I know about Pauline's sister,' I said. 'Your fiancée, your daughter, Grimsby, the six men.'

'You know nothing,' he said. He was calm again, his voice even and low.

'Where's Emily Carr?' I repeated.

'If you do know everything, then you've got nothing to give me in return, Rivers. And I've got nothing to lose by remaining silent until my more than capable lawyers start sorting all this out.' He sounded convincing and convinced, confident that he was reasserting himself.

'There isn't going to be any "sorting out",' I told him. 'You killed them, and your wife colluded with you. You're probably both going to prison for six times the rest of your lives.'

'What a simple little world you live in,' he said. 'And please, spare me your mawkish moralizing.' Someone spoke to him. 'That was ex-Detective Sergeant Brownlow,' he said. 'He's not happy that I'm talking to you. I told him I was calling my wife. Not much the poor little man can do about it – my legal entitlements and all that – and, anyway, he'll soon have his own enforced and impoverished retirement to think about so he won't be too concerned about what's happening today. He is, however, anxious to talk to me to determine for himself how he is currently being used by you and Mitchell, and also to work out the full and awful consequences of the error he's just made by listening to the two of you. So I'll say goodbye to you, Mr Rivers, and I hope—'

'She's gone to Oriel House,' I said.

He stopped abruptly and repeated what I'd just said.

'And you've just had your one phone call,' I said. 'The only call Brownlow will make on your behalf now is to those more than capable lawyers. You and your wife might have had a plan for all this, but I think she just abandoned it in favour of my own little arrangement with her.'

'What do you mean she's gone to Oriel House?' he said.

'I went to see her,' I said slowly. 'We had a nice long talk about everything. Which bit don't you understand?'

'You let her go?'

'Only briefly, so she could do what you'll probably never get the chance to do – see your daughter. She'll be back in Hull soon enough to tell Brownlow everything she's already told me. I do understand what a nuisance it must be, not having good old Alexander Lister there with you right now, but he'll be back later to hold your hand. Or not. Depending on which way the wind is blowing by then. I take it your wife didn't break our arrangement and call you en route to York. It doesn't say much for your plan, does it?'

'You stupid bloody idiot,' he shouted at me.

'Where's Emily Carr?'

'What? Forget her – she's nothing. When did—' He was interrupted as Brownlow took the phone from him and spoke to me.

'Look, Rivers, this is turning into a real fucking daisy chain of irregularities. I'm doing all this on Mitchell's say-so, not yours. If anything—'

'You're doing it because it takes your head off the block when Lister moves on and he has to take you out of his pocket and throw you back where you belong,' I said. 'You're doing it because you know that Mitchell is ten times the detective you'll ever be; and because he believes me and knows what's going to happen next. You can't interrupt Weaver's call like this – he knows that, and his lawyers will love it. Never forget – he'll be spending more on them in a day than you earn in a year. With or without your lump-sum pay-off.'

'I want you here,' he said. 'Now. And I want to know what's really happening. I'm not having you make deals with Weaver while I'm trying to do my fucking job.'

'Tell Mitchell to call me and get *him* to insist that I turn up. He'll do it, and that way you'll cover your own back. Do it now.'

There was a short silence, after which my own phone rang, and Mitchell said mechanically and loudly, 'Rivers, you're interfering unlawfully in Detective Sergeant Brownlow's investigation. I insist that you present yourself here, now, and that you stop trying to undermine him in his work.'

I started to thank him for what he'd done, knowing how humiliated he must have felt in front of Brownlow and his squad, but he hung up.

I left the agency and drove to the Queen's Gardens station.

Brownlow was waiting for me at the entrance. Several of his men stood close by. A photographer and a journalist from the *Hull Mail* were already there.

Brownlow came to me, told me to keep my mouth shut and pushed me inside.

'Careful,' I said. 'They're already taking their pictures and starting to write it all down.'

He took his hands from me and held up his palms.

'Who tipped them off?' I asked him.

'Fuck you, Rivers. And fuck them. This stopped being your game the instant I got my hands on Weaver. He's said nothing so far to convince me that—'

'He's said everything you need to know until Lister gets back to pat you on the head and take over,' I said. 'Stop worrying: he did it. Whatever else happens here today, whether Weaver tells you everything or nothing, be in absolutely no doubt whatsoever about that. Stop worrying about whether or not they spell your name right on the commendation, and start thinking about what you've got to do next.'

'Which is? His legal team are going to be here any minute. He's not saying a word until they arrive.'

'He had enough to say to me.'

'You rub him up, that's all. Plus he wanted me well aware of all the technical irregularities connected to bringing him in like this.'

'He might talk to me before they arrive,' I said.

'Which is something else I'm not at liberty to allow.'

'In which case, he'll sit on his hands until—'

'Until Lister gets back. I know.'

'Which is why you're going to go on bending the rules and let me see him,' I said, sounding more confident than I felt.

'The instant you answered his wife's phone he started to lose it.

And when he knew where she'd gone, he could barely control himself. He made a good job of it, but something definitely snapped when he heard that.'

'Have you spoken to Lister?'

'I called him as soon as we had Weaver back here. He told me he hoped I knew what I was doing.'

I knew that my chances of seeing Weaver now – before Brownlow started doing everything by the rules – would be improved by keeping Brownlow just as uncertain about his own prospects and role in all of this as he was about Weaver's guilt.

At the door beside us, the photographer pressed his camera to the glass and took several more shots. Everyone inside moved away from the entrance.

'You know what happens next,' I told Brownlow. 'We either get to do this now, quickly, before the feeding frenzy starts. Or we do it then, with all those lights and microphones and demands to be told what's happening.'

Mitchell and Ruth appeared at the far end of a corridor.

'I want them with me,' I said.

'You're in no position—'

I turned immediately and walked back towards the door. Outside, twice as many people had gathered since our arrival.

'Fuck,' Brownlow shouted. 'Come back.'

I went back to him.

'And even if you can't record anything that Weaver says to me,' I said, 'I want you – you personally – to sit and listen to everything he says. He killed them, and eventually he's going to tell you that. He's been on a quest, and that quest just ended.'

' "Quest"? What the fuck are you talking about?'

'And anything he doesn't tell you, his wife will fill you in on.'

'Well, how fucking cosy and all-round convenient is this all starting to sound?'

'And the first thing their lawyers are going to try and tell you is that the testimony of one is inadmissible in securing a conviction on the other.'

'Hey, why didn't I think of that?'

'Ignore them. You'll be handing this to the CPS on a plate. Pauline Weaver is going to do all your work for you. Everybody in this city is going to love you for ever for this.' We started walking as I said all this.

At the end of the corridor where Mitchell and Ruth waited, we descended a flight of stairs and passed along another corridor. Men stood on either side of us. There was an outburst of applause at Brownlow's appearance, and he pretended not to enjoy this.

At the end of the corridor, Brownlow indicated the door of one of the interview rooms.

'He's in there,' he said.

A man came to us and whispered to Brownlow.

'His lawyers have arrived,' he told me. 'I could have done with another half hour.'

'They won't get in the way,' I said. 'Weaver's back in control now. He'll tell *them* what to do. He needs this – me, you, now – a lot more than he needs all the predictable stuff ahead.' I looked at my watch. It was quarter to eleven. I called Oriel House and asked for Pauline Weaver.

She answered several minutes later.

I told her her husband had been arrested and that he was with his lawyers at Queen's Gardens.

'Will you still allow me the time with Angela you promised me?' she asked me.

I told her I would, careful not to reveal anything to Brownlow.

'Does he know where I am, that I'm with her?' she said.

'He does.'

'I see,' she said. She asked me if there was anything else. She told me she'd been with Angela when I'd called, and that she was anxious to return to her.

I thanked her for sticking to her part of the bargain, and then I hung up before she asked me what choice she'd had.

Weaver's three lawyers arrived in the crowded corridor. The man in charge introduced himself. The two others started complaining immediately to Brownlow about the technical and procedural irregularities he had already committed.

'Shut up,' Brownlow told them immediately.

The two men looked at him impassively, amused and encouraged by his outburst.

'Your response and concerns are noted,' the senior man said to him. The two others shared a smile. They were manipulating him. Whatever leeway Brownlow now demanded or expected of them, it would all be paid for ten times over later.

Brownlow saw the exchanged smile. 'That's good,' he said. 'Half a dozen bodies and you're smiling.'

The senior partner turned to the others and frowned.

After that, we all went in to where Weaver was sitting waiting for us.

The senior lawyer went immediately to him, shook his hand and started talking in a whisper to him. Weaver told him to wait, and then he raised his finger and beckoned the rest of us into the confined space.

It was the largest of the interview rooms and a dozen chairs had been placed around its walls. The lawyers sat together. Brownlow and three members of his team sat opposite Weaver at the table, and Mitchell, Ruth and I sat beside them.

Weaver kept his eyes on me alone as we silently arranged ourselves around him.

Brownlow was the first to speak, making it clear to everyone that this was not the start of Weaver's official interview, that Weaver had refused to allow that to happen until this preliminary meeting had taken place, adding that everything now was being done under the supervision and with the compliance of Weaver's lawyers. One way or another, he identified everyone present in the room.

Weaver continued looking only at me as Brownlow said all this.

'I waited until you left for the surgery and then I went in to see her,' I said to him. 'I know about the car in the outbuildings you used to abduct Tracey Lucas.'

'You don't have to respond to that remark,' one of the lawyers said.

Weaver didn't even look at the man.

'When did she leave for Easingwold?' he asked me.

'Where's Emily Carr?' I said.

'What?' Brownlow said. 'What's *she* got to do with anything all of a sudden? What are you asking him that for?'

'Because he's further ahead in all of this than you're ever going to be,' Weaver said to him, smiling.

'We interviewed her twice,' Brownlow said to me. 'She didn't see or hear anything.'

'At least nothing she told *you* about,' Weaver said.

'It doesn't matter what she did or didn't see or hear,' I said. 'Her father was one of the men on Weaver's list. She's four months pregnant. I last spoke to her twenty-four hours ago, and she hasn't been seen or heard of since.'

'Fuck,' Brownlow said, angry that I'd kept all this from him until now. And not because he was concerned about Emily Carr, but because what only a few minutes ago he had considered so certain and complete was suddenly fragmenting all around him.

'What makes you so convinced that she's still alive,' Weaver said to me.

'Because killing her was never the point,' I said, hoping and guessing in equal measure.

He smiled again at this.

Ruth McKenzie had watched him closely since entering the room.

He turned to her slowly, leaning forward over the table. 'Let me know if any of this doesn't fit comfortably into your predictable little profile,' he said.

'I'll wait until you've told one lie too many and then let you know,' she said, her eyes fixed on his.

Weaver turned back to me. 'Sorry. You were saying . . .'

'Emily Carr being pregnant was an unexpected bonus,' I said.

'Her father was a vicious thug who—'

'No – Don Lucas was a vicious thug. Everything else is debatable. What isn't debatable is that you were never brave enough or sure enough of yourself to go after any of the attackers themselves.'

'That would have been a bit obvious, don't you think?'

'And waiting over thirty years?'

'Ah, the sands of time. All those faded memories and severed connections. All those pieces of lost, unrecorded and uncorrelated information. All those scattering men and shameful secrets.'

'Including yours?' I said. 'Including Paul Dunn's? Because they're as much a part of this as anything else.'

He looked quickly at Brownlow and the other detectives.

'Where's Emily Carr?' I said.

'Oh, for fuck's sake,' Brownlow said, again to the amusement of Weaver's lawyers.

Weaver put his hands together and raised the tips of his fingers to his chin. 'Call whoever you have to call,' he said to me. 'But you need to have my wife picked up now.'

Beside me, Mitchell whispered, 'Do it. He knows something. This is his bargaining point.' There was a barely suppressed note of alarm in his voice.

I flipped open Pauline Weaver's phone. 'Where's Emily Carr?' I said.

'When I know Pauline is safe,' Weaver said.

' "Safe"?' Brownlow said. 'Safe from what?'

'After,' I told Weaver. I closed the phone.

Weaver rested his face in his hands for a moment. 'She isn't dead,' he said. He lowered his hands and looked directly at me. 'Now call the York police.'

'They're standing by,' I told him. 'It'll only take a minute.'

'Then *do it*,' he said.

'This counts for nothing,' I told him.

'Make the call,' Mitchell said, taking out his own phone. The gesture surprised me.

'Do it,' Weaver said again. 'Listen to Mitchell. He's ahead of you.'

Mitchell sat back in his seat, keeping his distance from me.

'Tell him,' Weaver said to him.

'Tell him what?' Mitchell said.

I flicked the phone open again. 'Weaver,' I said to him, drawing him back to me. 'I'm going to ask you one last time, and if you refuse to tell me, I'm getting up and leaving and your proper questioning starts. And once that happens, your options change, and in all likelihood you'll be told by the three wise men here to shut up and sit still. And even if you do tell me where Emily Carr is, I'm still going to wait for confirmation that she's alive before making the call. I made a deal with your wife. And I'm sticking to it because her testimony will be worth more than yours in the long run. No-one else is going to call her.'

He looked hard at me. 'You stupid man,' he said calmly, and then added in the same low voice, 'Fourteen Somerset Street. I own it. It's empty. She's in the attic.'

One of Brownlow's men immediately left the room. There was the sound of running footsteps in the corridor outside.

'She's alive,' Weaver said to me. 'Don't wait. Call Oriel House now.' He turned again to Mitchell. 'Tell him,' he said.

But Mitchell said nothing, signalling me instead with the slightest nod of his head to call the York police waiting close by Oriel House.

I called them.

Weaver ran a hand over his face and leaned back in his chair.

' "Ran a hand over his face",' Ruth said, pretending to write the words down as she spoke. ' "Crisis over. On comes the mask again".'

Weaver laughed at the remark.

'I need you to answer me one more question,' I said to him, expecting him to refuse me.

But he now seemed more intrigued than irritated by my request, and said, 'Go on.'

'I want to know why Lucy Collins died. I know you chose Paul Hendry because of his father, and because there was no other choice – no girl the same age as Anna had been, or anyone similar to her in the family – but why Lucy Collins?'

He considered this before answering me.

'Because I was seeing her,' he said.

The three lawyers looked suddenly alarmed at this admission and each of them told him to stop talking. But Weaver simply held my gaze and continued.

'Professionally. We came to an arrangement. My wife – if she has not done so already – will tell you in the nicest way possible that our marriage has been over for years. Well, to be honest, there is no "nice" way of talking about a marriage that is over, and where everything is done for propriety's sake, for the sake of appearances.'

'For your daughter?'

'Among other things. I told Pauline that if she divorced me, then I would reveal to the world that she was not Angela's real mother. After all those years, it would have killed her.'

'And she still controlled the purse strings.'

'As you can imagine, I had grown accustomed to a respectable standard of living by then, which would, to say the least, have suffered with the withdrawal of my wife's financial resources.'

'And Lucy Collins?'

'I met her when I finally tracked Paul Hendry down. Neither of them had the faintest idea, of course, of my intentions. I could smell it on her the first time I met her. I'd been Susan Hendry's doctor for years, and through her, her son's. Lucy Collins – and especially her being what she was – was just something of which I decided to avail myself while I waited. Sex, Mr Rivers. Nothing less, and certainly nothing more. She gave me what I wanted of her, and I gave her what she and her pathetic boyfriend continued to crave. A perfect arrangement.'

'And you killed her why? Because Paul Hendry found out?'

'Him? I take it you never actually met him. He was pathetic. I killed her because I found out about the abortion.'

Again, the three lawyers exchanged anxious glances and started whispering among themselves.

'And that was all?'

'What more do you want? I was already beginning to tire of her – there are hundreds of others out there – and then she dropped that particular dirty little bombshell.'

'And you were convinced the child was yours?'

'Of course it was mine. I'd been her only customer for the past year. I paid for the privilege. Hendry, it seemed, was particularly inadequate in that department. Hardly surprising, considering his "lifestyle". The child was mine. You've been listening too much to the boy's mother. Listening to her non-existent memories for when she's all alone in the world.'

I began to wonder at all the other connections he was making.

'It must have come as a surprise to find him there,' I said. 'In Nelson Court, living beneath Emily Carr. The two only children of two of the men on your list.'

He shrugged. 'It's Hull.'

'And Paul Hendry's overdose, having broken into your surgery?'

'The usual arrangement was that he came to see me, after hours, and I "paid" him for the whore's services earlier.'

'And he turned up on this occasion wanting whatever you gave him after you'd killed her, but without knowing what you'd done, and you couldn't let him go back to Nelson Court and find her there.'

'Of course I couldn't let him go back there. Even he was capable of putting that kind of two and two together. Let's just say I offered him something he couldn't refuse.'

'And you thought you'd given him enough to kill him.'

'It would have killed most people. All I needed then was for people like Brownlow here to start putting *their* two and twos together. Unfortunately, there were one or two minor unforeseen circumstances, but I appeared to have made a good job of things.'

'You're lying,' I said, already starting to calculate how much of what he'd already said he would later deny all knowledge of at his second interview.

'Am I?' He seemed genuinely surprised and offended by the remark.

'You anticipated at least half an hour before anyone responded to the surgery alarm being triggered. You'd set it off deliberately before and knew exactly how long it took anyone to get there. You did it the night you murdered Lucy Collins and injected Paul Hendry. You even turned it into part of your alibi for being where you were.'

'In my own surgery?'

'In your own surgery that had supposedly just been ransacked and burgled by Hendry. The alarm went off the night Alison Wilson was murdered. What did you do then – kill her and make your way back there to wait for the security firm man to arrive? Except he was late in getting there on that occasion because of all the police checkpoints.'

He looked from me to Brownlow and his men as I spoke. 'I have to applaud you, Rivers,' he said. 'I can see from the faces of our slower-moving friends here that they hadn't even started to work that particular little scenario out. Please, go on.'

'And after you'd stuck the syringe into Paul Hendry's arm, but before he was dead, the man from the security firm turned up because he was already close by. He was as surprised to find you there as you were to see him arrive so swiftly, especially after your trial runs.'

'It was rather disconcerting, yes,' he said.

I caught Ruth McKenzie's eye and she smiled and closed her eyes briefly.

'You covered yourself well,' I said to Weaver. 'You even let the security guard keep you company until the police arrived and went in to "discover" Paul Hendry, a known drug user who'd turned to burglary to support his habit, and who had then succumbed to temptation once inside the sweetshop.'

'They saw it because it was what they wanted to see.'

'And if the security firm had been true to form and taken half an hour to get there, then he almost certainly wouldn't have survived until the ambulance arrived.'

'No matter,' Weaver said.

'Meaning he's as good as dead now?'

'Who cares?' he said.

'Perhaps you should,' I said. 'Because by testing the security-firm response times, and by creating an unused alibi for yourself after killing Alison Wilson, you set up Paul Hendry's attempted murder in advance. Which suggests to me that Lucy Collins had told you about her pregnancy and termination before that day, and that you went to Nelson Court *intending* to kill her. Everything

Emily Carr thought she'd heard taking place between Lucy and Paul had actually been happening between *you* and Lucy. It was when you killed her. And it was what you'd gone there intending to do, knowing she was expecting you, knowing you were her little secret, and knowing Paul Hendry wouldn't show up. Lucy Collins's references to her "doctor" were nothing to do with her termination or the treatment she'd received afterwards; they were veiled references to you. It was why she insisted she didn't want Emily Carr with her when she planned to tell you what she'd done.'

'She was a foul-mouthed little whore,' he said dismissively. 'Whose only purpose as far as I could see was to keep Hendry where he was until I decided to kill him.'

'You killed her,' I repeated. 'And you went to Nelson Court intending to do it. And afterwards you took blood from her to spray all over Paul Hendry once you'd got him where you wanted him. And that way you even managed to make it appear as though Hendry had killed her. You broke the pattern. Sent everyone looking in the wrong direction, towards Lucy and not Hendry, who'd survived. You moved off your path and then you moved back onto it once everybody else was moving at a tangent. It must have affected you very badly – Lucy Collins's termination – to have made you alter your plans like that. Especially after having waited so long.'

'Not particularly,' he said.

Across the table from him, Brownlow slapped both his hands onto its surface.

'It appears that our time's up,' Weaver said. 'Our period of grace.'

Brownlow rose from his seat.

The senior lawyer stood up beside Weaver.

And I'd only been given that much time and access to Weaver because so far I'd been careful not to intrude on any of the evidence relating to the remainder of the murders, staying away from everything Brownlow would want to cover in the presence of Lister. I knew from Brownlow's face that he was now convinced of Weaver's guilt in these other murders and that, whatever the consequences of this brief and unofficial interview, he would now secure his conviction.

And although Weaver understood this better than any of us, in his own mind he was still in complete control of what was happening; and perhaps it suited all of us, his lawyers included, to allow him to go on believing that.

It occurred to me only then that it was possible that Weaver had never intended to kill Paul Hendry – just to ensure that he remained as he was for a long time to come and thus prolong his mother's suffering – just as his and Pauline and Angela Weaver's suffering had been prolonged following the assault on Anna Dunn. And because Paul Hendry hadn't died, everything that had happened at the Walker Street surgery and immediately beforehand was left confused and uncertain, the crime scene contaminated by the arrival and actions of both the security guard and the ambulance men struggling to resuscitate and then remove Paul Hendry.

Contaminated, confused and misleading. Just as the murders of Alison Wilson and Kelly Smith – two girls with ordinary, unconnectable surnames – had been misleading. It was only with the murder of Rebecca Siddal and then, later, Tracey Lucas that the significance of the names was ever likely to be understood, and even then only by the men concerned.

Just as the early killing of two known prostitutes had been misleading, sending Lister's investigation along a parallel track as Weaver then moved towards Tracey Lucas and Emily Carr. And an echo, perhaps, of Don Lucas's own self-serving insistence that Anna Dunn had been a prostitute on that street in Grimsby all those years ago.

Again, all of this could wait for Weaver's formal questioning. Just as the matter of why Don Lucas and Martin Siddal had been the only surviving fathers at the time of their daughters' deaths could wait. Or perhaps Weaver had known all along that Lucas alone had been chiefly responsible for the assault on his fiancée, and perhaps knowing this, and having started his killing, and because all but one of the other fathers were already dead, he had again broken his own simple rules to accommodate the murder of Lucas's daughter.

It even occurred to me that Weaver might have killed Rebecca Siddal *knowing* that the announcement of her death would coincide with Jimmy Boylan's solitary memorial to his four-years-dead brother – something to either prove his ingenuity, or to reassure himself that he remained far beyond all of Lister's attempts to catch him.

I had a sudden vision of him taking the two pieces of Alison Wilson's broken teeth from his pocket and throwing them to the ground beside her.

There was a knock on the door, and one of Brownlow's detectives looked into the room and beckoned Brownlow out to him.

In the interview room, no-one spoke.

Weaver sat watching the slow movement of his fingers on the table.

The three men beside him, I imagined, having listened to everything he'd just said, were already urgently reconsidering the nature and shape of his defence.

I felt exhausted.

Brownlow came back in to us.

'They found Emily Carr,' he said.

At the table, Weaver said, 'Ah,' and smiled broadly, first at me and then at Ruth McKenzie.

'You bastard,' Brownlow said to him.

'Careful, Detective Brownlow,' Weaver said to him. 'Our little period of grace just ended, remember?'

Brownlow restrained himself.

'What happened?' Mitchell asked him, rising from his seat.

But Brownlow ignored him. He returned to Weaver at the table and sat opposite him. His anger subsided and he smiled back at Weaver.

'That's right,' he said. 'Smile. Smile as much as you like. Because one *other* little period of grace also just ended.'

The smile fell from Weaver's lips.

'Hey, you guessed,' Brownlow said to him. 'Well done.' He started slowly to applaud.

And at the first loud clap of his palms, Weaver lunged across the table at him, trying to grab Brownlow's neck, but failing to get a grip on him and causing Brownlow to fall backwards off his chair. Weaver then scrambled around the table and tried to reach him where he lay on the floor, but the three other detectives grabbed and held him and forced him violently back down into his seat.

Struggling to his feet, Brownlow said, 'Nearly,' pointed a finger at Weaver and started laughing.

The detectives held Weaver's face hard down on the table as he struggled to free himself and to breathe.

The lawyers, all of whom had risen from their own seats and were now standing with their backs against the wall, looked on uneasily at what was happening.

Eventually, Weaver stopped resisting the three men and they slackened their grip on him, allowing him to turn his head from side to side and slowly to regain his breath.

'Let him go,' Brownlow said, straightening his jacket and brushing it with his hands. 'See, Doctor Weaver, it's not you who's in control now. It's me. I'm in control, me.'

The detectives moved away from Weaver, and though he was now able to sit upright, he kept his head down on the table, snorting rather than breathing, and with the fingers of both his hands rapidly opening and closing, as though trying to get a grip on the broad, smooth surface, and at the same time struggling to grab and hold on to something which, in that single sharp signal of a hand-clap, had moved suddenly and irretrievably beyond his grasp.

And it was then that I saw he was crying, that his breathing had slowed, that his eyes were closed, and that there were tears running in clear, unbroken lines from beneath his eyelids across his cheeks and mouth and chin.

I was still struggling to understand what had just happened, about to speak to him, when Brownlow grabbed my shoulder and spun me to face him, his pointing finger an inch from my eyes.

'No,' he said. 'Time's up. Out.' And he turned me further and pushed me towards the door.

35

I went back along the crowded corridor, left the station and sat on the wall overlooking Queen's Gardens, above the ponds, and only yards from where Tracey Lucas's body had been found inside its smouldering plastic bag four days earlier.

I called Yvonne and told her what had happened. Sunny took the phone from her and asked me how many members of the press were there. I told him about the rapidly growing crowd already clamouring at the station entrance. I didn't know which of these men and women were press and which were passers-by who had heard those first uncontainable whispers already spreading outwards through the city.

'I'm too busy here to come,' Sunny said. 'Lister's on his way back. Flying. He'll be home in an hour.'

'To snatch all the glory from Brownlow.'

'It was never going to be his. You and Mitchell knew that all along.'

I also knew that Weaver would tell Brownlow nothing now that his lawyers held him securely at their centre.

'Brownlow's going to feel pretty pissed-off,' Sunny said.

'He did the dirty work. It's all he was ever there to do. Lister will throw him a bone. No-one's going to come out of this smelling too badly.'

Yvonne took the phone back. 'I'm on my way,' she said. 'Wait where you are.'

She arrived fifteen minutes later in a cab, just as Mitchell and Ruth emerged from the station entrance and were immediately surrounded by the men and women there.

Mitchell announced that he had nothing to say, and that he had played no part in the investigation of the murders. Ruth carried on walking and came to where Yvonne and I sat on the low wall.

We all watched as Mitchell then extricated himself from the crowd, none of whom were willing to follow him away from the station.

He sat beside us and lit a cigarette, quickly smoking half of it in a succession of sharp draws. The smoke clung to his head and shoulders in the cold air.

'What's happening?' I asked him.

'He's clammed up.'

'Waiting for Lister?'

'Lister called Brownlow and warned him against doing anything that would jeopardize the interview. They're all just sitting in there, waiting, circling each other and looking for holes.'

'Sitting *and* circling,' Yvonne said.

Mitchell ignored her, shared a glance with Ruth and said, 'They found Emily Carr where he said she'd be.'

'Alive?' The word dried in my mouth.

'Alive,' he said. 'The house on Somerset Street was owned by Pauline Weaver. She has a portfolio of properties in the city.'

'I bet she does,' Yvonne said.

'And what?' I said. 'You think Weaver's going to say his wife abducted Emily Carr? No-one will believe that.'

He shrugged. 'I don't know what he's going to say. They found her chained to an exposed joist in the attic, gagged, blindfolded, unconscious. She's at the hospital now. She came round when they started cutting her free. She had no idea who'd done all this to her.'

'Thank Christ she's alive,' I said.

'Why? Because now her death's off your conscience?' Mitchell said.

It was still my belief that, since discovering Emily Carr was pregnant, *that* rather than Emily herself had been of greater interest to Weaver once he'd amended his overall strategy to take the events at Nelson Court into account.

'You'd better think again,' Mitchell told me.

Ruth put a hand on his arm, as though to prevent him from going on, but he pulled free of her.

'What?' Yvonne said.

'Emily Carr told the men cutting her free that she'd been preparing to leave Nelson Court for Withernsea, and that she'd gone down to the yard in which the bins were kept. Someone was waiting there for her, and whoever it was hit her from behind and knocked her unconscious. The next thing she knew, she was chained up in the attic. She was conscious for a few hours and then passed out again.'

'She was only missing for a day,' I said. 'It's unlikely there will be—'

'Shut up,' he shouted at me, quickly lowering his voice as several of the men and women at the station entrance turned in our direction.

He waited for them to lose interest in us before going on. 'While she was conscious, whoever had taken her to Somerset Street was still there.' He paused.

'And?'

'And she said that whoever was with her injected something directly into her stomach.'

'Into the baby?'

'They found the needle marks. Two in her stomach, one in her arm. She said they were painful injections, and that whatever it was, she then felt an excruciating pain until she passed out again.'

'Something to knock her out *and* something to harm the baby?'

'The doctor at the hospital was putting his money on a dose of insulin. It would cause foetal hypoglycaemia, which would only have to last a few minutes to cause permanent brain damage in the unborn child.'

'And Emily?' I said.

'Apparently they can reverse any symptoms in her by an injection of something called an insulin antagonizing hormone. She's going to be fine.'

'Is the baby still . . . ?' Yvonne said.

'They're doing what they can, but they're not hopeful.' He smoked the last of his cigarette and blew out the smoke.

I looked at Yvonne, who was now sitting with a hand over her mouth.

'Is that what Brownlow meant when he told Weaver that another little period of grace had just ended?' I asked Mitchell. 'Was Emily supposed to stay there and die both in pain *and* knowing that something had been done to her baby?'

He lowered his head and shook it. 'What the fuck is it with you and your saviour complex?' he said angrily, his voice low. 'You saved the girl, three cheers all round. No, it wasn't what Brownlow meant.'

'What, then?' I remembered Weaver's tears as his head was held down on the table.

Mitchell closed his eyes for a moment. 'What Brownlow was referring to was the discovery at Oriel House of Weaver's wife and daughter lying dead in each other's arms on the one bed.'

'Dead?'

'Each with enough morphine in them, by the look of it, to kill a horse.'

None of us spoke for a moment.

'How do they know?' Yvonne said eventually.

'Because they found the last two ampoules in a box which had held a dozen, and which Pauline Weaver had taken with her in her handbag from her home to Oriel House.'

The handbag she'd been carrying as she'd come back downstairs having put on her coat and scarf and gloves prior to leaving Bishop Burton. The bag in which she'd been pretending to search for her car keys as she'd come to where I was waiting for her. The bag from which she'd taken her mobile phone to hand over to me in yet another disarming gesture of intent before I'd allowed her to drive away from me and everything that was about to happen in Hull.

'That's how they know,' Mitchell said. 'The York police went in. Mrs Ellis led them to Angela Weaver's room, and that's where they found them wrapped in each other's arms on the bed.'

I remembered how anxious Pauline Weaver had sounded when I'd called her an hour earlier.

'First the girl, then herself,' Mitchell said. 'Pretty instantaneous, give or take those few very long, no-going-back seconds it took to die. One of the York men said he thought at first that they were just asleep. Apparently, Mrs Ellis went in and started shaking them. That's when they saw the syringe lying on the floor beside Pauline Weaver. She'd used those few seconds to grab hold of her dying daughter.'

'And now Brownlow blames me for letting her go there,' I said.

'He blames everybody for everything,' he said. 'But don't worry – he'll soon work out how to get everything he needs from this. It certainly won't do anything to harm his case against Weaver.'

I knew then, by the way he said it, and by the way he dropped his eyes as I turned to face him, that he had known or guessed that something like this might happen, and that I'd made the wrong decision in using Pauline Weaver's promised confession as a lever to prise open Weaver's own.

'You knew it would happen,' I said, when he finally looked up at me.

'Don't be ridiculous. How could anyone have known?'

'You knew.'

'Talk to him,' he said to Yvonne.

'If Pauline Weaver had kept her promise to me, her testimony would have convicted them both,' I said. 'Agreeing to her being allowed to see her daughter was the quickest way to the end of all this.'

'Right. And the end being what – Lister and Brownlow outside the Old Bailey in eighteen months' time announcing the guilty verdict to the waiting press?'

'Why?' I said.

'Why what?'

'Why didn't you at least tell me what you thought might happen? Pauline Weaver could have been stopped and brought back here ten minutes after she'd left me. Weaver would have been none the wiser. We could have lied to him and told him she was with their daughter.'

He shook his head at this.

And just as it had been beyond me to suggest that the murder of Lucy Collins had been substituted for the killing of Emily Carr, so it was beyond me now to suggest to Mitchell that he intended using the death of Weaver's daughter to get his confession in exactly the same way I had intended using his wife's testimony.

And even as all this occurred to me, and as I considered the implications of these final twists, these final released tensions in that solidified knot which had bound the past and the present so tightly together, and for so long, something else occurred to me.

'You don't even believe that her testimony would have been used against him, do you?' I said.

He pursed his lips. 'His lawyers would probably have seen to that. Changes in the law or no changes in the law. Brownlow might enjoy stomping around the room and shouting at them, but they're the ones who are really in charge now. I doubt if Lister will underestimate them the way you and Brownlow just did.'

'In fact, you think it would only have complicated and confused matters, don't you?' I said. 'How much of it was Weaver, how much was her? Was one helping or shielding the other, or were they equal partners in everything they did?'

'She only ever gave you her version of events,' he said.

'And you let her go to Easingwold, guessing what might happen, to avoid all these complications?'

'You heard Weaver. There was no real love lost between them. He would have made sure she dropped further down into the abyss than he himself was ever prepared to fall. If you honestly think they were equal partners in any of this, then you're a bigger fool than even he thinks you are.'

'And so you allowed me to let her go to avoid all these accusations and counter-accusations being aired in front of a jury.'

'*You* were the one who made the deal with her,' he said. 'Not me. Besides, she's not a stupid woman. She'll have left her good friend Lister something – probably with her own lawyers – to keep every-one moving and looking in the right direction.'

'And that's another reason why you let all this happen,' I said.

'Go on; I'm listening.'

'Lister.'

'What about him?'

'Too slow,' I said. 'Give or take a few hundred fallen women not worth the effort of redemption or salvation, and the grieving parents of a few murdered girls, everyone on your side of the fence now wants Chief Superintendent Lister up there where he belongs. It was what Finch meant when he said that nothing was going to be allowed to tarnish Lister's reputation. Figurehead of a new kind of policing. Law and order made to measure and on demand in the twenty-first century.'

'It's where we live,' he said. 'Go on, I'm still listening.'

'A bit embarrassing for everyone concerned if his good friend, charity fundraiser and stalwart police-liaison committee all-rounder Pauline Weaver was now to be charged with the murders he's in-vestigating, and in which he's invested so much, wouldn't you say? A bit of a blemish, that, on his otherwise spotlessly clean and polished record. Is that what your bosses told you to do – to clear the way for him, to get rid of all those unwelcome dirty tastes and smells?'

'You're being ridiculous,' he said.

I saw by the way Ruth McKenzie was looking at him that what I'd just suggested had not already occurred to her; and that if what I was suggesting was true, then she'd had no part in it, and was more shocked than any of us at hearing my accusation now.

She went on looking at him and he went on avoiding her gaze.

But Mitchell was wrong. The endings never really finished, and the abyss was always deeper, darker and steeper than anyone standing on its brink and looking down into it could ever possibly imagine.

By then, the crowd at the station entrance had grown to several hundred people. All of them demanding to know what was happening. All of them demanding to be told. All of them demanding to be allowed to participate, to be allowed to share their exaggerated and uncertain grief and to heal themselves.

Everything I'd just said to Mitchell was speculation and guesswork. Nothing could be proved and nothing could be disproved. It was just another narrow path in that labyrinth of empty, twisting spaces the law now inhabited. All done for the greater good. All done to convince and to reassure and to calm the public.

In less than an hour, Lister would be back in Hull and back in charge again. And an hour after that he would be in his seat centrestage in front of all the microphones, smiling to the cameras and telling all the journalists everything they wanted to hear, and feeling himself lifted higher and higher on the exalted swell of their questioning. Today would become the biggest celebration of his life.

I stood up from the low wall and told Mitchell I was leaving.

Yvonne rose beside me.

'Believe me,' Mitchell said. 'Everything that now needs to be done to convict Weaver will be done.'

Ruth continued to watch him closely, and he still could not bring himself to turn and look at her.

'Will it?' I said. 'Another three cheers for us, then.'

'Right from the start, you've been given all the leeway and ten times more than you've ever given back,' he said angrily.

'Right up until I made sure of that one little ending concerning Pauline and Angela Weaver?' I said.

He shook his head at the remark.

Yvonne held my arm and drew me away from him.

'Leave it,' she said, leading me down the steps and towards the ponds, where the dim, pale outlines of the fish still came and went beneath the surface of the water as our shadows passed like clouds across the sky above them.

36 ——————————————————————————————

I called Martin Siddal from Humber Street two hours later.

'I was expecting you,' he said.

By then, the news of the arrest of a man in connection with the murders had been announced at ten-minute intervals on all the local radio stations, and more detailed reports were promised for later.

'When did you work it out?' I asked him.

He composed himself before answering me, his voice low. 'The day after you came here,' he said. 'The Sunday morning, when I saw a photo of Don Lucas and his wife on the news. We watched them together, a day later, at their press conference.'

'Did you recognize him?' I said.

'I wouldn't have known him from Adam, but when I heard his name I knew it was him.'

'And only then did the names of the murdered girls start making sense?'

'If you're accusing me of having worked it all out beforehand, you're wrong.'

'Why – because you refused to accept that your daughter's death was connected to the others? Because some of them were prostitutes?'

'Think what you like,' he said. 'A year had passed, longer. And the next two to be killed were called Smith and Wilson. What kind of connection was that going to suggest to anyone, and especially after thirty years? If they'd called Alison Wilson *Boylan*, or if I'd seen that early mistake the newspapers made, then I might have guessed something sooner, but I didn't see it and I didn't guess. Believe what you want of me, Mr Rivers, but it's the truth. To be honest, I doubt if I'd have been able to remember the names of those five others, not after thirty years.'

It was his second lie to me, but I let it pass.

His first lie had been in telling me that it wasn't until he'd seen Don Lucas's picture in the papers that he'd started working out what connected the deaths. I'd told him I was working for Susan Hendry, and even allowing for the length of time which had passed while the police had insisted on Paul Hendry being a suspect rather than a victim, he must have recognized that name too, and started then to make all those scarcely believable guesses others were only now beginning to make.

'Does it have any real bearing on how or where Rebecca died?' he asked me, his voice drying even further as he said his daughter's name.

I told him about the assault on Angela Weaver three days before his daughter was killed. I told him I thought Rebecca's death had been made to look like suicide, or a game gone wrong, because Weaver had reacted in an uncontrollable rage upon discovering what had happened to Angela at Easingwold. Killing Rebecca was something he'd been unable to stop himself from doing. He'd started killing before he was ready to continue. That, and because, in all those perverse parallels, copies and echoes, the hanging of Rebecca Siddal had been made to mirror Anna Dunn's own suicide twenty-eight years earlier.

It was also why a year had then passed before the murder of Kelly Smith in the yard off Chapel Street.

And it was why – despite what he had insisted on when I'd

visited him in Cottingham – his daughter's killer would never have been found if the police had started searching for him fourteen months earlier, before all these near-invisible and rapidly fading connections had started being made.

'Do the police accept all this?' he asked me.

'They will,' I said. 'Have you told your wife everything you know?'

'Have I told her that our only daughter was killed because of something I didn't have the guts to stand up to thirty years ago, you mean?'

'No-one blames you,' I said.

'Don't they?' Meaning he blamed himself, and that nothing anyone tried to persuade him of now would make the smallest difference to how he felt, and how he would go on feeling until he died.

'For twelve years we tried to conceive a child,' he said unexpectedly. 'Twelve years. Yes, I've told her. And she hasn't said a single word to me since. She's at Rebecca's grave now. I offered to go with her.' He paused. 'Just when I thought I had nothing else left to lose.'

'The police will want to ask you about what happened,' I said.

'And what then? I tell them that the instant I saw Don Lucas and *his* crying wife – the instant I saw another of those mothers suddenly more dead than alive – that here I was, a man who knew who the *victims* might now be, but who had absolutely no idea whatsoever who the killer was. That must surely be a first in the annals of detection – knowing the exact victims, but having no idea how to make any connection back to their killer.'

'The victims were always the point,' I said. 'Not the way they were killed, or where they were found, or where they died. What mattered above all else to Weaver was *who* they were, and what they represented to their families when they were killed. It was all to do with the suffering of the families afterwards, with all that lost promise, all that unendurable anguish so suddenly brought into being, and for no apparent reason.'

'I know all about that,' he said.

And it also occurred to me only then that perhaps if Angela Dunn *had* died at birth or shortly afterwards, then she wouldn't have remained the constant reminder and justification to Weaver she later became.

And perhaps if I'd gone back to Siddal upon Tracey Lucas's body being identified, then he might have told me all this then – beginning with him recognizing the name Hendry – and perhaps he might have identified Billy Carr as the sixth man of the crew for me, and perhaps then I might have been able to do something to ensure that Emily Carr and her unborn child were better protected in the three days which passed before Weaver finally got to her at Nelson Court.

And if Emily Carr had been protected and saved, then perhaps even Pauline and Angela Weaver might not have died.

'I feel as though I'm standing up to my waist in the sea,' he said, again unexpectedly. 'And with the waves coming towards me getting bigger and stronger.' He spoke absently, to himself, as though he believed I might no longer be listening to him, and I wondered if he was asking me another of those impossible, un-answerable questions.

'I hope you and your wife get through all this,' I said. 'And that when—'

'Last night,' he said, interrupting me and then falling silent.

'Last night what?'

'My wife. The cemetery. She was there long after it had grown dark. Just her and Rebecca. She'd been there for hours. Someone reported her to the police and they found her there and brought her home. They knew who she was, what had happened. Told me they'd leave everything to me.' He started to breathe more deeply, and a moment later, after fumbling with the phone in its cradle, the connection was severed.

I considered calling him back, but decided against it, knowing that he probably wouldn't answer, and that each of the rings would pierce every corner and shadow of the empty house in which he stood alone and waiting to drown beneath those unstoppable waves.

37

The following day, I went to see Emily Carr in hospital. I arrived mid-afternoon and found her alone, the three other beds in the small ward empty. I watched her for a moment through the glass in the door. She looked asleep, but then, perhaps sensing my presence, she turned to face me. I imagined she might immediately turn away from me, but instead she raised her hand and beckoned me into the empty room.

I'd bought a bunch of flowers from the florist's at the hospital entrance, and I laid them in their cellophane cone on the cabinet beside her. There were no others in the room, no cards, no small presents or any of the other detritus which usually collects around the temporarily stalled and diverted lives of the hospitalized.

She pushed herself up in the bed and wiped the hair from her eyes.

'I'm sorry,' I told her.

'You shouldn't be.'

'I meant for not sorting the locksmith out for you. I promised.'

The remark surprised her. 'I'd forgotten all about it.'

'I should still have done it,' I said.

She turned the flowers to face her. They were large daisies, white petals with vividly yellow centres, a child's idea of flowers.

'They'll bring a vase,' she said.

It had been confirmed only an hour after she'd been brought to the hospital that Weaver had injected her unborn child with insulin. It had died later that same night.

'Even with the lock I would still have gone down to the yard,' she said. She drew her arms from beneath the sheets and laid them by her sides. The thickness of the bedding gave her the appearance of still being pregnant.

'Is there anyone I can contact for you?' I asked her.

'Such as?' she said. '*She* was here earlier.' She nodded over my shoulder back to the door.

'Who?'

'Susan Hendry. She just came and stood at the door and looked in at me. Probably thought I was asleep.' Meaning she'd done nothing to encourage Susan Hendry to go in to her.

'You could have spoken to her,' I suggested.

'Why? Because we're both in the same boat? I don't think so. Besides—' She turned away from me.

'Besides, what?'

'*My* baby's dead.'

And Susan Hendry still had that particular loss yet to come and to endure.

'She might be able to help you,' I said, though uncertain what I was suggesting.

'How? And then what? *I* help *her*?'

I was unprepared for this hostility.

'Apart from which,' she said, 'I daresay there are more than a few people who think that what happened to me was a blessing in disguise. What kind of mother would *I* have been, eh?'

The same kind of mother Lucy Collins might have been. The same kind Anna Dunn might have been. The same kind her sister had become. The same kind Susan Hendry was soon no longer to be.

'No-one believes that,' I told her.

'You don't sound too convinced. Lucky old me, then.'

She started crying and I leaned forward to hold her. She put her arms around my neck and went on crying into my shoulder. I cupped the back of her head in my hand.

When she pulled away a few minutes later, she wiped her eyes with her palm and then lay breathing deeply with her hands held across her throat.

It was beyond me to ask her what she'd already been told about the Weavers. It would have been beyond anyone to ask her if she believed, as I did, that she was alive now only because Lucy Collins and both their unborn children were dead, and because the perfect pattern of Weaver's plan had somehow to be maintained for it to go on making sense to him, and for his actions to remain justifiable.

'I went to Withernsea,' I said.

'I know. They were supposed to come and see me earlier, but they never showed up.'

She wiped the last of her tears from her face.

I told her I'd come to the hospital every day she was in there.

'Thanks for the flowers,' she said. 'Only next time, can you make it cigarettes.' She drew back the sleeve of her pyjamas to show me her patch-free arm.

I left her an hour later, ten minutes after she'd fallen back to sleep.

It was only four, but the day outside had turned to night during my short stay.

I went from one bedside to another.

Susan Hendry was sitting beside her son.

Lister had visited her personally with the news of Weaver's arrest, and the news that, as a consequence, every charge against her son had now been dropped.

'I think he expected me to be grateful,' she told me.

Almost a week had passed since Paul Hendry's ventilator had been briefly and unsuccessfully removed. There had been no suggestion since of any further attempt to see if he was able to breathe unaided.

She'd wept when I'd told her what had happened to Pauline Weaver and the girl she had treated and loved as her own daughter for thirty years.

For two days, both editions of the *Hull Mail* had been filled with the news of Weaver's arrest and the stories he was allegedly now telling to Lister. Filled, too, with the stories of all those other families struggling to stay afloat in his turbulent wake.

There were photos of all the dead girls. And new pictures of Karen Smith with her younger daughter. And the picture she had either given or sold to the *Mail* of the men who had chanced to be with her future husband in Grimsby all those years ago.

The day following Weaver's arrest, Don Lucas had been visited in Goole by Brownlow. Lucas had denied everything Jimmy Boylan had told me. Thirty years had passed. Nothing was going to convict him now. Lucas admitted his assault on Jimmy Boylan, but that was all. Boylan still refused to press charges, and Lucas announced proudly that he'd do the same again, and worse, given the opportunity.

Jimmy Boylan then spent thirty-six hours at Queen's Gardens telling Lister and Brownlow everything he'd already told me.

Lister had invited Susan Hendry to attend another of his conferences, and she had refused him.

At my arrival beside her son's bed, she rose and yawned and asked me if I wanted a drink. Guessing she wanted to speak to me beyond all possible hearing of her son, I said I'd been about to suggest the same.

I knew Yvonne had been with her at Park Avenue since the morning of Weaver's arrest.

We arrived at the small cafeteria and sat with our drinks.

'It's been six days,' she said. She meant since her son had been offered the unlikely opportunity to struggle back to life.

'Whatever happens, you'll still be the one who makes any important decisions,' I said. 'No-one else.'

'I know. And whatever I do, everyone will be watching me. Especially now. Whatever I decide, it will be wrong.'

The previous day, she'd arrived at the hospital to find two dozen people, most of them her son's age, on their knees in the waiting area outside his room, praying aloud for him, and telling everyone who approached them that God and Jesus and The Holy Spirit were now taking care of the boy, and would, given time and the power of prayer, ensure his full recovery.

I'd heard all this from Yvonne.

'I heard about the people praying,' I said.

'And did you also hear that I made a fool of myself by screaming at them to stop and to leave, and then that I tried to drag one of them out by his coat?'

'Yvonne just said that you'd been angry.'

'They tried to tell me that the time had come to remove the ventilator again. This time, Jesus was going to do Paul's breathing for him. I was angry that the hospital hadn't tried to get rid of them before I showed up. One of the orderlies told me to my face that I should be grateful for what they were doing for me and my son. "Why?" I said to her. "Because nothing *you*'ve been able to do for him so far has helped him?" You can imagine how good I felt about myself after that particular little outburst.'

I knew then that she was telling me she'd finally made up her mind what to say to the consultant the next time he approached her with his own carefully worded concerns for her son's future.

We sat together for an hour, and a crowd of others – visitors, out-patients, technical and nursing staff – came and went around us.

Eventually, she tipped what remained of her cold drink into a nearby bin and said she ought to return to her son.

I rose and we briefly held each other.

I wanted to suggest to her that she went again to see Emily Carr, but I kept the thought to myself.

She waited for a moment, her hands on my arms, as though about to say something to me in parting, but she, too, remained silent, and then she turned and left me.

Waiting until she'd gone, I went to the window and looked out over the city beneath me. From where I stood, I could trace all the major roads and lines of light leading back into the centre, where the glow intensified, and where the clear and simple pattern of the suburbs was lost, and where the confusion of lights looked like nothing more than the dying embers of a giant, untended fire.

And beyond the city itself lay the illuminated outlines of the bridge and the docks and the refineries, and beyond these the open levels of Holderness and the vast, empty spaces of the river and the estuary mouth, where the scatter of isolated lights grew further and further apart, and where the land and sky and water grew together, and where there now seemed to be no end to the world in darkness.